Everything Isn't Always As It Seems

(A Love Story)

Linda D. Catlett

Cover Design by Linda D. Catlett

Photo Design by Linda D. Catlett

ISBN-13: 978-0692700433 (Sister With A Pen)
ISBN-10: 0692700439

Printed in The United States of America

For

Margaret A. Catlett (Ma)

January 12, 1940 -- May 14, 2008

And

Lillian Jackson Catlett (Grandma)

June 8, 1911 -- March 19, 2008

The heroes in my life who were there for me at the most integrals times of this journey; from the beginning supporting me to see my vision through, and encouraging me to keep writing even when self-doubt, life, and writer's block attacked me.

Until we meet again, "I love you, I miss you, and thank you..."

Acknowledgments

First and foremost, Thank You God and Thank You Jesus for my life's journey, my family, my blessings, and my gift of imagination.

To Gladys Ward, my baby sister, thank you for always reminding me about the greatness in me, your unconditional love, your wisdom, and your sisterly protection, (*I love you, Sister*).

To Rodnesha Hill, because of your reaction to my first attempt at writing, and your chagrin when I halted our nightly readings; I realized that I just might have what it takes, (*Thank you Rah*).

Chapters

New Beginnings

"Q...Q...Are you okay girl?

" Aah...she'll be alright; she's probably just nervous."

"Shannon. Where's Shannon, somebody find Shannon"

"Oh God...Oh God...Oh God...please....please...please!"

"I'm here...I'm here. What's the problem?"

"Look at her," I heard Theresa say.

Feeling like I'm being shaken, but not sure.

"Oh my God, Sissy...Sissy, can you hear me?"

"Check out her eyes; all glassed over—naw, she ain't hearing a damn thing! You wrong now! Someone call nine one one. Female Meltdown I repeat...Melt down...Female Down!"

"Aw damn!—SISSY...Q...QUINCEE-JANE!"

That and the sound of feet running all around me were all that I heard before everything went...OUT!

Twenty-five Months

Earlier

Bamboozled

Now ladies, has love-hurt ever caused you to make promises to yourself, and in keeping these promises...you still ended up bamboozled?

August 31, 2005
River Park Towers
Bronx, NY 10:17 p.m.

"Ms. Quincee-Jane Catfire, Dre Frontlaroy here."

"Oh my goodness, what a nice surprise; how on earth are you?"

"I'm doing fair to middling. Still maintaining and making sure that the criminals stay where they belong and putting their crooked asses back in check when they get out of line.

Apologies for calling you so late, but it's taken me this long to get your number without baby girl getting suspicious. And you know I wasn't about to call dick-wad Danny for your information."

Quietly smiling at the comment, while ignoring the queasy sensation in the pit of my stomach at hearing Danny's name, I responded, "It's not too late, at all. And by the way, how is Tina?"

"Aah, Baby Girl is doing real well. She's working at the New Rochelle courthouse. She's the choir director at church, and she volunteers at the pantry every week. Doing all of that while going to school, my baby still managed to passed the bar exam the first time around, back in July."

"What! That's great news. Congratulations to her."

"Yeah, I'm proud of her. But she's been working so damn hard that she hasn't had time to relax, let alone celebrate. So, I'm planning a surprise celebration for her Friday night that's going to kick off our Labor Day Weekend Shindig, which brings me to why I'm calling. Will I be seeing you?"

"To be honest Dre, I didn't realize that I was still invited because I am no longer seeing Danny?"

"Damn, that's good news to hear, but I don't understand."

"Tina's friendship with Danny is so close. I don't want to intrude, or be where I'm not wanted."

"Listen, YOU are OUR friend, and YOU have an open invitation to OUR home at any time. So stop all this silly talk. Besides, Danny has no say-so up in here. I'll keep my gun close by, ready to pop a cap in *that* ass, if need be."

Openly giggling at the correction officer's allegiance to me, I responded, "Why thank you Lieutenant Frontlaroy for taking preventive measures for my wellbeing."

"Not a problem Miss Missy. It's my job to look after damsels in distress. So, are we clear on all that nonsense and I can expect your attendance?"

"Yes, we're clear and yes, I will be there."

"All right!. I know Baby Girl is going to be happy to see you. I need you to be here by six o'clock because she should be arriving home at seven, or there about.

Let me know when you're ready to take down my address."

"I already have it."

"Very Good, remember six o'clock."

"Dre, I know."

"Just saying…"

"Goodnight Dre."

"Goodnight Miss Quincee-Jane Catfire."

Hanging up, speculating if I would see Danny because I was initially invited to the weekend as a couple with Danny, by Tina. Shaking off the thought, I recited my Danny mantra.

Dear God…Thank you for all the love sorrow to be gone. I know who I am and I respect all the hurt that I've been through. I harbor no ill-will towards love, more importantly, I hold myself responsible for my own quality of life, in how I let love and people treat me. Amen

It's hard describing what Danny and I had. Our affiliation was just getting off the ground, when I walked away. There was no commitment agreement; however, something special had definitely passed between us and was blossoming into a powerful connection.

We had been seeing each other casually, for two and a half months. It was the type of groove where neither of us had to know where the other was at. We didn't have to be around one another all the time, nor did we bring our exes' baggage into our rapport. But I did know that there was someone in Danny's recent history from conversations I'd overheard from time to time.

Ladies, a face-to-face meeting of an ex is not offensive to me because we all have past relationships, no matter the length in between them. What pissed me off was the turn of events that occurred prior to meeting her, in addition to how I was treated in the presence of the gah-gah witch.

My mind flashed back to the infamous Friday evening. There were Danny and myself; Matt,—Danny's brother whom always been offensively cold towards me; Cheryl—Matt's girlfriend who treated me kind from the first time we met, and Toomey—Danny and Matt's rather unscrupulous friend that I do not like… at all!

After dinner at Michael Jordan's Restaurant in Grand Central Terminal, we decided to carry the evening further with a night of dancing. The plan was to make a quick stop at Cheryl's house—off Broadway and 97th street then head out to Red Hook in Brooklyn.

While waiting on Cheryl to change clothes, Matt served shots of tequila, and although my limit is one glass of any type of spirit, I was soon halfway through shot number two, and feeling pretty damn good. To add heat to my fire, it had been almost two weeks since I had last seen Danny, so the combination of liquor and a little bit of "missing you" on my brain made the perfect happenstance for wanting to be close. I did so, by scooting over so that our thighs made contact, but I was caught off guard when the hurt inducer inched away from me instead.

Playing it off because I was embarrassed and not sure if it was what I thought, or it was the tequila tricking me. I attempted my cat-call a second time, and received the same response, but more blatant.

Soon the bastard was damn-near sitting on the arm of the loveseat, trying to get away from me. Unable to hold my tongue and with danger dripping in my voice, I rhetorically inquired of Matt and Toomey, "Did you see that?" I know they did because they both were sitting across from me, looking like two stupid little boys.

Grimacing back toward Danny I whispered "You're acting like I have some kind of disease or something." Flabbergasted at not hearing "No baby", or "You're wrong," I continued "Oh, so that's how you feel? Okay, You Got It."

Matt and Toomey just sat motionless looking like dumber and the dumbest.

Bringing my emotional boil down to stillness, I mulled over my thoughts and smiled to myself as I inwardly commenced "the game", while staring blankly into the eyes of my opponent.

Turning my attention back to my drink, I gulped it down, and by then Cheryl was ready. Although she looked good in her tight jeans, with a white laced camisole, and her hair pulled up into two afro-centric bush-buns, and she was smiling and socializing, there was something that I picked up on that wasn't quite right with her.

Her golden complexion had lost its glow and yes we are the same height, 5 feet 6 ½ inches; yet, she appeared to be shorter from hunching over. We had been like two peas in a pod, up until the recent month. I made a mental note to call and check on her the following week.

Walking to the car, cringing at the thought of sitting next to Danny, I turned to Toomey.

"Toomey, why don't you sit in the middle?"

"And get in between y'all's shit...HELL NO!"

"I didn't ask you to say anything or suggest that you be a conciliator, just."

"Yo Dan, you know your woman's crazy, right?"

"I beg your pardon; this conversation is between you and me."

"And I just made it a three way."

"I don't know why I brother to have a civilized conversation with you. You're a jackass."

"Whatever! And like I said, hell no!"

Turning around throwing Danny a gaze that seethed, it would be in your best interest to leave me alone. Pissed off, I sauntered and slid my behind in the middle seat.

What I should have done was... take my agitated ass home. But...noooo...not me. Ladies why do we put ourselves in positions that we know damn well will end up being—not pretty?

I'll tell you why...Because of our desire to have our way; but more satisfyingly—to get under their skin—because we know how to.

Determined to indulge in some "get even", as soon as I set foot inside the club, I grabbed Cheryl by the arm and pulled her to the dance floor. When we were finished boogieing down, Danny and Matt where waiting for us at the edge of the wooden dance floorboards. Danny had my slow gin fizz with two cherries waiting in one hand, a handkerchief in the other hand and some sweet sugar that greeted my lips.

Yes ladies, I let the perpetrator kiss me; but, in my defense...it was my ego that had forlorn me.

I had this 6'3" light skinned alpha male looking down at me; hypnotizing me with grey/green eyes that were pleading, "I will do whatever you want me to." A spray of freckles dancing across the most innocent looking baby face, making me feel as if I was the only woman in the room. All while wiping beads of sweat off my face and intoxicating my nostrils with cologne that was saying, "Quincee-Jane, come and get me." Then to see and feel the envy of women all around me ...I just couldn't help myself.

We had been at the club for over an hour and a half, when my twins ran across my mind, and I wanted to check on them. Heading outside where there was less noise, also to cool off, I double back because I didn't have any bars on my cellphone.

Approaching our table, I saw Danny talking to a woman. She was stunning--of Brazilian, or one of the Latin heritage. Her olive-gold complexion was flawless. About 5'9" and model thin, she had long thick hair that was pulled back in a single cornrow braid that went down to her mid back. Her turquoise eyes stood out underneath the most full and perfectly arched eyebrows. She wore a little white spaghetti-strap dress and gold sandals.

By the time I was standing next to Danny and the women, apprehension was knotting my stomach.

All my curve-ah-licious sisters out there, I've fought with my weight all my life. As an adult, no matter my waistline size, I have style, grace, and class; I have never been intimidated by small or skinny woman.

"Excuse me Danny. I need to use....."

Never looking in my direction, and interrupting me, "I'll be right with you."

"No Dan, just pass me your phone...."

"I SAID I'LL BE RIGHT WITH YOU IN A MINUTE."

The non-look and the comment sent a chill through my body. I don't know why I was taken aback, especially coming off of the scene back at Cheryl's place; but, as the adage goes—it takes time to get to really know a person.

Everyone at the table was stunned at Danny's behavior; notwithstanding the women, whose pomposity appeared to marvel at my dismay. Indignation swept through me like a raging wind, but that manipulating sack of shit was not going to get begging, a confrontation, nor humility from me.

Ladies, when a snake rears its ugly head...you sever it from its body...The End!

Inhaling the fury into my belly; I snatched Danny's phone from the table, turned and walked into the packed crowd, zigzagging to avoid any attempts at being followed. Within seven minutes, I was in a cab heading to The Bronx, planning the next phase of my Danny-be-Gone project.

Shaking off the memory, I turned my thoughts back to the present.

Hoodwinked

Ladies…when I say in control, smooth, sexual, and mesmerizing, on top of being humble, refined, and a believer in God. Mmm…mmm…mmm…mmm!

Happily surprised to hear of Dre's loyalty to me, and feeling cocky at remembering my swift exodus from Danny's life, the Universe interceded; reminding me why I fell vulnerable, in the first place.

My mind drifted back to our first official date. It was on a Thursday night. Around 7:30 p.m., my phone rings.

"What are you doing tonight? Let me take you out pretty lady."

"Hello. Who's speaking", questioning nonchalantly.

"Girl, stop playing with me. You know damn well who you're talking to."

Incessantly turned on at the take charge attitude, ignoring the rush in my chest, I came back with, "Do you see what it's doing outside?"

"Yes, it is raining, and very hard I might add. The winds are blowing, what did the forecaster say; umm! 35 miles per hour."

"Oh, now you want to be a smart ass?"

"It's better than being a dumb ass, don't you think? But what does that have to do with anything?"

"Everything, I'm not traveling in that mess. Besides I'm not in the mood to go out. This is the type of weather where you stay home and be warm and cozy."

"How does this sound? I'll send a car for you around 8:30 and we'll eat in."

Ladies, do you see what I was working with?

Needless to say, I was done, did, and looking good by 8:20pm. I had on a baby girl pink cashmere sweater that laid off my shoulders and made my cleavage look peek-a-boo sexy, a pair of hip hugger acid washes jeans, and a wide burgundy alligator belt that matched my alligator boots.

Down stairs in my lobby, I was met by a chauffeur at the door with an opened umbrella, waiting to escort me to a limousine. The jazz music playing on the stereo, the rain crushing against the window, and my anticipation of the evening had me feeling aglow with perfectness before I even arrived to my destination.

As the driver was parking, Danny came walking out of a two story town house, opening the car door looking eat-em-up-good wearing a pair of jeans, a light blue long sleeved shirt that revealed those sexy ass biceps; and a pair of loafers.

Greeting me with an over-sized umbrella, a warm smile, and just as I was ready to receive a kiss on my cheek—my face was gently accosted by Danny's windblown jet black hair.

My grandmother's words came to mine, "Don't be courted by no fella who got hair prettier or longer than yours."

Cognizant of the effect it had on me, an invitation was extended "You can pull it anytime you want to", as I was guided up onto my tiptoes to receive sugar on my lips. I didn't know if the heat was coming from the kiss or from Danny's hand that was still lodged on the small of my back.

Upstairs in the house, I used the restroom as an excuse to get away and abate my growing excitement.

"Is everything okay?"

In the bathroom longer than I realized; trying to subdue the tingling sensation in my woman-flesh, I scurried out the door responding "Yes. I'm fine. Thank you. Where are you?"

"I'm in the dining room. Just follow my voice."

Walking into the dim lit room, I was immediately seated to a plate of filet mignon with mushroom and onion sauce, string beans, and miniature red potatoes. I was most impressed when I was asked "Would you do the honor and say grace."

Over dinner, my Quincee-Jane get-to-know-you inquiry, disclosed that Danny was thirty-five, single, with no children. Knowing nothing about basketball, I was a little embarrassed to find out that I was sitting across from a former college super-star and European pro basketball player.

Mr. TooGood senior made it clear that all the TooGood pups would be joining the family financial consultancy business. I did not have to worry about a convict history—no prison time, nor arrest, just parking tickets. Speechless and happy when I was informed, "I've never had any sex diseases. I can show you my latest Aids test if you like."

Being flippant I asked, "So how long ago was the most recent test, a year, six months ago?"

"No, I had one taken the next day after I met you."

Yes ladies, my bottom lip dropped, my 'She' trembled, and my defenses ran for the hills, like a bitch in heat. I had nothing. No comeback, no sass; I didn't even know where to look because it damn sure wasn't going to be in the eyes of the phenomenon sitting across from me.

The first thing that came to mind was to begin clearing the table. In the kitchen, placing the plates and utensils in the sink, I commented "If I had some gloves, I would wash the dishes for you."

"Not while you're on a date with me, you're not." Aroused by the indignant reply, I acquiesced, "You're the boss tonight."

"Am I?"

Feeling the sensual tension between us get thick enough to cut with a knife, I walked my happy hot ass out of the kitchen. Anywhere else was a safe place to be.

Following me back into the dining room with a tray carrying two glasses and a cheesecake from Juniors, I had something of my own to offer as well. Reaching down on the floor next to me, I picked up a marble gray bag that had black tissue paper poking out the top of it.

Accepting a glass of Drambuie, I extended my gift.

"What's this?"

"Look inside and see."

Watching the expression of intrigue change into an eight year old cool aid smile, and enthusing out "Cuban cigars...Flor de Cano Petit Coronas Cedros! Ahh, Very Nice! Thank you Quincee-Jane Catfire."

Pleased with myself, I egged on "There's more."

Pulling out the object, wrapped in a gray mesh sash, and opening it, "A candle... Mmm...this smells good. What flavor is it?"

Getting up to escape back to my haven in the bathroom, I replied, "Pussy." Reaching the doorway, stopping, but never turning around, while giving my exiting statement, "I wanted to warm your house with something that would remind you of me."

Not waiting or wanting to see what my comment brought, I high-tailed it out the room.

I had been the object of seduction since we had first spoken, earlier that evening, and this was my attempt at get-even.

Ladies, normally I hold my own, in the battle of a cat and mouse chase; but that night, I felt myself buckling under the pressure.

In the bathroom, talking my lady-fire down, while dousing my face with cold water, I had to reassure myself that my defenses were ready to stand guard.

Opening the bathroom door, I was startled to see Danny standing there. Stepping body to body close to me. The next thing I knew I was being swept up in those massively strong arms, succumbing to layers of softness from an exquisite tongue; exploring every crevice inside of my month. Caught up in Danny's Tongue Delight, my body purred sinfully, and left my defenses—abandoning ship.

Parting from the kiss that arrogant bastard had the nerve to turn me loose and say "I just wanted to warm you back," then walked away.

Still dizzy; yet, following behind like a love-sick puppy, but playing it off, I responded "I should be getting home."

Turning around to me and looking disappointed, I was let off the hook, "I'll drive you home."

Feeling my resistance to Danny's charm nowhere to be found, I was at a loss for words.

Sensing my discomfort, my knight in shining armor surrendered, "I'll have my driver take back you home. You look like you've had enough of me for one night."

The last set of instructions I received was, "Call me when you get home," then I was kissed again. Every nerve in my body was on edge. I had to call on the Lord for help.

"Dear Jesus, please give me the strength to control my libido, so that I can maintain what little dignity I have left…Aman and Amen."

Ladies there's nothing worse than letting a man see the power he has over your sexuality, especially if you like him…I was getting the hell out of dodge.

I thought we were a good fit; but all of that was water under the bridge.

Shaking off the sweet sojourn down memory lane because the afterthought of being hoodwinked still pricked at me, and I didn't want to give any more credence to Danny's existence, I headed to bed looking forward to visiting Dre and Tina for the weekend.

Fallen

(Alright men, we've all been there—where that one female that you did right by—just up'd and bitch slapped you in the heart.
Once it happened to me, I was finished with the four letter word... for good. Life was moving smooth for me, until cupid shot me in the ass with an arrow named Quincee-Jane Catfire).

Manhattan, New York
April, 2005
Thursday, late afternoon

Tired from a long day at work and an extra hard workout, looking out the second floor gym window I saw a storm coming that wasn't reported in the day's forecast. The streets were flooding; umbrellas were flying in all directions. A few of them even blew against the glass scaring at least three females who were on treadmills. Making up my mind that I was going home, I headed to the lockers, got my gear and was out the first set of doors.

Walking into the foyer, there was a woman standing and looking outside. I somewhat recognized her. She had been coming to the gym for a couple of months. She was quiet; we've greeted each other on a few occasions, when our paths crossed. I liked that she was focused, and worked hard. I never saw her give her trainer a hard time like a lot of females do. I was in no mood to talk, so I stood about three feet away from her watching the sky get darker.

Still looking straight ahead, she said "What did YOU do to bring all this rain?" then she turned and looked at me like I actually had something to do with the weather. It was a funny gesture at trying to holla at me.

I half smiled and told her "It wasn't me." Remaining focused on my plan, I added "get home safely" and I opened up the door. At the same time, a bolt of lightning lit up the sky, scaring the shit out of me and I uncharacteristically blurted out "GOT-DAMN!"

The woman had no embarrassment sharing her thoughts when I asked "Oh...you think that's funny uh?"

"Si senor"

I was moved by her honesty and the sweet grin on her face, despite her openly laughing at me.

"Okay, you got one up on me."

"Do I now?"

It was something about the way she said it that caught my attention.

BOOM...BOOM...BOOM! Thunder roared all around us. That's when she jumped, and in one movement, her shoulder was rubbed against my forearm.

Feeling vindicated I countered, "I think we're even."

"Yes we are."

Recognizing that she was genuinely frightened, instantly feeling like a dick for poking fun at her, before I realized it, we had been loitering in the lobby for a while, as the storm did its thing.

Reaching out for a formal introduction and shaking my hand, "By the way, I'm QJ."

"What do the initials stand for?"

"Quincee Jane", she proudly announced, looking real cute; doing so.

I had to admit, although a unique name, it fit her ass to the tee. Letting her name bounce around in my head for a second, I decided, "I'll call you Quincee."

"Everyone calls me QJ."

Arching an eyebrow and poking my chest out, I had to let her know, "I'm not everyone. I guess that means I'm special."

(Yo men, I don't know where the hell that came from. I wanted to kick myself in the ass. And I be damn, it got worse).

The next thing that came out of my mouth was "There is a Brazilian restaurant in the next block-- would you like to go and get a bite to eat?"

Without fumbling for words, "First you laugh at me then you offer me an invitation to dinner. I can't say that is the smoothest invite I've had, but yes I would like that."

We arrived at the restaurant soaking wet. Watching the beads of rain running down her face made me want to lick her dry.

Catching me staring at her, "W.h.a.t?" she asked, in a sexy nonchalant voice.

Ignoring her question, and posing one of my own, "Are you alright; being that I'm responsible for getting you wet and all."

"I'm fine, thank you for asking."

(Fellas, and fine... is what she is)

When she took off her jacket, my eyes damn near jumped out of their sockets. She had on a see through knitted blouse, with long sleeves that sat on the tip of her shoulders. The holes in the blouse were large enough for me to see what was underneath, but small enough make me stare at them longer than I should have. Under the pink piece of material, she had on a turquoise bra that was cut low and had a little gold snapped in the front. Her breasts were grabbing my eyes, and there were a damn a lot of them. Her jeans were tucked inside of a pair of authentic, but drenched moccasins.

Waiting to be seated, I was taken her in. She's about 5'6" with Hersey chocolate brown skin. Her hair is cut very short, and it sparkled with small, red, gold and brown curls. The more I looked into her light brown eyes; I saw a blue ring around the circumference of her eyeballs. Her lips are nice and smooth and I did want to kiss them.

The beauty mark underneath her left nostril had me itching to nibble on it. She has the prettiest petite hands that had me looking forward to holding them.

The woman is small by no means. In her thickness, she looks to be carrying about 30+ extra pounds, but she wears it damn well. I don't know what's going on with me because normally my taste lust for model thin, light and light-bright females with long hair—real or fake, shit I didn't care.

Seated with the menu in hand, I watched her study it for a few minutes then sit it down on the table.

"Okay, I am deeming you the expert, so what do you suggest? And I must tell you that I am holding you personally responsible for my dining pleasure."

Appreciating that she did not have a problem being led, I took charge, ordering a codfish appetizer; shrimp in Yuca Cream accompanied with Brazilian style rice and collard greens as a main course, and capped the meal off with Brazilian liquor made from sugarcane juice.

By the time desert came, fried bananas with cinnamon sugar, I had found out that she was thirty-eight, a single mother of 14 year old twins. She lives in the Bronx, but is a country girl at heart, did a stint in the Navy, she recently started up a consultation business, and she joined the gym to get in shape for her Master's Degree graduation.

She's not only sexy and independent; she's also intelligent and accomplished.

(Men, can you see how easy it was for me to have broken at least six of my own damn rules, just sitting across the table from her?)

Paying my rules no damn mind, I continued on with my questions.

"So tell me Miss Quincee, was your appetite satisfied and your desire appeased?"

"How do you know that I'm a Miss and not a Mrs.?"

For a split second, I panicked, but then she planted a warm smile between her lips and confessed "I was just messing with you. My satisfaction was pleased, and my desire…Well, I will never tell!"

Thinking to myself (*Oh but when I get to know you better girl, you won't have to tell me because I'll feel your desire while I'm satisfying you*), but answering "I am very pleased that you enjoyed your meal."

By the time we were preparing to leave, almost two hours had passed. She excused herself from me to make a call, and at the end of the conversation she asked "Why am I the luckiest mom in the world", and then said "That's right" followed by "You know it."

Watching me smile at her, she said "I have to let them know that my love for them exists at all times and that I'm glad that they are mine and that I belong to them."

I was moved by the sentiment. You see, I have always made it my business to stay clear of women with children. No bad experiences…just my preference. But a small voice inside my head warned that that was about to change.

We walked out of the restaurant into a dry night. I could have walked her all the way to the Bronx, but I hailed a cab for her instead. Before one came, I asked her for her phone number.

She had the nerve to tell me, "I'll give it to you the next time I see you. I'm making sure that you really want it, and not just asking because it's the polite thing to do after having a wonderful dinner and conversation."

She winked at me then slid her pretty ass into the cab.

Handing the driver a fifty dollar bill then watching the taillights fade, it hit me, I forgot to ask her when the next time she's going to be at the gym.

I had just met this woman, and she had both of my heads attention.

Quincee was on my mind all weekend, and it wasn't until Sunday night that I realized I hadn't thought about Ma'Haundra—at all.

That bitch was a pro at her game; she could knock a cat down to his knees. I heard on a many of days, "Fuck you. I don't give a fuck about you, or anything, or anybody. "

I hated the shit that she did. The way that she treated me was fucked up, and her attitude sucked—on a daily basis. For some reason I couldn't see past her beauty; shit, both men and women were always trying to push up on her and she ate that shit up. Plus she could be charming when she wanted something. And for some miss-guided reason her arrogance actually turned me on—in the beginning.

(*I know I'm not the only one who has dealt with a woman like that...come on brothers, fess up*).

Remembering her nastiness was one of the reasons that woke my ass up about her—after the fact, and motivated me to stay completely the fuck away from her.

We had broken up about six or seven times during our relationship because of her cheating. I've dabbed in pussy on the side, before I proposed to her, so that wasn't a big deal, but the straw that broke the camel's back was the Monday before Thanksgiving of last year. I arrived back in the city a day early from a business trip and decided to surprise her because I was missing her ass some kind of bad. By the time I got to her apartment door; my dick was hard as a rock and I had to concentrate on getting the key in the hole.

Tiptoeing through the house with two dozen long stem roses in my hand and a pair of black pearl earrings in my pocket, I was the one who got surprised.

Standing in the doorway of her bedroom, I saw that she had just finished giving some strung-out looking white bastard a blow job. Thinking to myself (*You nasty trifling bitch*).

With authority, I called her name real calm-like, "*Ma'Haundra.*" She darted her head up in shock. Just looking at her turned my stomach because the bitch had spit and cum all over her face. I turned around, took her keys off my ring, and dropped them on the counter as I walked the fuck out of her apartment and her life. It took a minute to get over that shit and even longer to stop wanting to have her ass knocked the fuck off.

Ma'Haundra and I were like oil and water, but I ignored her bullshit, probably because she was a super- super, freak in bed. But the bitch was dead to me, and six long months had passed, when I had gone out to dinner to Quincee.

It took my dumb ass going to the gym every day from Monday to Thursday before I saw her again. She was working out with her trainer. Watching her wink at me as she completed triceps kickbacks, with sweat running down her neck onto the bench, and her face contorting strain—my shit started throbbing.

Passing me on her way to the locker room, "Hey there" she said, touching my shoulder. I felt a heat go through me. The voice inside my head said (*Don't let her get away*).

"Quincee, do you have a few minutes to give me before you go home?

"For you… yes I do."

It was the way she said it; I felt the blood rush straight to my head…got-damn-it! She smiled at my beet red face that I caught a glimpse of in the mirror. I didn't like her knowing that she affected me, but I wasn't going to let that stop me from getting to know her better.

Ending my workout right then, and walking fifteen paces behind her, to show some kind of control, I damn near dropped a 50 pound dumbbell on my foot trying to keep site of her before she headed into the locker room.

Waiting for me down stairs at our meeting spot, she was wearing dark blue jeans that were hugging her thick hips and ass just right, a red sleeveless turtle neck that had me working hard not to search for her nipples that weren't even poking out, and a short olive green jacket that matched her belt and shoes.

Standing with both hands in her back pockets with her head tilted to the left she greeted me, "Hello Danny", in the sexiest tone that I think I've ever heard my name called in, (*Get a grip Dan. You know you're walking towards danger*), I thought myself. Clearing my throat and ignoring the voice in my head, "Hello pretty lady," I greeted then grabbed her hand and kissed it.

Smiling and inquiring, "What can I do you for?"

"Actually, I would like to set up an appointment with you to speak with my father about that systems thinking concept you were telling me about the other night at dinner."

"I can do that, I have to check my calendar before scheduling with you."

"Not a problem… at your convenience of course."

Not wanting her to leave, I broke the silence, "Do you have plans right now?"

"No"

"Would you like to get something to eat?"

"No, I am not messing with you. Because of my last meal with you, I got fussed out by my trainer."

"I apologize. That wasn't my intent."

"Apology accepted", and we both smiled.

"What would you like to do, in order to accept my request to spend time with you?"

"It's a beautiful evening; I wouldn't mind taking a walk."

We walked from 23rd street and Park Avenue South to Chinatown, and back up to Grand Central Terminal, where she takes the Metro North train home.

Within our stroll, I told her more about myself, about my parents, Matt, and my basketball team that I coach. I couldn't believe that I was telling her all my business. I felt like I was updating to a long lost friend.

At Grand Central Terminal in the tunnel at the track waiting for the train doors to open, bringing to her attention "You said that you would give me your number the next time you saw me. This is the next time, you're getting ready to leave again, and I still don't have it."

"Oh, but you do have them", arching a sexy eyebrow.

Throwing her a perplexed glance while complying with her instructions to, "Check your pocket." Sticking both hands into the sides of my blazer, I pulled out a piece of pink paper that had her home, cell, and fax numbers along with her email address on it. Before I could take in all of her information and comment on the red lips imprint, where she clearly kissed the paper for me, the train doors opened.

Stepping in, turning around facing me, she extended her hand out for me to shake.

Walking up on her, making sure that our bodies were touching (*Damn, she felt good on me*), I brought her hand up and kissed it then I bent down and planted a slow peck on her forehead.

As I did, she put her palms flush on the outside of both my thighs. She told me to call her that night to set up the appointment with her and my father. I did, and we talked for damn near three hours, and still, I didn't want to get off the phone.

The next time that I saw her was that following Tuesday evening. I kind of set her up. I didn't tell her that the meeting was going to be at my father's Park Avenue apartment.

Watching her walk up to me; I felt something tug at my chest, and made me throb all at the same time. She had on a fire engine red sleeveless dress that came about an inch above her knees. The neck of the dress was cut straight across her collar bone that showed off her trapezius muscle. She had on a see through teal, beige, and white scarf that hugged the front of her neck and hung down in the back. The colors of the scarf matched her snake skinned shoes and pocketbook. On top of that she had on a beige duster that was swinging in the wind behind her, with each step that she took. The cat-eye sunglasses made her look like a superstar—the woman's style is tight. She would make Quasimodo look good standing next to her.

Stopping way too close to me, to be a professional greeting, her perfume filled my mind with scenes of nastiness happening between the two of us.

Throwing me an mmmm look, and eying me as if she was reading my mind. I complimented her and lead her into the building.

Ringing the doorbell expecting Mary Rose, our caretaker slash mother figure to open the door, but it was my father.

Wearing the TooGood smile and a dark caremel cashmere smoking jacket (*Pops invented smooth*); the lapel and pocket flaps were chocolate brown, which matched his brown mock neck shirt, lounge pants, silk socks, and suede brown shoes.

Standing 6'4" with a muscled frame, salt and pepper hair and one of his many pipes in hand, for a man his age, he was a damn good catch and he had his share of young and mature women prowling around him.

"Hey Pop. Where's May-Rae?"

"She's visiting her sister in Florida who fell sick and was hospitalized Sunday night." "Wow, sorry to hear that." I made a mental note to send flowers to the hospital the next day.

"Dad, this is Quincee-Jane Catfire, also known as QJ."

"Sir, it is a pleasure to meet you", while flashing that gorgeous smile of hers. Thank you for having me to your home."
After strolling through the apartment, talking about the archway doors, the high ceilings, the floor to ceiling windows, and the super shinny marble floors, we settled in the living room.

Seated across from Pops, Quincee lifted out a plant from her patent leather red bag. Holding it in both hands as she walked and sat down next to my father in the loveseat; offering it to him, with her arms out stretched.

"This is for you Mr. TooGood. It is a Chinese good luck plant. May it entreat all of your wishes?" She glowed, as she handed it to him.

Zebudee TooGood II was speechless. "What do you prefer I call you?"

"Whatever pleases you sir."

"Well, thank you very much Quincee Jane."

I couldn't believe it; she had him cooing. Zebudee, the refined, mysterious observer being relaxed and showing emotion to a stranger, the voice in my head said (*She's special*).

Sashaying her fine ass back to the over-sized black leather chair, I enjoyed watching the expression on my pop's face that I hadn't seen in a very long time. Then they began to talk business.

"Let me preface by saying, I am not an expert, but I have put in many hours studying this concept and I have customized and implemented it to my company's fit. Systems' Thinking is a systemic method of running your business to enhance overall business operations and outcomes.   For example, think of your organization as a body. If a lung collapse, the body can't breathe; thereby, resulting in waning health. The problem must be addressed or the body will be predisposed to more illnesses. The same holds true for an organization. It can be predisposed to internal and external setbacks whether it is inefficient processes, employee dissatisfaction, or a drop in new client percentage."

After presenting her initial point, she inquired, "What is your goal for your company?"

"I pride some of my success on keeping up with cutting edge ideology. In doing so, my goal here is to fine-tune my core policies to facilitate stronger employee relationships to a cohesiveness that will generate more effective interdependencies and efficiency between my diverse businesses."

She introduced another concept and spoke a good half hour more, extracting input from my father; my girl was on her game. She wrap the session up with, "This would be an excellent organizational blueprint for you, particularly if you're planning to expand your business.

Although the meeting was a complete success, and I was pleased that my father had met her, along with him inviting us to stay for dinner, I wanted her all to myself.

After excusing herself to the bathroom, I damn near dove on my father, "Pop, would it be alright if I change our plans?"

"What do you mean?"

"I thought I'd take Quincee out to dinner."

"Ah, you want her all to yourself." Pausing then shooting me an affirmative grin. "That's fine with me. She is a very lovely woman, and intelligent to boot. I like her."

I was jumping on the inside like a kid on a hot ass summer day splashing in water shooting out of a fire hydrant. My father has never said anything close to those words about any woman that I have dealt with—ever. Don't get me wrong, he has never been mean or unkind; just indifferent to a few; Ma'Haundra, being one.

When Quincee returned, I informed her about the new plans, and asked her to join me for dinner. I showed all of my front teeth when I heard the excitement in her voice as she said yes.

Turning to my father with concern in her voice "Mr. TooGood, what are you going to eat?"

"Don't worry about me, I'll be fine."

"Can we bring you something back?"

"No my dear, you two run along and enjoy yourselves." Walking to her and shaking her hand, "I will have my assistant contact you for our next meeting. If you need anything from me beforehand, do not hesitant to call me."

"Thank You Mr. TooGood. It's been an absolute pleasure meeting you and I look forward to conducting business with you."

We said our goodbyes, and I was damn near pushing her out the door.

In the garage, in my truck, I asked her "Quincee, the plant... how did you know that we would be meeting at my father's place?"

"I confirmed the appointment with your father's assistant. I found out that the address you'd given me was your father's business residence here in the city."

Then with slickness rolling off her tongue, "I'm not a dummy. I know how to handle my business."

After picking my face up off the car floor, I responded, "Those very nice things you said to my father—thank you. You are a class act lady."

"Thank you Danny."

The ride up to the Bronx was a good one, we laughed, I told jokes, and we swapped funny stories about our youth. Everything was going good, and then it happen again. We were at a red light talking and laughing when she put her hand on my thigh and that familiar warm sensation went through my leg.

Looking at her, oblivious to my unexpected, but pleasant predicament, while the feeling was taking over me added more intensity to the blood flowing to both of my heads.

We ate Mexican food at a restaurant called Montezuma's. I enjoyed my experience there; but we could have had peanut butter and jelly sandwiches sitting on the sidewalk, and it would have been okay with me—her company was just that good.

Remembering our first night out and her sharing with me her life's philosophies about fairness, plus wanting to get as many brownie points as possible, I decided to let her select my meal.

(Men, women love it when you show them, give them, or do something that they said that they like. It lets them know that you are listening to them. Let me tell you...the benefits from doing those little things are far above what you can imagine—boo-yah!).

When the waiter came to take our orders, I gave him my menu, looked at Quincee and informed "I'm going to let you be the captain of my dining experience tonight."

I sat there taking in her surprise. She tried to be cool about it, I could tell that I got to her because she bit the corner of her lip so got damn delicate and sexy. That shit turned me the fuck on. I wanted a piece of her ass right then, right there.

For the appetizers, she selected guacamole dip and corn tortilla chips for herself, and ½ dozen clams on the half shell for me, (*how did she know I like raw fish*). For her main course, she had pescado relleno— filet of sole filled with shrimp and cheese—served with rice and sweet plantains. She chose for me, broiled lobster tails with green tomato and garlic sauce served with yellow rice. For desert, we shared an order of fried ice cream. The food was excellent.

All through diner, the conversation just flowed. We went from funny stories to political subjects to religion to current events then back to light subjects, (*I love a well versed woman*).

She definitely has lived a full life. She told me all about her family. One thing stayed in my mind. Several times while she was talking about them, she repeated "I am blessed with the best family in the world." And her face would light up. I don't recall ever getting that sense of family closeness with other women that I dated.

Back in the car, heading to take her home, she reprimands me for the food she had eaten.

"You know I got jumped on by Vay-Babe because of my Brazilian dining indulgence with you. Now I have to go home and make my body hurt. So if your left ear begins to ring...that will be me talking about you while I'm pumping the floor doing extra push-ups."

That statement had all kinds of shit in it that drove me crazy, not giving up my thoughts, "I am immensely sad for you, and I hurt with you. Do you accept my most humble apology?"

She just looked at me, bit the middle of her bottom lip, and was unsuccessful at hiding that she wants me.

(Mmm hmm...I caught her once again. Yes, I can be arrogant...all the shit that she has done to me and made me feel. As far as I'm concerned...we were almost even).

All of a sudden, the only conversation she gives up is directions. I didn't know what to make of it and not wanting to be on her bad side, I just followed her lead. About seven minutes later, she instructs me to, "pull over here."

Sitting in silence about five seconds, which seemed like an eternity to me, turning to me, she imitates a ring-masters persona.

"Sir Danny of Manhattan, I bring you here," by now she is getting out of my truck. Following her into a park, standing next to her watching her marvel; with her hands spread out in reverence she continues.

"You are standing on hallowed ground. The undisputable birth place of Hip Hop, Home to D.J. pioneers: Kojak, ICE, Kool Herc, The First Lady of Hip Hop--Cindy Cambell, Prince, Magic Man, Pee Wee. And the B-Boys: Spice Nice, Cadilac, Mev, Eldorodo Mike, Barretta, June June, and so many more. Ladies and Gentleman, I give you Cedar Park."

Standing in the middle of blacktop, I was surprised and glad that I wasn't on the outs with her. I applauded like I was a crowd. She explained to me in detail the history and her experiences with the park. We were out there for a while, traveling down memory lane with the songs and dances of the past. I felt like a kid again when she started humming, singing, then broke out dancing to Sugarhill Gang Apache of *Jump On It*. Feeling her flow, I jumped in with my best Manhattan B-Boy moves.

(*Men, I'm telling you. She makes me feel like no other women have made me feel*).

Before I knew it, an hour had passed and she said, "I better be getting home", which was literally up the block. Back in my truck and driving to the corner, she pointed to the street signs, Cedar Ave & W 179 St. "Remember, that's history."

Turning into her complex—River Park Towers, it was a community by itself. There is a school, supermarket, cleaners, discount store, barbershop/beauty parlor, and a deli shop. One thing that surprised me though was the amount of people outside side. I'm talking about young kids straight through to adults, and it was after 12 midnight on a weeknight.

There are six circular structures that have a tree planted within it, and built in cement benches encircled them. People were sitting on the benches, on the top of the structure; some were playing dice on the other side of the street by the garage, and others where in front of the buildings playing music.

Quincee must have read my mind because she said "Welcome to The Hood! It is not the best place to live, but its home and a part of me."

"I'm walking you to your door."

"You don't have to do that."

I just looked at her and she said "Yes Danny."

That turned me on...I gulped up her obedience. Before finishing my thought, she called this dark skinned, bald headed, big eyed cat over to my vehicle. I could have sworn she call him B Pong. She asked him if he would watch my truck until I come back down.

"Not a problem love."

"B Pong this is Danny, Danny this is B Pong" (*B Pong...what the hell?*), I thought as we shook hands. I watched as cat was undressing Quincee with those big ass eyes of his, and his mouth hanging wide open. She reprimanded him in a flirtatious way and then thanked him for the favor.

As we were walking into the building she told me that they share the same birth date, and that he is a close like family. True that may be, but I saw the midnight in his ass. What he wanted from Quincee had nothing to do with family.

Waiting on an elevator, I found out that she lives on the 35th floor. "I'm close to God", was her response to my momentary quizzical look.

Standing by her door, as she held it ajar with her foot; she turned to me, attempting to reach out and shake my hand again. I put both of my hands behind my back, and looked her straight in her eyes.

Looking up at me with an expression that I couldn't read, she began pulling me by my tie down toward her and kissed me softly on the lips with her mouth open. Then she kissed my top lip with both of her lips, letting me feel the warm and softness of the inside of her mouth, and she did the same thing to my bottom lip. *(The hallway, my brain, and my shit got hot).*

After she had her way with me, she let me go. While still real close and looking into her eyes, I whispered "Where have you been all my life?"

Looking all of six years old, throwing me sad puppy sexy woman eyes, she replied "Impatiently waiting for you."

I felt an energy that almost knocked me backwards, *(It actually scared me because I had never felt anything like that before).*

Then my chocolate queen to-be disappeared into her apartment. I was walking on air to get to cloud ten because cloud nine was two crowded.

(Men, I didn't give a damn, my nose was wide open...I had..... FALLEN).

Sideswiped

Sideswipe – noun; a glancing blow or a hit from the side (Dictionary.com)
Ladies…this doesn't always have to be a bad thing!

River Park Towers
Labor Day Weekend, 2005
Friday, Mid-Morning

Removing the last piece of fried whiting out the frying pan; turning off the burner to the sautéed cinnamon apples then checking the consistency of the cheddar cheese grits, the only items left to complete were to glaze the top of the biscuits with butter and squeeze the oranges for fresh juice.

Ten minutes later, in the doorway of the girl's room, singing to them; waking then up the same way since they were four years old.

"Har-mon-nee and Hope…Hope… Hope. Hope and Har-mon-nee…Har-mon-nee…Har-mon-nee"

Three choruses later both their heads darted up simultaneously. I chuckled at the aggravated expressions on their faces and their attempts to complain. Because before either one could verbalize a syllable, I witnessed them take in the aroma of breakfast. I swear it seemed like they levitated off their beds and greeted me with a peck on the cheek.

"Morning Mom", Harmony was first to reach me.

"Good Morning Mommy", Hope was close behind, as she zoomed passed me, on her sister's heels for their "You were first yesterday, It's my turn." "Oh Well, you should have gotten up earlier," daily routine.

Eight minutes later, we were sitting to a formal table setting, chowing down on a southern meal. Laughing, talking and eating, I listened to their hapless chit chat, as years prior, I remembered Dr. Phil saying "If you want your teenagers to tell you the big things, you have to listen to the small stuff before they get that age."

Mothers, I have listened to countless hours of dribble-drabble and I must say that it has paid off because my fourteen year olds have told me some things and have asked me some questions that have made my head want to spin around in circles.

Harmony initiated the next topic with her favorite two words, "Mom. Guess what?"

Having no idea as usual, she went on without waiting for a response from me.

"Me and Hope..."

I corrected "Hope and I"

"Yeah, Hope and I are entering the Double-Dutch competition across town, on Auntie Theresa's block. And we're going to blow everybody out the neighborhood."

"You guys are that good?"

Never lacking confidence, my first born affirmed "Yep"

"Yes"

"Sorry Mom; yes."

Turning to Hope, asking, "Is that right?"

My humble second born conceded, we're alright."

Shocked that I never learned how to jump double-dutch, I followed their crazy idea to move the living room furniture, making space so that they could teach me.

First, it took eighteen attempts before I managed to jump in. Then I couldn't get coordinated to the two ropes; thereby, never accomplishing a completed motion. Frustrated and embarrassed, my perfectionism kicked into to high gear. Determined to get this done, I followed Hope's instructions.

"Ok Mommy, stand in the middle and when I say jump. You Jump!"

"Okay"

"Mom, you can do it!" Harmony chimed in.

Simultaneously, they counted "1-2-3-Jump!"

Super pumped up, rocking to the rhythm of the ropes on either side of me -- I went for it. The right rope ended up hanging off my left shoulder. The left rope landed between my ankles. They were hollering in laughter. My feelings were hurt and the fun was over.

"That's it. I'm done. You two go get ready to go to your aunt's house."

I was so mad that I didn't pay any attention to their "Mom, Mom, come on we were just playing, or "Mommy, we're sorry, come on. Try one more time."

I cleaned up while they packed. Exactly forty-seven minutes later they were heading out the door, still snickering under their breath.

"Good bye Mommy. Have a great weekend. I Love you."

"I Love you too."

"Bye Mom. See you Monday night. Love You."

"Love You Back. Kick ass with the competition."

Simultaneously I heard, "We will!"

The door closed behind me and I shouted out, "My Time!"

Grooving to the song *Heaven* by Solo and singing way too loud to myself, while getting dress, my phone rings. It sounded like a woman, but then I heard an unrecognizable boisterous male voice in the background and then the phone went dead, just as the second line beeped in. I clicked over without checking the caller ID.

"Hello."

It was Eli and as soon as I recognized his voice, I hung up the phone and went back to basking in my "me time."

Ladies, Eli is the twin's useless father. I put him out seven years ago and he is still trying to get back into my life and home – NOT HAPPENING!

On schedule, I was walking out the door at 4:30 p.m. Fordham Road was so backed up with holiday traffic and pre-Labor Day shoppers that I missed the 5:35 train. Seated on the 6:15, it breaks down and it takes forty more minutes before an alternate arrives. Half way to New Rochelle on the replacement train, all of a sudden there was a loud thumping and scraping sound on top of the train then all the lights in the car went out. Debris on the top of the train disabled a piece of electrical apparatus; taking damn near another hour for the second replacement to come from the yard. So what was supposed to be a fourteen minute train ride, turned into a three hour fiasco.

Relieved to be in a cab on the way to the house, but I was still pissed off at not seeing Tina being surprised.

8:47 p.m. I'm walking up the driveway that was lined with stones on both sides of a beautifully manicured lawn that was befitting of the ranch style house made of beige, taupe and blue-gray masonry. Innocently jealous of their living quarters, I ring the Frontlaroy's bell.

Tina answered the door, warming me with an authentic smile and hug. I pretended that I didn't see a look, as if she were staring at a ghost. I entered into her home.

"Congratulations Miss Graduate. How are you? Damn, you look great..."

Never giving her a chance to answer me, I handed her her gift; a clear crystal paper weight that had her initials in calligraphy embedded in the gold, brass, and pewter background. Within a minute or so, our conversation was cut short by the doorbell ringing. She directed me to Dre, who had my bag in hand and escorted me to the room that I would be staying in.

Taking all of five minutes to freshen up, I headed to the party area. Approaching the room, I saw a familiar back of a head; it was Cheryl's chemical free sponge curls, pulled tightly back into one bush-bun at the nape of her neck. Then it dawned on me that I had never followed through to call her.

Walking around to the front of the couch, I see Matt first. Honestly trying not to be dry because for some reason that fine brown skinned handsome Maxwell/Lenny Kravitz looking bastard, never warmed up to me, no matter how hard I tried. Finally, one day I got tired and said "screw it." Our rapport consisted of; I speak and keep it moving.

Making eye contact, and calling out "Matt"

Reciprocating with a nod and "Q"

Bending down in front of Cheryl grabbing her hands, "Hey girl, ooh, it's so good to see you." Still stuck on stupid; I did not catch the ash gray on her face that penetrated through my glad tidings. I hadn't realized how much I'd missed her.

Interrupting our conversation was a woman sitting next to her, who extended her hand and said, "Hi I'm Lana."

Turning to her left side, she coo'd "And this is Danny", as I glimpsed them sitting intimately close. Thinking to myself (*What kind of fuckery is coming at me?*). I was cool on the outside though, as the next 60 seconds proliferated forward.

Knowing full well that I had no claims on Danny, nor any right to be affected; indignation ripped through my chest. It took extreme effort for me to take control of my emotions.

To the silent shock I saw on their faces at my presence, and the ambiguity of not knowing how I was going to react to this situation, *Ladies, I reiterate…I was cool.*

"It's nice to meet you Lana", mustering up a weak smile, but my "Hello" to Danny was indifferent; the bastard couldn't even look me in the eyes.

Standing up, I complimented, "Lana, I like your shoes."

"Thank you. I got them from….."

The shoes where just average and I had no idea what she was saying. It was part of my strategy for the game that had already begun. She turned to Danny and informed me, "My baby picked them out."

Still stunned, yet smoother than finely spun silk, I turned to Danny, "You have excellent taste", while gazing deep into the river of those beautiful grey/green lying eyes.

Feeling my strained decorum dwindling, turning away I bumped into Dre, the 6'4" dark chocolate, astute correction officer, with hands large enough to cover my entire face, yet had always treated me with the disposition of a gentle giant.

Taking all of three seconds to decipher the situation, the scowl on the Po-Po's face that was directed at Danny, on my behalf melted my heart. I walked away from the group feeling satisfied.

In the kitchen, Tina approached me. Seeing the empathy in her brown eyes for me and all of her 5'9" frame struggling for the right words "QJ, I just found out about you and Dan this evening and then to see Twink. I don't know what that's all about."
Reminiscing on the second occasion when Tina and I met, she continually pointed out how well Danny and I look together and that she'd never seen Danny that happy before, while informing me of her sisterly status to Danny.

I stored away all the uneasy thoughts that I felt about having a separate rapport with her.

"Tina, don't worry about me, I'm a big girl…I can handle it."

"It is not supposed to be like this. What happened?"

"That's a conversation for another time and another place. Tonight is all about you."

"You do know how Dre and I feel about you…right?"

"Yes. Yes I do."

Poking fun at her, "You should have seen the expression on your face when you saw me standing at the door." We laughed; I gave her a thank you hug and dismissed any further conversation about Danny.

Wanting to rid myself of the dull ached in my heart, my mind snapped back to…the club, and like healing water, I felt better.

A bonus for me was that I was looking and feeling, sexy personified. I had on a pair off form-fitting jeans with a turquoise top underneath a lace eggshell poncho, and turquoise sandals. I had no one to answer to, and I was in the mood to show my ass.

Ladies, you know how it is when we want to make them suffer for hurting us.

Feeling decidedly better, my appetite found me. With a plate of food in my hand, I re-entered the living room and sat in a chair directly opposite Danny and the group.

Full frontal view of my former crew--plus one, I enjoyed my meal scrutinizing them in my mind—Danny's girlfriend being the first one. If she was white, I would parallel her to a dumb blonde. I reveled at Danny's discomfort. The last attempt Lana made to be touchable close, the bastard looked my way then cringe at Lana's touch. Thinking to myself (*Yeah, I hope your skin feels like snakes are crawling all over your shady ass*).

Finished eating and nursing on a frothy frozen Margarita with brown salt that Dre had whipped up for me; I was feeling a little tingly -- when I heard a familiar voice.

"Hey, I know you."

Turning to my left side then walking my eyes upward I was shocked and simultaneously caught off guard by a pleasure pang that thumped my she-grotto. It was Stormy Wellington—the intelligent, no-nonsense, suave, funny IT Tech Specialist that I attended the University of Phoenix with.

Looking at the drop dead fine, short curly-haired, I know how to please you in the bedroom-eyed; yet, humbly handsome, sexy southern gentlemen who gave me goose bumps on the norm—also known as, the Quiet Storm.

Talk about being sweetly sideswiped. The Universe had thrown me a homerun. Ladies… you know, it was on then?

I hadn't seen Stormy since our graduation ceremony. We had promised to keep in touch, but up until that point, I guess both of us became too busy to pick up the phone and call one another. I was a bit disappointed in myself at not attempting to make contact, as I am normally very good at things like that.

That Fine Storm was wearing a lime green argyle vest that had navy blue diamond's that were thinly outlined in white; showing off those perfect biceps, also a pair of below the knee navy blue jean shorts, and a pair of navy blue leather penny loafers that matched the blue in the vest, with eye piercing shinny quarters in them.

Giddily responding "Hey, I know you too", gagging on the inside, while holding my composure. That's when I discovered that Dre and Stormy are cousins, (*It is a small world!*).

Squatting down meeting me face to face, I had to focus on not becoming memorized by the poetry that was before me. Smiling at each other in unbelievable surprise for a few more seconds, I decided that I wanted to be alone with the Surprising Storm. Standing up and directing, "Walk with me."

"Just-ah lead and I'll fol-lah City Darlin."

Outside on the walnut wood deck, making our way to the far left corner of the back yard where there was a very large oak tree that had two swings attached to it. Looking at each other, smiling we headed towards them. Stormy straddled the left swing side-ways, facing me and starring distractingly long. I sat forward in the right swing, moving it back and forth with my feet, trying not to let the heat accelerate in my jeans.

All was right in my world. After a few moments of silence, Stormy inquired, "So tell me City Lady, how are the young'uns?"

"They are doing well," sincerely meaning "Thank you for asking."

"What's life been do'n to yah since I last seen that purty face?"

Enduringlying turned on by Stormy vernacular spectrum. It extends from deep southern root-drawl to collegiate elite.

Screaming and creaming on the inside; but, pulling myself together and not without verbosely chatting about my life's happenings. Then I was hit with the one million dollar question.

"So tell me City Lady, are you gett'n any love'n?"

If that fine fuck had touched me at that moment, I would have orgasm all over myself. I reported the unfolding story about Danny and Lana, without divulging the participant's identification in the crowd. By the time I finished my story…you know how when a person is upset, but refrains from making a comment, passing judgment, or be overly compassionate, but you know they are ready to break bones on your behalf…that was the look on Stormy's face. I almost had second thoughts about sharing all that I had.

Reciprocating the question, the story that was unfolding before my ears was just as appalling, shocking, and sad, as mine was.

Stormy was involved in an on again-off again relationship with a woman named Jade. She is the type of woman that knows she is beautiful, her arrogance is bred from her family's old money, in other words— she's a narcissistic bitch. Their tumultuous relationship was currently in the off again stage.

Hearing how Jade had taken off with her not quite ex…ex, an investment banker, to San Tropez, for a week, and she hadn't contacted Stormy until the third day into the trip. I couldn't help thinking why do things like that always happen to the good guys. Not reading my thoughts well.

"Go-on, call me a fool. I know she's ah play'n with me, but I have been head oh-vah heels for the vixen, since I first laid eyes on-uh."

"That is so not what I would call you." Then I felt the blood rush up my face.

"Thank you fo-yah kindness, City Lady."

Hearing more of Jade's indiscretions throughout their relationship, it was my turn to be disgusted, angry, and ready to kick ass for someone who did not deserve malicious treatment , all in the name of love.

Swapping stories drained the both of us. In the midst of our individual misery and unbroken silence, we heard music come on from inside the house. I spoke up first, "I'm ready to dance."

Ladies, we have to pull ourselves away from strong negative thoughts. The process takes effort and discipline, but this is what we have to do for ourselves.

To all you Ladies, that's hurting right now….Come on—show me what you're made of.

As we approached the deck, Toomey stepped outside the glass door, startling me. "Where the hell did you come from?" bunching up my eyebrows in annoyance.

"Damn, well hello to you too—Quincee-J-A-N-E."

Turning to Stormy with an extended hand, "The name is Toomey,"

Then turning back to face me, "Can I talk you for a minute?"

Obliging and excusing myself, Toomey and I walked back towards the lawn, while Stormy headed in the house.

Dumbstruck at Toomey's presence, in addition to wondering (*what did we have to talk about*). Standing 6'3" mid- dark brown silky skin, sporting a Jeri-curl (*no juice dripping...thank God*) and looking like a Puerto Rican with a beige guallvera shirt, brown trousers, and closed toe sandals. Throwing me completely off guard and introducing the conversation with, "Hey girly, are you aw-ight?"

"I'm fine, thank you."

"I know you're fine, I can see that, but are you alright-- seeing Danny with that chicken-head, in front your face like that?"

Remembering why I consider Toomey an insensitive creodont, now looking through the hate-tolerate lenses that keep us perpetually at odds with one another. The one commonality that we shared was that we both considered our self the other's nemesis. So although the question was bluntly in my face, I did feel sympathy coming from my adversary.

"I have to say, I'm extremely taken aback by your interest, but I am alright."

"It's my job to be a pain in your ass. You always come off being a tough-ass. That's why I give you a hard time. Why do women feel they have to appear unbreakable?" Not waiting for an answer, "You're good people, and I just don't like the shit that I see."

About to say something mushy, I was interrupted.

"Don't be getting all soft on me. Go on with your damn long ass neck."

I said thank you and headed toward the house. In my wildest dreams I would have never imagined what happened next. As I stepped inside the glass door, a record from the seventies was playing "The Coldest Days of My Life" by the Chi-lites.

Toomey never letting my hand go, guided me to the dance floor, and encircled my body with those long, lanky but muscled, and unexpectedly comforting arms. I actually felt safe –it was weird, but reassuring nonetheless. Toomey let me lead. Barely moving to the music; my thoughts were all over the place.

Dear God, not again...Please help me hold it together.

A rush of hurt struck me in the heart and buckled my knees, just a bit. Willing back the tears that were welling up in my eyes was too much focus because my bottom lip starts to quiver. Toomey in sync with me held me up and looked down at me with that 'You are okay' expression.

I peered up at this person that I never really had nice things to say about, but who was canoeing me away from drowning in my own pool of despair.

Looking left then right, any direction as to not look into my rescuer's eyes, while the Chi-Lites sang *It was the coldest day of my life...I had to run for cover yeah, yeah, yeah.* The melancholy melody of the violins gently strummed my pain. That multiplied with a weak moment of feeling dejected by love itself, I buried my head in Toomey's chest and began to cry in incontrollable silence.

Ladies, standing your ground "for no bull-shit", does not reward you a pass to get of the madness pain-free.

Giving me only five seconds of raw emotions then bending down cheek to cheek whispering to me, "Don't give that yellow niggah the satisfaction of seeing you like this. STRENGTHEN YOURSELF!"

Grabbing my hand, leading me out of the room into the suburban night air, crossing the road to a dense forest of trees, that crazy ass said, "Come on, I got something for you to get your emotions right," pulling out a joint and lighting it up.

"You're going to get us arrested."

"Nawh, I pass on that. If the cops come driving pass us, which I doubt, we're going to duck behind these trees. Who's going to see our black asses in the dark?"

Suppressing the urge to say something slick, I went with the rationale and flow. I learned how to play "Boston—Take two Puffs and Pass."

Taking two long drags and letting the smoke take effect. Choking, coughing, eyes watering, and my nose burning; feeling like a sight for sore eye because Toomey began laughing hysterically at me. After recovering from my trauma and cussing, I became tickled and joined in.

Feeling the full effect of the smoke pow-wow, I mulled over Toomey's ulterior motives with regards to me.

"Why are you doing all of this?"

"All of what?"

"This…being here… coming to my rescue… taking care of me. Caring has never been your forte, especially when it comes to me. I don't get it."

Studying me intently, "Look, I don't know what the fuck happened between you Danny. All I know is that you just stopped coming around, and when I asked about your whereabouts, I never got an answer—which was my answer. Now I see you here today and shit doesn't look good. I see five against one. I include myself because I came with them. Yeah, I have my fucked up ways, but I play a fair game of ball."

"I appreciate that."

We talked for a long while and I learned some things about my former enemy. Then we made our way back to the house, got some drinks, and ended up on the deck around side of the house. I was observed, "You look better."

"Thanks to you;" commenting with a grin on my face.

"What are you smiling about—not that it's a bad thing?"

"I was just thinking, how God sends us mercy through the most un-likeliest of bearers."

"Amen to that."

The old Toomey then resurfacing and dismissing me, "Good, now that you got your shit put back together, I can tend to this call I need to make."

Bending down to plant a "thank you big brother" kiss on Toomey's wide forehead, Stormy came from around the corner.

"Hey. You ok?"

"I'm okay, thank you."

Throwing me a grand smile, "Good, see you back in doors."

Toomey gave Stormy one of those "What the fuck is up" looks, and snapped, "Yo man she's cool out here with me."

With both hands held up in mocked surrender, Stormy nonchalantly replied, "Not trying to stir up any dust."

Looking at me sexily and professing, "Just making sure the City Lady is faring well", then the Gentle Storm disappeared back around the corner into the house.

Gawking and inquiring of me, "What's up with that?"

"I hope something," arching one eyebrow in response.

There was a bonding that transpired between Toomey and I that evening. With a renewed sense of being, I headed back in the house, ready to do some damage.

Extenuating Circumstances

(Ok fellas, do you believe in loyalty? If you do, how far would you go to respect it and to keep your family relations in tact?)

East 19th Street, Manhattan NY
Wednesday before Labor Day Weekend

No one, in my circle, not even Matt or my father knew the bull-shit I was going through with Jimmy. He's the oldest…James Theodore TooGood, but the most irresponsible of all of my father's offspring. Jimmy is 5'8" with a scrawny build. He's yellow with curly hair, green eyes, pearly white teeth, dimples and a clef in his chin. His looks have kept him dick-deep in pussy and getting over on people ever since he was a teenager. My brother is a two-legged snake.

Bad things have always happened to him. The last game of his high school career, he broke his hip and tore the ligament in his knee in three places. There went his football scholarship to Iowa State (*the boy was fast as lightening…no one could catch him*). Recovering, he got hooked on pain killers, which led him to using all kinds of drugs.

I don't like Jimmy or how he chooses to live his life, but he is still my brother. He's always felt that our father loved me more, and he's taken a personal hatred towards me after Pop's named me successor to run the family business. That's one of the reasons why I keep cleaning up his messes. The last time I saw Jimmy was the day before Quincee dumped my ass. I had to give up $1900 to crack dealer that he owed.

Wednesday morning before leaving the house for work, I get a call. "Yo my niggah, I need a favor, seeing how you always got deep pockets and all. I need $750 cause I owe some bad cats some money, they gonna do some serious damage to me if I don't pay up, and I'm kinda dry right now. Yo, my mellow, I'm your brother. You know I'm good for it!"

"Jimmy, how many times I've heard that bull-shit; but, I've never seen one damn dime that I've shelled out for you. I'll get back at you later. I'm running late for work." I hung up listening to him scream into the phone, "Dan, I need your help!"

That night when I got out of my truck, two thugs walk up on me. The black burly one had craters in his face, two gold teeth in the front of his mouth, but was well dressed. He had on a black suit with a grey mock neck shirt, and grey suede shoes, and was accessorized with a Cartier watch and a fat ass diamond ring on his pinky finger.

His side kick gave off less of a presence. He was piss-color yellow wearing a pair of jeans with a long sleeve button down the front blue shirt, and a pair of black sneakers.

Caught off guard, but in full control, I gave both of them a questioning look. I saw the hand piece of the 45 glock sticking out the top of burly's pants. As calm as he was well-dressed he began, "Your brother suggested that I come to you for the collection of his debt."

In an even temper and straight face, I countered "My brother?"

The burly thug motioned for me to look across the street at the car that was parked directly across from my house. There Jimmy was, sitting in the car looking like a scared crack-whore. I could see sweat dripping down his face, and as I walked closer to the black range rover, I could see his eye twitching, which meant that he was practically shitting his pants. My first response was thinking (*How could that simple minded fuck bring these people to my home?*). Then I thought about his worthless life, so I asked how much was owed, and when was it due?

"Two G's, and yesterday."

All I had on me were three bills and give or take five hundred in the house. Thinking to myself (*This is Jimmy's last get off free card he's played with me*).

I told Head Negro In Charge, "I'll give you eight hundred dollars tonight, and you'll get the remaining twelve hundred by ten o'clock tomorrow morning.

Replying, "I'll take the eight tonight, and you'll have seventeen hundred for me tomorrow; twelve hundred plus five bills for tonight's accrued interest. By the way, little brah, will be staying with us tonight, just in case you start thinking…because you look like one of those thinking niggahs."

The shit-eating grin on his face made me want to shoot him square between those two fucking gold teeth of his, but I knew it was wise for me to go with the flow because now my home and my privacy was compromised. The meeting was to be in Brooklyn.

Thursday morning 9:47 p.m., I'm standing at the corner of Nostrand Avenue and Linden Boulevard. 10 o'clock on the dot, a car pulls up to the curb. The back door swung open and thug number two got out beckoning me in then he got in the front passenger seat.

In the back seat with Jimmy's simple-ass sitting between me and H.N.I.C, we hadn't rode to the next stop light before I had handed over the envelope, with the money, to thug one.

Grinning, and shaking his head, he propositioned "It's a pleasure doing business with you. If you are ever interested in making some investments, just let me know. I think that we could make a lot of money together."

"Naw partner, I'm straight. I'm not in your game."

"Partner...hmm...now that sounds good."

I looked that fat fuck square in his eyes to let his ass know—I'm not my brother—there was no fear this way.

Playing the staring game with me for a few seconds before announcing, "Our business is done." Then he signaled to Piss Color, who had been pointing a gun with a silencer at Jimmy's head the entire time. I opened up the car door dragging my dumb ass brother out the car with me.

On the street, Piss Color walked up on Jimmy, "If I ever see your ass again, I'm going to put a bullet between your fucking eyes, you dry piece of shit."

"What, you mad cuz your woman was looking at me and likes what she sees?"

I couldn't believe my brother; I wanted to beat his ass right on the corner of Nostrand and Eastern Parkway. Instead I grabbed him by the arm and lead his dumb ass away with me down the block.

After the range rover drove off, Jimmy started gloating; thanking me, and singing that same old song, "Yo man, you gonna get your dough."

Disgusted, I jerked his hand off my shoulder "Get the fuck off of me."

His arrogance never ceases to amaze me. I had just saved his ass, but he had the balls to say to me, "Oh you too good for me to touch you....the-fuck! Chill out. You act like I'm gonna rob you or something. I don't need your high and mighty, house nigger bullshit...the fuck."

Popping on the collar of his shirt with both hands, so that it stood up on the back of his neck then looking at me like he didn't give a fuck that I had just saved his life, he said "Later" then walked away.

Watching him stroll off, I stood there stupefied at his narcissism. I was so drained that I decided to take the day off. I went home and got straight in the bed and I didn't wake up until the phone woke me up later that night.

"H-i-i-i Danny. Danny... H-e-l-l-o-o-o?"

It was Lana, a.k.a. Twink. We have been friends ever since the fourth grade. She was high-yellow, boney, freckled face, and had a mop of long frizzy pigtails that kids use to love to pull. She was so damn shy that it used to piss me off because she would never defend herself when she was being attacked. I'd seen her bullied in school and in the neighborhood.

She and her mother—Miss Roberta were already living in the building when my family moved to the neighborhood on 93rd street. I ended up in the same class with her. She never spoke if she wasn't asked a question by the teacher and she was so damn scary.

In sixth grade, when we were old enough to travel to and from school on our own, I remember walking into the block and seeing a group of female bullies circling Twink. They were pulling her hair, and calling her all kind of jacked-up names, and she just stood there taking their shit. Then one of the girls hawked and spit in Twink's hair. Those little bitches were jealous because despite Twinks's disposition, she was a pretty kid.

Running up to the group hauling off and punching the spitter, right in her got-damn mouth knocking her big ass down then turning to her flunkies, "If I see any of you bitches touch her again, I'm going to fuck you up every day for a month." Then I said "Boo", and they scattered like roaches running from a turned on light.

Grabbing Lana by the hand, I didn't let go until we were standing in front of her apartment. While we were waiting for her mother to open the door, I saw a twinkle in her eyes that I never seen before—I started calling her Twink.

Later that night, Miss Roberta rang our door bell, introduced herself and told my parents the story that Twink had told her. She said that she wanted to thank me personally for protecting her baby. Truth be told, the pride that I saw in my parents faces that night set the course of me wanting to be a do-gooder for women and to them. From that day on, I protected Twink and she was good company for me. She was seven and I was eight when we met, and we have remained close friends and have stayed in contact over the years, other than the time that she and Ms. Roberta disappeared.

Twink considers me a big brother and when she have man problems; she calls me. I listened to her bitch and moan and cry and vilify her-self. Sometimes it's hard to dispute what she is saying because she is known for picking fucked-up men, plus she isn't capable of standing up to them.

Since she was so depressed; I decided to invite her to ride up to Tina's graduation celebration with me. I had to give it some thought because for the past year, I've noticed that every time she's going through something with her relationship, she had been making sly innuendos and passes at me; sometimes bluntly flirting, and one time she even tried to kiss me (*what the fuck!*).

Don't get me wrong, the years have been very good to Twink. Those long bulky unruly ponytails had turned into relaxed auburn curls. Her freckles were less pronounced on her face, and I didn't remember that she had huge beautiful tiger colored eyes. She had filled out in all the right places. She has the kind of ass that you could sit a glass on and it wouldn't fall. Bottom line, I see and will always love Twink as my baby sister.

The night that I invited her, she boldly asked me if I could be her date. It caught me off guard, but I said "sure" because her self-esteem was so got-damn low. So when she called reminding me, I felt like a jerk because I had forgotten that I asked her to ride with me.

"Hello Danny, are you there?"

"Yeah, I'm here"

"What's going on sexy?"

"I'm good, what's up?"

"I was just calling to see if we're still on for our date this weekend?"

(Shit… Think fast…Think Dan…. Awh….Fuck-it).

"We're still on. I want to be at Tina's house by 6 o'clock, so you should get to me no later than 4 o'clock."

I would have preferred to take Quincee, but she had made her position perfectly clear that she wanted no parts of my yellow ass.

"Okay, I'll see you tomorrow. B-y-e-e-e, for now."

Hanging up the phone from her goodbye, I felt a cloud come and stop at the top of my head.

(Men, tell the truth, what would you have done, if you were in my shoes?).

Friday afternoon at 2:30 p.m. Twink was ringing my doorbell. She was wearing too tight jeans and an even tighter, deep V-neck green blouse. The choker around her neck matched the two extra-large wrist pieces that went half way up her arm. I was curious, was it strictly fashion, or was she covering up something. I made a mental note to check her out when she took them off.

Attempting to greet her with a hug, she stood embarrassingly close holding on to me too damn long for my comfort; showing her intentions of promiscuity straight from the gate. I knew then that it was going to be a long ass weekend.

So glad that I had packed earlier; I told her that we were going to get on the road.

"Do you need to use the bathroom?"

"As a matter of fact; I do" she said trying to entice me by walking behind me and gliding her hand up my thigh and across my back.

"We're leaving soon as you're done."

Returning from the bathroom, dodging my plan for escape, "Do we have to leave just yet? I thought we might have a cocktail and chit-chat a bit," plopping down right next to me, avoiding all the other seating space in the room—a large couch, two chairs, and a window bench.

I felt like an eight year old boy trying to get away from a nasty little girl, who just happens to be my best friend.

Obliging her with a nice size brandy because she had always been a weak drinker, I reiterated, "As soon as you finish, we're leaving because I don't want to get caught up in traffic."

Huffing, she finally surrendered, "If you insist!"

"Yes Twink, I do!"

In twelve minutes, I had the house closed down, had our bags in the truck, and was pulling off. I was not going to let her catch my ass up in the plot she had planned for me.

The trip to New Rochelle was long, but it could have been worst. The drink that I gave Twink, knocked her ass out. She slept the entire way, *(Thank God)*. It gave me time for my own thoughts. I was looking forward to seeing Tina. It had been a while since we spoke because I was busy with work, and she had been so busy with work, school, and homemaking with Dre. The last few times I spoke with her on the phone, she sounded rushed, but refused to end our conversations.

"No, I'm not getting off the phone. I always have time for you."

The first time that I met Tina was back in college. It was the night that Matt and I took Twink back to her dorm, after Sammy went after her like she was some kind of got damn punching bag. Tina had pulled up in the dorm parking lot as we were getting out of my car.

Twink still had visible bruises on her face, so when Tina saw them through her the car window—I was the closest body to her— she jumped out of her Volkswagen and had her finger pointing square to my face, putting me through the third degree.

"What is going on? Who are you? Are you on the football team? I've never seen you before. Why does my friend have marks on her face? Are you responsible? I'm not like Lana, I will report your ass to administration in a heartbeat."

I had to smile because there was this short person that I was looking down at, who had pushed up on me like she was going to strike me at any moment. I was impressed at her loyalty on behalf of Twink---her friend...my sister.

When she saw me smile at her, she went livid. By the time Twink got out from the back seat of my car to calm Tina down, her face was blood red. She was ready to have my ass served on a platter. It took several minutes for Twink and I to explain and bring her gangster down to zero.

Finally aware of whom Matt and I were, she decompressed and was completely embarrassed. I have liked her from that day on because I don't know of many females who would stand up for their friends the way that Tina did for Twink.

I smiled as I was rolling up the highway. Then my thoughts went to Dre. We will never be friends. Cat doesn't know the true story, and will never find out from me. I hate that bastard so much that I changed my chain of thought.

My attention popped on Quincee and sadness plucked me when I passed her complex that is right next to the Major Degean Express.

(Little did I know that the melancholy I was feeling would turn into outright suffering?).

Everything I'm Going To Do Is All Bad

Retribution or karma—when either manifests itself to you, it's for damn sure, going to be good to you. Ladies, Enjoy the Ride!

New Rochelle, NY
Home of Dre and Tina Frontlaroy
Friday, late night

Nice and relaxed after leaving my sojourn with Toomy, I walked back into the house, and headed straight for the kitchen. Waiting for my second Margarita, I had no idea of the opportunity cost I would have to endure from Dre.

"Are you okay? What's going on with you and Dumb-Dumb? When did Twink come into the picture? Are you going to forgive that punk? Can I kick that mother suckah out my house because I saw you crying in the corner a while back?"

"I am okay; there's absolutely nothing between Danny and me; I don't know who Twink is; thereby I have no clue when they came to be, and it's up to you if you want to kick the mother fuckah out of your residence-- pardon my French, sir. You won't get any rejections from me."

I couldn't wait until my drink was ready, so that I could haul my behind away from this inquisition.

Making my way back to the party area, Usher's song "Truth Hurts" was playing. Moving my body to the music, gazing around the large beige airy room, I watched three couples grouped in the far corner laughing; then to the singles that were mingling on the opposite side that appeared to be scheming…then I spotted Lana. She was enjoying the song as much as I was.

Ladies, I don't know what came over me.

Walking over to her, reaching for her hand, I pulled her of the couch "Come on girl, let's dance."

The earlier hurt that I experienced was replaced with the bitch-in-me. I must reiterate I don't know what came over me. The beat was pumping, the margarita was kicking in, and both Lana and I were flowing to our own dancers beat.

When Usher was singing *"Whatever you were working, I hope that it was worth it baby."* I walked up on Lana and invaded her personal space. I then placed my right leg between her legs and stopped dancing. It's a move that I normally accost men with. The tipsy in Lana must have come out because she dipped down, bounced a couple of times then began caressing the bottom of my leg, up to my thigh as she return to the standing position; leaving me taken aback. She was going through her motion as Usher was singing *"Truth hurts...I got reason to believe that you've been fooling around!"*

While still gazing into Lana's eyes; I simultaneously flicked a pointed finger at Danny.

The song continued *"Whatcha you been doing and who you been doing it with... I hope that it was worth..."* Lana became more exotic with her dancing. Rubbing my thighs; gently caressing my arms, and then she turned around and began backing her behind up to me. I was too far in the game punk out. The four puffs of weed I had earlier definitely exaggerated my bravado.

Once the song was over, I thanked her for the dance and went outside to catch a breeze because it was most hot in the house.

The night moved on, and I was back sitting in the same comfortable caramel leather chair, when Luther's song "Never Too Much" came on—

"LUTHER, WE LOVE YOU AND WE MISS YOU!"

Everybody in the house was on their feet, dancing and pay homage to the musical superstar. I even saw a one woman with tears in her eyes as she sang out with the rest of the room *"Never Too Much...Never Too Much...Never Too Much!"*

Folks held up lit lighters. I have to hand it to the DJ, he followed up with Luther's "Having a Party"...the entire house was rocking.

Dancing and scoping the room, I spotted Danny and Lana; she was all over Danny like a bitch in heat. Honest to goodness I did not want to be affected by the situation anymore. It had been almost two months since the Ma'Handra incident. I caught myself just as I was about to get pissed off at myself for feeling emotions that comes along with love-hurt.

Ladies, if you are going through something right now and you are beating yourself up because you feel you should have known better –about him, about love, about being a fool---...STOP! Remember... You're only human and it's in our nature, as women to want to be loved, be protected, be made love to, and be in some ways, guided by the male energy. And you know what-- it is your God given right to expect it.

Lost in my thoughts, Stormy interrupts, inviting me to dance. Not paying attention to what was currently playing, I said "Yes", and headed toward the dance floor.

I believe I was set up because R. Kelly's "Your Body's Callin," was playing when I noticed that we were the only two on the dance floor. With intentions on being in the spotlight...I wanted to do it right, I walked back to the chair and took off my poncho; revealing my low rider jeans, with a turquoise bodysuit hugging my triple D's exactly the way I wanted it to. The horizontal diamond cut-out in the back, exposed my back from the bottom of my bra line to past the top of my jeans, which gave way to "ooh's and aah's. To add a little emphasis, I had on an extra-long silver necklace worn backwards, tucked inside my bodysuit with the silver and diamond cross touching the small of my back.

To all of my big booby sisters out there, we can be just as alluring from the back as our small endowed sisters who can wear us out with drop-dead gorgeous back-out attire.

Walking back meeting Stormy's "hmm" grin, I reciprocated with an 'I'm ready to play' glance. R. Kelly was singing "*I hear you calling...here I come baby to save you...uh oh*", just as Stormy pulls me up close and personal, looking deep into my eyes, (*I felt my libido being read*).

The very warm hand on my lower back implanted sensual energy throughout my body, on impact. I held my breath because I didn't want my heat to show—at least not completely. That Fine Storm caught a split second of received pleasure on my face, and winked at me.

Never afraid of a dance challenge or being caught at being a woman, I let the music take me at its will. I did a snake-like move, threw some energy at that fine country gentleman that landed like a bolt of lightning, while R Kelly sang "*My body's...calling... for yah.*"

Before spinning around, I explicitly returned Storm's previously ego-filled wink with one of my own while biting on my bottom lip implicating….yes my body is calling…what?

Turning my back to Stormy, I was facing Danny's group. I couldn't help myself; I looked Danny straight in the eyes and winked while out stretching my right arm across the back of Stormy's neck, as that fine chunk of yum-yum grabbed the sides my hips, and bump me…mmm… just-right, setting my ass on fire.

Danny's simple minded mud-duck ass got up off the couch and left the room.

Thinking to myself *(That's right; if you can't take the pressure then get out kitchen.; go ahead and run little boy…run!)*. The thought made me smile.

Looking towards the kitchen, I caught Dre's elation at Danny's suffering. Chuckling out loud as I was spun back around to Stormy, I reveled in our too close for comfort mating dance.
Lost in my own heat, I found myself becoming memorized by Stormy's presence, sexiness, and palpable lust for me.

Mouthing the words with R Kelly, *"You see I'm wise enough to know when a body's yearning… yearning for me"*, Stormy walked up on me again, bent down, kissed me gently on my cheek, and just stared into my eyes for about three seconds.

I felt indisputable care and boyish charm beaming at me in those country dreamy eyes. It was my turn to back up, but before I could do so, I was grabbed by my hands and led into the hustle.

My ego, my vulnerability, and my humility were being protected. Ladies I saw myself living in the country…and like, like, liking it.

Feeling all bubbly on the inside, we finished our dance like two old friends having fun singing to each other and making light of a heavily heated lust introduction.

Turning and walking away; when Jaheim's very slow song "Today's A Special Day for You" began playing. In one motion, Stormy jerks me caveman-like spinning me back around then gingerly pulls me in-- steamy close. Dizzying my nostrils with pleasure; taking in the smoky aroma of whatever kind of cologne I was inhaling.

Seduced by a mental rendezvous, my inhibitions surrendered without opposition, as Jaheim sang "What you want to do baby…think about it."

My hips are being guided in and swayed back and forth, from left to right into the lump between Stormy's legs. Feeling the calm, the mighty and the intensity all wrapped up into the Quiet Storm who was publicly working me over.

Jaheim sang *"Honest, honest, honest I'll do anything you want me to"* as Stormy is looking deeply into my eyes professing, "Guh, if'n you want it...you-can have it. I'll do anything you want me to."

I saw it coming straight from the soul in those country intoxicating eyes. The pang of arousal and the way I was called guh instead of girl had me smiling on the inside at that Accenting Storm.

Ladies, have you ever felt being absolutely craved for. Take the fork out of me, I was ready to cum.

When the record was over, we looked at each other and simultaneously turned and walked in opposite directions. Breaking away and heading to the kitchen, I retrieve my drink that Dre was watching for me. After letting the cool take over the heat that had risen in me, I returned back to the safety of my seat.

Nestled comfortably in my spot, Stormy grabbed a folded chair, and sat down next to me, commenting, "You're a nice bad City Lady."

With a blank catty stare I purred back, "Thank you for the dances Stormy Wellington."

"What am I going to do with you guh?"

"Why--keep me—of course," I Catfire'd out

Interrupting the nasty thoughts I was having, Dre walks over by us and began hooking up the stereo system.

"Bear, what are you doing?"

"I'm hooking up the Karaoke machine. My baby wants to sing, so y'all are going to be singing."

I couldn't believe it, but Tina likes stuff like that. Personally I thought it was corny. Little did I know how I would be drawn in. In a flash, Dre had the system loaded and then gave Tina the warmest and loving introduction.

Tapping on the microphone to get our attention, "Hello, hello everybody, I would like to take this time to thank all of you for coming to share this special occasion with me and the most beautiful woman in the world, the gentlest soul that I know, my motivator, my better half, the wind beneath my wings, and the love of MY life. Ladies and Gentlemen...I give you...Tina Frontlaroy." The room erupted in loud applause and shout outs to Tina.

Stormy turned to me and said "Cuz did real good" then began to applaud a whistle for the couple.

Tina approached the microphone, and Dre bent down and gave her a kiss on the lips as she blushed in the midst of joy. With the inner-glow of true love still sprawled on her face, Tina took the microphone from Dre, and thanked every guest individually and shared what we all meant to her. She spoke about Dre last.

Reaching for the Po-Po's hand, she began "Baby, without you by my side, supporting, encouraging, and sometimes pushing me, I would not have been able to accomplish all that I have this far, let alone obtaining my law degree. You said that I'm the wind beneath your wings. You are the force that gets the wind blowing…I love you."

It was a beautiful moment to share with them. Before ending her speech, she requested, "I don't know if everyone here knows that I'm from Alabama and I have relatives in New Orleans; The Ninth Ward to be exact. We almost cancelled this weekend because of Hurricane Katrina. I am so blessed that all of my family evacuated before she hit. I would like to have a moment of silence for the victims both the living and the dead; for the agencies that are fighting the good fight for them, for the honest police whom have forlorn their own families to protect and serve, and for the wayward—I pray that they be touched by the Holy Spirit to do the right thing."

The room went silent. With my head bowed, I heard the room fill up with whispered prayers as I said one of my own.

After a minute or so, Tina offered another thank you, and then she motioned to Dre to start the music. I had no idea that the woman had such a beautiful soulful voice. Facing Dre she said, "This is for you" and began singing Gladys Knight's rendition of "Wind beneath My Wings"

Looking at the love in their eyes for each other lit up the room. When she finished singing, Dre walked up to her, dip her backwards and planted a make-love kiss on her. I thought to myself, (*true love actually exist*).

A twinge of sadness strummed at me, as I thought about Danny, and what I thought we could have had.

Dre's voice interrupted my thoughts, "Okay yall, here we go", and the Karaoke recorder began playing *"You Know You Make Me Want To Shout"* by the Isley Brothers. Everyone was on the floor dancing and singing, except for Danny and Matt.

In the middle of the record, while still jumping with the rest of the crowd, I took a minute to smell the roses.

Dear God, thank you; for good friends, and times like these, Aman and Amen.

I was taken aback to see how many individuals were actually excited at getting on the microphone to sing. While Tina, her cousin, and her sister where wailing out "We Are Family" by Sister Sledge, I asked Dre what other songs where programmed in the system.

"Here's the list."

Browsing through, I notice a song that I have always loved, and something inside of me just needed to sing it.

Standing on the make-shift podium completely out of character and not at all nervous, I preamble with a request, "I'm a virgin at this Karaoke stuff, so please don't be too hard on me. The record that I'm about to sing is called "For Your Precious Love, sung by Linda Jones."

Looking sky-ward, I went on, "I would like to dedicate this to You, and You know who You are. This is my Ode to Our Love."

The song starts off talking *"Into each life, a little rain must fall. And you know every day cannot be Sunday."* By the time I was going into the next verse, Dre had put the word-play on mute, so all that was heard was my voice and the music.

I began to sing. *Your precious love means more to me, oh than any love could ever be.*

Scanning the room as I was holding the notes, I saw a couple staring into each other's eyes with love-smiles on their faces. They were definitely feeling me.

Back to talking and ad-libbing from my heart *"As I look around the room at the love that, for some reason has passed me by, I realize that it is time to shed my little girl fantasies, my grown ass woman desires, and the vision of love that I had for myself. But before doing so, I have to let You know, how I feel."*

Internalizing the words that were coming out of my mouth, cut my insides because I was also remembering how I had fantasized about being submissive to Danny.

Approaching the song's climax, dropping my voice with the beat of the music; throwing my head, my shoulders, and my arms back in surrender, I began singing...

"Darling. Darling Don't You Know That I Love You Too Much, Yeah...Yeah. Oh...Oh...Ooh...Ooh." Ad-libbing *"Mmm...Mmm...Mmm... Baby...Baby...Baby"*

My body jerked with every syllable, as I sang with all that I had. Unabashed sadness from my destroyed desire, poured out of me.

"For Your Precious Love, There's Nothing Darling, In This Whole Wide World That I Wouldn't Do."

With my hands raised above my head, and my finger pointed outward, I sung out into the universe. I refused to look directly at Danny because had I did, I would have implicated the both of us. Although I disliked everything about Lana, I knew it was the jealously in me, and that would not have been fair to her.

Ladies, just because we get over-taken by the green-eyed monster, that's no excuse to be malicious.

Tears were rolling down my cheeks by the time I screamed out *"BABY I WANT TO TELL YOU THAT I LOVE YOU, ONE MORE TIME, YEAH...YEAH FOR YOUR PRECIOUS LOVE"* Ad-libbing "YEAH...YEAH...YEAH. PLEASE BELIEVE ME WHEN I TELL YOU. IT'S YOU, YOU, YOU... YOU...YOU...YOU"

Lost in a trance, I imagined the microphone and stand as Danny. Palming the tip of the stem with my right hand, I began stroking down the stand; delicately holding it between my thumb and fore finger, and I sang to that mother fucka, but thinking *(Yes... know how much I loved you... you dirty, dirty sweet, smooth, fine son of a bitch. The hurt in me HATES YOU. The woman in me DESPISES YOU for making us miss out on our love-journey. I LOATHE YOU for not being my protector— the security guard to my heart. I DETEST YOU for your shortcoming of being my provider—the producer of harmony in my life. And I will deem you UN-FORGIVEN for leaving the gatekeeper position to "She" vacant. For all of this, I say fuck you Danny, in the worst way).*

Ladies, I was letting that salty bastard know....mother fucka...I love you and I miss us!

By the time the record was over, my face, my chest, and my back were wet with perspiration, my breathing was elevated. My energy was drained from pouring my heart out; and my soul was blithe because I bared the very essence of my love, unashamed, unafraid, and unpretentiously. It was freeing, empowering, and self-embracing.

Recuperating from my good-bye to Danny, I was unaware of the applause around me. Reentering reality, embarrassed and humbly thanking the room for my 15 minutes of fame, I exited the podium and did not stop walking until I was in my assigned room.

Enduring the day's emotional spectrum of exhilaration to shock, from hurt to falling on sadness's doorstep, had finally taken its toll on me. Lying in darkness and in the middle of the queen size maplewood post-bed digesting my performance, scrutinizing my motives for being here, and struggling with my feelings, I allowed myself a fifteen minute pity-party. Minute sixteen, I let my mind go blank because I didn't want to think about Danny, nor me not being with Danny, or anything that had to do with love.

Swinging my legs over and sitting on the edge of the bed, believing that my temporary sojourn from sanity had vanished because all the malicious thoughts of Danny were gone. I headed to the bathroom. All freshened up with a sleeveless turquoise micro-fiber mock neck blouse on and feeling emotional centered for the um-teenth time since I had arrived, I headed back to the festivities.

Making my way through the kitchen, I run smack into Dre, Danny, and Matt. Dre was busy at the counter mixing drinks. Matt and Danny were standing by the refrigerator --which I had to pass-- whispering, with what appeared to be an intense conversation.

Scanning Matt first, I saw a look of pity on that usually non-descriptive face. Thinking to myself (*I don't need any sympathy from someone who I know does not like me*).

I was caught off guard by Danny dabbing my arm and then just standing silently in front of me for about three seconds with the dumbest expression. I had to focus on keeping my cool from the heat of my re-lit anger, but more so from the sweet blaze that almost paralyzed me, from the mere touch of my enemy.

The fourth second hit and I was about to make my getaway, when Danny looked at me with puppy-eyed humiliation and proclaimed "Quince, Everything isn't what it seems."

Before realizing it, my tirade had begun with disdain reeking from every syllable "Your audacity blinds you. What makes you think that I want to hear anything that you have to say? Or that I would even care?"

"Quincee, you don't understand. Please…listen."

Ladies, what do you do when you know he's wrong, but he's begging--sounding and looking sincere, and your heart is imploring you to give in?...Been There, Done That.

Standing my ground, I continued "Listen to what…you making excuses about your new woman. If there's one thing that you should have learned about me…I'm neither a hater nor clingy."

Looking in need of absolution, but pissing me off instead, "Quincee, you have it all wrong."

Indignantly snapping back, "My name is Ms. Catfire, to you!" Then losing all control as I gesticulated towards the living room, inquiring, "So tell me, was she before, during, or right after me?" Cognizant of my self-betrayal at showing semblance of jealousy, I ignored.

"Quincee-Jane, I swear to God, I didn't know you were going to be here. I would never do anything to hurt you. And no there is nothing between Twink and me, if you would just hear me out."

Unable to stomach anymore of the denial and wanting there to be no mistake on this score, "You know what Danny…save your little self-effacing speech because I… DO… NOT… BELIEVE… YOU! Yes, you hurt me…but I've got love-scares so deeply bedded into my heart that your cruelty can't come close to matching, or your fake-ass love couldn't possibly melt them away."

Ladies, I think it is THAT pain that give breathe to the 'Angry Black Women Syndrome. Knowing that you have given love from every corner of your heart, but it still isn't good enough—that hurts.

"Quincee-Jane, Miss Cat….Quincee, I…"

I wasn't interested in hearing anything more. All I wanted was that lying bastard's pride…ALL OF IT! Then it came to me. Sticking my chest out in raw arrogance, pointing my eyes downward to the 'She' between my legs, I gloated.

"I'm the one who came out on top because you don't know what she looks like, tastes like, or feels like." Taking my conceit further, walking up on the pain creator so close that there was no space between us because I wanted all of my energy felt, whispering dignified-like, "Fuck You. Fuck Your Apology. Fuck The Very Air That You Breathe."

I thought I would feel retribution; instead, I felt the rawness of love-pain— the kind that actually makes your heart hurt.

Just then, that country fine Stormy flooded the room and caught a glimpse of me, and I heard the abject concern in, "Guh, what's the matter?"

I couldn't respond because my bottom lip was trembling so badly, and I was fighting hard not to let the formed tears trickle out my eyes.

Turning to view all the faces in the room, spotting Danny grimacing--I can safely assume that Dre implicated Danny as the love problem that I was experiencing-- Stormy turned back to me and instructed, "Get your belongings, you're coming with me."

Taken aback and opposing strongly, "No I'm not… I am supposed to be staying with Dre and Tina this weekend."

From behind me, I heard Dre happily retort, "Don't worry bout it. You are in good hands with my cousin."

With that being said and the country thunder-like command that Stormy issued, it was nothing left for me to do, but go and get my things. Before doing so, I found Tina and told her that I would be leaving with Stormy.

"QJ, I'm so sorry that all this happen to you. I…"

Cutting her off before she could finish, "How or why would you take the blame for something that you have no fault in? Look, this is your party, so just put me and all this mess out of your head, and enjoy the rest of your weekend."

"You are kind, QJ."

"No, I'm a realist, but thank you for the compliment."

"Dre will probably fill you in on everything."

"PROBABLY…you think," shaking her head at the thought of Dre's elation. Seriousness cloaked her face with her next statement.

"I don't know what happened between you and Danny, but I sincerely hope that the two of you can work it out."

If she had said that to me when we were speaking earlier in the kitchen, I would have inquired about Lana and Danny's relationship, but I had reached the point where I didn't care anymore.

Responding, "I really don't want to go there. I have to maintain some semblance of dignity."

"I know that's right." she concurred and then waved me off and said, "Go and have a great time, Stormy is one of the good guys. But remember, so is Danny."

"Yeah…Right!", I said shrugging my shoulders and rolling my eyes.

She didn't give me a hard time about it, and wound up our conversation, "I'll let Dre get a kick out of telling me the particulars."

Chuckling, I hugged her then headed off to find Cheryl.

When I met up with her coming from outside, I ignored the pre-occupied expression on her face as I told her about my plans. To my surprised, she looked disappointed.

"Cheryl, is everything ok? The last time we spoke you said that you needed to talk with me. Has that situation resolved itself?"

"No. I need to speak with you now more than ever. There is no one else I trust."

Messed up from her words, and concerned at the fear on her face, I asked "Does this have anything to do with Matt? Is that bastard treating you right?" I grilled her.

"The problem isn't Matt; just call me as soon as you can."

"I will call you Tuesday evening around 9:30. Is that good for you?"

"Can you make it earlier?"

"What about 6:30, 7'ish?"

"I'll be waiting for your call."

Troubled by the ominous feeling I had that her safety maybe in jeopardy, I showed her some extra love in my hug, told her to stay strong and to take care of herself then I headed towards the bedroom that had my belongings in it.

Never doubting my decision, I was actually excited about going with Stormy, (*Dear God, who would have thought our paths would have crossed again, whatever the outcome…I thank you.*)

Smiling at my reflection in the bedroom mirror, I headed back to the kitchen, with bags in tow, to Stormy.

Dre walked us outside to Stormy's car; a 2005 Lexus GX470, black onyx with gray leather interior.

"NICE Cuz," commenting to Stormy with a smile and a nod of approval.

"Thanks Cuz. It's a graduation present I got myself."

Turning, grabbing me up into a bear-hug and whispering into my ear "You will be alright with my cousin?"

Whispering back to Dre, "I know I will, with your bad ass."

Smiling, I got in the car.

While Stormy and Dre ran their mouths, I took the opportunity to call my mother and inform her of my change of plans.

"Hey Ma."

Quincee-Jane, Eli has called here four times today looking for you. What's wrong now?"

"Nothing, he's just probably upset because when he called me earlier today, I hung up on him."

Laughing at Eli's stupidity, my mother summarized "Well, if he calls here again, I have some choice words for his ass."

"Thanks Ma. I'm calling because I......."

"I don't believe this. This is Eli calling again. Call me later."

"Okay chica...bye. I love you Ma."

A few moments later Stormy and Dre hugged, then Stormy got in the car.

Making our way to the highway in silence, I was taking in the view of the beautiful homes and landscapes in Westchester County, even in the dead of night.

After re-entering the car from filling up the tank, Stormy inquired, "Are you alright?"

Reciprocating without responding, "What are you doing?"

As sharp as a country tack and still accent free, "I'm protecting you because right now you're not doing such a good job."

There was nothing that I could say, as I did feel protected.

"So where are you taking me?"

"With me."

"And where would that be?"

"Crystal City"

"Crystal City, DC...Crystal City?"

"That'll be the one."

Pondering for a minute, with no doubt infiltrating my thoughts, acquiescing to my Country Protector just seemed like to right thing to do.

Before the end of the New Jersey Turnpike, I asked Stormy to make a pit-stop for me.

Still feeling warm and tingly on the inside when we pulled into the rest area, opening the car door, the cold air slapped my body, and I began shivering.

Stormy—on point, got out of the car, went to the trunk, and returned with a long sleeve sweatshirt.

"It's ben wore'n. Ah had it on while play'n ball earlier."

I was so cold I didn't care. Having the shirt pulled over the top of my head, catching a whiff of musk and cologne—I was turned, all the way on. Still under the influence, I asked nonchalantly "Are you coming in?"

"Naw, Ah'll be rat-chere wai'n on yuh. Ah'mah gonna rest mah ah's ah-bit."

"You look exhausted."

"Ah-mah tuckered. Ah was on duh row'd bout 3 dis maw'n, fix'n to have mah momma n place fo mah auntee's breakfast go-n's on, honoring huh at dah UFT or TFU, sump'n tah du wit fed-ation ah teachers, at 8AM.

We gat chere tah duh city bout 6:45 or so witch gave me jus nough time tah shauwer an all. We ded'n git out yonder til one, or so. It sem lak all dem foks wan-nid ah piece of my aun-tee, an she be'n who she is n all, spok-en wit dem, an hurr'red nay-ah one of-em."

Chuckling at the annoyed expression on Stormy's face, while being turned on by the thickest accent I had ever heard passing through those sexy southern lips, I continued listening.

"From thair Ah tuk all'er bud-dees' home."

Stormy began to laugh, and went on to say, "At ah point Ah felt all-ov sey-em years ole wit dem tree'n me lak baby boy Joe-Joe, but it was ah pickle hang'n out wit-em. I wint tah dah park fo ah quik two games, den wint bak to auntee's house, shauwered, put mah git-up on an hed-it to Dre and Tina's."

"Whew, you poor tired baby", I said moving in close.

"Guh, yune betz to scoot from me."

When I saw that fucka's heat rise; I hurried up and got my ass out of the car. Heading inside, I got an idea, and made a call.

"Hey Shannon, I need a favor from you."

"What you need, Sissy?"

"Can you book a room at the Philadelphia Westin for tonight and late check-out tomorrow, for two?"

"I thought you were going to be in New Rochelle for the weekend?"

"Change of plans, girl. I'm with Stormy."

"No..oo..ooo. The one I met at your graduation?"

"Yes girl!"

"Stop playing!"

"I know!...I know!...I know!"

"Okay, I'll call you right back."

Shannon is twelve year my junior, and also my rock. She stands all of 5'3", light brown skin with a 26" waist and a Beyonce Booty. Her no-nonsense personality of "telling it like it is", is not to be mean or critical, it's her position of, "I have no time for anything else but the truth" that actually have people afraid of her. I once dated a guy who was six foot two and weighed an easy 275. He was scared shit-less of my sister. Her other side is, she is the most giving, wise, and straight-shooting, honest hearted being that I know. I love her with all that I am.

Did I mention that she is one of the smartest people that I know and an exceptional go-to person...for anything?

Standing on line at the Burger King counter getting something to drink for Stormy and myself, Shannon calls back.

"Sissy, I made the reservation and put it on my credit card.

"Thanks chica, I'll transfer the money back to your account on Tuesday."

"No problem, "Luh Yah."

"Love you back."

Walking back to the car, I could see through the window, Stormy was leaned back in the seat...fast asleep. I felt so bad and a twinge of fear crept on me, (*can we make the trip to Philly without Stormy falling asleep at the wheel?*).

Inside the car, I took several minutes just watching my Protective Storm sleep ever so peacefully. Reaching dangerously close because of the fire that had already been lit between the two of us, I cooed "Hey there", while gently touching those smooth cheeks, with my nose.

"Mmmm...Ah der, rat bak at-cha."

"I have new plans; I've booked us a reservation at the Philadelphia Westin, in downtown Philly."

"Hav-yah now?"

I couldn't tell if it was a "Have you now…okay baby", or an "How could you make a decision without speaking to me first."

"Well since you are so tired and DC is another couple of hours away, and you definitely need some rest…so there, you have it."

That sexy fine Tuckered-Out Storm just looked at me and said "Then Philly it'll be."

Back on the New Jersey Turnpike, traffic had thickened and for about 30 minutes we crept, due to an accident. I made it my business to watch Stormy like a hawk and kept continuous conversation so that sleep would not overtake either one of us.

Relieved to finally be approaching South 17th Street, Philadelphia, I couldn't wait to get that sweet Tired Storm into bed for a good night's rest.

Two of the highlights of the hotel are the Heavenly Bed and Heavenly Bath, and let me affirm, that is a definite truth.

It is one of my top favorite hotel chains. It sits in the middle of the block like an enclave with a circular driveway area that is grey marbled. Guests are greeted by a doorman in a red coat and black top hat. The entire staff caters to you with exceptional customer service. All facets of The Westin; from the gold mirrored elevators to the traditional decor, are beautiful and permeates an ambiance of elegance.

The receiving agent was extremely gracious and was amused as she listened to Stormy chastise me for the pre-payment arrangements. My sister's account was subsequently credited after Stormy produced a gold American Express card.

When we got into the room, I saw the fatigue wash over Stormy's demeanor. Grateful for the care I'd been given thus far, I headed straight to the bathroom. I ran a steamy bath and added some Carol's Daughter almond cookie bath oil to the water. Watching the tapioca pearls, pearly everlasting, and angels' wings flowers float in the water, had me wanting to jump myself. The room was lit with the vanilla scented candle that I brought with me.

Getting Stormy into the bathroom was practically a feat; I had to physically push the lug through the bathroom doorway.

Staring at my little storm cloud take in the eye appealing brown onyx marble floor and countertops, the double-headed shower head, an extra-long bath tub that was filled with scented oil soothing our nostrils, along with the steam heating the room temperature to lullaby-just- right, all the gratitude came pouring out.

Hugging me appreciatively and lusciously, I just barely heard "Awh, City Guh. This is just what I needed."

Winking, I exited the bathroom.

Thirty minutes passed and I'm relaxing in the lounge chair when Stormy came out the bathroom. I took a quick glance, and then turned my head away. Why, why did that fine specimen of yum-yum-eat'm-up come out the bathroom soaking wet, wearing nothing but a towel that was about ready to fall from a six pack ab'd waist?

The water droplets looked like they were ready to pop with pleasure. That coupled with seeing Stormy body's in its natural state for the first time, the lethal combination both terrified and had me too turned on!

Pondering whether to play it safe by going to soak in the tub, or take a big risk and stay and chit-chat; Stormy read me like a book, and commented an inquiry, "You scared to lay with me City Lady?"

The bitch in heat in me, is always ready for a good challenge, so I got up and sauntered my ass towards the bed, all the while thinking, (*alright girl, you know you're walking in the red zone*).

Lying on the bed semi-wet and glistening with body oil; hands clasps behind that thick neck, exposing those sexy ass biceps; I scooted down beside the tired but Yearning Storm. One second, I was sitting on the bed and the next I had been pulled on top of that hard, slippery soft body. Being engulfed by firm; yet exquisitely gentle arms, my socks were being rocked with the softest fullest lips that were treating my mouth with tender loving care.

Backing away from the kiss, after approximately twelve seconds, my nerves were completely wrecked. Looking up and seeing pure tiredness in Stormy face, I ordered "Baby, get some sleep."

My Exhausted Storm responded "Mee-cha in the morn'n City Lady", and was sleep in a matter of seconds.

It was then my turn to wind down. By the time I finished with my bath and had slipped into the bed, it was well after 3 a.m.

Feeling Stormy get out of the bed, glancing at the clock, and seeing 4:58 a.m., I pulled the covers over my head, curled into a ball because it was cold in the room, and I dozed back off.

In my sleep, I felt myself being pulled. When I opened my eyes, I was in the same position on top of Stormy as the night before when we were kissing. Then I heard....

"Now where were we? M-m-m-m...rhat chere."

I was being kissed exactly the same way, but longer and with a lot of extras. My back was being caressed, my neck massaged, my chin licked, while my 'She' was being grinded on with just the right amount of groin pressure. The room heated up to sauna hot and every craving that my body beseeched, Dr. Storm appeased.

Averting my eyes sideways, as to not be put into a trance by the sexy eyes that were looking back at me and one step away from searing into my soul; I lost the battle.

Turning my chin forward, "You are beautiful Quincee-Jane Catfire. Do you know how long, I've dreamt about having you in my arms?"

So engrossed in feeling good, I couldn't even pull a response out of my toes.

Positioning me on my back and whispering bedroom love in my ear, that Candy-Taker pulled my thong to one side, spread my legs and slide a long finger up the middle of my wet opening--stopping at the little girl in the boat—inducing the room to smoldering.
Ladies, my libido was under attack by the pleasure monster. Did I mention that I had not had sex in two and a half years? I was in critical condition.

Heat dripping from every word "Damn... Guh... Ah lady-pearl should never be this hard", while circling and pulling on the tip of my clit.

Peering up, witnessing the pulsating neck vein expanding and contracting; informed me of the restrain that the Controlled Storm had to muster to keep composed because I know the dick was thumping to my cadence.

Knowing my pearl's value, normally my bedroom banter is 100% on target, but the QJ Bitch in me came out, and I responded, "I know, so tell me something new.", and I attempted to squirm away in mocked disobedience.

Rising up to a sitting position and looking down into my eyes; for a split second, I saw a Perplexed Storm, but then I was set straight in no uncertain terms. Meeting me eye to eye, the Agitated Storm sarcastically chided, "I know you hurt'n and all, but I'm not the enemy. That dirt belongs to that damn Yankee. Right now, you're here with me and you're mine. Pitch away that salt and let me care for your ailing."

Scooping me around my thighs and lifting my behind up into the air, so that only my shoulders and head where still on the bed; I tried to make a move to get out of my predicament, but I was confronted by a bedroom baritone voice Storm guiding my body down gently on the bed accosting me with, "Billee-Jane Yankee, Johnny Southerner here… ready to answer that cat that's- ah calling me. So hold your playing with me guh and let me take care of you and the puss-ee!"

The Lollipop Licker defeated my alter ego, first by kissing the insides my thighs then biting the outsides of my woman lips, in precursor to gnawing on their insides. At the onset of feeling my clit being suckled on, and my threshold entered by a nasty country tongue that made me moan in apologetic pleasure.

Hearing the automatic Storm Pilot, "mmm…sugar, sugar, sugar aaaaaaaaaaah, yeaaaaaaaaaah City Guh", I melted like liquid butter. When my mind felt like it was going to explode from all the shit Stormy was sensually assaulting my ears with, that master of tease flipped me back on top and said "I'm yours…Take whatever the fuk you want."

No soon as I heard that said, I wanted to hear moaning in my ear. Ensuring that the Storm Front didn't try to slide up inside me, carefully I sat astride the dick so that my lips hugged it like a warm bun encircling a big sausage.

You see ladies, I have never met a dick that I wanted to sit on and ride. Sorry boys; but, if you want that from me, you're gonna have to take it!

Rotating my pelvis backards and forward, sliding up and down the length of Stormy's shaft, so that the dick could feel my contented wetness, while intermittingly I planted sweet kisses on my more than eager Enslaved Storm.

"Groan for me." Commanding as I lifted my hips then dug in with 'She' so that my syrup could be felt with each flick of my clit, along the entirety of Stormy's candy and abs of steel. I felt like a nasty girl licking on a forbidden caramel lollipop.

After bending down kissing both of those sexy closed eyes, I started kissing every inch of that small cute right ear, before licking it; then whispering into it "Do you feel 'She' answering you?"

At first I heard a sigh slip out "Ah." Then I focused just on the tip. I let 'She' talk to it with her wet and juicy—slurping, squishing and clapping sounds.

Gone were the arrogance and ego—the Ejaculated Storm moaned and groaned for me, "U-m-m....A-h-h.h.h.h...M-m-m-m-m-m-m-m," then organism out, "Q-U-I-N-C-E-E J.A.N.E!"

A rush of power shot through to my psyche. My body felt like it was in a forbidden place, looking down on a perfect specimen of wonton want for me. My venery intellect continued to be stroked by Stormy's humbled submission.
Talking some more... "I'm your pain releaser. You just make sure that the next time that you and that bitch get together—and you will— make sure that she makes you feel like this."

Sliding down I began to slather Stormy's tip with my wetness in a circular motion. The absolute control that I had over the libido that lied underneath me, filled every cell in me with power and had my body aching to explode, but it was my turn to maintain an even strain.

The sweet scent of sexual charged pheromones dangled in the air, adding three dimensions to watching Stormy's face sliding down to meet my crotch, and the warm hands that spread my behind cheeks apart exposing my open lips; uncovering my readiness.

Ladies, you know that feeling when the air hit's your clit! My pussy was on FI-YAH!!!!...Cut out the lights and call The Law!

The Hungry Storm's long fat tongue darted inside my woman-hood, which further aroused the nasty in me. I rode that tongue better than a fifty year experienced high-price whore who knows how to ride a dick. I mop my essence all over Stormy's face, and in return that Starving Storm sopped up all the heat that was in me and my juices.

Within less than a minute, my body was shuddering, as the Relishing Storm ate me and muttered a chorus of *"mmm hmm's."* Then with a bit more firmness, I felt my clit being sucked and I popped right then. It had been so long since my body felt an orgasm that it hurt....but so...so…sweetly good. Stormy had worked me over so splendidly that I couldn't move any part of my body. I just laid there and drifted straight off to laa-laa land.

While in a deep sleep, I was awaken to my cell phone ringing.

"Quincee-Jane, it's Michelle. I have some exciting news. Remember the property in Brattleboro that you adored, but it was too pricey for you. Well, the owners are in the process of getting a divorce and are offering a quick-sale. They have dropped their asking price by 30k, but the catch is you need to come and see it today.   I got the call late last night from their agent. I haven't put the word out yet, I'm giving you first dibs. Quincee-Jane...Quincee-Jane. Are you there?"

"Mmmm! Yes, I'm here. That is exciting news." I could hear Michelle, yet neither my body nor my lips were responding as quickly as I would like them to have. I believe that my mind wanted to stay in Stormy Land, but the real world was calling me.

Clearing my throat to respond, "Yes I'm interested, and I'll make it up there today. I'll get back to you and let you know what train I'll be on."

Within 15 minutes I was back on the phone, "Michelle, I'm taking the 9:53 out of Philly and arriving in Brattleboro at 5:10 this afternoon. Is early evening too late for them?

"No, I'll pick you up at the station."

Immediately looking at the clock, I saw 8:07 a.m.

Ladies, you have to hear the story about...STORMY!

It's Not What It Seems

(Yo Chiefs, Love pisses me off because it can castrate a dick. Finding myself holding that bag; I didn't know who the hell was looking back at me in the got-damn mirror anymore. All in the name of trying to keep hold of the woman who had my heart on cruise control and my dick on lockdown).

I was stuck on Quincee-Jane Catfire because I liked the way she made me feel about myself when we were together—I mean, all the time.

(I know I'm contradicting myself, but men—give me a break... hear me out).

You know how women want to know—where you're going, who you're going with, how long you will be out —but not Quincee.

I remember one Saturday when the crew was hanging out—me and Quincee, Matt and Cheryl, and Toomy with a crazy-ass female. Toomey reminded us about the Diego Corrales vs. Jose Luis Castillo boxing match that night, so the three of us decided to cut the evening short and go to Matt's house to watch the fight.

Toomey's date started in first with the whining, "Aw come on Toom. It's still early. I thought that we were...."

Toomey chopped her ass up. "Oh hell no! I'm not having any of that bullshit. You and I have been together ALL day. I've giving you everything that you've asked for. Now plans have changed. I'm going to watch the fight tonight with my boys. End of conversation." The skeezer jumped up from the table six shades of pissed off—then stormed off to the bathroom.

I was surprised to see Cheryl's face frown up. Matt said, "Baby I'll have the boys go to Dan's house and we'll go to the movie or whatever you want," kissing her hand and meaning every word. My brother is smooth personified, but Cheryl never opened her month, so I had no idea which way brah was going.

Almost afraid to look at Quincee, but when I did, she was staring back at me, looking so got damn fine wearing a plain white bodysuit that showed off her neck. Some black jeans and the black pearls that I had giving her, and she said, "Have fun. Just leave me with some goodies to keep me on the straight and narrow before you go--" winking and leaning into me, waiting for something.

On the regular tip, I am not into public displays of affection, but that night I would have done anything to her, anywhere she wanted it, and anyhow she wanted me to do it. Grabbing her by the back of her neck and jerking her to me, I bit her jugular vein soft enough to make the pussy warm, and hard enough to warn, 'Don't fuck with me!'

Kissing me soft on my upper lip then expertly nibbling on my bottom lip and mouthing, "Mmm…I'm going to keep it warm for you", right then I knew that I wanted her all for myself--always.

(Fellas, its shit like that –no pressure AND encouraging a man to hang out with his boys. Don't women know that'll keep a man wanting to keep his woman happy? I didn't give a shit-- my nose was wide open).

I like Quincee just as much as I lust after her. I was seeing her fine ass on the regular. Everything was good with us, until one night I saw Ma'Haundra at a club. The whole got-damn night was a series of misinterpretations that lead to Quincee leaving my yellow ass.

The first thing she was wrong about was I had been walking around for a couple of weeks with an extreme case the blue-balls ever since she put a strip-tease whammy on me the last time she was at the house. So the night that we hung out, from the moment I saw her; I went from having blue balls to a having a hard-on, strong enough to cut steel.

We had made a brief stop at Cheryl's house before continuing the evening. Quincee and I were sitting on the coach and she touched my leg. I swear to God, there was an energy surge that went all through me that made everything in me, feel perfect. I had never felt anything close to that before. Not even the feeling, when she gives me goose-bumps. In order to keep cool, I slid away from her.

I could tell she was not happy about my movement, but staying true to her nature, she played it off. Why did she move up on me again?

In order to not show how she was affecting me; because I was about to cum—real hard, I inched away from her a little further.

All her civility flew out the got damn door and she went off on my ass. I wasn't about to let my secret out, so I just sat there and took everything that she spewed at me. Once the urge to cum was gone, her anger started turning me on. All I wanted to do was grab her up in my arms. It would have been okay if she left it at that….but not my Quincee.

From the time she came out of the bathroom, she wouldn't talk to me let alone, look at my ass. On the ride to the Brooklyn, she was damn near sitting on Toomey's lap trying to keep as far away as possible from me. She wouldn't take my hand to help her out the car.

As soon as we got in the club, she showed her natural ass. The first thing she did was rig her bodysuit to make it show more cleavage. Shit, personally I liked the look. Upping her game, she told me that she was going to use the ladies room. Damn near twenty minutes had passed and no sign of her, I went looking for her ass. Walking towards the restroom, I saw some half wanna-be baller leaning all up in her neck, and she was grinning all up in cat's face.

When she saw me walking towards her with my hand stretched out for her to take, she stayed cool as a cucumber. Grabbing my hand and introducing "Baby, this is Randy, Randy this is my other half."

"Yo man, I'm sorry. No disrespect. I was just admiring the perfume she is wearing. I had no idea that she wasn't alone."

I told cat "Everything's good" and I lead Quincee's ass back to our table, wanting to ring her pretty-ass neck. I let her get that one because I left her hanging, back at Cheryl's house. I made it perfectly clear that from that point on, when she walks—I walk with her.

She stayed in her seat until she went to make a call. Soon as she left, Swear to God, out of nowhere, Ma'Haundra was standing beside me at the table, *(And no I didn't know that she was going to be there).*

Even though the next day would have been our fourth year anniversary, had she not fucked up? Seeing her meant nothing to me. While she was running her mouth, I was thinking about Quincee, and wishing she was by my side.

The conversation with Ma'Haundra was no more than two minutes tops, and besides, she was with her new man—Brian somebody. She was wearing a white jump-suit that showed every curve on her body. She looked good and she knew it, but she wasn't going to get a compliment from me, *(those days were long gone!)*.

Truth be told; one, I don't remember snapping at Quincee and two, I will never go back to Ma'Haundra. All I remember was Ma'Haundra appearing and me thinking (how much time am I going to let her into my space and the next thing I know, Quincee was beside me and then she was nowhere to be found in the club.

Initially I didn't think anything of it because she had played the disappearing act earlier. But within five minutes, I was up looking for her. I covered the entire club three times. She was just…gone. I felt like shit because I could only imagine what she was thinking.

Guilt gnawed at my ass for a long time. I thought that I would hear from her because she was staying at my house that weekend, and when we left for the club, all of her things were still at my place.

I called her for two weeks straight. I left messages on her home phone, on her cell phone; hell…I even sent her a fax. She never returned any of my modes to contact her. A week or so later, she had the audacity to send me a postage pre-paid box to return her belongings, (*Men, that's some cold shit*).

I ended up calling her sister. Shannon is about 5'2", brown-skinned, with dark hair and dark eyes. She is extremely sexy and intelligent, no-nonsense, and wise for her age. She is also exceptionally protective over Qunicee despite being the junior sibling. She pulled no punches with me, and made her position very clear, the night that I took her and Quincee out to dinner to meet Ms. Shannon.

She came right to the point, "What are your intentions with my sister? You know that she is a single mother, and that her twins come first? She is soft down to the core, and if you hurt her, I'm coming for you…because I don't play that when it comes to Sissy."

I was a bit thrown off guard, being chastised for something I had not done, nor plan to do. I respect Shannon's gangster and appreciate the love that she proudly shows for her sister. We developed good friendship. So the night that I called her, she patronized my ass and talked to me for damn near an hour, (*Big-ups to you Baby Sis,*).

The biggest misconception Quincee had of me is the day that she saw Twink and me at Tina's celebration. If I had any idea that Quincee was going to be there, I would have stayed my yellow ass home. No, I take that back. Twink would just had to have been pissed off because I would've went stag and let her get her shit off on me some other time.

I had no idea if Twink had it bad for me, or if she just needed a boost of self-confidence, at my expense.

Truth be told; that was one of the top worst days of my life. I thought I was going crazy when I first heard her voice, but didn't see her. Then when she entered the room, I'm not going to lie, my heart must-of skipped four got-damn beats. She had jet-black braids in her hair that came down to the middle of her back. That together with her creamy chocolate skin and the Gucci sunglass that she was wearing, made her look like a glamorous movie star. I let out silent exhale in order to get some blood flowing through my heart and brain.

What made a bad situation worse, was Twink introducing me has if we were a couple—fucking my position up with Quincee to the tenth power.

When Quincee acted like she didn't know me… that shit hurt! Twink was killing me.

For the next hour, I tried to think of a way to approach her and to explain the situation. She never let on to Twink about us, while letting Twink ramble on like a confused teenager, high on speed.

From there the evening didn't get any better. That fucking Dre's cousin rolled up in the house. She was flirting with that mother fuckah from the jump; cat never stood a chance. They went outside and sat in swings that gave me a direct view of them; rubbing my face in it. That mother fuckah wanted my girl. They were out there talking for a long time.

By then, I had no clue what Twink was saying. I didn't care what she wanted or what she was going through. Any debt I had with her was paid in full. Playing along with her charade was killing me on the inside. After this weekend, the record would be set straight, (*Could things get any worst…HELL YES!*).

That got-damn Dre walked into the living room where we were sitting, acting like the gracious host, but I knew down inside the wildebeest wanted to fuck with me. The Kujo looking Sasquatch glanced outside at Quincee then turned to me and smiled a shit-eating grin, and asked me, "Yo man, you enjoying yourself? Can I get you anything?"

I thought to myself, (*Yeah, you can get me a bat so I can wail up side your fucking head*). Instead I said, "Naw man, I'm good."

"You sure, you know what they say…music soothes the savage beast. Let me play something for you."

In seconds, I heard Nelly saying *"Cuz it's all in my head, I think about it over and over again. And I can't keep picturing you with him...and it hurts so bad."*

My heart took the 4 express train straight to the pit of my stomach. I felt nauseas. When Clint Black came in singing *"When I realized I was going down"*, I saw that asshole Dre smile at me then looked toward Quincee and that country bumpkin she was with, and then back at me again with a smirk that made me want to break every piece of furniture in the got-damn room.

I really hate that jolly black cocksucker. I sat there and held my rage, while half listening to what Twink was saying, and wishing she had a muzzle on her mouth.

Wasn't it enough that I had to watch the woman that I love be all up in another cat's face; plus have my childhood sister- friend want a piece of my ass--literally; and make me look like the jerk amongst all of my peers. That should have been it—right, *(Not the case)*.

I look up and see Quincee being escorted outside by Toomey...of all people. What was my so-called friend up to? It pissed me off because whenever the two of them share the same space, they go at it like a cat and dog.

They were outside for a good little while. I thought that one-sided bastard had mellowed out, but I guess not because it was obvious the dog was on the prowl. I planned to take care of that situation when we get back to the city too.

Still half hearing Twink's gibberish in one ear, ignoring the pounding in my head, and nursing a double Hennessey, Quincee walked back in the house, and the bitch was gorgeous.

(I normally don't call women bitches, but with all the shit I was going through for the sake of loving her...all my manners are out the got-damn door!).

She looked different though. The strained control that she had been walking around with was gone from her face and she was seeping sexy appeal.

My heart took a B-turn from my stomach and went straight into my ass. So I dug it deeper in to the couch because I had a very bad feeling that I was headed for a bumpy ride.

Queen Quincee performed. I guess she decided that she was ready to shake her ass, and I was not at all ready for what happened next.

Dude asked her to dance. She took off her poncho and when I saw all her bare flesh then to have another cat—right in front of my face, touching all over her; I wanted to crush, kill, and destroy every fucking thing in sight.

Watching her being pulled in close, I saw myself with my hands around that mother fuckah's neck (*What kind of name is Stormy anyway....the country mother fuckah*).

I couldn't take anymore. I got my hurt ass up and headed for the bathroom, wanting to fuck Dre up for bringing the two of them together. I was so fucked up that I had to hold onto the sink for balance. I felt like puking; shit felt like it was churning up to my throat, but more pitiful than that, I felt tears welling up in my eyes, from the bottom of my heels that made me hurt all over, (*Quincee had me fucked up!*).

I splashed some cold water on my face and talked myself down before I was able to stop shaking. I couldn't even look myself in the mirror, (*My dick was completely limp*). I have no idea how long I was in the bathroom before I managed to pull my shit together.

Not ready to go back to the party, I went outside in the front yard to take in some fresh air.
All I could think about was the record that fucking Dre played and cat touching on Quincee.

Feeling the need for a cigar, I walked to my car, pulled out my cigar case from the glove compartment, only to see the cigar that Quincee had gotten me as a house warming present; stirring me up all over again. I'm not a believer in fate, or any of that mystical crap, but that day, there seemed to be something out to get me. I lit the damn thing and took a few long pulls and was finally able to settle down.

Relaxed and back in my own head. I had made it in just enough time to see Tina making her celebratory speech. She deserves all the best in the world. I am happy for Tina and I'm proud of her and all of her accomplishments, but as I watched her look goo-goo eyed up at the Hela-Monster, for the life of me I will never understand what she sees in Dre.

They are like night and day; oil and water; and snakes and kittens. Shit...that's like Halle Berry marrying Pee Wee Herman.

Seeing the joy in the smile on her face and then hearing her sister's begin to sing, interrupted my negative train of thought, so I just sat back on the couch and turned my attention to their perfect harmony. Aah, things were finally calming down…*didn't I wish!*

Sitting through karaoke was not one of my favorite pastimes, but over the years of knowing Tina's love for entertainment and singing, I had built up a tolerance for it. I was surprise to be enjoying all the vocalists in the house. There had been four other sets of singers…And then Quincee got up and walked to the microphone.

When she first began speaking, I didn't hear a word that she said. I was in awe of her elegance, her grace, her style, her beauty, and that shy little girl expression on her face. She had my heart and my nuts in her hands, and she didn't even know it.

Wincing to get my ears to stop failing me, I heard unfamiliar music begin to play, and when Quincee named the record and artist, I was still clueless. I felt like I was going cum, while experiencing heart attack-like chest pains when she said "I would like to dedicate this to You, and You know who You are. I call this, my "Ode To Our Love." (*She was talking about me, about us!*).

(*Fellas, women need to understand, this is why we just play, and not get our feelings involved because all that hurt shit is not worth their desire for our love.*

Women, you need to realize that's why we dread those four words "we need to talk", and why we run as fast as we can when we hear talk about commitment. Come on, what man wants to see his balls dis-attached from its sack?).

That being said, listening and watching her belt out her love eulogy to me, I felt myself falling more and more in love with her despite her musical goodbye to us. Lost in her trance, I was interrupted by that damn Twink—scooting closer to me, putting her right arm around my neck and her left hand on my thigh. She turned to me with a vex attitude, and says. "She's got it bad for somebody." Then she screams out to Quincee, "I say fuck him. Go on girl, sing that song. I feel you. Fuck, fuck, fuck him!"

I thought to myself (*Why me?*), while struggling with the urge to tell Twink to shut the fuck up.

Witnessing Quincee perform her musical soirée to me affected me because she confessed her love to me. She sang with everything she had. Arching her back and dipping her head backwards, she belted out a note in a pitch that had the whole room feeling her pain.

When she swooned out "*I got to tell the man that I love him*", her torment stabbed me in the heart making me suffer with her, and informing me of the agony she felt from loving me. All I could do was silently tell her (*Baby I hear you, I feel you, I'm sorry, and I love you back*).

The more intensity that she sang with, the faster my heart pumped; the harder my dick got; and the lower I felt. I wanted her to know that her love had a chain over my heart and that she's the only woman who has the key.

When she was finished singing, she looked like a superstar. Standing at the microphone, I witnessed her being lost in her own sexy-ass world. The entire room was on their feet applauding her stellar performance. I just sat paralyzed in my seat feeling like a pile of shit. I thought I was at the lowest point I could be at, *(It wasn't!)*.

Having a need for another stiff drink, I headed to the kitchen. It was a good thing Dre was nowhere in sight because there would have been words between the two of us.

My head was still spinning from Quincee's love admission. Despite her completing ignoring my ass, my instinct never stopped feeling the connection between us, and it felt damn good hearing her admit her feelings for me.

Waiting for Tina's oldest sister to stop running her mouth on the phone and to finish fixing my drink, left me with too much time of idol thinking.

Reviewing the entire day's events, nausea started churning in my stomach again. What made things worst was that I kept hearing conversation from the other room about Quincee.

"Damn she's not only sexy, but she can blow her ass off too."

"Who is that chocolate fine thang?

"Is she here with anyone?"

"Naw man, I saw her walked up in here alone."

Almost losing it when a colleague of Dre's inquired about Quincee, and that giant asshole began advertising Quincee's single status. I was heading towards Dre, when Matt walked up and pulled me back by my shoulder, offering up advice.

"Yo man, that's not the way."

Sulking in my crushed world, I don't think that I had ever fought back the urge to kick anyone's ass as hard as I did at that moment.

Reading the expression on my face, Matt asked "What do you want to do? If you want to get her back, you need to handle your business."

Before I could take in what my brother had said to me, I saw her walk into the kitchen. From there, things went from worst to catastrophic.

My intentions were to make amends and to gain some re-formed respect in her eyes for me. I even would have accepted pity from her. All I said was "Quincee, everything is not what is seems."

Then all hell broke loose. She cussed me the fuck out. I wanted her so bad that I didn't even care that she did it in front of Dre.

(*That was a small price to pay because my eyes were on the prize...Quincee Jane Catfire being mine again*).

She spewed out "Mother fuck you and you apology." She even called me a simple minded dip, which bitch slapped me in the face. Under normal circumstances, there was no way in hell that I would accept bull-shit talk like that from any female, but my focus was unbendable, so I took it.

What hurt more was that after her tongue assault, that country bumpkin walked in the kitchen, took one look at her, and I saw the lust in those shady ass eyes for my woman. Quincee looked so fragile and broken—despite the lion that had just bit my head off and chewed my balls up only seconds before.

From Quincee's response, I knew that mother fuckah would be getting my baby's cream. The thought made my stomach churn; causing me to swallow vomit that had spumed up to my throat.

Watching that Rainy fuck take control over Quincee pissed me off; to know that she was being protected from ME! As soon as she left out of the kitchen, I bolted for the bathroom as smooth as I could.

Behind the closed door for the second time, I had to grab a hold of the sink for balance because my head was spinning from trying to control the Quincee-pain that was caving my chest in.

Looking in the mirror, my eyes were bloodshot redder than if I had just smoked a blunt. Watching snot run down onto my top lip faster than the tears rolling down my face, I didn't know or like who the fuck was staring back at me.

(*It doesn't make any sense for women to have that kind of control over men. It's shit like that that makes men want to stay uncommitted. Fellas, am I lying?*).

My chest untightened then the hurt turned into anger. Then a phone started ringing. I looked down on the counter…it was Quincee's cell. I opened the receiver.

"Hello…"

(Men, retribution can be just as sweet as victory. Oh Yeah!). Feeling better, I headed straight to Twink. She was in the living room talking to Tina. "I'm leaving. You can stay or come with me. Personally, I don't give a damn which way you roll."

Of course, she chose to leave with me, and when she started her shit; putting her hands on my chest, and asking, "Baby are you okay?" I put a stop to it.

"Twink, cut the bull shit."

I was safe the entire ride home. I nipped all of her shit completely in the bud before I dropped her ass off, at her spot.

STORMY

Does This Dance Have to End

Ladies, always remember...One Monkey Don't Stop No Show!

Philadelphia, PA
With my Rescuer

Hanging up the phone, silently cursing at having my morning interrupted. Lying in the bed watching the peacefully Sleeping Storm, my mind wandered to what my life's weather would be with a Country Storm. Reveling in juices of our early morning love-fest had butterflies dancing in the bottom of my belly.

Subsequently I went back to brooding over having to leave my sojourn that I wanted to last at least two more days. But that's the way it goes sometimes—high yield, high opportunity cost, so I cleared my thoughts to develop a plan for the day, *(Take a shower, get dressed, and pack within 30 minutes. Phase two—wake up Stormy, purchase and print out ticket from the business center downstairs—20 minutes max. Phase three—give or take 20 minutes to check out, get something to eat then have Stormy drop me off at the train station—leaving me with 16 minutes to board the train).*

I wanted to stay underneath the covers and snuggle up to Stormy's warm body. Instead I raised my unhappy ass up to put my plan into action, only to have my body held down by one astonishingly strong muscled arm.
"Where are you going sweet pah-tootie?"

In Scarlett O'Hare imitation, "I do declare Sir, such a charming salutation for little ole me?"

Rett Butler retorted, "Why yes ma'am...for you Ms. Quincee-Jane Cat Fy-Yuh because you are juicier than dripping honeysuckle and you taste sweeter than its sap dripping down its pedals."

Then in a sullen voice I was asked, "Why are you leaving me?"
"Baby, I don't want to go, but I have to take care of some business in Vermont."

"VERMONT!"
"Yes My Love."
"Does it have to be today?"
"Yes Darling."

"Stop aching my heart with all your gussie appellations. If you're going to let me down, do it like you city-slickers normally do—all raunchy-like!"

Seeing disappointment creep upon my face from the uncalled for assertion, my Abandoned Storm with a corrected disposition inquired, "Baby, I'm sorry. What kind of business are you taking care of in Vermont?"

Somewhat apprehensive I began sharing my objective of a vacation home in Vermont and why.

Looking into my eyes and appearing enthralled with my increasing excitement, Stormy conceded, "City Guh, go on and git, while I calm my dick down."

"Ooh, you are nasty…I'm telling my mama on you."

Exuding absolute confidence while omitting allegiance to arrogance, "That's quite all right because your momma will love me."

"We're mighty sure of ourselves aren't we?"

Utterly serious, "Yes we are because your momma would read my eyes and see straight into this ole yearning heart at how much I want nothing but the best for her baby."

Ladies, looking at the Earnest Storm looking back at me with pure care and want-to-do-right to me…I was tingling on the inside… yet again…damn…damn…damn!

I hate when my thoughts are so transparent because no soon as I looked into Stormy's eyes, I was flipped over onto my back and my lips where being kissed, nibbled, and sucked on.

My libido was being lulled by a slow Approaching Storm. I felt like a lioness in heat, whispering polite request into my Quenching Storm's ear, "Ease me out of what you're doing to me."

That curly-head, crazy-about-me, Cum-Pleasing Storm picked my chocolate behind up; positioning me on my knees at the head of the bed, bending my torso over, placing my hands in front of me, arched my back then began licking me from the back while stroking my clit, (*hum-min-nah…hum-min-nah!*).

I was being eaten slow and sucked even softer—to the point that the seed of my impending orgasm faintly registered in my brain. The Storm Custodian was outstandingly maintaining and extending my sexual energy.

The more I begged for harder and faster, the more I received gentle and prolonged. When I was ready to explode, my Thirsty Storm brought down my rain-cream and drank it as if it was life sustaining magic juice.

The feeling of wonderfulness was exponentially met when I went to make a move in reciprocation, but I was exquisitely rejected, "Come here and let me hold you guh cause this is all about you!"

Ladies, isn't it supreme when you're basking in the afterglow and don't have to worry about a dick being shoved in your mouth, or in your behind, all in the name of making it even.

Lying there next to Stormy ready to drown in relaxation, or possibly go another round, I get nudged, "Come-on girly, it's time to get up if you want to make your train."

Glancing at the clock; it was 8:37a.m., but not ready to move just yet, I stayed in bed while Stormy got up and ran the shower for us.

Beckoning me with, "Alright Ms. Quincee-Jane, your company is wanted in here with me, right now, front and center...and if I have to come and get you, you're going to be in trouble."

The rebel in me wanted to remain stationary to explore the notion of what trouble actual consisted of; instead, I inched my satisfied ass out of the bed and headed towards the bathroom. Standing just inside the threshold, I was transfixed at the silhouette that stood on the opposite side of the shower curtain. I did my best not to carry my gaze downward, *I failed miserably!*

Ladies, you know that feeling you get when you see him in his natural state---lifting and washing his manhood, and it looks so good watching him do so that you begin thinking of all kinds of goodies—like licking on a lollipop.

As if reading my mind yet again, the Psychic Storm extended out a wet forearm to me and summoned "Come on in here guh. I got sumpt'n for yuh."

Feeling my orgasm bubbling at the base of my lust core, I was ready to do a running hurdle over the shower rod to get my hot ass over to Stormy. Instead I calmly let myself be lead into the tub the way a lady should, (*holding up to the particulars in my mannerisms*).

Water from the shower head was running down Stormy's shoulder dripping onto my face. More than ready to be taken, I listened intently.

"All right Missy, you have seven minutes and seven minutes only to be in here."

Before I could make a comment, I was turned around and had my arms pulled firmly behind my back, as I was glided into the warm water that sensually accosted my body from my neck down, while my left nipple was being played with. Feeling Stormy's hard body pressing up against mine then biting me on the left side of my exposed neck was just a preamble. I was moved away from the water, and kissed so tenderly that I didn't want it to end.

The Lubricating Storm then lathered me up with my Oil of Olay Body Ribbons liquid soap. I was completed covered notwithstanding my koochie, when the foam launcher lifted my right leg placing it on the side of the tub and began soaping 'She.'

Ladies, when I say fingers like butter....I'm talking about that room temperature soft kind. All I wanted to do was make my pussy available for whatever. It was shameless.

Spinning me back around, picking me up with my legs spread full eagle, the Rinsing Storm immersed my "she temple" under the showerheads.

Train…when?...Vermont.…where?...property…what?.

Being held up by massively powerful arms, while the water beat down on my spot perfectly, I was about to have another orgasm that I didn't know was ready to drop. Before my climax was fully formed, I was removed from the water, taken out the tub, carried and sat down on the countertop, and dried off.

Not wanting to hear, "all right sweet pah-tootie you need to get dressed, so I can get you to your train on time."

Screaming inside my mind because secretly I wanted to stay and be taken. Interjecting my thoughts, the Extinguishing Storm elaborated, "City Guh, I can easily see myself love'n and want'n you for the rest of my life, knowing all the while that I have to swim up stream for yuh."

I shot out an inquisitive glaze.

Standing in front of me, inching closer between my legs, the Rational Storm chided "Don't look at me like gat because dumb…we ain't! I'm talking to Danny and Jade. They have our hearts wrapped around there fingers, you and I both know it."

Bowing my head in acquiescence of complete humility at our precarious positions, there was nothing left for me to do; but, to get dressed.

Although I had put myself together nicely with a greenish Capri acid wash jeans and crop jacket set, a tangerine halter top with 3" tangerine wedge heel lace up the leg shoes, I was feeling melancholy.

I became downright bitter when I saw Stormy's fine ass wearing a soft red tee-shirt that had a khaki colored portrait of the tree of life, eight pocket khaki knee length shorts, leather slide-in shoes, and a rawhide choker with the piece sign made out of shells; giving off that natural afro centric look.

Standing by the mirror and staring at our reflection—we looked good together. I wanted nothing more than to hang around Philly/DC—where ever, to be seen, laugh, cajole, make love, and enjoy myself with my Rendezvousing Storm, but that clearly was not going to happen.

On schedule, 9:17 a.m., we were checked out and waiting on the valet to bring the car around. Wanting to get the leaving part over with, once we were seated, I requested, "Baby, please just take me straight to the station."

Cringing at the disappointment in the Sad Storm's face, "If that's what you want City Lady. Your wish is my command."

By 9:37 a.m. we had parked the car, and were walking hand in hand toward the 30th Street Station, when all of a sudden, Stormy stops and yelps out, "Aah Dang!"

Concerned while inquiring, "What's wrong?"

"I have to make a call."

"Excuse me?"

"I call my mum-mah every Saturday morning between 8 and 9 O'clock."

Relieved, and countering, "I guess you'd better make that call then!"

"I tell you what; I'll ring her up real quick then tell her I call her back later."

Ladies, I was taught by the women in my family...You can tell a man's character of how he will treat you; by the way he treats his mother. I couldn't believe this is what I was walking away from.

Giving Stormy some privacy, I strolled inside the station to the departure board, and saw that my train was delayed. Instantly calling my realtor, hoping that this would make the plans fall through, (*of course it didn't*). By the time I ended my conversation with her, I was walked up on from behind.

More than happy to part with my information, Stormy was just as excited and suggested while rubbing my belly as if I were carrying Stormy' Jr., "Let me feed you?" Bending down to my right ear and whispering, "It'll be my desert because I've already had my main course", following that by biting the tip of my ear.

Enjoying myself and feeling alive with giddy delight, Stormy's phone began ringing off the hook.

"You're not going to answer the call?"

"No."

"Why?"

"Because it's Jade."

"Oh!"

"She has called me damn near thirty times since yesterday morning."

"Aren't you the least bit concerned?"

"No."

"Anxious?"

"Nope."

"Intrigued?"

"NO! I'll get back to her when I'm ready."

Exuding sex appeal by sounding definitive at not being in the mood for my line of questioning, I quickly changed the subject.

"I have a taste for some pancakes. Let's go back to the dinner by the hotel and get take out."

"Yes Ma'am" was the response I received. I loved the fact that I had a wish grantor at my disposal.

In the car, heading back to the train station, feeding my Chauffeuring Storm a Philly cheese-steak sandwich, I was increasingly being turned on. Each time I drew my hand back from those sexy ass hungry lips, my fingers were being either kissed, licked, or sucked on—in no particular order.

Once parked in the station's garage, I was happily escorted out of the front and into the backseat. Before resuming my feeding expedition I frivolously scolded "You need to leave my fingers alone, and be a good boy."

With genuine inquisitiveness, I was asked "Why?"

For the life of me, I couldn't come up with a reason, so back in full-dress Scarlett O'Hara character, I gushed out, "For sweet sake of mercy, Mr. Wellington, I do believe that you are taking liberties with my virtue."

The Honey-tongued Storm conceited "Your mine til I escort you on the train, so I have the right to take whatever liberties I want…including a bit of your virtue that I still have in my mouth… Miss Quincee-Jane Fy-Yuh…!"

The arrogant tone and sincere demeanor sent shockwaves directly in between my legs, like an arrow hitting its bull's-eye. The un-abating attraction filled the air in the vehicle with sexual electricity.

Still floating on that cloud, I was instructed, in a soft, calm, yet firm pitch, "Come here."

More than ready for the kiss that I was about to receive, I had my tongue barely out of my mouth, when that sugar taker bit it, then began sucking on it like it was the sensitive part of my lady button.

Ladies, ladies, ladies….I was in the mood to perform a public act of indecency in a car, in broad daylight.

Once the world stopped spinning and I collected myself, I reprimand my Kissing Storm, "I am so not messing with you anymore! Do not kiss me, do not touch me…don't even look at me!"

With the disposition of an eight year little boy not receiving the bicycle that he wanted on Christmas morning, the Pouting Storm's comeback was "Miss Quincee-Jane, did I do something wrong? How can I make it better?"

Segueing into man-handling me, by grabbing me by the back of my neck, pulling me body to body close; then finishing up with, "Now come here and let popah make it better."

I was drawn into an enchanted abyss of pleasure, watching Stormy's tongue kiss mine.

Bringing me back to reality was that damn phone ringing again. I attempted to withdraw from our kiss, but my Adamant Storm was having no part in that, and held me tight until I was motionless. The phone sang out twice more before I was let go.

The first words that came out of my mouth were "You need to answer your phone."

Giving me a peck on my lips then asking "For what?"

I was trying not to be affected, and quickly rebuked "Because it's obvious that she wants to speak with you. Besides, something could be terribly wrong."

"If it is, I'll find out when I call her. But for now, I'm with you and I have no aim of her interjecting herself onto us. Why…you tired of me, or something? What I do you for that you're giving Jade more of your attention than me?"

Feeling lost, hurt, and sad for the both of us, I just stared out the window.

Ladies, have you ever been in a situation where you were in love with one man who, for all intents and purposes was no good for you; yet, simultaneously there was another man in the wings—a good man that you know would love you and do anything for you, but your heart was stuck on number one…aka stuck on stupid?

Stormy and I were both members of the tortured-hearts club, and because neither of our hearts had the wherewithal to forgo the down-trodden title, the next conversation was easy to latch onto.

Taking hold of my hand and rubbing it gently, my Apropos Storm conveyed to me, "Do you know that I would ask you to marry me in a heart-beat—knowing that I'm number two, if I thought that you would say yes?"

Flattered by the sentiment and hopelessly unhappy at our reality, I responded, "Do you know that I would say yes in less than that same heart-beat knowing that I wouldn't be the only one you wanted to love-down for the rest of our lives?"

Looking into my eyes and squeezing my hand a bit tighter then offering, "For your consolation prize guh, I would give you everything this world has to offer. As sweet as your yonder downstairs is, my dick would be only for you. I would make sure that you cum big-strong every-day of the week, and every- night I would hold you in my arms and tell you how much I love you until you fall off asleep."

Reluctant to respond, I chose my words carefully, as we were tight-roping on the brink of crossing a line that had the ironic potency of being omni-satisfying or righteously enslaving to and for us.

"Why does love have to be so complicated?", and before I could finish speaking my thought, the melody to Al Green's *"How Can You Mend a Broken Heart"* infiltrated the newly sullen atmosphere.

Karma can be so cruel. It doesn't care who its victim is. The innocent caches its wrath just as ferociously as the guilt-ridden. So ladies, when it barges through your door, let it do what it does.

Succumbing to the forces, Stormy leaned over the seat and turned up the volume to the stereo. We sat there drinking the words of the song as I pondered my new options, while reeling in self-pity, and swallowing the mild sickening flavor of love-hurt. Just after Al crooned out *"How can you mend this broken man… somebody tell me, how can a loser ever win?"* I turned to my Proposing Storm whose thoughts were a million miles away from where we sat.

Marveling in the warm feeling enveloping my body, contemplating being Mrs. Stormy Wellington, my daydream sojourn was interrupted by Stormy asking, "What's going through your mind, City Lady?"

Caught off guard, I responded "Uh."

Grinning with curiosity and gawking at me mischievously, "You have the prettiest smile that's making your face glow. What were you thinking about?"

Openly honest *"You"* I replied.

You see, it's the pure emotions of love that is the life-blood of a relationship. It's the force that will have a woman always wanting do right by her man. And it's what a man needs to keep doing right by his woman.

Matching my desire, I was instructed; yet again, "Come here guh," pulling me body to body close.

Finagling my way over and landing in between Stormy's legs. In the hot seat with my body outstretched and my feet dangling in the air, I laid there in majestic contentment, as I was held and rubbed unimaginably gentle by the Tender Storm.

My eyes closed, and inhaling the joy of the moment, I was nudged and asked, "So?"

I didn't get it, "So…What?"

"Will you marry me?

(D…U…H). I felt like the host of an idiot convention, but I recovered nicely, "Will you regret not giving Jade one last chance before making a commitment of that magnitude to me, or any other woman?"

"I don't want to hear a question about…"

Over-speaking my Annoyed Storm, I politely interjected "No…
listen to me. This is too important to both of us. I believe all that
you just told me that you would do for me and be to me. So if we
were to take our rapport to another level, I would do my part as your
friend, your woman, your lover, and your wife. And I would expect
you to do the same from your position on and for my behalf. You
see, with me, I don't have any reason to look back. Danny has
already moved on…you saw that for yourself!"

Sympathetic to my plight, but agitated nonetheless, "I know
what you're going through; guh, that's why you're here with me. I
don't understand your attitude towards us, and your devotion to
Jade."

Feeling myself wanting to fall head over heels madly in love
with my Misinformed Storm, I quivered out "Stormy, this is not
about me. What I've been referring to with regards to Jade…is all
about you. In the three years that I've known you, I've come to
admire, respect and really…really like you—as a person, a team
member, as a child of God, a southern gentleman, a maestro in the
bedroom, a son any mother would be proud of; I could go on and
on."

Looking into the eyes of my Blushing Storm, I had to refrain
from rubbing my head up against that sexy-ass neck, which smelt
some kind of good with who knows what kind of colon. I continued
my position, but not before shaking my head to get the intoxicants
out of my brain.

"I have no doubts in my mind that I could open-heartedly move
forward with something anew with you, but I want you to have the
same opportunity that I've had, of being absolutely certain. I care so
much about you and want nothing but happiness for you and
possibly for us.

I think that you need to speak to Jade before you make a move in
any direction. Look at it this way. If something is wrong, wouldn't
you want to have done everything to the best of your abilities? So if
you choose to walk away…you do so with a clear conscience. You
know that will fuck her head up on so on many levels."

Looking at me quizzically, I offered up, "The first to go would be her ego—to know that you don't care anymore will deflate her conceit. Two, she will no longer have power over you and her former control will turn into self-doubt. Her blanket of arrogance will be swept from under her feet. Three, you know the old cliché "You never miss the water until your well runs dry." By you being AWOL (Absent without leave) in her life, she will begin to think about the up-rightness that you brought into her life."

Smiling from ear to ear, I coo'd on, "And speaking from experience, she will most definitely miss your sex. We women are just like men—the vision of another woman making you groan is going to drive her ass crazy."

I watched my Digesting Storm stare out of the front windshield in deep concentration. I kept on with my aspect, "On yet another level, suppose she is really missing you and want to do right by you. Don't you think that she will be sick on the inside just thinking of all the unkindness that she has ever done to you. Also engineering how she is going to move heaven and earth to get you back. Tell me that you wouldn't want to be there to participate in that exchange, even if it's just your ego wanting to hear her say that it's all about you?"

As if the universe and Jade were waiting for me to finish speaking, Stormy's phone rang out... again. Feeling nausea well up in my stomach, struggling back the tension that was in my vocal chords , in order to summon up words that I did not want to verbalize; barely audible I managed out, "Answer your phone baby."

Turning my head away and biting the inside of my mouth to prevent my bottom lip from quivering,

I felt myself letting go of; maybe one of the best chances at happiness to ever come my way. Ladies, I was sick on the inside.

Gazing down into my eyes, "NO... I'm Not Going to Do That to You!" Then sighing, "Look at-cha...You have the same damn hurt'n on your face like back when I snatched you up from Dre's house. Guh, I kan't.... Damn, this shit aint suppose'n to be hap'nin. "

Fleetingly, I was tickled, at the drawl that had been going in and out since the rest stop last night, but I toiled on with my orchestration enjoining Stormy and Jade in conversation. When the phone stopped buzzing, we looked at each other with mutual relief.

Digging deep for the sake of goodness, "If it's in our books of life to be together, then this is something that you have to do. I'll wait until Tuesday to hear from you."

"Whoop-de-doo. Ah whole three days."

Ignoring the cynicism and unblinkingly answering back, "You can be sarcastic if you want to—with your sexy ass, but you know Damn Well that your heart already knows what it wants. It's your ego, you and Jade's history, and the unknown that's keeping you from picking up the phone!"

Feeling a bit ticked off, snapping on, in a pleasantly nasty way, "If you are so sure about your decision to marry me, what's preventing you from confronting, or listening to what Jade has to say?"

Surprised at the calm response, "I'm not afraid to confront Jade; actually I'm looking forward to it because there's a lot I have to get off my chest to her. Far as listening to her…that will depend on the mood I'm in. If I feel like hearing what she has to say, I will, if not—then she's shitty out of luck.

I didn't take her call because I have anything to hide; I'm ignoring her because she doesn't get to take away any of my time with you."

Watching embarrassment wash over the face of my Retracting Storm, "Quincee-Jane, I apologize… for that three day smart-ass remark I made. The thought of not see'n or speak'n to yuh for that long, bumped me off my stump. Do you forgive the salt I showed yuh? I apologize City Lady…It won't happen again."

Searching my eyes seeking absolution, I answered a genuine "Yes."

I felt myself falling and lusting all over again, and although our ulterior motives were different, I was ready to abandon my goodwill speech as my Pardoned Storm leaned towards me, looking at my lips.

Ladies, you know that look in his eyes he gives you just before he lays a really nice kiss on you? Mmm…I was ripe for the picking.

Waiting for contact with those sweet ass lips, my lady-bump starting jumping, my heart was pounding…damn near out my chest, and my body was trembling—noticeably so, and no soon as Stormy's warm tongue made its way between my lips…the bitch called again.

That was it…reality hit me like a torpedo slamming into the side of an aircraft carrier and I thought, (*It would be real nice if life threw me a sweet curve ball like Stormy. And yes, I may be a little down about Danny, BUT! I'm not hard up for dick or for love, and I will for damn sure, not be number two to anyone, for any reason, or for any period of time, anymore!*).

Feeling strengthen, grabbing the tormenting electronic device from the back dashboard, flipping it open, and whispering "Here" while passing it to Stormy. Following up with placing my forefinger across my lips, mocking "ssh— and murmuring "She doesn't have to know that you're with anyone."

My Acquiescing Storm looked at me, matching my sorrow and we stared at one another not knowing if that was going be the last time that we see each other.

Love-pain attempted to paralyze me as enigmatic confusion poked at my senses. That coupled with my potent sexual desire for Stormy meandering between my G-spot and my energy core, along with massive disappointment waddling through my limbs— all welled up within me so big that it felt like it was going to implode inside my chest and crush me…But only if I let it!

Ladies, when love-hurt has had its hold on you like this, what did or what would you do….sink or swim?

My tears were free-flowing; however, I was determined to remove myself from the hazardous situation. Easing my way out from the lap of sweet-melancholy, I reached over the front seat, grabbing the car keys out of the ignition.

Standing in front of the trunk of the vehicle, I heard nothing while trying not to feel the despair that was gripping me, and as I reached for my suitcase, out of nowhere I saw those country-strong muscled arms lift my suitcase over my head and place it on the ground—the Universe was toying horribly with my might.

Before I could react or respond, "You Yankee women are something else. Always busy try'n to be fast…mmh."

Smiling on the inside, I chastised my Disobedient Storm.

"You're supposed to be on the phone engrossed in conversation."

"No, I'm exactly where I SUPPOSED to be… rhat-chere with you. Don't you know that a southern gentleman walks a lady door to door and in your case— from my car door to your seat on the train. Besides did you think that I was just going to let you walk away from me like that?"

Ceremoniously grabbing me up, and eyeing me gentlemanly and genuinely "Guh, all you have to do is say it, and I'm yours for the take'n…foreva. Please Believe That!"

All caught up in Stormy Wooziness, I confessed, "I believe you." Then the got-damn phone started ringing again! Pissed off to the highest, I was fed up and ready to put my self-induce torture out of its own misery.

Jerking back and uttering out "Handle your business. If I hear from you on Tuesday…cool. If not…I understand, I wish you and Jade all the best."

Sauntering my riled ass to the station, not once did I look back, not even when I heard, "But Quincee…Quincee-Jane Catfire!"

Throwing one hand up in the air stating for me, I don't want to hear it—determined to stay my course.

The one element the Universe gave me was that after I bought a cup of coffee, my train was ready for boarding. Seated by the window in the middle of the car, sunglasses on, Bose ear-buds in place, pen and pad in my lap, cell phone beneath my right thigh, —I was ready for my trip. Despite my disposition, it was a beautiful day and I love travelling by Amtrak.

Reliving the past half hour events with lingering vestiges of Stomry's face in my mind, scent in my nostrils, and tongue imprint still on my both pairs of my lips, my mind wandered into analytical thought.

(I do not think that I was being played because I saw, I felt, and I witnessed the authentic emotions that were poured on, direct at, and offered to me. However, I do believe that the situation itself was a game, and that Stormy and I were forfeited contestants ready to live out our lives as consolation prizes to one another).

Given the type of individuals we are…that would not have been a bad thing because Ladies…That Man-hooded Storm is a catch for any women… STOP PLAYING!

(But the reality is that we would be settling, nonetheless. Stormy and I are the pawns with Jade and Danny as the Game-Keeper and Ring-Master of our hearts).

Being down this road before and not vying for a redo, I was somewhat irritated with myself for falling gullible to someone else's fantasy, but I was also pleased for terminating condition-red immediately.

As soon as a smile materialized on my lips, my phone rang. It was Michelle, "Quincee-Jane, where are you? Have you left Philadelphia yet?"

"No, but I'm on the train, and we should be pulling off any time now…Why?"

"Damn it! I'm sorry Quincee-Jane; but, someone bought the property."

"What…what do you mean bought the property? How could you not know about that until now?"

"I know and you're right; but, some mysterious person topped your offer with $5000 in cash and no inspection required."

"I've been going back and forth with these property owners for four months. Then they promptly make me an, "it's yours" offer then pulled out…just like that. You know what…. I'm done with Vermont."

"Quincee-Jane, don't make a decision right now. Your emotions are getting the better of you. I know how much you want a vacation home here. And I know how much time you have put into this project. Please, just give it some more thought before you decide. I will do my do-diligence on this end. Please don't give up just yet."

Feeling defeated and too obstinate to sulk, "Michelle, don't worry about it."

"I feel God awful for interrupting your holiday and not being able to give you any more information than I have…."

Letting her off the hook, "It's not your fault. If it was meant to be it, it would have been. I'll give you a call in about a week or so. Enjoy the rest of you holiday…and relax…stop working…get some PLAY time in."

The train began rolling as our conversation was ending. My attention was drawn straight to somebody whistling and screaming, "Hey, Stop, stop! I thought to myself, (*sorry buddy, you will not be making this train*), as the locomotive began moving faster.

Just then, my phone rang. Flipping it open…it went dead. In no mood to speak to anyone, I put it in my bag, cuddled up in a ball and slept the entire way back to New York.

By 12:40 p.m. I was in a yellow cab heading home. I decided then that I was going to stay in bed the entire holiday and I was actually looking forward to doing so because it had been a long time since I had a lazy weekend.

1:20 p.m. I was entering my house, and it felt good being home. Walking directly to the kitchen and connecting my phone to the charger… immediately it began ringing. Complaining aloud before answering, "Damn it, I just walked through the door; Hello?"

It was Stormy.

Perturbed at my excitement, I calmed my demeanor before speaking again.

Interrupting my plan, I was asked.

"Didn't you hear me calling you?"

"Huh?"

"At the train station; I was going to surprise you and take the trip with you. I was flying down the stairs yelling for the train to….."

"That was you?"

"Oh, so you did hear me."

"Everyone in the train-car heard you." Tickled at the memory, I had to maintain my composure because I thought it inappropriate to laugh. Then it hit me… "You came for me."

"Yeah, I did. Did you think I wouldn't?"

"Not saying that you wouldn't. It's a grand gesture…is all that I'm saying."

"What have I been telling you and trying to show you all along? It's all about you Quincee-Jane Cat Fy-Yuh."

I felt like a school girl, all wishy-washy on the inside, twirling my index finger around the charger chord with my toes bobbing up and down a mile a minute.

Ladies, I felt myself oozing. It was absolutely ridiculous.

"Don't be alarmed, but I blew up you cell phone."

"No alarm taken. I think I would have been affected if you hadn't."

"Is that right?"

"That's a fact."

"Were you punishing me by not picking up my calls?"

"No baby, not at all— my phone didn't have any juice left. I forgot to charge it last night, and this morning, well… I was busy."

"You damn right, you were. By the way, you should know City Pants…it was my mother who'd called me when you walked off all high and mighty. She and I had been having bits and pieces of conversations all day--shoot and that's her again now. I'll be calling you rhat back City Catfire. You hear me?"

My brain failed my lips for words. Then when I knew what to say, my lips failed me out of shear embarrassment.

"Do You Hear Me?"

"Yes… I hear you."

"Ah-ight baby guh." Then the phone went silent.

All kinds of pleased with everything, a light bulb moment flash in my mind. *(When I surrender to situations that I have no control over to the Universe, the outcome is in my favor, and my opportunity costs aren't anguishing.)*

Ladies, we as innate 'fixers' are always trying to control conditions, verdicts, etc. The next time you find yourself in that predicament, step back and give up your charge —then watch and take note of what happens.

Damn near skipping to my room, I turned on the television, and saw the classic "The Imitation of Life" would be coming on at 2 O'clock. Excited because it's one of my all-time favor movies, I hastened my pace to be unpacked, undressed, and in the bed prior to its coming on.

Removing my lingerie from the suitcase, I spotted Stormy's lime green boxers and was surprised by my appeal to them—and yes, I did put them on. I swear it felt like Stormy's hand was stroking my nakedness underneath them. I shook Mr. Feel-Good out of my head and from between my legs, and focused on me.

By 1:47p.m., I was situated comfortably in the middle of my Craftmatic bed with the head and feet in the up positions, the massager on rolling waves, and sipping on a frothy pina colada. The butterflies were still active in my belly when the phone rang again.

I pick it up to hear, "I Miss You. You're All Up In Me! I See You In My Mind; I Smell You Every Time I Inhale; I Can Still Taste You. Damn Guh!"

My loins were shouting *u…u…m…h*!

In a Catty mood and smiling I commanded a "What?" that was dripping with sexiness, but the response that was reciprocated was sexy—personified.

"What do you mean What? You are My What, My How, My Why, My Where and The Want of my focus. So tell me Miss What, How is your Why doing? And Where do you Want me?"

Taking great pleasure in our mating game's war of words and wit, I shot back, "Because you can't be WHERE I Want you to be, I refuse to answer any of your questions...SO THERE. What do you have to say about that?"

"Touché" and from that point on there was no more talk of a sexual nature. My bluff may have been called and I was ticked off about it, but I was still enjoying Stormy's company, no matter the capacity.

For the next half hour or so, we talked about everything under the sun— school stories, work, Dre and Tina, our summer happenings, until finally I couldn't take it anymore—curiosity was killing my nosy ass cat, "Have you spoke to Jade?"

"Yes, she was going on about some....."

My damn doorbell rings, interrupting my concentration. I had forgotten that my neighbor, Evelyn was coming to bring me some food. My Dominican sister can cook her ass off.

"Baby, this is my neighbor, I'm going to call you right back.", and I hung up the phone, not waiting for a response.

Looking at the clock, I saw that it was almost quarter to three; thereby, validating the miss-meal cramps rambling in my stomach. Anticipating scarfing down some carnelon (shells stuffed with a minced chicken mixture); arroz y habichuela (rice and beans); arroz y camarones (rice and shrimp); and tostones (fried plantains)-- my mouth was salivating.

Swinging the door open-- it was Stormy, standing in front of me looking finer than when I stomped my hot-tempered ass off that morning. Additionally adorned with a kaki baseball cap sported backwards; a pair of top-gun sunglasses that reflected off iridescent turquoise, midnight blue and amber; and a smile that lit up my life, I was overcome.

Greeting me with "Hello City Lady", The Surprising Storm extended long stemmed red roses in my direction.

Eyes tearing, my heart filled to capacity, and thanking God for absolute happiness, I responded, "Hi there Country Gent. Welcome to my abode," as I stepped back and eloquently swayed my arm in a summoning manner.

Ladies, you know he is trained well, when he takes his hat off as he is entering into the house. No more thug want-to-be's for me.

My brain still in the clouds, as I inhaled the beauty of my flowers and the essence of my rendezvous-er strutting pass me.

Getting right to the point, soon as the door closed behind us, "I know you want to stay in bed all weekend, but where do you want to be in bed at? Are you good here? Do you want to go back to Philly—because I like that hotel, or I can take you to my place in DC?"

Caught up in the options that were put to me, I started to respond, but then thought better. With a slight attitude I questioned "Wait a minute…wasn't you supposed to be dealing with Jade first."

Taking my hand a leading me to living room, we sat down on the couch. Looking me square in my eyes, "I did. The thirty seconds that I spoke to her, she was crying and babbling on about something. I was in no mood to hear what she had to say, so I told her that I would talk her on Tuesday."

Wondering how Stormy knew the direction to my living room then letting the question fade in my mind, I indignantly cross-examined "Just like that?"

"Yes ma'am, just like that."

"What was her response?"

"There was no response because I hung up."

"How pompous of you", I snorted with my nose turned up in disgust. "Stand up to your convictions because if nothing else Stormy Wellington, I've always know you to be fair and honest."

"Whoa…Slow down my City Flower. I'm not the bad guy here. Have you forgotten the conversation we had yesterday? She is the one that has put a piece of hurt'n on me. She's been a thorn in my side and a royal pain in my ribs. I can't trust did-ly that she says, a dang thing that she does, and as far as sleeping with her goes, I don't know when I'll be keen on touching her again… but I do know that I love her skinny wicked ass.

Thank you for goading me into taking a look at the mess I got myself into and the monster that I'd created."

"Do you want to marry her?"

"Honestly speaking, I'm not ready to look that far down the road yet, but I plan to forgive her, take her back and the whole nine yards, but today is not that day. I made it perfectly clear to her not to call me this weekend. In fact, I let her know that I was with you."

Horrified at the thought and denouncing, "That's cruel. You didn't have to go there."

"Yes ma'am, I did because she needs know that it was because of You that I even bothered to take her call in the first place. And besides, she needs to feel some pin-pricks, for a change."

Witnessing my disposition turn into apathy and my attention turn away, I was inoffensively instructed "Look at me…look-ah-here!"

Melting at the second request, begrudgingly looking up at The Elucidating Storm, I gave my undivided attention.

"I took on the role of your rescuer, when I lead you out of the den of pain that Yankee was putting you through last night. And I'm here now to hold true to my place. City Lady I'm all yours, whatever you fancy me to do, I will do. I'm not going to let anyone or anything stop me, and that's how is going to be."

Looking into the eyes of the lover that I will never share love with, I was captivated with infatuation and sadden with misfortune. Numb from Stormy's words, I indifferently commented, "I knew our conversation about you and I being together was too good to be true. But it was nice while it lasted."

"City Cat Fy-Yuh, you have to believe me—everything I've said is true guh. I've been sweet on you since our second class together."

With and arched eyebrow and sarcastically remarking, "If that's true, it definitely isn't helping me now." I turned my head away again.

The heat of the hand that I felt under my chin stirred up the fire that was building underneath the boxers I was wearing. I willingly accepted the untouchable connection that was growing between the two of us.

My women's intuition sensed discourse in the future with regards to Stormy, but I shrugged it off because I was in the here and now and I had all intentions on enjoying My Storm with what little time that I had.

Witnessing an honest without arrogance expression appear before hearing, "I see you have been thinking about me," then flinching at the boxer's waistband snap on my skin.

Feeling the blood rush to my head and my temperature rise with excitement, I bashfully commented "You came for me!"

My whole body felt the pure relief and raw sex appeal of the "Yes Guh, I did…for you and only you."

Eagerly ready to continue my ride on the wild side, but slowing down my reigns long enough to create Rule #1 before letting myself be enchanted by Stormy's spell.

Briefly backing away, I decreed "I'm going to keep you pure just in case you do decide to marry that woman."

"And how do you propose to do that Quincee-Jane Cat Fy-Yuh?"

"By making you keep your dick outside of me... Stormy Wellington!"

"Are you sure that's what you want?"

"You heard the words pass through my lips, didn't you?" I retorted egotistically.

Absent of hesitation, malice and charade my Subservient Storm replied, "If that's what you want, then that's what I'll give you, or should I say...not give you."

The attitude of obedience alone, made me want to throw myself on the floor and do the nasty, by having the nasty done to me.

Ladies, respecting love may be honorable, but it can also be a difficult and lonely road.

Concurring with me so easily pissed me off and the she-bitch in me arose from thin air and I replied. "You just make sure you do, or don't...you know what I mean!"

Meeting my arrogance with mildness, the treaty was sealed.

"On all the love that I have for Mah'Dear; that's what I call my mum-mah, I will keep my dick outside of you...there! Do you trust me now?"

A wave of embarrassment tore through me instantly making me regret my snide comments because Stormy has never been anything but open, honest, loyal, and most of all...trustworthy. Grounding myself, I apologized, and of course I was made to feel like I committed no offense.

"Guh nothing you do to me this weekend you have to be sorry fo...yuh hear me?"

My sisters, I was ready to slap the shit out of the she-bitch in me, my own damn self.

Refusing to allow my disappointment of a no-dick weekend reveal itself, I averted my gaze down to my hands, only to have my emotions and mind read like a beguiling Love Story.

The recipient of my unyielding desire showed true gentleman-ship by letting me off the hook, "I'm going to grab my bag out the car, and I'll be back."

Saying thank you with my eyes, I inquired, "Can I do anything for you?"

"Yes Ma'am, you can have a hot bath ready for me when I get back."

Filling the tub was the second thing I did; after cleaning up the cream that had my thighs craving for some up-close personal Stormy attention. Afterwards, I turned the television to the R&B Music Classics station, and began clipping my roses to prepare them for the ruby red vase I had taken out to place them in.

Thinking about the past 24 hours, the bell rang. Literally skipping to the door, with my heart beating thirty thousand times per second, I had a big ole cheesy grin on my face, and a daddy's home sensation filling my womanliness.

Re-entering my apartment, I get an, "M...m...m." I was being sniffed—all around my eyes, my nose, my mouth, and my neck?

Mentally shaking off the trance-like effect and refusing to not go out like that, I half-ass indignantly retorted, "What are you doing?"

"Appreciating how much you and your city heat are like'n me."

Then the fine fucker stood in front of me, holding my hips with a firm grip, kissing me nice and soft-like on my lips before asking directions to the bathroom.

Feeling myself flush beet red and conceding to defeat, I pointed and walked in the opposite direction to the safety of my kitchen to finish arranging my flowers. They were spectacularly beautiful. After marveling over them for a few minutes, I prepared an ice mug of Heineken and a glass pina colada, I grabbed the food that Evelyn brought over and joined my Soaking Storm in the bathroom.

Taking in the view, I had no shame in splitting my gaze between the handsome face and the clear revealing water. The ambiance was simple and the mood was comfortable—the light off, the door open with me sitting on the floor next to the tub. We ate, we snapped, we envisioned, reminisced, and talked about everything from my tiny bathroom to what each of our dream homes will look like, to childhood stories, our parents, and our professional aspirations.

After three tub refills, two more rounds of drinks, and one Wrinkled Storm, I excused myself and retired to my bedroom. I had to because the alcohol had my toes tingling, my knees weak, my she-part thumping, my nipples hard, my tongue hungry for a kiss, and I was feeling exceedingly compelled to do something very un-ladylike.

The next thing I remember was waking up into darkness. Sitting up, glancing at the cable box and seeing 10:37p.m. I had slept the day away. Cobwebs still fogging my brain then jumping at the movement that I felt next to me; I completely forgot about my guest. Gently guiding me back down, and whispering into my ear, "What's all this noise fo? Me love'n you up is the only reason you should be making them there kinda sounds guh."

Without warning, I was flipped over onto my belly and had my arms extended outward on either side of me. I felt pressure on my upper thighs as I was straddled. In between the love kisses that were planted on the tip of my right ear, the sweet nothings that were subliminally attacking my rationale as I listened to "All I want to do is make you feel good."

My sensibilities were being broken down as my eardrum was accosted with, "M...m...m. Make a milk river, so I can drink you!"

Before my mind could respond, my body began thrusting back and forth and I shrieked out, "Move... Get off of me!" It was a poor attempt to terminate the control Stormy had over my body.

As calm as peace is, my Tranquil Storm slid down on the bed next to me, complying with my outburst. No soon as I was unbound, I tooted my ass up in the air, and my lips were shamelessly begging, "Touch Me!"

Guiding me down towards the base of the bed to be positioned behind me then pressing down with firm hands on the small of my back and saying "Stay right there... don't move." I was expecting to feel a hot tongue greeting the other me (*Not!*) Instead I felt my left she-lip being inhaled and then kissed. After communicating reciprocity to my right she- lip, my openness lapped at its breath being drawn out, making me moan "*m...m...m...h!*" in satisfied pain/pleasure...I couldn't decipher. I was spread apart and the air give my clit a heartbeat, while sweet malleable kisses made her hard and hornier. My inside walls had long since unclenched their grip, so when my Cum Collector beseeched "Milk for Poppa", I complied like a good little girl by pumping out cream with each squeeze of my she-muscle.

Still not having had the pleasure of Stormy's tongue in my mouth or in me, I attempted to antagonize my tormentor by flopping down on the bed and ending our foreplay tryst—*didn't happen!*

The she-bitch in me was force to forfeit her appearance by way of Stormy enlarging my clit with continual tender kisses—the back of my leg, my heel, my arm, the palm of my hand, my fingers, my neck, my elbow, my shoulder….. The more I was touched, the steeper I arched my back exposing my most sensitive flesh. Out of nowhere, my stomach growled loud and long.

Tickled pink and before I finished giggling, Stormy directed, "Come on, ghet up and ghet dressed, I'mah put some vittles in yuh belly."

Flopping down on the bed astonished, "What?......Now?"

"Yes guh, now."

"You're joking…right?"

"No City Lady, no joke'n."

Pissed off and ready for a heated debate, I was asked every so sweetly.

"Do you trust me?"

In horny hell, I did not want to surrender my vulnerability to the perpetrator of my unwanted predicament.

"Do You Trust Me?"

Having had my rebellion shut down, nodding my head while looking beyond the bed, my chin was guided upward by one finger, so that we were looking into each other's eyes. My Pledging Storm oath to me,

"If you hold onto that bone and walk with it for me, I promise yuh, when we get back home, my dawg is going to come and fetch it from yuh cat. Do you believe me?"

Before I could open my mouth to respond, my koochie assented *yes…yes…we believe you …and we will wait for you…. yippy;* by way of a series of pleasure pangs that bought a smile to my face.

Within twenty-five minutes, I was locking the door to my apartment. Dressed in a canary yellow tube-top, and light blue bell-bottom pants, I accessorized with sterling silver teardrop earrings and choker set that matched my slinky silver over-the-head shawl that draped the bottom of my shoulders ever so sensually, and a pair of silver alligator-skin sandals. I had my braids pulled back in a tight ponytail at the nape of my neck to top off my look with an air of sophistication.

Making a mad-dash back into the house to turn the radio on, then scurrying back towards Stormy waiting by the elevators for me and looking too damn sexy to be outside of the bedroom, in straight leg dark colored jeans, a sleeveless button down the front hooded shirt that sported horizontal colors of pumpkin orange, hunter green, sunshine yellow, medium gray, and black, and a pair of black leather loafers. We really made a good looking couple. It took hard work not to get myself all hot and bothered again.

By 1:35 a.m. Sunday morning we were in the car heading home with stuffed bellies of glazed Hennessey ribs with mashed potatoes and green beans and bread for Stormy; lobster tails, ribeye steak, baked potato and salad for me.

Opening my front door—I turned on the light before entering into the apartment. Stormy right behind me locked the door, flicked the light switch back off and said, "Close your eyes."

I didn't see the sense in it, as we were already in the midst of pitch black, but going along with my Playful Storms' flow, I concurred by standing at attention like a sailor on an inspection line.

Lost in my thoughts for a minute or so, I was startled when I felt movement at my feet. I silently giggled at myself as my left leg was lifted and my sandal was removed. I leaned on the wall for support with my left arm while the same gentle steps were taken to remove my right sandal. I felt like a queen looking down at my servant who was preparing me to have all of my imperial desires met.

Standing up and facing me, I was instructed to "Hold your arms up."

Letting my hands flop down after my shawl and top was pulled over my head, I caught a feel of Stormy's rippled abs, and just as I was about to speak, I was interrupted, "Poppah didn't give his guh any sugar in a bit." then I was grabbed up.

I inhaled at the full tongue that gingerly and continually onslaught my mouth. Exhaling in the same breath, I felt the dick that I had banished, press into my abdomen.

My friend Cree's motto popped into my head. "I ain't running from no dick...Fuck That!" I could not bear witness to her words because it actually pained me to look down at it. Nor did I want to think of the possibilities of what the dick could do to me. Pondering and desperately hoping that I wasn't kept to my pledge of being dick-free.

My body was trembling and I felt my knees about to buckle underneath my feet, just before I was swooped up, carried into the living room and placed down on the couch that had been lined with my forest green microfiber comforter. Then I had my jeans peeled off me like I was a first-place prize that had to be handled with extreme care, as my treasure was being unveiled.

Up to that point I hadn't paid any attention to the music coming from the radio, until Stormy asked me, "May I have this dance?"

That's when Patti Labelle's voice materialized in my ears *"Somebody loves you ba...bey. Oh...oh...oh somebody loves you ba...bey."*

When I stood up, I felt the plush comforter beneath my feet, sweetening the mood even more, and for a second I cringed because I knew this was a one-time show that I will always remember and possibly forever crave.

I jumped at making body to body contact with the dick that was hard as the sound of thunder is loud. Looking down at me and showing concern for my plight, I was twirled around so that my 'She' was safe from the dick. I automatically lifted my hands and held my boobies up because triple D's are no joke carry around.

I was ordered in no uncertain terms to, "Put Your Arms Down!"

Complying, I slide my hands down my body, onto my thighs, and over to clasp the outsides of Stormy's legs of steel.

In turn, I felt one hot hand glide down my neck, making its way to lay atop of my chest, while the other hand slid across and massaged the bottom of my baby pouch abdomen.

Although I had been working out, and had lost a good amount of weight, I was still a tad bit insecure about my lower belly in the nude, but the way that it was being caressed, I not only felt sexy, but explicitly wanted.

As Patti aspired out, *"Wanting instant replay of Yes...ter...d...a...a...a...h...e...y"*, my breathe was snatched from me as my arms were pulled close together behind my back, just like yesterday morning when we were in the shower.

Obeying Stormy, relishing the sultry music, and feeling Patti's words—all intensified my heat. I melted on, in continued excited enchantment—being rubbed up against, and swayed sinfully slow. In doing so, I was becoming more and more lost inside of Stormy's sauce.

Moaning out, and having my personal space further invaded, I heard, "Is that for me? M...m...m I accept it!!", and then the Heated Storm began to lull my sexual energy. Spinning me back around and listening to Patti sing, "*I don't want to break free. You can make a slave out of me*", which was how I really felt in my heart, but then I thought (*Hey, wait a minute; this is supposed to be a what-Q-want weekend. Then why I am the one that's being flipped around like a love doll?*).

No soon as my thought was completed, I was being sniffed again, and BANG! Stormy's country yummy tongue was in my mouth.

Trying to maintain some sense of leverage, I backed up pleading, "Stormy, stop tugging at me."

Taking a step back and looking quizzically at me,"What do you mean guh?"

"I mean stop messing with my heart...This...all of this," sashaying my arms around referring to everything that was going on between us.

Looking down at me seriously, "You don't think that you're not pulling at my chord too. City Guh...no can do you fo. This weekend is mine with you too, and I'm going to love you and show you how I would have loved you for the rest of our lives?"

The words were being said, all while still leading my body in slow dance. In one smooth move, I was being kissed again, and I was dripping at the same tempo-- nice and pain-sweetly...slow.

When our kiss ended I heard "Cum on... my City Chocolate Forget-Me-Not, give it to Poppah" and I winced in sex-pain.

Ladies... that Cum Coaxer was talking to my energy...Ooh, I say Fuck You Stormy...just thinking about you right now.

My mouth was entered yet again by that engaging tongue which felt like apologizing rolling thunder, as the sides of my tongue were struck again and again and again by it.

Then miserably unexpectedly, I was rest-a-sured by the Orgasm Summon-ner "Don't worry City Guh, I'm keep'n my promise— my dick is stay'n outside of you", as I was spun out for the second time away from the dick.

Go ahead ladies, say it...I'm stupid. I know! And for those of you who say, "Serves me right", I say...give a sistah a break because it was a hard pill swallowing.

Soaking up the good with the bad; entrenching every morsel of the encounter into my brain as we moved to the music in silence. When Patti chorused out, *"Somebody loves you ba...bey"*, as the music built up climatically, and she screamed out her release *"I...I...I...It's Me I...I...IT'S M...E...E...E...E...E...E!"*, my body was pulled closer into Stormy's and in my ear my Sharing Storm imparted, "No... It's ME!"

Hearing the directness, turning my head and seeing the sincerity, in addition to feeling the wanting in the statement—all had me panting unabashedly. Just as suddenly, I was twirled around, yet again to face my Pleasure Pacifier, dancing out the rest of the song, with me being held hungrily-soft just-right.

Our next musical jaunt was to Smoky Robinson's *'Cruising.'* Touching skin to skin, my head amid Stormy's chest—with the city's and the George Washington Bridge lights illuminating my living room, I looked up into my Dancing Storm's eyes and became so overwhelmed with emotion that tears of joy stung my face.

The sensation, my thoughts, my energy, all attached to what I was experiencing, elevated my spirit to a higher level of emotional being. As our foreplay dance continued in silence, an electrical, chemical, and physical charge magnified itself so potently inside me that I felt my energy drawing to and sopping up Stormy's sexual power and intentions towards me.

Hearing *"And if you want it you got it forever, this is not a one night stand ba...bey"*, pricked at my decision making skills because I chose my ill-fated destiny and sojourn with Stormy via a nasty disposition followed by my big ass mouth.

Ladies, women, and sisters in heat you have to believe that those weren't my objectives. What had happened was...my everything was longing for a Stormy love-dick down, by way of being sexually man-handled. So in my snippiness, I actually wanted and was attempting to be put in my place by Stormy—caveman style. But of course Stormy being the perfect country gentlemen—stomped all over my plans by complying with my surly words.

That messed me up!...I admit it. And after the love of Momma comment was made, there was no way I could fess up the truth because that would have been in poor taste. Like an adult, I put an "H" on my back and had handled it.

Wallowing in all that, and listening to Smoky sing out, *"Let the music take your m...i...n...d, just release and you will f...i...n...d"*, I felt like I was being choreographed because my mind was lost in the music and I was more than ready to be released from the overload of pressure that had mounted up in my woman flesh.

Smoky crooned out, *"Baby let's cruise, let's float, let's g...l...i...d...e. Ooh, ooh. Let's open up and go i...n...s...i...d...e"*, a heat-flash of bitterness burned my ego, and I shot back by taking a nicely firm bite into Stormy's chest.

Witnessing the grimace on my Tortured Storm's face, I smiled then laid my head back down in the very spot that I had just assaulted.

Ladies, how many men do you know of that would let your envy run a-muck at his expense?

Feeling sick on the inside because I had not only pushed this one away, but also talk my way into a continued dick-drought.

Still caught up in our sensual lullaby, as Smokey was wrapping up with *"The music is played for love... cruising is made for ...I love it...I love it...I love..."* all I could do was to stand in place and let Stormy rub my heat, and churn it into an even deeper frenzy, which preluded the next level of our foreplay excursion.

Wordlessly pleading with the universe to stop mocking my bad decision practices regarding Stormy as the melody for *"Do Me Baby"* by Meli'sa Morgan filled the living room. Just as I mustered up the courage to look into Stormy's eyes, Meli'sa began sauntering *"Here we are in this big ole empty room....staring each other down. You want me just as much as I want you.........so let's stop fooling around."* By the time she got to the chorus of *"Do me ba...bey.... like you've never done before!"*, I was wound up so tight that all I needed was to feel the head of Stormy's dick kissing my opening with its presence, and I would have popped, on contact.

Looking down and observing my face, my Torment Releaser, began massaging the sides and back of my neck in attempts to quasi-free me from my build-up.

Closing my eyes, twisting my head, and bending my neck to meld my tension with Stormy's soothing fingers, I couldn't help moaning out, "mmm...mmm."

Every word drenched in concerned sincerity, my Appeasing Storm soothed out, "Come on, Poppah's got sumpt'n fo yuh!", as I was lead to my round dining table.

The top half of my body was bent over, with my arms spread across the width of the glass.

Snuggling up close behind leaning down on top of me, my Relief Taker first, kissed the top of my back before returning to massaging my neck then adding my shoulders. By the time those country feel-good hands had made their way down to the small of my back, I was ready for Jim Dandy to come to my rescue!

Involuntarily heaving my female-ness upward, the Gnashing Storm spread my upper thighs apart, moved in closer to me, dipped down and began bumping my meat with the dick that I would not have the opportunity to personally know, to the words and melody of *"DO ME!..DO ME! ...DO... DO...DO Me Ba...bey! Just Can't Wait No More. Oh give to me! Do Me, Do Me Do...Do...Do...Do Me"*, while continually kneading the nape of my back.

I didn't know where my desire began, my satisfaction ended, or when my sexual frustration materialized. Unable to think, hear, or yearn any deeper, I managed to agonize out, "P.l.e.a.s.e!"

Immediately, my Temporary Baby went into action. First my arms were slid from the outstretched positions to 12 o'clock above my head. Then stepping back and pulling the dining chairs up close to me on each side. My right leg was hoisted up. Holding my balance for me, my knee was placed in the chair ---ever so carefully.

Sisters, have you ever been treated as if you were as delicate as finely spun china? My heart, my mind, my pussy, my nerves--- EVERYTHING!!!!---was on love-fi-yah.

My left side was looked after with mutually exquisite care followed by Stormy attentively scooting the chairs apart from one another; thereby, naturally spreading me open wider.

Adhering to my instructions "Don't move", I peered through the glass table and watched my Preparing Storm sit down on the floor; with feet facing outward, head facing upward, then pulling me downward, and sliding my thong sideward.

Howling out the gratification I felt from the first stroke on the candy between my legs be licked and pulled on. Everything around me froze in time; the only element that I was aware of was Stormy's tongue—feeling bigger than life itself.

My first orgasm came within less than ten tugs from Stormy's mouth on the tip of my she-heat. Sighing out my satisfaction when it ended, I was grabbed and held a little tighter.

The second time around, my entire clit was swallowed in the hollows of Stormy's hot, soft, and skilled oral cavity. My climax may have been Johnny-Cum-fastly, but it was also much stronger. Jerking out the last throws of my orgasm, I was in need of a blissful break …(didn't happen!).

Attempting to lean back on my knees and lift up, I was asked, "Where you going? I'm still hungry!"

Stammering out, "Umh…I'm….But…Baby…I was going to…m..m..m!"

For the last edible-giving apex that fulfilled my Insatiable Storm's appetite, my position was changed. In the midst of me fumbling to articulate a sentence, Stormy had pulled up a chair, bent my torso belly-down back onto the tabletop, sat down in the chair, and lifted my be-hind up, then kissed me on my right butt-cheek and mumbled, "Hold tight City Lady, this isn't it."

Walking over to the couch and grabbing the rust colored silk and antique gold linen throw pillows, then returning back to me with a kiss on my left butt-cheek. The silk pillow was situated beneath my head, the gold one was placed at the edge of table with my right knee positioned on top it, and my left knee was still planted in the chair.

Taking a seat again, scooting up to me, slightly nudging my right leg forward on the table so that we were koochie to mouth level then moving my thong further to the side, I heard, "Ah, yes guh, this'll do."

I started being licked from the front of my mound to the end of my she-gap.

While sucking up my heat, my desire, my juices, and my flesh", my Ingesting Storm mumbled out, "Damn guh, you taste sweeter that maple syrup on homemade biscuits. Gim-me It...Got Damn!"

My ass instinctively obliged. I tooted it all the way up in the air toward that fine country face—front and centered, and announced "All hands on deck—Take It, Got damn it!"

Appreciating me back, that mother so-and-so began lapping up my protruding tunnel like you would slurp up dripping ice cream off the side of the cone, all the while making those indecent glirping sounds that were driving my yen to want more.

Just when I was at the point where I couldn't take the tease any longer, the entrance of my temple was poked by Stormy's tongue that was stiff as the dick that I wanted so desperately to show it-self. Starting out with shallow jabs, further rendering me absent of control over my own body, I was then prodded deeper with increasingly quicker strokes.

Announcing my commencing orgasm, abruptly I felt nothing more on my 'personal'. That followed by, "Not yet City Lady...I'm not finished with you."

That was the second time that I had been cut off...just like that! It was becoming a pattern that was out right pissing me off.

Bending up from the table, readjusting my thong, and standing up, I affirmed out "You Can't Keep Doing This To ME!!! Who Do You Think You Are?" At that point, I, my ego, and my orgasm were ready to spew venom at Stormy's malicious intent of playing with my horniness.

Unruffled by my hyped demeanor, and gently taking me by the hand, I was told "Slow down City Lady. I'm not playing with you— I'm loving you. What's wrong with wanting to make you feel good and making it last guh?"

Feeling embarrassed like Fig-Mo; but, still hot in the ass, and unwilling to concede to another Stormy defeat, I jerked my arm away with all my might and headed toward the couch.

Before I could take that second step, my arm was grabbed and I was snatched back even harder; making me feel sexy as fuck, and turning me on, intensely deeper.

In that same tranquil tone, I was asked "Why you being so salty guh?"

Determined to keep my charade going, I barked out "I'm not one of your play things that you can just do anything to. You're just like......"

And as gentle as sun shower raindrops falling on my face, my bottom lip was met with Stormy's forefinger and I was politely interrupted.

"Guh, you are so beautiful in heat, but the words coming from between yo lips are more sour than a rotten pickle. It's not good enough that yuh have my dick rhat where yuh want em—on lock down?

I didn't feud with you about it because I'm just a good ole country boy trying to give a city lady what she wants. Yet you come back with accuse'n me of mistreat'n you? And that's after you let your defiance write a check that your lust and my manhood have to pay fo."

Having heard ample information about my current disposition, I rambled out, "What do you mean?"

Sounding disappointed in me, "Yuh still not will'n to let go of that acid, uh?" ; while lifting up my hand, kissing it, then attempting to continue, but getting acrimoniously cut off by me.

"I don't have a clue as to what the hell you're talking about or… referring to."

Ladies, I know…but my sexual frustration had turned into infuriated scorn, and it tipped my mad ass off the deep end, and at that point, I couldn't help myself.

In spite of my offensive conduct, still as calm as the quiet is before the thunder, Stormy chided "Well let me make it clear for you City Lady. The reason you're holding on to all that salt is because of shame."

I was gasping in indignant shock.

"You KNOW you were wrong. And I don't understand why you won't admit it, or why you're willing to carry all that vinegar to your heart –just so to hurt me?"

That last statement messed me up because ultimately that wasn't my intention—the tears instantly began pouring down my face.

Unmoved by my humiliated admittance, my Thundering Storm spoke on, "And You know damn well what I'm talking bout. When was the last time you were made love to? Either you were holding out on that Yankee, or you've be lying to me because your sweetness is so tight around my tongue, I KNOW you haven't been touched in a city minute."

Secretly pleased with the assumption, but shocked at the statement, I sounded out through my tears "WHAT?"

In a stern, but settled tone, my position was put on permanent hiatus.

"Take that scorn you have for me to the outhouse; cuz that dog aint hunting no more. In the little time that I've spent with you, I know yuh body, yuh sex, yuh needs, yuh signals, and from what your body's been telling me, that kitty between yuh thighs is craving my dick... real hard....but because of your acid, you can't have me the way you want me; yet you blame me fo it; that aint fittin."

Ladies, I was so sick of myself. I wanted to throw up because I was super-sonically cold-busted.

Adjourning my disgrace, I was drawn in closer.

"Guh. I don't wanna bicker with you. So stop fret'n and let me give you what I have for yuh."

Suffering like a chastised daddy's little girl; I buried my head in the nakedness of my Tolerant Storm's chest.

Trying to keep the whinny seven year old out of my voice, I apologized.

"Stormy, I didn't mean...I don't have bitterness in my heart for you. I was just... I'm sor...I'm so sorry."

Afraid and embarrassed, I composed myself then looked up directly into the sexy ass eyes that were staring back into mine, biting the bullet, I continued, "Stormy, please forgive me. There's no excuse for my behavior or my ill-manners. You didn't deserve any of it. Do you accept my apology?"

"All is already forgiven City Lady."

By that time the tears were streaming rivers down my face, snot was preparing to run out my nose, and I felt the on-set of hyperventilation glinting in my chest—I was a deflated mess. To add insult to my discomposure, Bobby Womack's slow jam *"If You Think You're Lonely Now"* jump out of the surround sound speakers and teased my plight. Karma's sword was out in full force, showing me no mercy or pardon....*But Stormy did!*

Giving me the opportunity to recover from my fall from grace, my Acquitting Storm pulled me closer and sexily asked, "May I have some sugar City Lady?"

I tip-toed up and humbly gave myself wholly over to my Merciful Storm, and was kissed undeservedly splendidly in return.

Bobby asked out *"When it's cold outside, who are you holding"*, I buckled at the Universe's jab of retribution, and I appreciated it being silenced as I was encircled by Stormy's massively strong; yet gentle hold around my shoulders and waist as waves of softness were pumped into my mouth.

Concurrently, I was sensually caressed down my back while bursts of Stormy's tongue continually penetrated my lips. I ingested it, as a willing subservient participant. And, yes, I was equally compensated for it.

Ladies you know those primal grunts of pure lust he spurts out when you make him feel a certain way—So much to the point that it sounds like he's in pain. M...m...m!...yeah—those!

The love-music was so funky in my ear that it sent quakes of pleasure through my desire's essence that rip a hole in my sex-core.

Detaching from one another, my libido was completely wrecked. My throat was parched, my body was wet, and my thong was soaked.

Excusing myself, it took no time for me to return refreshed wearing a shear sunshine yellow baby doll nighty set that had lace ruffle straps with a matching ruffled see-through thong, and smelling good with Fracas perfume by Robert Piguet.

Walking into the kitchen I noticed the clock said 4:37a.m. Paying no mind and poking my head into the living room, asking "Would you join me in having another cocktail?"

"Don't mine if I do." was the response, which made my uterus flutter, and a pang of fear yanked my body.

Cognizant of my panic, walking straight to the stereo, I attempted turn the station, but Stacey Lattisaw's "*Let Me Be Your Angel*" was too much competition—I was politely asked, "Baby, leave it be." Steadfast on my road to penance, I obliged.

Sitting down on the couch, my emotions attacked me and I immediately offered another apology because I felt dreadful on the inside, but I was instantaneously cut off with "*shhh!*"

As if the Universe saw the sincerity of my redemption bound heart, the melodic groove of Ghetto Heaven, by The Family Stand filtered the room—breaking up my tension.   Calling out accolades "A...a..a...h. I haven't heard this in years", shaking my head and swaying my shoulders.

"Girl, what you know about that?"

We simultaneously jumped up and began singing, dancing, laughing, clapping, and taking it back to old school moves. Stormy's spontaneity at having fun is an endearing quality that is a rarity.

Ladies, you know how it is when he is so comfortable with you that he can be his natural self—you see pure silliness in his actions and on his face, and you hear raw happiness coming from that care free eleven year old in him.

We danced to, *Everyday People*, by Arrested Development, and *O.P.P*, by Treach. It felt like we were in a club. By the time we sat back down, I was wet from sweating all over again, but smiling from shear merriment.

Preparing to raise up and get a towel for us to dry off, I was stopped short. Scooting over invading my personal space, I began to be feed spoons' full of my frozen pina colada.

Affiriming,"This'll du", as a droplet was overtly spilled on my chest then licked up. My heart was beating faster than the drink was cold.

Kismet continued its meandering as the music of Rolls Royce's I *Want To Get Next To You* began strumming my ears. Watching Stormy reading my body language perfectly, ordered, *"Cum-ere guh"* as I was pulled closer—leaving no space between us.

Listening to the words *"Sittin' here, in this chair waitin' on you, oh baby, to see things my way, but not a word that you say"* as my strap is painstakingly strip teased off my shoulder. Shivers spiraled down my spine. I felt naked as a newborn, venerable to love, and exposed to the passionate ambush that I was under. My head was tilted to the left side, licked with Stormy's full tongue, kissed real soft and then bitten hard enough to leave teeth impressions that literally made my fingers tingle as I rubbed the indentation.

Unable to contain myself, I involuntarily reached for the forbidden bulge, and received a smack on my hand along with full drawl vernacular "Ah'm not let'n you fuk wit'em no-mo", pointing to the dick that looked hard enough to fight thunder.

Offering up consolation goodies in its place, I was informed, "Poppah's got sumpt'n fo yuh."

I felt like a sitting duck with its tail pointing up in the air. Having my heart pilfered and my genitalia seduced by the Storm Bandit, I did not know how to react because I didn't want to repeat my ugliness, so I just sat there motionless.

"What's wrong City Lady, don't you like me anymore?"

Depleted of any kind of fight in me, I melancholy'd out, "You know that's not the case."

I was feeling that country bastard so powerfully at the moment that it actually hurt to speak.

Reading the pain in my face, "Baby don't! Do you want me to stop?"

"N...o...o!"

Knowing exactly what I needed and finally putting an end to my suffering, my left leg was lifted and placed over the arm of the couch. My right leg was placed over the lap that held the steel rod that I wanted so desperately inside me, and I sighed in mourning as my thigh lay down atop it.

Whispering in my ear before kissing me, "M...m...m, got these legs cocked open just the way Ah wan'em!"

My breath palpitated from the intoxicating banter and for my intense need of wanting more of Stormy's love-joy. Amid cherishing every inch of the kiss, I was penetrated with one of Stormy's long full fingers. It felt so good that tears trickled down my face.

Sliding in and out of me... "Got Damn Guh!...your lady feels good on me. Cock open more for me."

I spred my legs wider and stuck 'She' all the way out. The tip of my little boy in the boat was being caressed along with feeling Stormy's slow strokes in me, I lasted no time--I came.... and I came plenty.

As I'm screaming out my surrendered orgasm, my ears are filling up with "Drip all your juice in my hand!"

I swear my orgasm started all over again, and in the middle of it, that Torturing Fuck pulled out of me, cutting my apex short.

Before I could simulate the thought to the feeling, repositioning in front me on the floor, on bent knees, I was being inhaled. My Sniffing Storm compelled out, "Guh, you smell fresher than a loaf of Sun-dey morn'n baked biscuts. Gim-me some more!" then kissed my creamy opening.

Ladies, you know how your koochie makes slurping-clasping sounds when she's happy. It was horrible...Stormy was having a conversation with her...and she was all too eager to run her mouth.

After what seemed like an eternity of talking and teasing, my clit was sucked up and I was simultaneously poked with two of Stormy's fingers. The more I came, the more I was licked dry, and when my button was too sensitive to be touched any longer, I was kissed in a trail that lead all the way up to my forehead.

I was then guided down on the floor, put in the inner spoon position, and held tight until I fell off to slept, which was sometime a little pass dawn, as I remember looking up toward the lavender sky when saying my prayers.

"Dear God, thank you for this day. Thank you for my children and family, thank you for my health, and strength, and thank you for always keeping us safe. And Dear God may you bless Stormy with the happiness of a million angels wading in your water…Aman and Amen."

Waking up that afternoon at 1:17 p.m., I felt light as a feather in mind, body, and spirit. Lying there with my eyes still closed, taking in the aromas that permeated my nostrils. Flashbacking to my childhood in Virginia, where the Sunday morning ritual was a big country breakfast at either Grandma's house or Aunt Jo's trailer, in the back yard, listening to gospel greats such as The Williams Sisters, The Gospel Keynotes, the Five Blind Boys, or Tommy Ellison and the Singer Stars—afterwards my cousins and I scurried to get ready for Sunday school. Life was so carefree back then, which was how I was feeling at that moment…and then I began humming.

Coming into the living, looking domestically-fine wearing a wife-beater and light blue pajama pants; kneeling down beside me on one knee. Startled at seeing me crying through my serenade, "Baby Guh, what's wrong?"

"You know the old saying, when you hum, the devil don't know what you're talking about. I am so happy right now; I'm humming so that he doesn't take it away from me."

Empathizing with my joyful sorrow and looking at me with appreciated wonder, I marveled at my Praying Storm.

"Dear Father and most merciful God,
I come to you on this glorious Sunday afternoon as a sinner, but a true believer in you. Thanking you for loving the world so much that you gave us your only son—the savior of mankind—the Lord Jesus Christ. Thank you for another day of breath, and I thank you more--for your child who is sitting next to me. May You hold her happiness in Your bosom and keep her in Your favor. In the Lord Jesus Christs' name, Ah-men, Ah-men, and Ah-men"

I cried aloud in gratefulness because I knew I was so not deserving of such a grace as that. Not for the lack of loving or believing in God, but because there are countless lovers' of God who walk a more devout path than I, and I never want to feel bigger of myself than I actually am in His eyes.

Uncontrollably my head began shaking from side to side, the spirit shook my body, and I began calling out "I'm not worthy, I'm not worthy… I'm not worthy, but Dear God thank you for blessing and loving me anyway."

Continuing in the midst of my outburst with red eyes and a pale face, Stormy looked at me with conviction, "You are loved, You are blessed, and YOU ARE WORTHY!"

My mind grappled with the possibility, and a feeling that was greater than the compilation of all the joy, happiness, and goodness that I've ever experience in my lifetime—touched me. For a mili-second, I felt something better than this life has to offer, and I will forever be grateful to Stormy for exalting my spirit to that level.

Bending over and kissing me on the forehead and saying, "Thank you"

I was honestly baffled, I questioned, "For what?"

"For taking me to church guh…it felt good."

"No…thank you for what you gave me", and I went on to explain my experience.

"What am I gonna do with you? You're a God fearing spirit along with everything else that I'm digg'n about you. Are you sure you don't want to tie the knot wit me. Look…we can be in Vegas tonight, and by this time tomorrow, you could be my wife."

I took the proposal with a grain of salt, smiled genuinely, and jovially responded, "Get away from me Country Boy. You are just too damn fine for me to keep turning you down, so don't ask me anymore because I may not have the strength to be upright the next time."

Cherishing the good-guy in Stormy, a peaceful feeling came over me, and I had to share my thought, "Storm…I really do wish for you all that you want with Jade. And all jokes aside—the only reason why I'm not packing for Las Vegas right now is because I know that you love her, and that there might be hope for you guys."

Ladies, I couldn't be mad because truth be told—I had a glimmer of hope in my own heart about Danny.

Before the conversation got any deeper, I switched subjects to lighten the mood. "M...m...m it smells delicious in here, kudos to the chief."

And just like that, we let the 'us' conversation benevolently die; but, not the remainder of a memorable weekend because although the dick abstinence was still in place, the chemistry between Stormy and I kept bonded the non-intimate intimacy of 'us'.

After luxuriating in the bathtub, reliving my pre-dawn orgasms while washing off the remnants of my love jaunt with Stormy, I slipped into a ruby red tank top and lounge pants set.

Arriving in the living room to find a picnic buffet set up on floor. Happily impressed, I sat down Indian style and gorged my face on eggs, bacon, home-fries, applesauce, and drop biscuits, (*Yes, the boy can cook!*). I washed it all down with orange juice and coffee—all the while engaging in fun lighthearted conversation.

Even the clean-up was a treat. Stormy gathered up the food and brought it to the kitchen; I stored the leftovers in bowls. I washed— Stormy dried. In between it all, we had a water fight, a robot dance-off to "Dancing Machine" by The Jackson 5, and a laughing binge when we both slipped and fell on the soapy tile. Feeling good and having fun, where there were no expectations of sex, or pre-conceived lows of knowing that that was our solo weekend sojourn. Staying true to lackadaisicalness, I fell asleep while Stormy was watching a sports program. I was awakened at the sound of, "What kind of play is that?"

"Umh...what..."

Touching my hip and apologizing, "Baby, I'm sorry; didn't mean to wake you."

Before I could rationalize a response, I realized that I had no pants on.

Honest to goodness ladies, it was a platonic unconscious occurrence. You see, I've always had a habit of taking off my clothes in my sleep, when I get hot.

Instantaneously dismantling my embarrassment, my Alleviating Storm began rubbing me down the side of my thigh and inquired "Pretty sleeping dandelion, how was your nap?"

I couldn't answer for gazing at my nakedness. Continuing the one sided conversation and attempting to put my uneasiness to rest.

"You have no need to worry, I was a perfect gentleman. But baby I got to say, I've never been party to a strip-tease by a sleeping beauty before—I really enjoyed it."

Protecting my innocence, I half-heartedly accused "So you mean to tell me that in my slumber, you entertained yourself at my expense?"

"City Lady…You offend me with malicious character assignation."

Feeling a bit heel-ish, I made nice because in my heart of hearts I know that Stormy is made up of first-class stock.

Putting on my girlish charm, my apology was accepted with a kiss on my hand and a "You know dang well that I forgive you, but you have to do something for me."

Taken aback at the conditional attachment, I let my apprehension fad as I was assisted up and sat on the couch. Stating real sexy-like while leaving the room, "Ah'll be rhat bak" and returning before I could contemplate what was in store for me.

Peeking out at me from the kitchen, I was ordered to.

"Close your eyes."

When doing so, I felt something placed over my face—it was my lavender and chamomile anti-stress pillow that's been keeping space on the cabinet shelf. I groaned when the Up-Close Storm slid behind me, down my back; poking me all the while.

Next, leaning me a bit forward, my neck was massaged followed by my right shoulder; the spot that holds all my tension. The soothing aroma hitting my sinuses along with the perfect amount of pressure around my temples and on the bridge of my nose, collectively with the kneading sensations of the massage, triggered a spiraling wave of relaxing euphoria that worked its way down to every muscle, every nerve and every cell in my body.

Sinking into the couch and feeling all kinds of good. My body, as comfortable as room-temperature jelly, I surveilled Stormy moving around and repositioning me. Spreading my legs shoulder length apart, and although the movement startled me, my state of calm, surrendered me contently motionless.

Now sitting in front of me, my right leg was raised and stroked by tender firm hands. My toes were individually massaged in a circular then pulling fashion. The sole of my foot was kneaded with just the right amount of tension, and my heel was squeezed with tender loving care.

Basking in regaled bliss after the other leg was addressed, I thought, (*this is living*). My left foot was placed on the floor. When I was in a state of lethargy, Stormy nonchalantly suggest.

"Now you can apologize to me fo cuss'n me out in your head when I told you that you had to do something for me."

Without hesitation, I directed my attention to my masseuse sitting before me, and I coo'd.

"Mr. Wellington, please accept my apology for the error of my thinking. Now come here and let me make it up to you."

Getting up and bending down over me, smelling good enough to eat. All I could do was part my lips, and hot digity dog that ready to be licked tongue buried itself all up in my mouth. And I sucked on it like a calf pulling on its mother's teat for the first time; demonstrating all kinds of Quincee-Jane appreciation. Unable to do anything more, I stretched out and fell asleep.

Waking up on the couch at 7:45 that evening and feeling more refreshed than dawn itself. I was endeared when I opened my eyes to see Stormy laying on the floor next to me staring adoringly into my eyeballs.

Making funny faces at each other until I couldn't take it anymore, reading my mind once again; I flipped over onto my back and my belly pudge was kissed—yum-yum nicely, dissipating all self-conscience feelings that I have about that body part. We went from smooching to dry-humping to me moaning and groaning and ready to open my legs.

Stormy rose up off me and in controlled frustration "Guh, yuh take me from zero to thousand in-ah drum-thump. I'd follo yuh in the woods blind-folded and bare-footed."

No Ladies, I do not know what a drum-thump is, but I knew what was being reveal to me.

Rising up on my elbows and feeling a burning hole being planted in my soul from the look of love plastered all over that country-fine face—I confessed,

"I love you back."

I wanted to say, "I'm ready to go to Vegas", so bad, but catching a side glimpse of those country tears, I scooted down on the floor and buried my head in the pillow to hide the water running down my own face. Our silence was interrupted by my phone ringing. Obliging for the get-a-way, I dashed to the kitchen and retrieved it. It was Harmony.

"Mommy, I don't believe Daddy."

"What did he do?"

"I was walking out of Auntie Theresa's building when I saw him. So I called him and asked him for a dollar so I could get some french-fries from the Chinese restaurant. Mommy, tell me why daddy started running up the block away from me? And I couldn't run behind him because I have on flip-flops."

Mothers out there, my children's father is a Grade A certified Ass-hole.

I know my child was stressed out and needed nurturing and consolation from me, but my funny bone was tickled chocolate pink, and I starting laughing hysterically, (*It was awful*).

"Mommy, it's not funny."

"Baby, I know. I'm not laughing at you. I can't believe that your father would do something like that. It's just that I can see him plain as day running from you, looking like a supersize jackass.

Harmony, baby, I'm sorry that you're having this experience. Wait a minute, I gave you and your sister money. Don't Tell Me That You've Spent It All?"

"No mommy, I have all my money, I asked daddy just to see what he would say because it's always you taking care of me and Hope, and it's not right."

I was beaming with pride at my child's words. It's moments like these which me think, (*damn, I did something right*). Then I asked her, "Do you want to come home?"

"No!"

I talked to her until she had calmed down, told her that I loved her, and then we ended the call.

Hearing my conversation, I was chided by Stormy and I took it because I still felt a tinge of guilt. When I revealed the whole story, all I got was an arched eyebrow from Stormy regarding Eli's behavior.

The rest of the day went by with no more sexual manifestations of any kind—we ate the leftovers, watched a few movies, I got my toes polished, we laughed, talked and cuddled until we feel asleep.

Waking up Monday morning, I was filled with dread because I knew that my love sojourn was coming to an end, and as much as I tried to shake off the negative energy, the cloud of doom weaved itself deeper into the fabric of my psyche.

At quarter pass ten, I couldn't take watching Stormy peacefully sleep any longer as my mind raced with bitter thoughts of jealously and resentment.

Taking my unhappy ass into the shower, I let the water saturated my face, so that I had to focus on my breathing and not the hurt that had welled up in my heart and had begun working its way into my bones.

I don't know how long I had been in the bathroom when, out of nowhere I felt Stormy's naked body press up against mine. Enwrapping me within the arms of pure serenity, protection, and love… and what did I do? I jerked away.

Ladies, God does not like ugly.

I not only started choking because water entered into my windpipe, but I slip and probably would have broken something had Stormy not caught my evil ass.

Looking and sounding like the protective father, I was asked.

"Cat Fy-Yuh, are you okay?"

In full snippety regalia, I replied "I'm fine, thank you" and I attempted to exit the tub, but was gently tugged back.

Looking at me while clenching my chin with one hand and holding the small of my back with the other,

"City Lady, I'm going to remember this weekend for the rest of my life. Thank you."

A deluge of emotions crashed my mind and before I let the dam of tears flood down my face, I turned around toward the on-pouring water.

A ceremony with the two of us washing each other in sad silence, yet with evocative care just added to the treasure trough of our too short and confined liaison. I wanted so bad to be kissed; however, not trusting my self-control, I settled for a long passionate hug.

Ladies, its events such as these that makes love a taboo to me because I know that inevitably hurt will be knocking on my doorstep. And the pain is akin no matter what the parting terms are. Danny vs. Stormy equaled the same heartache.

Giving me my space to sulk, Stormy followed my lead cautiously walking around on eggshells. When I realized the effect that I was giving off, I made an honest attempt to loosen up because at that point, I hadn't spoken not one word since I gotten out of the shower.

As soft and natural as I could muster, negating all adversity in my voice, I asked as I was lotion-ing my legs.

"What time are you planning on leaving?"

"Whenever yuh ready for me to go."

Observing me struggle for words, my soon-to-be Departing Storm sat down on the bed beside me and offered,

"Quincee, I could easy see myself here with you another week and still not be ready to go. But like I've been say'n---it's not about me. If it'll be easier on you for me to leave now then that's what I'll do."

My mind was screaming at me, *(Bitch...Las Vegas, what the hell is wrong with you. Pack our shit and let's go get married. You're going to fuck around and turn us into a lonely old bitty...ooh we hate you!)*

Not sure what to make of my expression, Stormy spoke up, "Quincee, what do you want me to do?"

My mind still a million miles away in flux, it wasn't until I was nudged that I became cognizant of the question. Once again, taking a dive off of sanity's cliff –as if I was outside of my body watching stupidity reign over me, I retorted.

"I don't believe this. You whirling me up into your love scheme like I'm some kind of mercy piece of ass."

Seeing ambiguous fury cloak those fine ass eyes, but steadfast incredulously calm, I was told "Dad burn it Yankee Woman, you need to put on the breaks—guh!"

All the hurt, resentment and love that I was feeling for Danny *(ooh, where did that come from? ... I meant Stormy)* was transformed into incensed rage, and I gutted out.

"Why...because ...you don't want to hear the truth? So... you disagree that you were my knight in shining armor who swept me up from the throws peril on Friday--which made you an instant hit of the party?"

Waiting for an answer that never came, I continued "This Is All Your Fault!"

Scooting away from me and getting a clear view of my face, I was told...

"You got it all wrong. This Is Not My Fault! Instead of thinking about us when I asked your beautiful ass to marry me, YOU were the one who planted the seed of Jade and me, in my head.

Then you poured water on the two of us with your '*I don't want your dick, but I'm going to fuck with your country ass to my please'n*. I let you give me the short end of the stick cuz I'm feel'n yuh, and yuh know it.

Now that your Lady is fancy'n my dick, yuh hard-on is ruffling up yo feathers. Because you know you can count on my promises that I will give you what you want from me. Be mindful of what comes out of your mouth City Lady... the shit is hurtful and it aint fit'n."

Humiliated fury accosted me. Ready to lash out; but, before I could speak in my own defense, I was muted.

"Oh no, there will be no more of that...Calm down...My Yankee."

The nasty in me bypassed the nicety and I responded "FUCK YOU!"

"EXCUSE ME? Never mind don't repeat it, but I want you to hold that thought."

Leaving me alone in my room, I didn't know what to think, or do because the last time I saw such a strong reaction was back at Dre's house and it was directed towards Danny.

Yes ladies...I was scared. Did I mention that we hadn't gotten dress; we were still in our towels.

Regurgitating the conversation over and over in my mind and cringing at the choice of words that I puked out at Stormy had me questioning whether I had a secret quest of sabotaging my own happiness.

Maintaining a low profile because I was too shamefaced to step-foot out my room, I decided to change the sheets on my bed. Practically finished, I was bent over smoothing out some wrinkles on the furthest edge, when I saw a towel fly across my head, landing half on my arm and half on the bed.

Before getting my footing and erecting my posture, I was swung around with Stormy standing in front of me—butt ass naked, looking a cross between angry and hurt, (*and sexy as fuck*).

Yanking my towel off me and poking me in the belly with the dick that had my name on it, my Retribution-Bound Storm stated.

"I'm going to bury this bone right now" then guiding my hand and commanding, "Touch him! You know that's what you been want'n all the while."

And of course ladies… when I'm finally offered the very thing that I've acted like a complete idiot for, I get stage-freight…UN…BE…LIEVE…ABLE!

Dumbstruck for verbalization, my Fed-up Storm was not trying to hear any rebuttals nor refusals of any kind from me.

"Zip it with the bull-shit because you've dug your claws into me for the last time."

Trying to save face, I cried out.

"You can't do this…"

Cutting me off,

"Yeah I can and I am going to my Yankee Rebel… remember you're the one who woke up this dawg."

Before I was able to think another thought, I was turned around, bent over onto my bed, and had my legs spread open, all while hearing.

"You've had your fun punishing me Yankee. Now welcome to The South…Here."

Sliding the dick of thunder in between my woman-lips back and forth—but never letting its head stop near my opening sent my want… past the point of comprehension. Grabbing a handful of my braids and pulling them hard enough to invoke a spasm of pain, my Behest'n Storm muttered out.

"Moan for me!"

Avowing "mmm…mmm…mmm" in transported agony, feeling the veins of the country bridled dick ripple over my clit.

Beseeching for more, my aforementioned nastiness rounded full circle and became my biggest tormentor.

Thrusting me over onto my back, but then kissing me mercifully tender and afterwards leaning up and gazing into my eyes with sweet restrained composure, my Concupiscent Storm announced.

"Not this time around, City Flower."

Ladies, you know when he's pissed off at you, but he can't stay mad at you—and all you have to do is look at him innocent-girly-like? Unfortunately for me, that was not the case.

I witnessed Stormy's transformation from a Southern Gentleman into a Country Monster that I knew not of. Lifting my legs up and pressing my knees into my chest harder than need be.

"You better hope that Jade acts right because if she doesn't I'll be back on Friday. And when I knock on your door, you better answer.

Make no mistake, I'm coming to make you mine, but more than that, I'm com'n to Fuck You because that's what you need."

Bearing down and putting pressure on my lady-ship, and following up with, "This hot ass cat-slit is going to feel my dawg's bone, along with every other hole you're carrying around. Yuh hear me? M...m...m, yes suh... poppah's going to put you out of both of our suff-rin."

Agog with anticipation at the possibility, my heart was beating cardiac arrest fast. But my desire to have my Gentle Storm return to me had my mind racing even quicker. In a docile southern belle's accent I appealed, "Kess meh!", *(I couldn't believe it...it worked)*.

Taking hold of my face with tender care and filling my mouth with a billowing pile of softness, I basked in the amour of our oneness...then I remembered my fate—our fate, and my wet agony slowly began rolling down my face.

Ladies have you ever had your tears licked away and your face dried with his kisses?

That was followed by lifting me up to a sitting position on the side of the bed. Aggrieving for my pain, my Empathetic Storm queried.

"Quincee-Jane, how can I stop yuh hurt'n?"

By then the second wave of tears begin trickling out.

"You can't. You and I both know it. "

Sinking down on one bended knee between my legs matching my melancholy, I was implored, "Baby Guh please stop cry'n."

Collecting my thoughts, and wanting to come across without maliciousness or cracking in my voice.

"I...uhm...uhm...I know that I'm just a forerunner, and that this weekend together is a prelude to your life of happiness with her!"

Attempting to cut me off, but refusing the stoppage, I pressed on.

"No Storm....hear me out...Please. I appreciate you wanting to take my hurt'n away, but this is my struggle."

Appealing to my position, "City Lady, let me share this with you."

I was moved by the sentiment and wanted to say I love you; instead, I forged ahead with my interrogation with clear thoughts, a strong voice, but with continually free-falling tears.

"What do you propose that will ease my loneliness from you? As much as I want you to come back to me on Friday, I know that you're not because Miss Thang is going to do anything and everything that you want from her—I feel it in my bones.

And how can I fault any woman for wanting you, especially after what you've shown me these past few days? S...H...I...T!"

The full weight of dejection was about to debilitate me—my mind started fogging up, my chest began tightening on me, and my heart was physically hurting. Turning my head away in disappointment, sadness, and self-pity, I looked up toward heaven and lashed out my frustrations.

"When is it going to be my turn? I've always tried to do the right thing, and still I get the short end of the love stick. God...why? No, I take that back. Dear God, please strengthen me."

I felt the Holy Spirit save me.

As quick as a flash of light, my spirit began burning a creed into my mind-- *I love ME more than wanting or missing love that come from someone or somewhere else.*

My female sinew kicked in, empowering me—stripping away all the enfeebling manifestations that were attempting to cripple me.

Collecting myself, I began to view the situation through different eyes, but more importantly with a peaceful heart, and I reasoned out, "It's time for you to take your fine country ass home"--and I was sincerely okay with it.

Unaware if I was series or not, my Bewildered Storm questioned "Uh?"

Chuckling at the ambivalent response, pulling my soon-to-be Absent Storm close to me and continuing, "It's time for our dance to end."

Comprehending the authenticity in my words,"I can't leave you like this City Lady."

"It's okay Country Boy—I'm going to be just fine" I reassured, still feeling the comfort of the peace-be-still feeling in my heart.

I don't know what came over Stormy but the next thing I knew, I was being pushed onto the middle of the bed. Startled and aroused I inquired "What are you doing?"

"Quincee, I got to make this even." By that time I was on my back with my legs readily open. In a hurt and compassionate tone, my ever Surprising Storm mandated "I got to suffer this out with you."

When I looked down, I saw the verboten dick coming in my direction, and I yelped "No, we can't do this. You'll never have your momma coming to me in my dreams… and beating… my ass."

Ignoring my comment completely, "Guh, stop play'n."

"I'm not. I'm serious as a heart attack."

Taking alpha-male control of the situation, getting me to keep still with my legs opened in the right position, and looking candidly into my eyes.

"Three things; first, I want you to know what I feel like."

Ladies, my 'She' started itching and I inched my legs apart just a wee bit wider.

"Two, I want you to know that the first time I lay Jade down, I will be thinking about you and what she has made me pass up, with you.

And three, I don't want to wonder what your sugar lady feels like all up around my dick."

That was followed with my 'She' lips being spread apart by the head of that golden colored rod of thunder then being placed at the onset of my mass of creaming honey.

As soon as it made contact, just sitting there, on my opening's doorstep, EVERYTHING STOPPED!—time, my breathing, my hearing, and it wasn't until I felt the dick circling the circumference of my clef that jolted me back to reality.

When my senses returned, my entire body felt like it was on fire. Immediately, came a rumbling sensation that began inside the depths of my libidinous cave that transformed into a slow welling up.

As the wonderment made its way towards my chest, I looked up and saw Stormy's face contorted in pain, pleasure, and desire. That joining my own lust and the dangerous game that we were playing had me feeling like we were on the precipice of etching an affinity between us that might not ever be broken.

Making eye to eye contact, the connection was so powerful that our body's spasm which thrust the head of Stormy's dick onto the threshold of my impermissible woman passage. It felt like pure sin and B…O…O…M!

There was a surge of energy that actually thrusted Stormy up off of me and onto the floor, while leaving me temporarily immobile. I was experiencing a euphoric pulling-drawing-fluttering sensation in my loins that I've only had the pleasure of knowing twice before in my life. It was doing me so good that I didn't care that I was otherwise paralyzed.

Jumping up off the floor, dashing over to me, looking shaken, but more concerned about me "Quincee, Baby, Are You Okay? WHAT THE FUCK JUST HAPPENED?"

Not wanting to interrupt my feel-good phenomenon, I whispered what was still occurring to me. Seeing horror in the eyes that were, draped with anxiety for me, turn into raw aphrodisiac. In a soft raspy whispered voice to me-- "Guh you could make me lose my religion."

Still focused on my personal encounter, I was informed in a professional tone, "Here, let me take care of that for yuh!"

Within seconds my Illicit Storm was back between my thighs, spreading my lips open, exposing my vulva to the air, and then sucking on my muscle.

W...H...A...M! A deeper intensity of my climax immediately materialized.

The sexual cheese that had been pinned up in me was being drawn from my neck, my heart, my spine, my lower belly, and from my G-spot; all headed towards the vortex of Stormy's thirsty mouth. My Begotten Storm drank my satisfaction until I was dry. After my female serum and energy were drained, my limbs were massaged back to life with the care of a guardian angel and the expertise of a master masseuse.

Crawling upward and laying atop me for the last time, I licked off my juices that were gleaming on the face that was satisfyingly gazing down at me.

Staring into the eyes of my no-longer lover, I declared. "We're Even."

I had to close my eyes and re-open them to summon up the strength to say, "Walk now, while I still can let you go."

Watching my Parting Storm dress and pack in silence, I had the urge to put on black because I felt like I was in the midst of a funeral, and walking to my front door was symbolic to closing the coffin.

Ladies....it was hard!

Standing face to face we didn't kiss—not because we didn't want to—there was something in the energy between us that vibe'd—we had done enough, so we just stood for a moment forehead to forehead telepath-ing the love that we have for each other that we were closing the door on.

Unable to keep the cracking out of my voice, I managed out as best I could.

"When you get home, ring my phone twice, hang up, and repeat it, and I'll know it was you."

Concurring to my instructions with a nod, I felt my Parting Storm's tears as I was kissed on the inside of my wrist and told, "I love you City Lady."

My eyes where just as wet as the ones that I was staring into when I reciprocated, "I love you back, Country Gent."

And we parted ways.

When I received the second call that night, I cried like a baby until I fell asleep because I knew in my heart of hearts that Friday, Stormy was going to be a 'no-show', (and THAT was the case).

What I'm Getting Into --Is All Bad

Ladies, by nature, I have always been scared of courage, intimidated of spontaneity, and horrified of standing up and fighting for myself. However, there comes a time when even the weak hearted have to take a stand. It's a wonderful thing... to be 'Afraid-No-More.'

Tuesday after Labor Day
7:27 p.m.

Sitting up in bed with papers scattered all around me, I was deep in thought working on Mr. TooGood's project; preparing for our next meeting, when I remembered that I was supposed to call Cheryl.

Just saying, "Hi Cheryl, it's QJ... Girl, how are you doing," made her cry.

"Cheryl, Cheryl, Cheryl. You have to calm down. Come on, breath with me. Inhale...1...2...3. Exhale...1...2...3." It took two more sequences before she could speak.

"I don't know where to start." she responded, still sniffling.

"How about... at the beginning."

She blew her nose, took a deep breath and began her story.

"One night on my way from a friend's house in upper Manhattan, my car stalled on me, and I managed to get it to curbside at 145th street and San Nicholas Avenue. I was outside trying to get the hood open, when this man approached me and offered his assistance.

Silently chastising myself for letting my opinion slip out, "A stranger, Cheryl—No!"

Agreeing with me and forging on through a stressed voice, "When he stood beside me and I didn't feel discomfort or warning signs of any kind, so I let him look under my hood.

After a few minutes of tapping and finagling on gadgets, he asked me to try the ignition. When nothing happened, he had me to place my hand on something while he tried the ignition. Not thinking or knowing anything about cars, I did as he requested.

I became frustrated and call my friend to see if she could meet me. I walked away from the car to the sidewalk while I was on the phone. When her voicemail came on, I decided to leave the car there and have Matt have it towed for me.

I walked to Grimes—that's his name, thanked him, and I was about to get my belongings out my car when I realized that I had locked myself out. Grimes said that he had a friend who is a locksmith, and that he would call him, which he did. Grimes invited me to his house, which he said was right up the street, and that it may take twenty minutes to a half an hour before his friend would get to me."

Gasping at the thought of her going to a stranger's house, I passed no judgment. I had decided that I would hear the entire story before asking any questions or commenting. I continued listening, but there was a long pause. Finally breaking the silence, "Cheryl, are you there?"

"Yes, I'm here."

The choking in her voice was palpable, and I gave her silent kudos for her strength.

"After debating whether to go to his house, I convinced myself that I would be fine and safe. But deep down I know it was pride. You see, from time to time Matt's told me to learn some common fixes about my car, so that I wouldn't be stranded if something ever was to happen to my vehicle. Plus I forgot to renew my Triple A insurance." She started crying again.

My heart was hurting for her, but more frightening was the menacing feeling that had knotted my stomach.

"After convincing myself that I would be safe. I let that be an excuse because I had to go to the bathroom very badly. I used the bathroom then I walked back into the living room. He was on the phone with the locksmith person. I even spoke with him, and he said that he would be there within fifteen minutes.

While waiting, Grimes offered me something to drink. I accepted a closed bottle of water, and within minutes of drinking it, I began to feel funny. The next thing I remember is waking up. I checked my watch to see that it was 1:35 in the morning. My head was killing me, my mouth felt like cotton, and my body felt strange; although I was still fully dressed. I didn't pay any more attention to it.

As I was getting off the couch, Grimes came in the house. Handing me my car keys and informed me that my car was running. I tried to pushed $70 in his hand, but he said not to worry about it and that it was his pleasure to help me. I thanked him for his help and for him being a perfect gentleman."

Up to that point, I didn't understand what the problem was, other than I think there was missing time in her story. Then she hit me with the bomb-shell.

"About two weeks later I received an envelope in the mail. I opened it and there were twelve 8X10 pictures of me and him in all sorts of sexual positions."

She went on, fighting back the cracking in her voice.

"I was mortified and disgusted; I actually became sick to my stomach. He had attached a note stating what a wonderful time he had with me, and how delicious I tasted, and that he looks forward to more encounters with me. The note also stated that he knows where I live, where I work. He mentioned landmarks of both my home and job, of different outfits of mine. That meant that he had been following me.

Going back to that dreadful night, I believe that he drugged me because I now remember the water tasting funny, and the bottle top opening up very easily. I believe after he did those God awful things to me, he went in my car and got all of my information from my identifications in my wallet."

I am such a stupid fool."

"Don't say that. You're human. We all have, at some point in our lives, made a bad decision. Why didn't you call the police?"

With absolute conviction, "I'm not going to the police."

"Cheryl, you can put his ass away for life."

"I don't care. It's not going to be me. So QJ please don't ask me again."

"Fine, I won't mention it again, but what about Matt?"

She flew into a panic. "Oh God no, I can't tell Matt...I just can't....I ...I"

"Alright....alright. We'll figure something out."

Then she said "There's more. He has been making me go to him once a week for the past few months."

"WHAT. Cheryl, why haven't you called the cops?"

"I can't take that chance. For one, it has been too long since it all started. You know how victims of this nature get victimized all over again by law enforcement."

She had a point there.

"Secondly, the note also stated that he would post the pictures on the internet, and make sure that copies end up at my job. QJ, I would not be able to withstand the shame. I completely shut down when it first happened. I didn't go to work for over a week. I couldn't get myself out the bed; I didn't take any calls other than Matt's. I didn't eat, barely slept... I didn't wash my body.

But the main reason why I haven't said anything is because he threatened Matt's life."

"How does he know Matt?"

"Probably from the photos I have in my wallet of Matt and myself, and if he was stalking me, Matt picks me up from my job, frequently."

At that point I think we both felt defeated. I apologized to her several times for what she's been going through.

"Remember when I saw you at Tina's house?"

"Yeah, and you didn't look right then."

"I called you early that afternoon, while I was at his house because he didn't believe that I had plans.

Instantly remembering the short-lived connection, I felt like a piece of crap for not being there for her. Attempting to apologize but she, interrupted me and continued her horror story.

"The only reason why he let me go was because Matt called, after making me put my phone on speaker, and listening to my entire conversation.

"The week before that, when I went to Grimes, he forced me to have sex with him and two female crack-heads."

"Cheryl, I am so sorry" I wanted to cry, but got mad instead. "Don't tell me anymore. That mother fucker needs to be stopped and put out of your misery. Matt must be told, so that mac-nasty fucker can be handled. How dare he do this to you? I'm just surprised that Matt hasn't picked up on anything, or can't see that something is wrong with you."

"Maybe so, I don't know, I've just been in my own world. My baby is so sweet, and I just can't even imagine the thought of what will happen if....if" and she started crying uncontrollably again.

"Cheryl, you have to stop crying and center yourself. Have you got yourself tested?"

"YES! I have. Do you think I am that malicious as to place Matt's life in danger?"

A bit taken aback by her defensiveness, I apologized for the question.

"There's no need to apologize, it's me. I apologize for snapping at you. We haven't had sex since all this madness began. I told Matt that I am having female problems and that my doctor advised me to not have intercourse for a while."

"Smart move."

"I feel so dreadful about lying, but I have to protect my baby. I am so messed up."

"So what do you want to do?"

"I want all of this to end. I want control of my life back. I want to stop hating myself for volunteering to go meet Grimes. Every time that monster touches me, I have increasing thoughts of suicide. I am walking around like a zombie, and I can't take it anymore."

I let her continue until she was able to vent out all of her emotions.

"Oh God, if feels so good to get this off my chest. Here lately, I really thought I was going to lose my mind, literally. Thank you so much QJ"

"I didn't do anything, and to be honest, listening is the easy part especially if you want to stop this mother fucker in his tracks. If he is doing this so proficiently to you, there's no telling who or how many other victims he has out there.

Can I ask you a question—Are you ready to do what needs to be done to get that grimy bastard out of your life once and for all?"

"I don't know…I know I should be….I guess I am."

"Cheryl, there is no time for indecisiveness. That is why he is able to prey on you because of your weakness. Before you make any type of move, you must strengthen yourself. I can't make any decisions for you, but you can best-believe that I have your back."

"QJ, why would you put yourself out there for me?"

"There have been many times in my life where I've had help, sometimes from strangers. It's my duty as a human being, child of God and as a woman to be here for you."

"QJ, I don't know what to say, but I do appreciate just being able to share my nightmare with you."

"Tell me, what do you want to do?"

I heard the mustered bravado in her voice when she said, "I'm ready!"

"Okay. When is the next time you are supposed to meet him?"

"This Friday at 5:30 p.m."

I repeated what she said in a questioning tone. "I know it's a weird time, but he has me come at different times of day and on different days of the week, as not to arouse suspicion."

"I have to give it to him; he is a smart sexual offender—all the more reason to stop his monkey ass. How would you feel if I showed up with you?"

After a long pause "I don't feel comfortable at having you pulled into this."

"As far as I'm concerned, I've been in from the moment I asked you what's wrong."

"You would do that for me?"

"I'm not playing when I said; I have your back, and yes I would, but we're not going over there without a plan.

Are there any other people he have around him when your there? For instance—a partner, or look out person, or a body guard?"

"There's this guy named Jake that comes by, and now that I think about it; it's always after Grimes finishes with me."

A chill went through me, but I concealed the emotion as best I could and let her continue.

"But he hasn't come around the past few times I was there. I don't know what type of rapport they have."

I asked her if Grimes was a drug dealer, or partake in any other undesirable business or behavior.

"I don't know. You know what; I take that back because he always makes a point to show his knot of money, and it's a big one. So he's probably into something illegal."

"Do you know where the closest precinct is?"

"No, but I can find out." She broke down sobbing again and said, "I hate drawing you into this."

"You're not; I'm just helping out a sister in struggle."

She cried harder.

"Cheryl, you have to shake off the guilt and the tears; it's keeping your judgment cloudy. This bastard doesn't feel bad about what's he's doing to you, so fuck him…and fuck fear."

This is what I think we should do; I'll meet up with you in the 145th train station, you'll call him and have him come outside because we are NOT going into his house. There you can inform him that you won't be going to him anymore."

"What if he doesn't come outside?"

"Then we leave and go straight to the police, or tell Matt. I see no other way out. Bottom line, it's your call. Whatever you want to do, I'm with you 150%."

"QJ, what should I do?"

"Sweetie, this has to be your call."

Taking a deep breath and concurring, "Okay, we'll go with the plan on Friday."

"Are you sure?"

"Knowing that you'll be with me, I'll be ready by Friday."

"Cheryl, You...CAN...Do... This! He has won long enough. Stay strong, I love you, and know that we're in this together... to the end."

Hanging up the phone with her, I had a major headache and questioned what did I just get myself into?

Friday came within a blink of an eye. It was a beautiful day. The temperature was about 70° degrees, the wind was calm, and the sky was beautiful. Unlike my mood and thoughts of dread regarding the afternoon's pending event.

Ever since my conversation with Cheryl, I had an ongoing headache, my shoulders felt like they carried the weight of the world, and my stomach had been in knots, while continually replaying our plan in my mind's eye.

I packed some backup tools—a mini machete that Eli had given me and pepper spray.

All was going according to plan. We met at the A and D train station at 5:15PM. Before we left out, Cheryl put in a "hello" call to Matt because she was about to turn her phone off.

Walking arm and arm down 145th street and turning left on San Nichlas avenue, I was pumping Cheryl up with encouragement.

"You can do this. I know you can. You don't want to continue living, as you said, like a zombie. That's no kind of life. Besides, your spirit can't take it, and your mind will end up having you institutionalized somewhere saying bah...bah...bah...bah."

I was pleased with myself because I got a chuckle out of her. By that time, we had turned up 146th street and Cheryl had just pointed out his house, when someone walked up behind us.

Jerking around, I was facing this big dark brown skinned man who was about 5'9" with nappy hair and beard, crooked teeth that match the smile on his fiendish looking crater-filled face. He was wearing a plain black long sleeved shirt, pants and sunglasses.

After getting a view of the madman, and feeling Cheryl dig into my arm, I immediately commanded "BACK THE FUCK UP OFF ME…." and then everything went black.

That boogley looking mac-nasty fat bastard did something to me, (*How can something that horrible happen to a woman in broad daylight and not draw any attention?*).

Waking up in a room, I heard sounds, but couldn't make them out at first. As I tried to open my eyes and focus, I was unable to spread my right eyelids apart, and the left one had a glaze over it, and it burned. Raising my torso up was a failed attempt because of the sharp pain on my left side, so I melted back down on the floor.

My mind was racing, think back! Then it came to me, Grimes had approached us, and I became very still with panic. Reattempting to gain clarity with my vision to locate Cheryl, I strained to refocus all of my senses.

Picking up the scent of refer and another odor permeating the room, I also smelled extra pungent urine. I began to make out the space; it was a studio apartment. I was lying on my right side in front of a fireplace, half on and half off the mantle. The kitchen was towards my head, a bed was directly in front of me, and to my horror I saw that Grimes had Cheryl laying on a table with her dress bunched up to her waist, while holding her legs together straight up in the air and he was raping her (*Oh please God…help us*).

Just then I heard him say, "Ahh yeah, this is what I'm talking about…fucking all…that…ass."

Thinking to myself, (*Oh my God, he is sodomizing her*).

He was pulling her hair so hard that I saw the cringing and tears from her profile. Thinking to myself, (*Quincee-Jane…think fast*). I remembered what I had in my bag. Thank God that I had it draped across my body, and it was still on me. I attempted to move again and I thought that I was being silent, only to draw the monster's attention.

Without missing a stroke in Cheryl's rectum, he looked at me and said "Ah, the brave hoe is coming back to life. Just hold on because big daddy has something for you too."

Fear piercing everything in me; shot my adrenaline level to maximum, manifesting rage and much needed courage.

I had to move fast because it sounded like he was about to cum. I had 10 maybe 15 seconds, if I was lucky to open my bag, find the pepper spray, and have it ready for action. Positioning my bag almost brought tears to my eyes from the pain. I got it turned around to face me; my hands nervously fumble around the bottom for the can, (*Oh shit he's walking in my direction...Fuck! he spotted me out*).

When he was about a good six steps from me, I had the spray in my hand, and was pulling it out of my bag. Once he saw that I was fiddling for something, he charged at me. The stupid ass took about two steps, slipped on an article of clothing on the floor, his feet went up in the air, and he bust his ass. My adrenaline was flowing too fast for me to enjoy the moment.

Jumping up to my feet, I was wobbly, but just glad to be standing. By the time I fully recovered, that mother fucker was back on his feet. He kicked me in the lower part of my stomach and I fell against the wall of the fireplace, dropping the pepper spray.

He then stood over me with his nasty uncircumcised dick swinging in my face, and said "You dumb bitch, you want to take on The Grimes...you piece of shit", and then he began urinating on me—all over my head, my face, and down the front of my torso. As he was doing so, he scream out, "This is what fake ass wanna-be tough bitches get."

With all that was in me, I prayed...

"*Please God, give me strength, if not for me...for Cheryl; that I can get her out of here to safety.*" A scripture came to mind "Isaiah 41:10 "*Fear thou not; for I am with thee: be not dismayed; for I am thy God: I will strengthen thee; yea I will help thee; yea, I will uphold thee with the right hand of my righteousness.*"

With that I said out loud, "*THE DEVIL IS A LIAR*", and I felt a force rush through my spirit and I was on my feet again, and had backed away from him.

Eli's boxing training instructions also resounded in my ears, "A fight should last no more than three seconds", and "You have to be able to take a punch in order to give one."

The mother fucker already had two up on me. I swear I felt no pain by then. When he came for me that next time, I could tell that he was still in a state of comfortable aggression. More of Eli's words came to me "Let your opponent's arrogance be to your advantage."

When that gruesome fuck charged at me, I held my ground and when he got arm's length, I punched the cocksucker right in the throat. As he grabbed his throat and gasped for air, I kicked him in his rape-infested swinging balls. As he was going down, I hit that mother fucker with an upper cut. Spasm shooting through my knuckles, awakened all the other pains in my body—my head, my face, my back, my ribs, and my stomach.

While he was down on his hands and knees trying to regroup, I retrieved the pepper spray I spotted on the floor, and sprayed that disciple of the devil all in eyes, nose, and mouth.

I then turned and headed for Cheryl. She was still on the table curled up in a fetal position, rocking herself. I couldn't run, but I held a steady slow pace. Reaching the table and hurting like fuck, I pulled her up. We looked at each other, she was crying, I was crying, she was bleeding from her private area, and I was bleeding from my mouth and other areas that I didn't know where.

Still worried about being in that house and not knowing Grimes true condition; although I could hear him gagging, which was music to my ears, I scramble around to find Cheryl's underwear and pocketbook. Lifting her up and helping her off the table shot a wave of pain in my side that had my ears throbbing.

Now standing on the floor, we held each other up and made our way to the outside door, only to find that it was dead bolted from the inside. Horror struck both of us.

I knew Cheryl didn't have it in her to go back into the apartment, so I whispered to her, "Just stay here, but be prepared for whatever may happen because we might have to break the window if I can't find his keys."

Scared as shit, but riding on a small high from my prior Laila Ali performance with the incarnate of vile, I made my way back to his apartment, but stopped short at the doorway. I spotted the crazy fuck immediately; he was crawling towards the bed. His breathe was still labored and I could tell that his sight hadn't returned by the way he was using his hands as a guide. He was mumbling incoherently with foamy spittle leaking out of both corners of his mouth.

As he was climbing on the bed, I surveyed the room for his keys, but was unable to locate them. I silently thanked myself for bringing the pepper spray.

Ladies, it is important to know that there's a difference between pepper spray and mace. Pepper spray is an inflammatory agent that not only causes temporary blindness, nausea, and has the propensity to cut off all but life support breathing, but it also renders an offender disabled longer—up to ten minutes. It also affects lunatics who are under the influence of drugs and alcohol, whereas mace may or may not have an impact.

Unable to determine how much time had lapsed from when I first pepper sprayed Grimes. Still at his doorway, everything hurting, feeling defeated, and wanting to cry; but, believing that I was still cloak under the protection of prayer, I cross back over the threshold to his apartment. Glancing over the room for his key, I spotted them on the floor under the table.

Taking a shallow breath that burned my side with pain, I tiptoed sickeningly slow towards the dining table, trying to make as less noise as possible and carefully maneuvering my way as to not step on vomit and the other unidentified liquids that were in sporadic areas on the floor. The stench almost made me throw up.

Approaching the table, bending down—that's when the tears came, grabbing the key chain with a tissue that I pulled out of my jacket pocket, I stood up only to trip over a fallen chair. I hit the floor hard and landed with something poking in back.

My mind was screaming to lay there and waddle in my pain, but fear told me to get the fuck up! However, it took me about three seconds to move the pain out of my consciousness. I didn't look at him or wait for any kind of response. Running fast as I can, but feeling like I'm moving in slow motion, I heard him attempt to laugh, but uttered out instead, "He's coming."

All in a split second, I froze then turned around and looked into the face of the child of Lucifer, and a chill ran down my spine as he sat up on the bed with puke and spit laced over his face, and staring into his own darkness. He sniffed into the air, while turning in my direction attempting to get up, but then grabbed his stomach and began throwing-up on himself.

Feeling confident that he was incapable of inflicting anymore harm to me, I took a sigh of relief only to hear him choke out "I'm going to kill you" then gutting out a boding evil laugh, just as Cheryl screamed, "Quincee-Jane.

Horrified with terror and anxiety, I jetted towards Cheryl's voice, only to run nose first into the door frame of the apartment. Not stopping to wait until the stars disappear in my vision, or to wipe the flowing blood running out my nose, or to pass out from the pain.

Reaching Cheryl standing flush to the wall, she clenched onto my arm, crying out, "Hurry up, hurry, hurry, hurry, hurry", while looking diagonally out the door window. "I see...see Jake. He...he...he's coming down the block!"

It took me only a second realize who she was talking about— Grimes' flunky. My hands became rubber, and I began fumbling with the keys as Cheryl rattled on, "Come on, come on, come on, hurry, hurry, hurry, please, please, please." She was making me more nervous, and I wanted to tell her to shut up, but couldn't bring myself to do so.

Annoyed and experiencing the most frightening minutes of our ordeal, I finally got the right key to unlock the door. Before I could take hold of Cheryl's hand to assist her out, she had grabbed a hold of the back of my blouse and was holding on for dear life, intensifying the pain in my side.

Midway down the outside steps, Jake spotted us and began walking fast towards us. Cheryl panic, lost her footing, and fell down about four steps just as a cab pulled in front of a brownstone two doors away from us.

By the time I got her back on her feet, my eyes were going blurry from the pain shooting around my insides. I saw a small framed African woman with a baby get out; along with a tall robust Puerto Rican cab driver, who was retrieving a stroller from his trunk. I yelled out to the cabdriver, "Hello, hello... Please can you take us?"

Catching sight of us, I saw concern grip his face, and he responded "*Adio! Meo. Que' tienes*?" just as Jake was walking pass the cab, saying something into his cellphone, he slowed down to a normal pace.

The cabdriver pulled out a steel baseball bat from the trunk of his car and blurted out something else in Spanish then Jake stopped dead in his tracks.

I couldn't distinguish Jake's nationality, but he was a short scrawny, pimpled rat face looking man—wearing a wrinkled and stained emerald green sweat suit that was just as disheveled as the black tangled and matted curls on his head and his dingy white sneakers. He's a punk because he was two steps away from us, throwing up his hands in surrender to the cabdriver, before even turning around to face him.

The bat still in a striking pose in his right hand, standing one step from Jake and never taking his eyes off of him, the cabbie reached out gesturing for me and Cheryl with his left hand.

Taking hold of his large meaty warm palm, with Cheryl beside me holding onto my arm with a death grip, we were allowed free passage. I swear I saw an angelic glow around our rescuer's head.

Jake standing with his arms still stretched out in an arrested position looking at me with indifference, but he winked at Cheryl. Tightening her grip on my arm, she sped up our pace as we passed him. The cabdriver backed away from Jake, with the bat remaining in swinging position, the entire way to ensure all of our safety.

Inside the vehicle that smelled of cilantro and chicken with a baseball game being announced in Spanish on the radio, the doors were locked, the windows were up, the air conditioner was on, and we were headed down the street. It wasn't until then that I knew that I would live to see another day.

The cabdriver asked us if we wanted to go to Harlem Hospital, and Cheryl flew into a temporary frenzy, "No…no, no hospital. I just want to go home! Please just take me home."

"Ju sho? E be no pro-lem."

"Cheryl, you can't go home. You don't know if that crazy fuck will come for you, or…"
Not completing my thought to her because I saw her shrinking into desolation right before my eyes. Cognizant of her state of mind, I instructed "We have to tell…somebody; if no else, Matt needs to know."

Watching her stare into space, wrapped in her own agony made my pain seem like a dull ache. Retrieving her phone from her pocketbook, I dialed Danny's house number. Hearing "Hello", I hung up then gave the cabdriver Danny's address. Looking confused, he asked "Ju sho. I can to ta-kah ju to la hospital."

"No thank you, we'll be fine."

"Ju got it senorita."

Gently touching Cheryl's leg "Okay, this is what we're going to do; we'll tell Danny first. This way you'll have me and Danny as buffers when you tell Matt. I'll be right by your side the whole time."

Looking pass me she dropped her head in my lap. I rubbed her forehead like how my grandmother used to soothe me when I was a little girl.

After she was in a calm or catatonic state, I gave praise, *"Thank you God, for my life and thank you for Cheryl's life, and most of all, thank you for sending us an angel...Amen."*
Like being shaken into fright by the sound of thunder, the thought occurred to me that I/we hadn't thanked the cabdriver.
Embarrassed, I called out, "Perdón (Excuse me)."

He interrupted me, "I am Vek-tor."

Leaning forward, ignoring my pain and placing my hand on his shoulder, I offered, "Victor, please forgive me, I haven't thanked you. Mucho Gracias, thank you so much. Thank you for saving our lives", and I started crying uncontrollably.

"No mommy, por fovor no...no...por favor don't cry... eet's ok, eet's ok."

By the time we hit the red light at 137th Street and Edgecomb Avenue, I had settled back in the seat, was still crying, but to myself.

Cheryl was a pliable wreck because even though her head was lodged between my lap and stomach, she showed no signs of anything.

Looking at me through the rear view mirror, Victor commented, "Ju got son people?" The expression on his face read; shit needs to be handled. Turning his eyes back towards the street, he mumbled "ese fuckin puta."

His words and anger brought about a welcoming peace, and I was able to finally lay my head back, closing my eyes, willing the pain away until we get to our destination.

I was awakened to the sound of Victor's horn blowing and him arguing with a yellow cabdriver. We were on the FDR and were around 42th street, when I caught a whiff of myself, and I became paralyzed with embarrassment; realizing that I was funk-ing up his cab with the odor of Grimes urine on me and my clothes.

Opening the window to let some fresh air ventilate the cab, I spent the remainder of the ride dealing with the physiological effects of Grimes' piss assault. I couldn't get the stench out of my nostrils, and then urine began to burn my skin. My entire body felt like I had microorganisms crawling inside me. Next the itching came and at one point I thought I was going to break the skin, I was scratching so hard, but the thought of his urine streaming through my veins caught my attention—real quick. I truly began rubbing with aforethought.

Spotting Victor observing my discomfort from his rearview mirror; he was merciful to me, "Mommy, no pra-lem. La carro... I can wash. Ju don worre about la."

"God bless you Victor."

Turning away from his view, the rest of the ride was a blur, until we turned onto the corner of Danny's block, when I inadvertently yelped out, "SHIT", startling both Victor and Cheryl.

Sitting up in a panic, my thoughts racing for a Plan B because I saw Matt's truck.

Looking like a hopeless ragdoll, I watched Cheryl continue her implode into her own world. Her face went expressionless, her eyes went blank, and her body went jelly-like.

Pulling out my cell phone, I starting dialing--"Hello, Danny...its QJ."

"Baby, what's the matter?"

"I need you to come downstairs, but don't say anything to Matt."

"Quincee, what's going on?"

"JUST COME DOWN STAIRS....please!"

"I'm on my way."

Coming out of the front door, and looking fine...fine...and more fine, wearing a faded grey tee shirt and khaki cargo shorts with grey socks and grey sport flip flops. My mind took a temporary break from the current devastating state of affairs. My heart skipped a beat in the name of my true feelings, and then a pang of sadness blew over me, for all that was lost between us.

Ladies, have you ever been in the presence of that one man that you least want to be around, and his magnetism still has the power to put butterflies in the pit of your belly. And he pisses you off even though; he doesn't hesitate to be at your beck and call?

I hated the thought, but that was my reality.

Not looking forward to what was to come; I begged "Cheryl, you have to get out the cab." My poor broken friend was immovable. The more I tried to push her up out of my lap, the more I realized the amount of pain I was in and I wouldn't be able to get her out by myself.

Turning around in his seat, speaking his best English, Victor was trying to coax her out, and looking like it would pain him to upset her, even one little bit.

The closer Danny got to us, the more I tried to keep my face looking down to the floor of the cab. For a split second, regretting my plan, but then rolling down the window turning toward Danny and I went with it, "I can't get Cheryl to get out of the car."

The look on Danny's face is one that I will never forget.

"WHAT THE FUCK? QUINCEE, WHAT HAPPENED TO YOU?"

Fighting back nausea and unidentified anger, while instructing "Danny, please, not right now. Just help me get Cheryl."

Oh how I wanted to throw myself into those strong, sexy, comforting arms, but I didn't...that's probably why my ass was so damn heated. Ladies, I can admit it.

Turning my attention, "Victor how much will that be?" Holding his hands up in a position gesturing that he wasn't accepting any money and before I could oppose, Danny was standing at the driver's side window, placing a hundred dollar bill in Victor's hand, saying something in perfect Spanish dialect.

Victor got out of his cab still looking gravely concerned when Danny opened the driver's side back door to usher me out and walked me to the sidewalk then having to physically get in the vehicle in order to get Cheryl out.

Standing in front of me was this, fair-skinned, brownish black wavy haired man with the thick mustache and warm comforting chubby hands. Humbling me even more by taking off his hat in reverence, I gave him as best hug that I could and thanked him from the bottom of my heart because I will forever be grateful to him for me and Cheryl's lives. I got his card, said goodbye, then turned and followed Danny, who was carrying Cheryl toward the house.

With her head buried in her chest, and holding on to Danny, I felt a glimmer of hope that she was coming out of her mental torpor. As soon as the door closed behind us, Danny turned around and looked at me...I saw the horror in the face that was looking at me.

In seconds, I felt the dry air in the house intensify my burning skin. Looking down and seeing whelps all over my arms and chest, I terminated my plan of explaining everything to Danny before we go upstairs where Matt was.

"Quincee, What Happened?"

"Dan, please just let me go to the bathroom and wash first....Please." I was begging.

Reaching the top of the stairs, Toomey—of all people—was in the kitchen and caught a glimpse of me. Putting my index finger up to my mouth, gesturing "shh" followed by placing my hands together, silently pleading "Don't say anything." I received a perplexed nod indicating that our secret was safe.

By the time I had dragged myself into the master suite bathroom, Danny had sat Cheryl down on the bamboo cushion seat that was next to the shower.

Turning to our rescuer "I will tell you everything when we come out, but give me some time with Cheryl. Plus I need to get clean as well."

Trying to prolong the conversation, "Quincee, what happened?"

Aggravated and snapping out in the need to feel some type of control "CAN'T YOU SMELL ME. I SMELL LIKE A GOT-DAMN URINAL. LET ME GET THIS SHIT OFF OF ME, AND TRY TO PREPARE CHERYL FOR WHAT WE HAVE TO TELL YOU AND MATT...GOD!"

"You are in pain and both of you are fucked up, I can't help but ask."

Not wanting to respond, closing the bathroom door and severely hurting, I started my slow walk over to Cheryl.

Softly exalting "Hey girl, you did it?"

Simultaneously catching a glimpse of myself for the first time, I froze then began peeling my clothes off.

Catching my reflection in the mirror, I observed a black eye, spots of dried blood on my forehead, hairline, nostrils, and lip; splotches of dry urine stains; in addition to a big bruise on my right side that stretched around to my back, and oversize whelms everywhere.

My body was hurting so bad that I just wanted to go and get in Danny's bed and sleep for three days straight. Instead I managed to sit down next to Cheryl and undress her; she didn't resist. I was afraid for my friend.

Leading her to into the shower stall, I centered us directly under the gigantic water-head. Not knowing what to say, I just kept quiet, and held her with one arm. I was thankful because I let the streaming water masquerade my tears that were rolling down my cheeks from the physical and emotional pain that I was experiencing.

Not knowing how much time had passed and focusing on how lucky and blessed we were, still holding her, I whispered "Cheryl, we made it. We made our way out of hell, with our lives. You're safe, I'm safe, and we don't have to worry about him anymore."

I held her with one arm and began to pray.

"Dear Lord, God, and Heavenly Father, we thank You for our lives, our sanity, and our friends. Thank You for giving Cheryl the strength to rise to a challenge that was un-understood, un-just, and un-warranted. Thank You for making me a conduit, so that she didn't have to make the entire journey alone. Thank You for making her whole again. Thank You for renewing her mind, rejuvenating her spirit, and for awakening her consciousness. You are our Alpha and our Omega, our Savior and Rescuer, our Doctor and Lawyer, our All and All. In the Holy name of Jesus we Thank You, we Thank You, and we Thank You... Amen and Aman."

I knew I had reached her because the dynamics of her body shifted, and she began to cry again.

Feeling really bad because my body was unable to rock her; so, I just lulled her to a peaceful place, "Shhhhhhhhhh...don't worry. You are safe now. God didn't get you this far to let you go. Come on now, do you think that Matt is going to let anything else happen to you, or let Grimes get anywhere near you?"

She began crying harder. "You are so brave. I don't know if I would have been able to endure all that you have. I am so proud to be your friend, and I am even more honored to have been in your corner when you stood up to that madman."

She sank down to the floor, and I un-believably followed. I thought I was going to pass out from the pain, trying to hold my friend up. We just sat there silently for a good fifteen minutes or so, letting the water wash away all that was bad.

Ready to clean the stench and filth of evil off me, I said in a comedic tone "Okay, I'm ready to wash-my-ass."

Somewhat looking up at me and speaking in a barely audible voice, I think I heard *"Okay."* Washing her first, I did so in the same fashion as a mother would wash her newborn baby, for the first time. I don't know what sickened me more, all the bruises that I saw, or the zombie-like state that she was in.

By the time I got to myself, my legs were about ready to give out, but God made a way out of no-way for me to finish showering, dressing Cheryl and myself (*I thank You...I thank You...and I thank You Amen and Aman*).

Back in Danny's bedroom, I noticed the two sets of tee-shirts, sweatpants, and socks on the bed. There was also a piece of paper with two pills on it that read. "Take these for the pain. No backtalk."

Sending thanks and kisses into the Universe regarding Danny, I instantly got pissed off all over again because we were supposed to be together.

Dried off, dressed, and sitting on the bed, I patiently waited until I thought that Cheryl was ready.

Glancing at me when she thought I wasn't looking, and I told her "You can do this. It may be hard, but the worst part is over." (*I had no idea that I was telling a lie*).

Leading her to the door, and opening it, Danny was standing there looking at us with concern and anxious ambiguity.

Turning towards Cheryl, taking a short breath, grabbing her hand, the three of us walked toward the living room.

Let's Talk

(Have you ever had a dream that you were marching towards hell, only to realize that you're not sleeping?)

A week after I see Quincee leave Tina's home with Cloudy, or whatever Cat's name is, she shows up at my house with Cheryl. Quincee's face is bruised, she was having trouble breathing and she was wincing in pain. I noticed all that just by observing her through the window of the cab.

Holding my shit together, while literally peeling Cheryl out of a cab, and thinking (*What the Fuck Is Going On?*). She was totally gone, I had to carry her. I'm trying to keep my cool, so that I can find out what happened, but Quincee shuts me down. I tried to push the issue, but she lets me know that she's in charge. I went with it because some bad shit has gone down, and I was going to need details, before taking this shit Matt.

Waiting for them to come out my room, now I'm fucked up because all kinds of shit started popping in my head. I'm ignoring Toomey trying to signal me for information, and I'm lying to Matt after being asked three times, if I was alright? My chest is about to explode because I'm ready to do somebody in.

Shutting down the interference, I told my boys that I had to make a business call and I went and sat outside my bedroom door and waited on Quincee and Cheryl.

Over an hour, after she slammed my own door in my face, Quincee opened it. Immediately on my feet and really getting a good look at them. They were fucked-up. Holding hands and looking like school girls with my long white tee-shirts that went down pass their knees and my socks that were way too big for their feet. I wanted to call an ambulance, but Quincee promised me that she would go to the hospital after they talk to us.

I wanted to wrap my arms around her and tell her that I'm going to protect her from the world for the rest of her life; instead, I grabbed her hand and the three of us took a long slow walk to the living room.

Matt's face initially smiled when seeing Cheryl, but then contorted as we approached closer. Standing up and walking to her, "Baby, what's the matter?"

Cheryl cowered behind Quincee, and I saw it confuse my brother even more.

"C-lah... baby, talk to me", but the poor thing just stood behind Quincee, not moving or speaking.

Matt was infuriated.

"WHAT THE FUCK IS GOING ON?"

Walking over to my brother I attempted to defuse the hyped emotions that where flying through the room.

Jerking away from me, and in a tone that was full of controlled anger, but more with hurt, "Dan, what the fuck is up? Is my girl fucking around on me?"

"Man, something has happened. I don't know what it is, but they are going to tell us now. When I met them downstairs, they both where pretty messed up."

"Downstairs....what the fuck do you mean, downstairs? How long have they been here?"

Ignoring the frustration I read in Matt's face, "Yo man, just let them talk. This is some bad shit."

Matt sat down in the lazy-boy, and Toomey and I stood on either side of the chair—I was there for my brother, no matter what the fuck we were about to hear.

You could hear a mouse shit on cotton; it was so damn quiet, while we waited for either one of them to speak. Taking her time, Quincee sat Cheryl down in the brown butter leather loveseat then sat beside her. My baby put her right arm around Cheryl's shoulders and held her close then spoke up because Cheryl appeared to be too far gone in her own world. Watching my girl wince in pain put me in agony, but I had to just let her be.

Looking at the three of us individually, Quince was almost begging "Please just let me tell you the whole story before you say anything, or ask any questions.....please."

We all agreed.

"Tuesday after Labor Day Weekend, Cheryl and I spoke on the phone and ...."

By the time Quincee got to the part about the pictures, I was sick to my stomach and I was fighting hard to keep my legs from buckling, but that wasn't shit compared to watching Matt sink down in the chair. I swear to God, I felt my brother's sanity slide into darkness. Toomey and I moved in closer, for whatever kind of support we could offer.

"What the fuc…?" I cringed at hearing the loss in my brother's soul.

Quincee then produced the pictures. Not looking, I passed the pile to Matt. God knows, I didn't want to.

Matt took a look, went deeper into a blank place, jumped up out of the chair before I or Toomey got a chance to hold cat down. "MOTHER FUCKAH, WHO IS THIS…HE'S A DEAD WALKING MOTHER FUCKAH!"

Toomey said "Calm down, Man."

"FUCK YOU! WHAT THE FUCK YOU MEAN…CALM DOWN!"

Toomey's hands were thrown up in the air, saying "You got it. I check myself. Shit…I understand!"

Turning to me and not trying to receive any of the empathy that I was offering, "FUCK YOU TOO. They've been here all that time, and you never once opened up your fucking mouth, not even to give me a heads-up as your boy, as your brother, or at least as a niggah that you know from the street? Get the fuck outta my face."

Then without warning, my brother hauled off and punched me in the jaw. You have to know the rapport between me and Matt to understand the seriousness of the reaction.

I love Matthias Fernand Dollingwood. We met back in my short-lived thug-lover-wanna-be, days. Before my trust fund kicked in and still living by my father's rules of, "You will know how to appreciate a dollar…just because I have money, that does not mean that you have money" days. From the time my friend and partner was willing to go to jail by taking the rap for me, I've considered us brothers ever since. I actually wanted to do the blood brother thing—Matt doesn't believe in "that shit."

Another reason why I love Quincee is because of how she treated Matt, despite the distance between them. My boy just doesn't warm up to people and understandably so; but Quincee always respected Matt and my relationship. Never once did she give me a hard time about the amount of time Matt and I spend together and I never heard any of the slick-ass comments that females can make about best friends.

So when Matt punched me in the face, I was caught off guard because nothing like that had ever passed between us, but shit, I probably would have done the same thing, if the shoe was on the other foot.

Quincee tried to jump up, but remained seated and yelled "Stop Fighting. This Is Not The Time For That."

I didn't know what the hell she was talking about…there was no fight. I was the one who got japed in the face; no other punches were thrown.

Turning her attention to Matt, "Cheryl doesn't need this…look at her. She's withering right before our very eyes."

Matt dropped back down in my favorite chair, and Toomey and I took our original positions beside our falling brother.

Quincee went on to tell of her brilliant plan to confront the mother fuckah. I couldn't believe that she would do something so stupid. I was pissed off, but there was no way that I was going to voice my opinion about it…I continued listening.

"The next thing I know was, I waking up in his apartment."

My blood running cold, everything in me numb, not wanting to, but needing to hear all that happened to her. I waited for the silence to end.

All of sudden, Cheryl sat up straight like she was sitting on the witness stand, talking for the first time since I carried her in the house. Speaking as if she was outside of herself, her eyes were vacant, her body was stiff as a board, and she stared straight ahead, looking at none of us the entire time that she spoke.

"What QJ doesn't know is that he punched her and knocked her out. He picked her up and carried her into his house."

Enjoying the feeling of hatred running through my veins, I wanted to ask Cheryl why didn't she scream for help, but I knew it was better to kept my mouth shut.

She went on to say "He made me smoke crack with him and then he made me give him a blow job."

I cringed, and when I looked down, I saw tears rolling down Matt's face. I felt helpless as a brother and hopeless for my brother.

Reaching out in attempt to console Cheryl, but realizing she wasn't ready. After witnessing Cheryl go into a panic; shaking her head back and forth and screaming "Don't touch me, don't touch........ Matt sat back down in the chair.

Cheryl continued "and he raped me for like the hundredth time", then she lost it.

"Was it rape because I didn't fight or disagree? I didn't stop it, but I didn't want it...I was scared, I couldn't tell anybody. I couldn't tell you."

Looking a Matt, she continued to lose it some more "What would you think of me? I just didn't want anything to happen to you because he said that he would kill you and I...", and then she started crying hysterically.

A first for me was seeing Matt cry and I mean buckets of silent tears.

Dropping out of the chair crawling on the floor towards Cheryl, saying "C-la, I'm sorry I wasn't there to protect you."

But the poor thing jerked her legs up onto the loveseat, like she was afraid and cuddled onto Quincee. Matt just broke down in the middle of the floor and I witnessed my brother crying like a baby.

Quincee removed her hand from Cheryl's, inched her way down the chair onto the floor. Cradling Matt's head on her lap, she started apologizing.

"I am sorry Matt. I'm so sorry. She called me for help...and...and I didn't...didn't protect her the way that I was supposed to, the way that I had planned to. Matt, P.l.e.a.s.e....P.l.e.a.s.e ..... F.o.r.g.i.v.e. ...M.e."

My baby could barely get the words out because she was crying that hard, along with Matt. Tears started falling from my eyes, and I looked at Toomey trying to go undetected, but it was too late, I saw the water.

Quincee kept repeating, "I'm so sorry."

Matt's hand was less than five centimeters away from Cheryl's leg and reach out to her, but Cheryl jerked her limb up on the seat , saying "Don't touch me...I'm too dirty."

I watched my baby stroke my brother's rejection. Seeing her wince in pain, I moved towards her, but she waved me off—I respected that and stood back at-arms beside Toomey.

Quincee guided Matt more onto her lap, sitting with her back flushed to the couch, stroking my brother's head and shoulders—big rock size tears pouring down her face encouraging, "She is going to get through this. I promise you. Just hold on." Out of anguish, I witnessed a bond forged between my brother and my lady.

(For the longest I wanted the two of them to get along, but got-damn—not like this. And yes...I said my lady...that's how I feel in my heart...I don't give a good got damn what anyone thinks).

Turning towards each other, Toomey and I in silent agreement understood our roles as we stood side by side, to stand guard over our downed brother.

Matt was helping Quincee up off the floor; I didn't realize that I was rocking back and forth until Toomey whispered in my direction, "What, now I got to keep my eye on you too?" I regain control of my shit...only for a couple of seconds though.

Sitting back next to Cheryl, Quincee picked back up the story. "He peed on me."

(WHAT! This mother fucka would be handled. Every man, thug, geek...all of you out there with a women to protect...you know what the fuck I'm talking about).

Tapping my leg glancing up at me with a "Man, I'm sorry about what Quincee went through" expression, I shook my head agreeing, "Me too."

Quincee finished the story with their escape and the cab driver. As if on cue, when she spoke the last word, Matt ran out the room headed to the bathroom. I'm in there a few seconds later, watching my brother hugging the toilet—crying and dry heaving, all at the same time. Stooping down to be some kind of support, then sliding down the wall, I sat there in silence—and I waited.

Pulling it back together, Matt said "You know that mother fuckah got to die."

"Yeah, but the first move is to have them checked out." We said simultaneously "Faye."

Faye Tyler is another family friend we go way back with. She was nasty when we were teenagers. I learned what a ménage tois was, after she propositioned Matt and me. We turned it down, but I did get some of her on another occasion, by myself. Faye is a GYN Doctor, and she has a successful practice on Park Avenue South, in Mid-town.

Still sitting on the bathroom floor, I called her, "Faye, this is Danny. I need you to call me back. It's urgent. I'm looking to hear from you girl."

Thinking out loud I said "She looks good."
Looking at me like I won the stupid award, Matt said "Faye?"
"Naw man—Quincee. I know she's all bruised up and shit; actually she's pretty fucked up, but I think…she just…you know…never mind! How do you want to handle this?"

"I want to get some more information first."

"It's your lead?

"I'm ready to get back to Cheryl.

Feeling better about Matt's state of mind, which never strays far from alpha dog, we headed down the hall into my living room.

Toomey was still standing guard beside the chair. Quincee had both hands in her lap, appearing to be in pain, but whispering something to Cheryl, who actually looked a bit better than when she first came in the room. The zombie look was gone, but she still looked far away.

Matt and I took our original positions. Wasting no time, I asked Quincee and Cheryl "Is anything left in his apartment that could place either one of you there?"

Quincee spoke up "I'm pretty sure that I have all of my belongings, but I will check my bag to make sure."

Directing her focus on me, Cheryl said "He never gave me back my wallet and I don't know if there's…umh…if there are any…"

It was clear that she was struggling with bringing up the pictures. I interrupted her, "I hear you. That's fine" while pushing down on Matt's shoulder, suggesting, "Go easy boy."

Quincee hit us with the powerhouse, "I still have his keys." I wanted to leap over to the other side of the room; draw her fine ass up into my arms, and kiss the shit out of her soft sexy-ass lips.

Instead, I glanced down at Matt, and from the corner of my peripheral vision I saw Toomey's wide-eye grin; our minds where in sync; a plan was being conjured by the three of us.

Cheryl went to move and fell back down on the couch. I couldn't tell if it was from exhaustion or from pain. Matt rushed to her side, and she was okay with it. They hugged and started talking and crying. I was so got-damn happy for my brother.

Giving them some privacy, I escorted Quincee off the loveseat and walked her to my bedroom. Toomey following my cue, headed downstairs to the first floor.

Lying across my bed with her head on the edge, staring up at the ceiling, the women that I love looked exhausted. I knew she was emotionally tired, and physically fucked up.

Sitting down next to her, picking her head up and gently placing it in my lap, I started massaging her forehead and temples.

Unable to hold my piece any longer, I had to ask "Quincee, why didn't you call me?"

"Why would I do that... considering the last time I saw you? Give...me...a...break?"

She caught me out there. I wasn't expecting her anger to still be so hard. I couldn't say anything because this was not the time to get into that shit regarding Twink...or Ma'Haundra.

I was getting ready to say something stupid like; I miss you, but my phone rang and my ass was saved by the bell. It was Faye.

"Hello there Doctor Tyler, how are you doing? Thanks for getting back to me. I have a situation that needs you."

I gave her an abbreviated version for the house-call then I filled Quincee in about Faye and informed Quincee that both she and Cheryl would be checked by Faye. Within a half hour she was ring my doorbell.

At first Cheryl resisted being examined, but with coaxing from Quincee and Matt she finally conceded. It seemed to take forever before Faye came out of the room to speak to Matt and me.

Worried at the concern on her face, she reported.

"Let me start off by saying that you know I am breaking my doctor patient confidentiality by what I'm about to tell you!"

I thanked her, Matt didn't say a word.

Starting with Cheryl, "Well, there's been damage. Her vaginal and rectal walls are in bad shape." She stopped speaking, aware of Matt's torture, but I summoned her to continue.

"There's evidence that she has been burned on the inside of her labia perhaps with a cigarette, but those scars are in the healing process. I told her to come to my clinic and get tested for STD's. She informed me that she has been tested because the guy didn't wear condoms on any of the encounters.

My heart dropped; Matt just stood there expressionless with icy hatred lifeless eyes.

"I think she should continue to get tested every six months for another year and a half, or so just to be on the safe side."

Reaching into her bag, pulling out a pill bottle, and placing it into Matt's hand, "Here is some Vicodin for her for the pain. I'm also concerned with her mental state. She looks to be just barely holding on. This is a number of a colleague of mine. Her name is Chantay Cooke, and she is the best in her field. I will brief her about Cheryl, but it is ultimately up to Cheryl to take the first step.

Honestly, I don't think she's ready yet, but there's hope for her. I've treated and referred, unfortunately too many women who have gone through similar situations of abuse to Chantay, and with counseling and a support system from family and friends, they are leading healthy lives once again. I'm not saying it will be easy, but with time, normalcy can be attained."

As for QJ, she needs to get her ribs checked out. I think there bruised possibly a fracture, but only an x-ray will determine the severity. She did say that she would go to the hospital, which is a good thing. In the meantime have her put an icepack over the wounded area ever 20 to 30 minutes until you get her to the hospital. Make sure that she takes deep breathes to expand her lungs. That will prevent infection from setting in. Also she needs her eye checked. I see some broken blood vessels. You want to make sure no other damage was done."

Checking her watch, she said "I'm sorry that it's these circumstances that I am here, but it is always good seeing you two. We have to make plans to get together." She gave Matt a kiss on the cheek and I walked her down stairs. At the front door, she faced me.

"I'm concerned about Matt. You and I know what....."

"Don't say it. But, yes I know."

"I'm going to keep an eagle eye watch out for any signs of....well you know."

With her hand on my face, looking more worried than I wanted her too. I kissed her hand then led her out the door.

Back in Matt's room –we have a room in each other crib-- where Quincee and Cheryl were sitting on the bed. Matt was talking to Quincee, and she was holding Cheryl's hand.
Matt bent down beside Cheryl.

"I'm not going to the hospital!" she flat out let all of us know.

"Baby Quincee is going, you can go with her", Matt pleaded.

"You go with her. I'm not going. Just take me home!"

Standing up and sounding adamant "C-Lah, it's okay, you don't have to go to the hospital tonight. But You're Not Going Home! I'm not letting you out of my sight---That's Not Happening Anymore. Let me get you in bed, so you can get some rest. Dr. Tyler gave me something to get you out of some of your pain."

She agreed then held out her hand for Matt to take it. They both started crying again. My heart was turning in a knot for them, but I was happy because there did seem to be some hope for Cheryl.

Quincee and I gave them their privacy then I led her into my room so that she could prepare for the hospital. After everyone was out of sight, Toomey approached me, "Yo man, this is some baa...baa...bullshit. What's the plan?"

Still taking everything in; "I'm going to take Quincee to the hospital. Can you stay here and watch Matt and Cheryl for me?"

"You got it. When are you gonna start making them calls?"

"I have to take care of Quincee first."

"I hear you."

We left the house around 9:30 that night heading to Metropolitan Hospital, riding the entire way in silence. I didn't care; I was enjoying just being around her. I felt as if nothing bad had transpired between us. She let me hold her hand, and she let me speak for her and didn't interrupt me when I took over the conversations with the doctors.

(*I know it was being selfish, but that's my disposition when we're together. After all, it's a man's nature to take charge and protect his woman*).

After spending three hours in the emergency room, we found out that Quincee had a concussion, two bruised ribs, spasms and bruising in her lower back. There was no internal damage to her eye or to her insides where that mother fuckah kick her in the stomach, (*mmmmh*).

The doctor's diagnosis was, "I expect her to recover fully with minimal effort. I'm giving her a prescription for muscle relaxer for discomfort."

I knew she had to be in big pain, but from the time she and Cheryl arrived at my house up until, standing here with the doctor she never once complained. I would see her wince, catch her breath and blow the pain away, but that was about it.

Doctor's orders were, "she needs rest to heal her ribs. Work is out for the next seven to ten days. It can take up to three to four weeks for them to heal completely. Ice pack, avoid lying on that side, pain medication, and most important", looking at Quincee he said, "You have to keep your lung expansion and don't evade coughing because infection or pneumonia can set in. It will be uncomfortable, but it's necessary."

Then turning to me and continuing, "For the concussion, she needs to be monitored. If you see any signs of weakness, numbness or decreased coordination; if she gets a headache or vomiting and nausea that persists; her speech begins to slur; if she goes to sleep and you have a hard time waking her. If she has problems with recognition and of course if she experience seizures or convulsions, or loss of consciousness, get her back here ASAP. I don't foresee that happening, but keep watch, none the less. Right now, she shouldn't be in that much pain. I gave her 7.5 milligrams of Vicodin. She can follow it up every four to six hours as needed for pain."

Quincee seem preoccupied, as the doctor shook my hand and walk away. I think that her focus was on Cheryl because she had called back to the house about twelve times checking on Cheryl while we in the emergency room.

Spending another half hour waiting on prescriptions— Ibuprofen and vicodin—the chest pad would have to wait until tomorrow when the store opens. We got home a little after 2 a.m.

Making sure that Cheryl was okay first, Quincee then let me get her settled into my bed. The pain killers looking like their doing their job because she was wincing less. Kissing her on the forehead; "Try and get some rest. I'll be back in a few to check on you."

With our woman taken care of, it was time to get down to business. In the living room, Matt and Toomey were having a drink. Sitting down to join them, Matt started the conversation.

"Thank you."

Toomey walked over and slapped Matt on the shoulder "Yo man, I ain't did nothing yet, but I got your back all the way up in THIS SHIT!"

Matt just nodded.

I replied, "You know I love you Brah." Then turning to Toomey I asked, "Can you stay here and watch Quincee and Cheryl? I don't want them alone and I trust you."

"Sorry cuz, I can't help you on that one…I want to be part of the action. I've already made some calls."

Matt and I looked at each other.

I came up with plan B. Turning back to Matt, "We'll take them to pop's apartment." Matt nodded okay.

Always being the got-damn devil's advocate, Toomey asked Matt "How are you going to get Cheryl to leave this house, and you not being with her. I don't mean no disrespect, but…"

Matt shot Toomey a nasty 'I'll deal with her', look.

Hands in the air again surrendering, "You got it dawg; like I said—no disrespect."

We sat about fourty-five minutes finalizing the plan and taking shots of tequila before Matt and I went to tell Cheryl and Quincee of their temporary dwelling arrangements.

Before opening my room door, I had a two week itinerary set up for Quincee because I wasn't going to negotiate with her ass, or try to wear her down.

Standing in the doorway looking at her laying there with her hands clasps together staring at the ceiling, she looked perfect and I was falling in deep for her all over again. But, it wasn't about me, so I avoided my thoughts, walked over to her and went straight to the agenda.

"I want you to call your mother and tell her that you will be staying with me for a week and from there, you have a business trip—I don't want her or the twins to see you like this."

"You scared they are going to think you did this to me. Ooh I'm going to tell my momma that you gave me a black eye."

I actually panicked for a second, "WHAT???"

Then she let out a small giggle.

"That's not funny Quincee."

"Yes…yes it is Danny," still facing the ceiling and with a big ass grin on her face.

It turned me on, hearing her call my name.

"I'll get some money to her for the girls."

"No Danny. You don't have to do that."

Ignoring her and continuing "I'll get some money to her for the girls. Then I want you to get yourself together because Matt is going to take you and Cheryl to my father's apartment."

The look I gave her, she knew to…just comply. She asked "How does Cheryl feel about going?"

"She doesn't have a choice!"

(Men, when a woman doesn't hesitate to get down in the trenches to show love to your people, then go along with the program that hasn't been explained to her. You got to respect her Ride or Die…Got Damn…I love that woman).

Within a half hour, I was walking Quincee to Matt's truck. I held her hand the entire way there. She looked saintly and tough; but also scared and worn out. All I wanted to do was to take her in my arms and let her know that I'm going to protect and love her…forever *(DAMN!).*

Instead, I whispered in her ear, "I love you."

She whispered back "Fuck you."

I had to suck that shit up, but it just made me want her more. I said a silent prayer.

Dear God, if you give me a second chance with Quincee, I promise You, I will do all the way right by her. Aman

Ignoring just being dis'd, " I'm going to call you as soon as I can, but don't get pissed off at me if you don't hear from me in a few hours," kissing her forehead then I let her hand go.

5:04 a.m. I watched Matt's truck until it disappeared around the corner. Back in the house, Toomey started in "Is this mother fuckah gonna know that you'll don't play that shit?"

I threw a confirming look.

"Now that's what I'm talking about. I've made a couple of calls. If you get the biatch, I've got a place to take the mother fuckah! Are you cool with that?"

Not feeling awkward about Toomey's attempt at retribution for Matt and my plight, I ask, "Are your people good like that? Can they be trusted?"

Looking indignant, "I don't know who the fuck you think you're dealing with and I know you're all fuck up in the head after all the shit that's happened to your lady and all, but know this… I'm on your side. Why the fuck would I get myself involved, if I thought any of us will get fucked up in the process?"

Calmly replying, "You finished?"

"Yeah, I've said my piece."

"I gave your ass the benefit of the doubt when you first mentioned making calls because when it's all said and done, this is Matt's and my problem. If you come in, you assume the risk that goes along with the resolution."

Retorting sharply, "You think you talking to some kind of got-damn new-be? Do you have somewhere to take this mother fuckah, or are you gonna continue to insult my ass with your bullshit questions? What the fuck you want to do because I don't have time for games?"

Responding indifferently, "We also need a clean car."

"You're pissing me off because I got you covered. I got a car AND a legitimate body mobile. Don't fuck with me."

All I could do was laugh and seal Toomey's participation in our project, with a hand shake.

5:51 a.m. Toomey left to prepare and would be returning within two hours. I had no idea where Matt was headed.

The first order of business for me was to get rid of the throbbing headache that had been fucking with me for the past nine hours.

Sitting down in my favorite suede lazy boy chair where the seat has conformed to the shape of my ass, with a glass of brandy in one hand and a splif in the other. I didn't stop drinking or smoking until the glass was empty and the blunt was nothing but ashes in the gray marble ashtray beside me.

Feeling better than nice, walking back to my room, laying on my bed letting the intoxicants work their effects. My headache was gone; the brandy had burned the heaviness out of my chest. Thoughts of Quincee's ailments had me blood-thirsty excited about this mother fucka's demise.

Thinking about her, I picked up the phone and dialed her number.

"Hey pretty girl, how are you doing?" I got stiff hearing the happy surprise in her voice.

"Hey there yourself, I'm okay."

"How is Cheryl?"

"She's sleeping"

"You should be too."

"Are you telling me what I need, or what to do?"

"Yes I am. Is there a problem?"

"No. I was just asking."

My meat started throbbing at her obedience. "Do you need anything?"

"No, I'm fine. Miss Delores is taking good care of us. She is a character."

"That she is. She's the next door neighbor, and ever since she found out that my father is single, she's been on his jock strap. So I knew that you and Cheryl will be in good hands."

Thinking about the time, I first saw the small frame light-skinned former dancer push up on my pops, made me smile.

"Baby, try to get some sleep. And no, I'm not telling you what to do, I'm just suggesting. You might not want to hear it, but I do know what's best for you."

"Oh do you now?"

"Girl, I know how to protect you…if you let me." There was a moment of silence. Thinking to myself (*I know I got her with that one…she felt me*).

"Get some sleep and I'll call you sometime late afternoon."

"Okay. Good night Danny."

"Good night baby."

Feeling good about my conversation with Quincee, and not knowing what Matt had planned, all left for me to do was wait for my partners in crime to return.

The Project

(Men, When Taking Care of Business....Do It Right!)

6:17 a.m. Toomey returned first.

"What up D? Matt back yet?"

"Naw...I'm still waiting."

In less time that it took Toomey to smoke a blunt, Matt called, "I'm using my key."

"Come on up."

6:31 a.m. Matt was standing in the middle of my living room.

Watching Toomey look awkward trying not to sound concerned, "Man, you alright?"

Looking aggravated at having to answer the stupid question, Matt blazed, "What the Fuck Do You Think? Let's take this ride uptown."

Checking out the stranger standing next to me that had jump into darkness, between the gaunt eye circles, the zombie expression, uncombed hair, the wrinkle clothes, not to mention—standing damn near hunched over--I don't remember seeing my brother this fucked up before....ever. For the first time in my life, I was afraid for Matthias.

Fronting like I wasn't worried, but more so to freeze the got-damn creeps that were crawling underneath my skin, at 7:12 a.m. the three of us were out the door, and pulling off in the 2002 black Honda Civic with tinted windows that Toomey provided.

Parked directly across from the brownstone in an up-kept block between Saint Nicholas and Convent avenues; we scouted out the temperature of the street to complete the logistics of the plan we partially had formed back at my spot.

Into our second hour of surveillance, the block was quiet, not more than fifteen people passing through; teens and middle aged people out with their pets, a group of senior citizens--power walking. The only element out of order was a young cat looking up to no good. It was his third trip pass us since 9:15 or so. Each time he was on the phone, but never talking, and was holding his head down like he was trying not to be noticed. I was thinking, (mother fucka, we see you).

11:00 o'clock hits, traffic picks up. Two heavy-duty, (*I mean no disrespect, but they were big girls*) were walking down the block with shopping carts, (*I'm talking about the kind you use at the grocery store---swear to God*), full of laundry. A nice looking older teenager was running down the block with a baby in one of those straddle waist things, trying to catch up to a two or three year old, yelling "Kwisee, wait… don't you run out in the street. Kwisee, Kwisee!"

Checking on Matt through the rear view mirror, I heard Toomey yell, "Oh shit," jump out of the car, and in one motion, grabs the kid just as a black hummer jetted by them, at top speed. The woman ran up to them thanking Toomey, and yelling at the boy.

Closing the car door and cussing "I can't believe these got-damn females. If you can't watch your kid, keep the little bastards in the house—got-damn babies having babies."

I extended my hand to give a "well done" dap. That crazy fuck dapped me five then cussed for another three minutes. Save a life then get pissed off…but that's Toomey.

Deciding that we'll leave at noon, just a little of 11:30, two crack-head looking females in their early thirties walked up to the door we had been watching. One was Spanish with long stringy hair. About 5'2", her curves showed threw the ugly ruffle purple top and shorts she was wearing. The entire time she was waiting, she never stop moving. When she did sit down on the stoop, her legs where shaking like a dope fiend.

The tall black female looked to be at least 5'9' or 5'10" and was a stick. Her dirty black jean-shorts and gray tee-shirt just barely fit her bones.

She wanted in that door bad. Watching their every move; ended up they were looking for the psycho. The tall female attempted to peep inside of his window that was completely covered with black material. She had the short female hold her by the waist of her pants for support, while she stretched her long torso over the cobblestone banister, reaching for Grimes windowsill.

Right after Toomey got out, "the bitch need to fall…just for the sake of stupidity!" Curvy lost her footing, and fell backwards on the landing, while bones fell over the banister, under Grimes' window. The shit was hilarious Toomey and I bust out laughing, Matt, in the back seat was unmoved.

It was even funnier to see Bones jump straight up like a cat. Pissed off and screaming at Curvy. I cracked my window, so that we could hear their conversation.

"You stupid spic; all you had to do was hold my black ass up!"

"Ain't nobody told you to be no black Spiderwoman."

"Well, you sure Ain't no Robin...FUCK YOU!"

"Yeah aw-aight, but who's stuck...FUCK YOU TOO!", and Robin is...Batman's sidekick. Spiderman is a lone superhero...Dumbass." Then she started walking down the steps.

Toomey and I were rolling.

"China, Yo hold up. Look, I'm sorry...my bad. I just need to get my nerves calmed...Where the fuck is this nigga at? Please help me get my black ass out this whole."

Toomey was laughing so hard that I had to roll up my window. Watching Bones try to climb up the rough surface, while curvy was bent over the banister pulling on her arms grunting, was some funny shit to watch. After three or four attempts, she actually made it back up.

Bones spit in her hands and wiped her knees and elbows. Then she stuck up the fuck-you finger to Grimes's window, and both females starting walking down the steps to the street.

Crossing in front the car, Bones was still inspecting the scrapes on her elbows, cussing Grimes and Curvy was laughing and showing off her dingy teeth.

Into hour four and three quarters, rubbing the cramps in my legs, Toomey spotted "There's that freak again. Hold up, he's turning in towards the building."

Matt and I sat up at attention.

"I bet you that's...mmm...what did QJ call the other one?"

"Jake" Matt said with death dripping off the one syllable.

We watched the trick stand on the stoop peeping towards Grimes window, looking frustrated at not making a connection on the phone. After about ten minutes, he left.

Letting a half hour go by to see if cat would pass by again, Toomey being Toomey, "Have yall mother fuckah's got enough of what we came up here for? Cause I got to take a piss, and I'm ready to bounce from this fucking spot...shit...got-damn...come on!" Matt nodded from the backseat, Toomey started up the engine, and we rode back to Manhattan in silence.

At 1:17 p.m., we were double parked in front of my spot. The plan was to meet back at my house at midnight. From there we all went in separate directions. Toomey went home; I don't know where Matt was heading because I was ordered, "Look after my woman, I'll check in with you later."

After giving each other our secret hand shake, I jumped in my truck headed to see Quincee and to check on Cheryl.

Exhausted from the past seventeen hours, my body felt like it was on its last leg, but the closer I was getting to her, the more spurts of energy rejuvenated me.

Waiting on the elevator to take me upstairs to my father's apartment, my chest was pounding and my shit was jumping. Just the thought of being in her presence had me going.

The first thing I did was take a shower. I had to be in the bathroom for a good hour. Letting the hot water relaxed my muscles, while I relived the past night's events, and strategically planned for the upcoming project. I was not going to have the woman that I love, be in fear... period.

Tip-toeing through the house, so that I wouldn't wake up Quincee or Cheryl, I headed for my room. Opening the door slowly so that I wouldn't startle my sleeping princess, I walked in and saw her lying in the middle of the bed, on her back with her arms out stretched on either side of her. Her knees were bent and she was staring up at the ceiling.

Walking towards her, I addressed her softly "Hey you."

Only turning her head in my direction, I got stiff hearing her reply "Hey there yourself."
She was wearing my robe, and from the top of her thighs to her feet, was exposed bare skin—I had to fight not to get caught staring at her.

By the time I had reached the bed, she had uneasily moved over and made room for me to lay next to her. It broke my heart to see all the pain that she was in. I told her "Baby be careful", while assisting her into my arms.

It took some time for her to get comfortable, once she was, I asked "How are you feeling?"

"I'm okay."

"I know you're okay, but how are you feeling?"

"I feel like baby doo-doo. I hurt all over, but I'm still here, so...I'm good." Then she rolled across me, and got up.

With unintentional panic in my voice and before I could stop myself, I blurted out "Where Are You Going?"

"I'm just going to the bathroom", responding in a gentle tone; pacifying my open nose. She held her right hand up and commented, "I got it", just as I was getting off the bed to walk with her.

Watching her make her way back in the room is what made me look forward to "the project." By the time she reaches the bed, I'm sitting on the edge and I assisted her back to her same spot.

Looking at me she says, "Ooh, you've got a boo-boo." Touching my face with her soft ass hand and reaching in and kisses me on the spot where Matt clipped me.

(*Men, swear to God. I have never felt physical pain and pleasure together the way Quincee had me feeling*).

All I could do was look at her with my mouth shut because had she even just called my name, I would have spurtted on myself.

Before I realized it, I opened her robe, (*wait...let me get it right*). Quincee let me open up the robe, and I took in all the bruises and discoloration on her body. Then, I kissed every spot that I saw.

(*Brothers, retribution is a bitch...I saw blood in my eyes for the dead mother fucka to be. Any of you out there been where I'm going...do you feel me?*).

Once I finished, she began guiding me to her unseen pains. "*Right there*", pouting as she pointed to the inside of her wrist; "*here too*" leading me to the top of her thigh; "*and back here*" she said, looking like a seven year old little girl sulking, indicating to her lower back.

I got down on my knees and I kissed all of her boo-boos like a father kisses his daughter's hurt away. But when I kissed her on her back, she moaned like a woman, (*who was in too much heat*).

After hearing the matting sounds escape her lips, my shit instantly begin throbbing again.

I stopped kissing her because her body physically could not withstand the convulsing, and definitely not what I had for her.

While still on my knees, I turned her towards me and I laid my head beside her belly, and she stroked the back of my shoulders. Eventually we ended up in bed in our previous positions.

Concerned, I asked "Have you gotten any sleep?"

"I just haven't been able to close my eyes", she replied with aggravation in her voice and back looking up at the ceiling.

I didn't respond. I just carefully scooted closer to her. As she tucked her head in the crest of my arm, I could feel her brain churning.

"Girl, you scared me. That was some dangerous shit you pulled. I want you to promise me that if anything happens in the future, I don't give a damn what it is, you will contact me first before you make any moves."

The wench had the nerve to ponder before finally saying "I promise" with a smile and a wink. I returned the smile and bent down to kiss her. She attempted to kiss me back, but groaned in pain, so I stopped my advance.

Looking deep into her eyes, I confessed "I love you Quincee-Jane Catfire."

"Fuck you Danny TooGood."

"I take that…but that doesn't change how I feel about you", I countered.

Peering at me with un-assurance splatted on her face, "I know", then she laid her head back down on my chest. Within minutes, her head had fallen into my armpit, and she was softly snoring.

Sprawled across me with her right hand on my chest and her right leg stretched out over my thighs, there was no other place in the world I'd rather be than right there with her. Feeling like the protective king, with my queen in my arms, that shit made me smile, and I feel asleep, on top of the world, (*No shame in my game*).

Hearing a knock at the door and a small voice call out "Quincee", I saw through foggy eyes Cheryl's head peeping in the room. Beckoning her to come in, she walked over cautiously, looking like a child with Matt's oversized NY Giants jersey and socks that looked to be 6 sizes too big for her small feet.

Motioning for her to come over, I was relieved that she felt comfortable enough to do so, and surprised that she snuggled up beside me. Wrapping my arm around her, I let her know, "When Matt is not around; I am here to protect you. You will never be left alone again? Do you understand me?" I could see that she felt my truth. I've always like Cheryl, but that's when our bond solidified.

Nodding her head and crying, she just barely got out "I apologize for getting QJ mixed up in…"

Cutting her off, looking her square in the eyes, "You own no one an apology. I mean No One. If anyone has a problem with it, send them to me."

She started to say something, but I couldn't distinguish if she was lost for words, or if she just choked up. I told her to get some rest. I guided her head to my left shoulder and she closed her eyes. Lying there with my girl, and holding it down with Cheryl for Matt, I held them with care while they slept.

My thoughts drifted back to Grimes, and my blood went cold. I smiled with anticipation at the thought of that mother fucka's death, and then drifted back off to sleep.

When I woke up, it was 5 p.m. and I was in the bed alone (*Got damn it, where are they*), I thought. I went from the bed to the door in two steps, searching through the house like a Navy Seal on a mission and found them in the kitchen eating ice cream.

Wanting to remain un-noticed, I was falling more in love with Quincee watching her whisper and giggle to Cheryl, while ouch-ing from her pains. It was apparent that she had taken another pill.

She was saying, "I can't believe I have a black eye. I've never had one before", as she gave Cheryl a profile view. It was also clear that she was proud of it. I just shook my head, smiled, and thought (*That's my girl*).

Watching them in their female element was a good thing to witness. It had been a long time since that room was filled with any kind of laughter. I cleared my throat to get their attention, and not to impose on their conversation.

"How long have you been standing there?" Quincee asked.

"Not long."

"Did we wake you up? Were we talking to loud?"

"I woke up because I didn't feel the two of you next to me." Catching her blushing, I instantly changed the conversation, but I was more surprised to see Cheryl lucid.

"Ice cream, is that all y'all could find to eat in this place?"

Quincee speaking up, "Didn't you know that hurt and ice cream go hand in hand, and it's hitting the spot very nicely...thank you very much. Would you like some?"

Declining as I walked over and sat on the stool beside her at the island then turning to Cheryl, I asked "How are you doing?"

I couldn't believe the change in her from last night to the small face that I was looking into. Not that she was smiling or even talkative—her voice was still hardly audible. It was good seeing her appearing to be re-connected to the land of the living. But I was still concerned that that is a temporary break; that she might pop back into crazy-land.

Realizing that I hadn't eaten in almost 12 hours, I ordered diner for the three of us.

6:15 p.m. I called the girls into the dining room. Quincee came in first, looking delicious, wearing my royal blue silk Polo pajama top, *(all I felt like eating was her)*. But wishful thinking has never gotten a brother anywhere, so I just smiled and lusted after her in silence.

Then Cheryl entered the room, and I was glad that she had an appetite, however, small it was. Quincee had no problem devouring the shrimp, garlic spinach, and pasta; tomatoes, mozzarella, basil and olive oil; and garlic bread.

6:50 p.m. Cheryl received a call from Matt. Once she left the kitchen, I asked Quincee about Cheryl's emotional state. Quincee's relaxed demeanor immediately turned into concern.

"She admitted that the worst part of the whole ordeal was lying to, and worrying about Matt's safety. She is terrified at the thought of Matt thinking less of her, and not loving her anymore.

Her self-esteem is shot to hell. She thinks of herself as being tainted and unwanted. She confessed that "the thought of losing the best thing that ever happen to her" had put her in a state of depression, and that she was ready to end it all."

That shit scared me, and made my heart hurt for both her and Matt.

Watching my reaction, Quincee put her hand on my chest and rubbed it. The heat from her palm implanted itself in my brain that made me want more of her, *(She had control over all of me, and I didn't give a damn. I had to force away the thought of what I wanted her to do to me)*.

Continuing, and unaware of the effect she was having on me, "She also shared with me that she is going to make an appointment with the therapist that your friend suggested."

"That's good news."

"You damn right it is. She's going to pull through this. I know it."

"And what makes you so sure?"

I am a firm believer: that love—not greedy, selfish, jealous, or hurtful love. I'm talking about real love—can get you through anything."

"Really?" I asked her with sincere intrigue.

"Yes really!" replying with equal conviction and staring me square in the eyes.

"For example, when bad things happen to a woman, but she has someone in her life that will be there to protect her fear; reassure her security with strong comforting arms that she can feel wrapped around her. Having that person uplift her self-worth with encouragement by being her biggest fan; who will also stand by her side with any decision that she makes whether they agree with it or not; and who will not judge her actions, consequences, or the relationship....Shesh...

Matt has that type of love for Cheryl, and I would bet all that I hold dear that they are going to make it through this tragedy. Matt's going to hold her up."

"Is that a fact", I questioned.

"Yes, because love like that has its own coat of armor that will protect them from the nay-sayers and evil wishers, and it will guide them with and by its potency."

Watching her unfold her philosophy to me in the sexiest matter-of-fact tone, I couldn't help day-dreaming that it was the two of us in the example that she was given.

Although I was drawn to her every word, I commented, "You put a heavy burden on love. Do you really believe it can do all of that?"

Looking at me with conviction and responding "Don't you know how powerful love is. It can manipulate a sane man's mind into insanity. It can turn a good spirited law abiding individual into a psychopath. It can make the strongest of men... weak, and turn the most docile good natured woman into a raving lunatic.

On the other hand, it can transform a wild beast into a gentle lamb, and a blood thirsty killer into a saint-like protector. So to answer your question...YES, I believe that love is that wonderfully powerful.

At that moment, I had to fight back the feeling of wanting to ask her to marry me; instead I reciprocated nonchalantly, "Well...you have definitely given me something to think about."

She continues to have a natural ability to catch me off guard without even attempting to.

Checking the clock on the wall, it was 7:35 p.m. Time was ticking by fast. Avoiding her gaze, to prevent showing the sadness in my eyes, I commented "I have to be leaving here no later than 9 o'clock."

It pleased me to see disappointment on her face, but also being true to her witty nature, she came back with a smart-ass comment.

"Okay, I'll make sure that I have your fine ass out the door on time."

I actually felt myself blushing at her words. The rest of the time that I spent with her was straight up feel good for me.

Walking back to my room holding hands, Quincee giggled as I shared some house secrets. At one point, we were both silent, and as she lay in the bed next to me with the city lights shining on her face from the opened curtains, I couldn't help but take in her beauty.

Staring at her coughing and wincing, I decided to have her cough more—doctors orders. After a few minutes of looking at her look at me like she wanted to smoke my ass, she announced that it was 8:50. Then she moved on top of me and kissed me.

Receiving her, I ran my hands under the pajama top that she was wearing, and I gently pressed up to meet her body. She felt like rare silk ready to be meshed into my spinning wheel, (*Her heat was imprinting itself onto me*).

As she squirmed for me, I adjusted my legs so that she could fit herself comfortably in between them. (*I wanted her pussy to feel me*).

Her kiss was soft, intense, dick hardening, and long; but it also felt like it would be the last time that I would ever taste her. The feeling threw me off so much that it motivated my ass out of my father's house…lightning fast.

9:34 p.m. I was parked in front of my house, but decided to drive around a bit more to shake off that uneasy feeling I had, back at the house with Quincee.

At 9:53 p.m. I'm walking into my living room, as the phone rings. It's my father. "Hey Pop."

"Danny, what's wrong?"

"Nothing's wrong…why do you ask?"

"DO NOT PLAY GAMES WITH ME!"

"Dad, I'm fine...I promise." Not believing a word that I spoke to him, he asked,

"Whatever that is NOT going on, can you handle it?"

Feeling like a thirteen year old idiot, I answered "Yes."

Attempting to casually drum up another conversation, "How are you doing Dad?"

Not taking any of my bull-shit, he commanded "All is well with me. Danny...Take care of your business, and I will call you when I get back in the city tomorrow night. I love you", and the he hung up the phone.

Thinking (*how the hell does he know anything. Then it hits me, it's that dang Miss Delores*). Not appreciating being chastised, I headed to my room and changed into all black—mock neck sweater, pants, sock, boots and scully cap.

10:45 p.m. I'm in my chair, with another glass of brandy by my side and smoking a Rock Patel cigar. My mind was racing with all kinds of shit; how am I going to get Quincee to love me again? How the fuck come I wasn't there to protect her from that psycho mother fucka? How much revenge will I be able to inflict because the worst damage was done to Cheryl, and I know what my brother is capable of. Did I make the right decision to bring Toomey into this shit? What is the worst thing that could happen? What would it do to my father to lose two more children? Where was my father going because he has been taking unexpected trips out of town for the past couple of months? Is his health alright? What would I do if anything happened to him? The questions just kept coming.

At 11:12 p.m. my thoughts were interrupted by the doorbell. Toomey walked in the house wearing black pants, shirt, hoody and sneakers. That crazy bastard also had on a dreadlock wig with a red, yellow, and green bungo, which is a rasta tam made up of crocheted yarn (*shit, I had to give it to cat, for creativity*).

"What's up? Am I the last one in?"

"Naw man", I said while still laughing at that fool's get-up.

Ignoring my amusement, and asking with concern, "How is baby brah doing?" (*That is a term of endearment that Toomey uses referring to Matt, but only in the company to the two of us. Toomey wouldn't have the balls to say that to Matt's face*).

"Honestly man, I don't know. We haven't had a chance to sit down and talk. But I can tell you one thing, the mother fucka is dangerous. Anything is possible at jumping off tonight. I'm prepared to roll with the punches, and I suggest you be ready too."

Walking over to me gesturing for a fist pound, Toomey replied, "Now that's what I'm talking about. There's going to be a hot time in the ole muh-fuckin town to…night", so joyfully that a chill went through me. I definitely had to be on guard and watch both of them, so that shit didn't get too far out of hand.

By the time Toomey settled down on the couch with a corona and a blunt, Matt was walking thru the kitchen door wearing a black sweat suit, tee shirt, and timberlands, carrying a knapsack, and 'The Sword.'

Toomey and I gave a report on what was in place so far. I knew shit was going to get real deep when Matt said "Are you'll ready to take a ride on the Green Fairy?"

I hurried up to turn down the offer, "Naw man, I'll have some after the job is done."

Toomey looking confused, but interested; watched Matt take a swig right out of the bottle. After a few minutes, Toomey still looking dumbfounded asked "What the fuck is a green fairy?"

"Absinthe" I replied.

"What?"

"Absinthe, it's a French high level alcohol; the content is between 50 and 75%. It is spirited from leaves and flowers of the Artemisia Absinthium, aka the wormwood plant along with other herbs, such as anise, licorice, fennel, veronica, angelica, and lemon balm. The distillation process turns the liquor green from the chlorophyll content of the herbs…aka giving it its green in color. The powers that be, deemed it a highly dangerous addictive psychoactive drug, and associated it with the likes of opiates, cocaine and weed. It's been banned in the United States since 1915, as well as European countries, except in France."

Looking scared to take the ride, Toomey stated "I'm with Dan, I'll have some of that shit later man." Then turning to me asking, "What the fuck, you some kind of walking dictionary?"

"No, I use to date a French woman, and she loved the shit."

Indifferent to our rejection and ignoring our conversation, Matt took another swig, sat down beside Toomey on the couch, and said "The countdown starts now."

Toomey and I looked at each other then back at Matt and we simultaneously nodded in agreement.

I brought Matt up to date of Toomey's contribution and the resources that I had gathered. Initially I thought Matt would have a problem with Toomey entering into our secret world, but the opposite occurred.

Matt turned to Toomey, offering an out-stretched fist, and said *"That's some good shit"*, took another swig of absinthe then got up and walked to the window and stared outside for the longest time, in deadly stillness.

Knowing that real bad shit was going to go down, Toomey and I just sat and waited in silence for Matt to give the last bit of the plan. When my brother returned back to the earth, Toomey and I had moved to the dining room.

At the table, we finalized everything within an hour and a half. That included making calls to confirm all the players involved— checkpoints, the time schedule, and alibis, (*A.K.A; capture, retain, terminate, and disposal.*)

Looking at Toomey and me, Matt extended a way out for us, "If you want to back out, now is the time to do it. I hold no judgments, no bad blood."

Toomey and I both gave my brother an "ARE YOU STUPID!" look. There was a brief silence, then the three of us joined fist as a show of solidarity. Matt backed away first and took a nice size guzzle of the Green Fairy and said "Let's move."

(*Project Execution has commenced*).

Project...Execution

(Retribution wasn't mine for the taking!).

2:15 a.m., walking out the door, I paid no attention to the early morning chill, but for some reason, I was pissed off at not seeing stars as I stared at the full moon. Waiting at the car for me, Matt was standing gazing into blackness. Toomey on the other hand looked ready as a dear-hunter headed for his first kill of the season.

We made it to our first check point—3rd avenue, in less than fifteen minutes. Pulling up to the corner of 123rd and parking next to a fire hydrant and in front of a 1980 non descriptive dirty navy blue utility van that was waiting for us. Switching vehicles with the cat that was out the van by the time our vehicle had stopped. Looking inside, all of our equipment had been transferred into it.

Toomey got in the driver's seat, I was in the passenger seat, and Matt sat on a crate behind Toomey, still staring into nothingness.

The next stop was 146th street. Ironically, we pulled into the same spot we were at, less than 24 hours ago. We sat in the van for almost fifteen minutes to determine the block's traffic. No one had passed through.

A minute or so after, Matt got up and ordered, "Let's go." Toomey was thrown of guard, startled at the patch on Matt's left eye.

"Holy shit, niggah! You scared the fuck out of me...looking like..."

In mid-sentence, Matt shot Toomey a look that left Toomey saying nothing else. I knew what the eye patch meant.

What Toomey doesn't know is that when Matt was nine years old, cat's addict infested mother almost took my boy's eye out because Matt didn't want to suck some trick's dick for heroin for that bitch fiend of a so called mother. Matt wore an eye patch until the age of fifteen, and walked with the philosophy "Dan, mother fuckahs don't know, when I have my patch on, all of my other senses are heighten. This is my third eye. The Kamikazes taught me well. Mother fuckahs will talk behind my back, but no one has the balls to say shit to my face...fuck everybody."

The Kamikazes were a Japanese martial arts group that Matt train, fought, and ran with back in the day before we met. Needless to say, Toomey felt Matt's wicked disposition, and changed the subject—real fast.

"Fuck, I almost forgot. Let me put my shit back on."

The somber mood was temporarily broken, as I snickered at Toomey's dreadlock disguise. "Mi dun waan fa be rec-kog-nized. Ya no? Mi face muss be unintended... to Babylon."

Un-moved by Toomey acting like a buffoon, Matt spearheaded a review of the plan. Confirming that it was mutually embedded in our brains, we put on black gloves, grabbed what was needed, and went into code silence as we exited the van.

Cautiously we made our way unnoticed up the brownstone steps. Getting into the three doors was a piece of cake; made possible by Grimes keys that where given to me by Quincee.

Before 3 a.m. we were walking through the doorway of Grimes nasty ass infested apartment. Quincee had described it perfectly, and it appeared to be in the same condition as when they escaped less than forty-eight hours ago.

Looking at me pissed-off and disgusted, jumping around like a hop-scotch player attempting to avoid stepping into the unidentified substances on the floor, Toomey pulled out a handkerchief and began breathing and mumbling into it.

Almost paralyzed by nausea, from the funk of vomit, urine, shit, and rotten food, I had to force the bile back down that had risen in my throat because I had no intentions of leaving any traces of my DNA in this hell-hole.

Walking up next to Matt and bumping shoulders I felt like I was standing next to pure evil. Oblivious to my presence, I silently prayed that my brother would return to the land of the sane when our objective is completed.

Standing ten feet beyond the doorway, we took ten seconds to survey our immediate surroundings, each of us looking in a different area of the studio apartment.

Toomey turned back towards the door to check the kitchen area. I viewed the dining room area to my left, and Matt's sight was straight ahead on Grimes. The look of lust for murder cloaked my brother's profile.

Eying Matt walking towards Grimes, Toomey and I followed in sync.

Looking like a corpse already, the psycho fuck was lying motionless on the bed, while flies were having a field day on the food and vomit that lay on and beside him. The asshole was floating in and out of conscientiousness, and I couldn't determine what type of stupor he was in.

Based on all the shit I saw on the table; white and brown residue, buds of weed, pills, crack rocks. Shit…the dumb fuck could have ingested some of everything by the looks of the paraphernalia—a crust infested spoon and lighter, an uncovered needle and syringe, blunt roaches, pills sprawled over the table, and about ten empty crack vials.

Jerking up to a sitting position, his eyes still closed, sniffing out Matt's presence, Grimes barked out, "WHO THE FUCK IS YOU?"

Bending down directly into Grimes' ear, coldly replying in a whisper that I heard, "I'M YOUR GRIM MOTHER FUCKING REAPER!"

Then Grimes' went to sleep, as Matt's covered the ass-wipe's nose and mouth with a chloroform soaked rag.

Within less than a minute and a half, Grimes had been slammed in the wheelchair that Matt brought in, his face had been covered with a hospital mask, and his knocked-out ass was ready to be transported to the van.

As the lookout, Toomey headed out first. Matt followed—wheeling Grimes' ass, and I was in tow as the wingman. Before exiting, I scrutinized the apartment to make sure there wasn't anything that could tie Quincee and Cheryl to the dead-to-be bastard.

Skimming over a cluttered bookcase, and seeing a stack of brown manila envelopes on the bottom shelf, I scooped up all that I saw. Opening up the first one—there were pictures of a woman with the sick fuck doing nasty shit to her, along with what appeared to be the female's address book and other personal belongings.

The third envelope that I opened…bingo… was Cheryl's dossier. There was a hand written note that had Cheryl's driver license information; pictures, which I avoided looking at; a shit load of negatives; car insurance booklet; job ID card; and a picture of her and Matt. Feeling satisfied for hitting the jackpot, I locked the door and turned to catch up to my partners in crime.

Walking into the foyer stopping next to Matt, waiting on Toomey to give us the 'clear to go' signal, I was silently hoping that we get Grimes' stink ass in the van without a hitch. About three minutes later, which seemed like an eternity, Toomey swung the door open. Matt wheeled Grimes down the steps, making his body jolt with each step that the wheelchair landed on.

Surveying everything right of the building and Toomey had the left side, within four minutes, I was sitting in the driver's seat, Toomey in the passenger seat and Matt had rolled Grimes up in a rug and was using his body as a foot rest.

Before starting the ignition and feeling nauseated at what needed to be done, I passed the manila envelope back to Matt, "Here man. Don't open it."

Then I asked the same stupid ass question that I already knew the answer to, "You alright?"

Seeing no response, but clearly viewing that one hatred eye staring back at me, "You didn't..."

Not waiting for the complete question, "Naw man, for your eyes only. I pulled out her job ID, that's how I knew." Not wanting to extend the conversation, I started up the van and we were out.

Waiting for the light to change at 145nd street and Broadway, Toomey called the contact. We were informed to drive to 133rd Street and 12th avenue.

Waiting at a red light on 139th street and Broadway, turning back towards Matt, Toomey inquired, "Yo man, will that mother fuckah wake up anytime soon because we have to leave his ass in here alone for a minute?"

Filling the van with ice, "He's staying knocked the fuck out until I want him to wake the fuck up."

"Au-ight. You just make sure that happens because my people are in place to move his ass, and if the bitch does wake up, they are going to do his ass right there!"

Matt's tone went deeper and colder, "I don't need you to tell me how to handle my mother fucking business, you just make sure that your part..ners do what the fuck they supposed to do!"

The atmosphere was thick and claustrophobic. A quick risk assessment; Matt was mad at the world and nothing would be almost right again until Grimes was dead. Toomey had a case of the jitters—no man can be 100% sure when doing bad deeds with new people, for the first time. The issue went both ways because we didn't know Toom's people either. Absolute trust wouldn't be bonded until the entire job was completed. I didn't play mediator. Letting them blow off steam now was better than at any point forward of what was going down.

As fucked up in the head as I was too, there needed to be at least one of us in the group using a rational mind. It might as well be me because my gangsta was on lockdown. My thirst would never be quenched with retribution of making Grimes bleed by my own hands, for what he did to Quincee because this was Matt's kill.

Parked on 12th avenue between 133rd and 134th street, waiting for the next phone call, Toomey was about to take another jab; Matt's phone rings.

In a blink of an eye, transforming from pure evil to speaking tender, "Hi baby… No, I'm never too busy to talk to you. C-lah what's...are you sure? How are you feeling? I'm taking care of some business right now, but I'll call you as soon as I can....yes, I promise."

In a more definitive tone, Matt said to her, "I Love You", and "You're never going to be alone again. Right now I want you to try and get some rest. Where is Q?...put her on the phone."

Appreciating my girl, my brother inquired, "How is she doing? That's the best we can expect for right now. "Watch out over my baby for me." There was a pause then Matt choked out a "thank you", and then turned off the cell phone.

Cheryl's call was the catalyst that shut down the combat of two stubborn egos. The confrontation seemed to be over and there was silence in the van, until Toomey spoke up.

"How is she doing?"

"As good as can be expected."

"She's going to come out of this shit just fine. She's going to need some time, that's all. I've been putting my prayers in for her." Then turning to me, "Quincee too."

"Thanks, man, I appreciate that."

Toomey was quiet for just a second.

Looking at Matt through the rearview mirror Toomey sanctioned, "Au-ight niggah, you ready to get jiggy with this mother fuckah, with your Cyclopes evil looking ass."

I tried to hold back my snigger, but couldn't.

Toomey then got serious…" Yo Matt, about all that shit I said. Man I…"

Matt interrupted, "We're good."

By the time that conversation ended, a dark blue Honda Civic pulled up beside us. Toomey got out the van, slapped the driver five then motioned for Matt and I, and the three of us got into the back seat.

Pulley, the driver was black as night, with a bald head that touched the roof of the vehicle. His neck looked to be an easy 18 to 20 inches wide because of the two rows of fat at the back of it. His ham hock size arms and hands made the stirring wheel look to be toy size and his back and ass were far too big for the single seat.

Joey, the cat in the passenger's seat was Pulley's opposite. He was sporting a 1970's red afro. The windbreaker jacket looked too big for his scrawny chest. He's about average height, and from the back seat, he looked scared as shit.

Watching Pulley drive with his fat head tilted to the left side, and then looking over at his cohort's nonchalant expression…they reminded me of Laurel and Hardy. The shit was damn funny.

We rode a short distance. Inside a warehouse size building, Pulley parked in a holding area, where we got out the car.

It was there I felt and saw just how huge the cat was. Sitting in the middle seat, I was the last to exit, so when Pulley waddled his fat ass out the seat, I felt the car spring up about four inches. He had to be between 6'6" to 6' 8" and damn near 400 pounds.

I thought to myself, (*where the fuck could he go and what could he do, and not be conspicuous…nowhere and nothing*). I got a sagging feeling in the pit of my stomach.

I shook my head then got the fuck out the car, and watched the big man walk down one hallway, while Joey lead Toomey, Matt, and me down another. We ended up in the back of the building in a blue room that looked like it was lit up with 300 watt bulbs. It had a couch, some chairs, and a large metal picnic table with benches, a big screen television, a kitchen area, and a bathroom. We hadn't even sat down good, before Joey disappeared out the door without opening up his mouth.

I don't know which was more aggravating, the damn bright ass lights or the continuous clicking sound above my head. To defuse the noise in my brain, I thought about Quincee, and I wanted to call her, but I knew now was not the time.

Instead, I began reminiscing of being with her earlier--Damn, she felt good in my arms. Her smell, her softness, her body, her heat, and the feel of her lips and the taste of her tongue-- shit I couldn't wait to get back to her.

Then reality stabbed me and my mind took off racing in another direction-- *(Am I back in her life, or is this just a situational thing? How the fuck am I going to make her mine again? Will she let me? How am I going to make things up to her; all the crazy shit that was between us-- Ma'Haundra, Twink, Jimmy, and now this?)*

Rage penetrated my skin at the picture of Quincee being violated by that mother fuckah, and blood thirsty thoughts pounded my mind that brought on a monstrous unneeded headache.

My mental chaos was abruptly ended when Pulley busted into the room. As soon as his ass hit the bench, Matt produced an envelope and slid it towards Pulley.

Matt informed him "Six thousand is here. You'll get the remaining four when the job is completed."

Pulley nodded a pleasing concurrence then extended his arm to shake Matt's hand across the table and said "Then we're all set."

The plan was moving like clockwork and we were ready for the next phase. Pulley continued, "Joey will bring yall to the office and I'll meet you up there in about fifteen minutes or so."

A few minutes later the door swung open with Joey dragging in and requesting, "Follow me," leading us up one staircase level and into a drab grey painted room that had only a desk, a chair and a phone. Waiting until we were all inside, he handed us badges and exited back out of the door. Turning over the card that was in my hand, it was an identification badge that had my picture on it, *(how the fuck, and when was my picture taken?)*.

About two minutes later, entering with another employee, allocating automotive directions, and before sending the older man on his way, Pulley patted him on the back offering accolades. The fat man made a quick call then looked at us and said, "Time to go."

Following Pulley to a staircase, walking down two flights, we met up with Joey again. Continuing through a long corridor towards the back of the building we came to a large garage area where an unmarked white van was parked. There were no windows on the sides; just two small ones on each back door where I saw Grimes' ass laid out.

Before getting into the van, Pulley handed us three plastic wrapped gray jumpsuits and instructed, "Here put these on."

All suited up, we loaded in the van—Pulley in the driver's seat, Joey in the passenger seat, Matt, Toomey and I entered through the rear and sat on a metal bench that was attached to the right side of the van.

Across from us was Grimes, wrapped in a body bag and laid out on a coroner's gurney that was attached to the floor of the vehicle. *(From the time I sat my yellow ass down until we arrived to our destination; I hoped like fuck that the maggot stayed sleep)*.

We drove up the ramp out onto the street, toward the Westside highway—headed for the George Washington Bridge. Everything was still going according to plan—so I sat back and listened to Toomey and Pulley talk, and from the sound of it, the two of them go way back.

Toomey asking, "How's your mamma doing? Is she still making thum slamming ass ham biscuits?"

"Yeah man, and there better than ever."

"Shit I got to get down there and see her."

"Yeah niggah, you should. She asks about your ass from time to time."

Midway thru the New Jersey Turnpike, Pulley and Toomey were still yapping like we were on a pleasure trip, when all of a sudden we heard a sharp pop against the back of the van. It sounded like a pebble ricocheting off the vehicle. After we were all comfortable that that was the case, Toomey and Pulley went back to their conversation.

About a quarter mile into Delaware, we heard sirens behind us. Looking through his rear view mirror and shouting, "SHIT", Pulley pulled over to the roadside, commanding "Nobody talk, I got this."

Diving into assess mode, I observed that Pulley was composed; Toomey looked concerned by collected; and Matt was indifferent, but did remove the eye patch. What concerned me, was Joey. The scary bastard looked like he could possibly fuck us up.

Pulley had picked up on that as well. Looking at Joey asking "Niggah you au-ight?"

"Yeah, yeah man, I'm...I'm cool."

"Then what you sweating for?"

In seconds, a state trooper was tapping on Pulley's window. It was a brother, which did not make me feel any better because sometimes, they are the worst ones --a black man with a gun, licensed to shoot or kill another black man.

Looking like a country bred rock that could move trees with his bare hands. The cat's muscles bulged out the side of his perfectly creased uniform, and his neck was bigger than Toomey's head.

In a laid back tone, Pulley initiated the conversation, "Good morning Trooper Walker, is there a problem?"

Ignoring Pulley's question; commanding, "Driver's license, registration and insurance", which Pulley produced immediately. Taking the card, but before looking at Pulley's identification, the trooper flashed a light inside the van.

I nervously watched it dance on Joey's face, shoulders then on the floorboard near my feet. Pulley immediately interjected the trooper's light inquisition, and in the same non-aggressive tone stated "If you will notice, I also handed you my mortuary license", pointing to the rear, accounting for our presence.

Pulley continued, "These are my trainees."

With unforced and unnecessary condescension, the trooper requested that the rest of us produce identification as well. Passing Matt and my ID cards to Joey, I was silently thanking Pulley for his criminal-minded business tactics.

The trooper then turned his attention back to Joey.

His skinny ass was so nervous that Joe Law decided that he was going to run Pulley's license plates. After the trooper left the van, Toomey asked with contempt, "Yo Pull, is your license clean?"

"Clean as a mother fucking whistle."

Pulley turned and lit into Joey, "Niggah if you fuck this up, I will kill you myself, then at your funeral, I will sit on the first pew with Aunt Christine and Uncle Harry, and I will cry harder than the both of them put together, about your dumb dead ass."

Toomey burst out laughing and joined the conversation, "He has always been a punk; I don't know why you brought his ass along in the first got-damn place."

Joey never responded to Pulley or Toomey, he just sat there holding his stomach like he was in pain.

As the trooper returned to van, he heard Pulley going off on Joey, "Niggah if you shit in my car, I will put your ass out on the side of the got-damn highway. Go ahead---fuck with me. I told you not to fuck with those cheese enchiladas… you stupid ass."

Pulley's roar was interrupted by Ice-Brick being unable to hold his professional stance and ended up returning all of our documentation back to Pulley, and barley got out why we were stopped.

"You're driving with a broken right tail light."

Explaining what happened back on the turnpike, Pulley added, "I will have it taken care of right away officer."

Looking unmoved by the excuse, the trooper smiled as he handed Pulley a ticket and said "You do that. You don't have to appear in court. You can mail your payment to the address on the ticket."

Looking down at the ticket and blurting out, "$150 dollars!"

Hercules smiled and responded, "Have a good morning", and headed back to his patrol car.

Before pulling back onto the highway, Pulley made a call, "It's me. I need you to get Jerry to make a pickup…Joey… Yeah…I'll call you back with the exit number…Naw man... Au-ight…Later."

Flipping his cell phone closed and turning to Joey, "I'm dropping your dumb ass off at the next rest stop. Jerry's coming to pick you up."

When we pulled to the curb of Roy Rogers rest stop, Joey had barely gotten out and closed the door when Pulley peeled off. Toomey taking the passenger seat almost fell to the floor, as the van was rounding a curve, at a good speed, heading back onto I-95 south bound.

Pulley went in, "That pussy mother fuckah. His punk ass always wants to be in on shit, but then bitch the fuck up…all the mother fucking time…shit", as he beat his fist on the stirring wheel. Within three seconds he took a deep breath, held it in, blew it out, and had his cool back on before placing the next call.

When he was finished, Toomey asked, "What's up with your boy, and why you keep his ass around you; almost having all our asses locked the fuck up?"

"For two reasons, the skinny fuck is resourceful; he can get you anything that you want—women, guns, a clean social security number. He's a master at breaking codes—shit he once tap into FBI files unnoticed. But all that shit aside, he is my father's favorite sister's boy." Then he looked at Toomey like—I'm stuck with him.

Toomey changed the subject to the scene with the state trooper. "What's up with you Mr. Credential?"

"Fucking A, my shit is tight. I keep all my licenses current, I still go to all the industry's forums; symposiums the trade shows, shit like that. Sh.i.i.i.t, if I'm going to live a criminal life, I'm going to use my brain, along with all the resources I have available to me. Pops being an undertaker and all...the shit has its perks."

Within fifteen minutes we were getting off the highway, and in the next fifteen minutes or so we were riding down an unlit, narrow, bumpy, curvy dirt road. Pulley stops and hands us blindfolds, instructs us to put them on and not to take them off until we were told to do so. I was agitated at not being able to see anything, but I kept my mouth shut and put the damn thing on. We rode another fifteen minutes and came to a stop.

Pulley said, "Hold tight, I'll be right back."

Waiting in the back of the van, ignoring the fact that I hate being blind folded; I'm getting pissed because I'm feeling like one of the three blind got-damn mice Pip, Bip along with Dip in the front.

A few minutes later, Pulley's voice trails to the back of the van. The door opens, he climbs inside and hand us some articles, "Here put on these rubber gloves and footies.

Matt and I did as ordered and we were lead off the van by two more of Pulley's people. I got out first, feeling disoriented and uncomfortable. Stepping down and walking a few extra steps away from the van to hone in on my internal compass and to stretch my legs.

By that time Matt was out of the van, I heard Toomey cussing, "Damn niggah, you ain't got to be up on me holding me and shit. I got this…..A.a.a.a.a.a.a.a.h!" That crazy ass tripped and fell.

"Get the fuck off me. I know how to stand up on my own."

Paying no attention to Toomey, Pulley ordered his man, "Get his ass out."

I heard Grimes' body being slid towards the foot of the van, and being hoisted up. Right after that, the three of us were lined up single-file in hand on shoulder formation.

We were lead up steps, into a building, through several corridors, and finally into a room, where we heard the door slam closed behind us.

Pulley announced, "Ya'll can see now."

Taking the blindfold off slipping it into my pocket and adjusting my eyes back to normal, looking around, smiling while my chest was engaging an adrenaline rush, I thought, (*we are in the right place*).

Before walking into the corner with Matt, Pulley ordered his men to remove Grimes from the body bag, and place him on the metal gurney that was set up in the middle of the room.

While that was taking place, I took in the view. All the windows were covered with black material. Stainless steel sinks, countertops, and cabinets lined the walls of the entire space.

A minute later, Matt walked over to the countertop where the extra-long blue duffle bag was.

I watched my brother pull out three cups, a gallon bottle of Poland Spring water, a small box of sugar, and the bottle of Absinthe. Once the setup was complete, Toomey and I walked over to Matt. I know the drill. Toomey imitated me; taking off my glove and pouring sugar in my palm.

Looking at the green liquid that was measured into three servings, Matt pick up the first cup, made a toast, "Here's to another mother fucker headed to hell"; licked the sugar, and downed the drink. Toomey and I followed.

Making sure to be the last to drink, I wanted to be cognizant of their reactions to the madman's fluid. The Green Fairy wasn't a good experience to me by any means. The smell burned my nose and eyes. The licorice attacked my mouth with the taste of bitter. By the time the last bit of the second shot hit the bottom of my stomach, the hairs on the back of my neck stood up as the temperature in the room dropped to freezing cold then heated back up at double the speed to a higher temperature. Then the room tilted sideways on me.

Toomey and Matt repeated the ritual twice more than me. I witnessed a bond forge between the two of them, as they stared deep into each other's eyes, reciting a mantra that I couldn't hear. They looked like two opposing drunken gang members about to head into battle as allies.

The hypnotic cocktail took more effect on me. Right before my eyes, Toomey materialized into a straight up hit-man, looking ready to kill for free. I saw a flash of light that I couldn't determine if it was coming from a gold tooth, which Toomey doesn't have, or a gun which, none of us are carrying.

Attempting to shake the image out of my head, turning to Matt, who looks like a medieval executioner, complete with a mask and an axe. Now the room is glowing like hell fire colors and feels like it's well over 110°. All I want to do is get out of the got-damn jumpsuit that is suffocating me.

I don't know how much time had passed when Toomey was standing beside me, and we watched Matt reach back into the bag and pull out a small brown glass bottle then pour the liquid substance into a piece of cloth.

Taking in a un-conscience whiff from the rag, Grimes woke up in confusion. "WH...WHA...WHAT THE FUCK? ...WH...WH... WHERE THE FUCK AM I ?... WHO THE FUCK IS YOU? ... GET THE FUCK AWAY FROM ME...YOU PIECE OF CROW SHIT."

Rising to the sitting position, the befuddled fuck was knocked clean off the gurney and out cold, when his face made contact with Matt's spinning round house kick, by way of black steel-toed Timberland work boots.

Matt nodded to the two attendants. They walked over and picked Grimes up, put his stink ass back on the table, and bound his arms and legs.

Before waking his funky ass up again, Matt did some preparation work on Grimes. With rubber gloves back on, Matt bound Grimes's head to the table with gray duct tape, cut off all his clothes, then bent down on one knee and began praying.

"Dear God, please forgive me for not seeking you out more in my life. Forgive me for all that I have done in my past. Please forgive me for what I am about to do, for I know what I am doing is against your law. And most of all, forgive me for not getting caught...Amen, Amen, and Aman."

Still bent down on one knee, my brother reaches over and picks up the pearl handled sword that's resting beside the duffle bag on the floor. Sliding it out slowly from its blood red case, I swear, I see the gold dragon swaying and smoke permeating from its nostrils that dissipated into the black embossed Chinese markings on the thick blade.

Kissing it in ceremonial fashion; looking like a combination of a ninja warrior and a reckless pirate; in one motion, standing up, grabbing hold of Grimes' dick and chopping it off with a swish of the sharp blade.

Blood flooded the gurney, spattered across the floor, over the sick fuck's lower body, and on me. Toomey jumped back like a scared bitch from it.

My shit was jumping to know that his body would be leaving this world without the dick that caused damaged to those close to me. Laughing at the horror on the bastard's face then to see him want to scream, but couldn't because his words were stifled by his own shit-stained draws that Matt had stuffed in his mouth, (*I love when justice is served....It is a sweet taste of mother fucking everything*).

Matt's next move was funny as hell. I was doubled over laughing, in my mind when Matt placed Grimes dick on his own neck. Toomey yelled out while pointing to dick-less, "Where's your dick...mother fuckah?", then started singing "Oops, there it is...Oops there it is*"* while pointing to Grimes' neck.

Looking at Matt, I saw nothing in that one eye that was exposed, as the dark angel sniffed Grimes blood that coated the sword; before I could finish enjoying that sight, Matt sliced Grimes' ear off.

My shit got hard watching the almost dead fuck's torture—blood was dripping down onto the metal slab, his body still shaking in pain. Matt bent down, reaching inside the open wound and pulled out some exposed fleshed. The bitch started leaking piss ... and everyone in the room, except Matt, backed away. Then he starting shitting and it smelted like something had crawled inside of his ass and died.

My brother was all the way gone by that point; I cringed when I saw Matt take Grimes's shit and stuff it in his nose.

The two attendants grimaced and turned their heads.

Pulley mumbled "Damn Man."

Toomey frowning, said, "Cuz…that's some bold shit," smirked then cheered Matt on, "Do his ass!"

I got off watching Grimes' trying to blow the shit out of his nostrils, only to have some of it land on his lips. When he looked like he was about to pass out, Matt gave him a whiff of the wake-me-up rag. Looking into Matt's one lifeless eye, a chill ran through me again.

Matt motioned towards the two workers then turned and nodded to Pulley, who beckoned his workers towards the steel table. By the time the two reached it, Matt had produced ten crisp $100 bills and gave them five hundred a piece, and snarled "For your trouble."

Taking the money enthusiastically they forgot all about the nauseating smell coming out of Grimes' ass. One knelt down unhinging the gurney from the floor, preparing Grimes' transfer to another area, while the other one began pouring a substance that smelt stronger than bleach, over the blood stains on floor.

Pulley turns to the three of us and instructs, "Lights out", pointing to his eyes; indicating to put the blind folds back on. In the got-damn dark again, (*I didn't like that shit at all*).

Back in single file, hand on the shoulder, were lead out the door. Walking between thirty to forty feet in the opposite direction that we came in, and down a flight of stairs, we entered the second hot room.

Once we were given the okay, I took my blind fold back off. I thought I was in a storage room because of all the tools, rusted equipment, and stacks of dank smelling boxes. But when we were lead around a corner, I saw an old brick furnace that was lit up and ready to cook some flesh, (*The blind fold shit was a small price to pay*).

Not caring about subtleties, Matt asked Pulley, "What's taken so long?"

"Got to get an X-ray in, to make sure the bastard doesn't have any metal inside him, pacemakers and such because I don't want no explosions."

The response appeared to appease my brother. Less than ten minutes later, Grimes was rolled in front of us. He had already been placed in a large cardboard coffin shaped container that sat on top of a gurney that had wheels instead of a flat surface. His hands and feet were tied; he was still gagged, and he hadn't made any attempts to move because the bitch was too busy crying.

His was stinking so bad that Matt wasted no time, in taking care of business. Pulling an object out of the pocket of the duffle bag then walking over to Grimes, Matt held a picture up in front of Grimes' face, and said, "Remember them...they are why you're dying tonight Mother Fuckah."

(I love my brother. Although I couldn't get my hands wet, I felt a small taste of retribution, by Matt including Quincee)

The almost dead fuck must have forgotten about his amputated body parts because he was begging for his life with his eyes, with no signs of pain in his movements. When cat saw that he was in the wrong crowd looking for mercy, he mustered up some courage and tried to rise up out of his death box.

Appearing excited, Matt growled "Where the fuck you going?" and grabbed Grimes up in a choke-hold. The bitch started flailing his knees, trying to get some breathing slack.

Matt let Grimes' head go, and just when the stink bastard sighed relief, looking like he had a minute of reprieve, Matt begin moving the board forward into the furnace.

Putting on the mask that I was given by worker number two, I was laughing as I watched Grimes' last attempt to cheat death, when he started rocking side to side in his coffin.

In one movement, Matt slid the sword back out of its case; fashioned the blade right on top of Grimes' adam's apple and announced into dirt-bag's only ear, "If you move, I'LL SAW YOUR MOTHER FUCKING HEAD OFF WHILE YOUR FEET BURN."

He got the message because the bastard lay back down and settled in for his death procession. Matt picked up Grimes' dick and threw it into the flames while eulogizing a denunciation to Grimes. "Now the demons can fuck your hole like you're a bitch for the rest of eternity," then rolled his ass into the fire.....slowly!

I have to give Grimes credit; he lasted until the flames were damn near at his thighs. The bitch had to have been on some REAL GOOD drugs.

The more the muffled screams came from him, the better I felt. We watched his body jolt in agony....and then...nothing. After he was out from either shock or being dead, we stood there and watched him turn back to dust.

While his ass was ablaze, Matt, Toomey, and I got out of the jumpers we were wearing, and tossed them into the fire, along with everything except our foot-ties and gloves.

Watching our clothes burn, Pulley walked over and tossed the ID negatives into the flames, and said "I know yawl not", closed the furnace door then walked over and stood between Toomey and myself. Matt never moved from the bird's eye view of the furnace window until Grimes was ashes.

Three blunts of official Hawaiian Bud and a gallon of water for me; plus 4 shots of absinthe for Toomey; and damn near the rest of the bottle for Matt, which came close to three hours. Grimes ashes and small pile of bones had cooled down and was placed in a plastic bag; ready to be transported to his final resting place.

Taking the patch off, Matt was in a daze, but I also saw relief in those cold, treacherous eyes. I walked next to my brother and asked, "You alright, man?"

"What Do You Think?"

"You look like you are getting better."

Worker two walked over and handed Matt Grimes' ashes. Matt looked at me and actually smiled and commented, "Your right." We gave each other a dap and looked over at Pulley who was motioning for our attention.

The cat pointed to his eyes again, (*that dark shit was beginning to get to me because after fucking with the Green Fairy, I was having a hard time with my coordination and I was seeing some bad shit in my mind*).

Back, though, up, down, and out the building, we were lead outside to a different vehicle, where we rode in silence for about twenty-five minutes before stopping. Pulley announced that we could uncover our eyes.

Stepping out of the black Toyota, I swear I wanted to put my blindfold back on. We were in a grave yard (*I hate those things. I hadn't been to one before or since my mother's death*).

Creeped out and pissed off, I was ready to do the damn thing and get the hell out of there. Walking pass me was Pulley's worker, followed by Toomey and Pulley laughing about their earlier years hanging out in cemeteries. When Matt passed my ass, I picked up my pace.

The four of us standing around a small hole that worker number one had just opened in the ground. Matt kissed the bag, whispered something that I couldn't hear; dumped Grimes' remains from out the plastic into the ground, poured water on top the ashes then turned and walked away.

Pulley took a step forward as the presider of the funeral obsequy, "You're dead. You're buried…Amen."

Toomey standing beside him hawked and spit on the mud, eulogizing—"Mother Fucker, I hope you rot in hell", then followed behind Pulley.

Some sick shit was going through my mind (*If this hadn't happen to Cheryl, Quincee wouldn't be back in my life*). I was struggling because anyone who thought well about any part of this situation had to be a sick fuck. Needing to break up my thoughts, I caught up to Matt.

"How are you holding up?"

"All good bro."

Then out of nowhere, I was asked, "I thought you said that you got rid of all the shit that she gave you! That did include jewelry didn't it?"

Dumbfounded at the inquiry and thinking that my boy was losing it, "What Are You Talking About?"

Feeling my chest, and realizing what the for-seer was referring to—the chain I had on—I was ready to run. I had just put the chain on that night-- I wore it as a good luck charm that Ma'Haundra had gotten for me, when I roll out into situations such as these. The hairs on the back of my neck stood up because the gold chain and charm were underneath my clothes, I was alone when I got dressed, and at no time was it exposed.

"How the fuck did you know I had this on? Throwing my hand up in opposition while trying to shake of the creeps that were crawling on my skin, I retracted "You know what…don't tell me. I don't want to know."

Damn near sprinting over to Grimes' grave, yanking the chain off my neck, rubbing off any traces of my prints, I pitched the damn thing into the hole that was being covered up by Pulley's man. I was shocked at how much lighter I felt with the piece of jewelry gone from my neck, realizing that even symbolically, Ma'Haundra was a weight on me.

By that time I walked back to Matt, Pulley had just received his last payment installment.

"It's a pleasure doing business with you. If you need me in the future, Toom knows where to find me." He shook Matt's hand and announced "Alright fellows, you all know the drill."

Before he could pronounce the d in drill, I was already headed back to the vehicle, following worker number one, with my blindfold out, anxious to put the shit back on.

"Where's the car?"

"Yall gonna be using the blue car."

I turned and saw the Honda Civic pulling up to us. I hopped in the back seat. It was a better ride because it was just Matt and I in the back. Toomey rode in the front. Lights out until we heard…

"Yall are alright now."

Taking the sweaty ass blindfold off, I remember being in the same spot when we were first given them.

Entering onto the highway heading north, feeling relieved that Cheryl and Quincee don't ever have to worry about Grimes, and confident that no one will connect him to us; I sat back and closed my eyes conjuring up Quincee in my mind. My nasty thoughts with her were interrupted by the Toomey and Pulley.

"Why the fuck you got us in this small piece of shit ass car? You got like six mobiles, shit I would even prefer the meat wagon to this."

"This is my repellent."

"Repel…my ass. My neck is going to have a crook in it from leaning to one side. My got-damn knees are going to have dashboard burns from rubbing up against it. This shit is whack."

"Say what you will. When I drive ole girl, I look like I don't have a pot to piss in. So when the law passes me smirking and probably thinking (ugly black broke nigger); I give them a cowering nod, while driving dirty with drugs, dead bodies, and kidnapped mother fuckers right under their red-neck and nigger noses."

Smiling at Pulley, Toomey conceded, "You the man, I shut the fuck up."

About three more conversations, we were exiting the highway midway on the Turnpike. I got out to take a leak, and decided to make a detour to Burger King before heading out the door. As I was sweetening a cup of coffee, Pulley walks up to me and handed me the keys to my truck.

"You're ride is parked four cars away from mine to the right."

Smiling and thinking back when Toomey asked me for my truck keys, I told the fat man, "I like the way you handle business."

"It's all about exceptional customer service." He shook my hand, and was out.

I waited at the front entrance for Matt while Toomey was talking to Pulley. I brought Matt up to speed, and inquired again, "You alright?"

Looking completely out of it, my brother calmly stated, "Get me home because I see six of you, and all of you are wearing nothing but a purple flower."

"O...k, you need to get in the car, preferably in the back seat". I whistled for Toomey to come on because we were ready to roll. As soon as Matt's head hit the seat, cat was out.

Toomey and I talked the entire ride back to the city.

"Yo Dan, I'll never forget that mother fuckah's face when he realized that he was going to die, the scummy trick. I wanted to walk up to him and put my hands on him, at least once because I hate a nigga who does shit like that to women."

"Yeah man, I feel the same way."

Talking with Toomey and not paying attention, I missed the Lincoln Tunnel exit, and we ended up taking the George Washington Bridge into the City. Toomey suggested that we get something to eat. It was close to 8 a.m. The sun was shining bright in my face, Matt was out for the long count, so I headed to a soul food restaurant my father had taken me to years ago—Jimmys, on 169th Street and Clay Avenue, in the Bronx. After I had parked the car, Toomey was standing outside looking unimpressed at the eatery's curb appeal; my phone buzzes. It's Quincee, (*My shit starts throbbing*). I couldn't pick up her call fast enough.

"Hey pretty lady. I'm getting ready to get something to eat. What can I get you?"

"Mmmm....I'm not really hungry. I'll just munch off of what you have, if that's alright with you!"

"You can munch, get or have anything that I own."

There was a sexy pause then she commanded "Get home to me safely."

Everything in me lit up from her comment. I dashed my happy ass out the truck and informed Toomey of a change in plans. One of the things that I like about Toomey is that the cat is flexible.

"No problem just let me order something....are you sure about the food in here because the décor doesn't look too advertising."

"You're going to be satisfied...Man, just order your food."

Toomey's smart-ass said, "Yo my niggah, calm down, she'll be there when you get to her. She ain't going anywhere."

Ignoring the on-target jackass, I placed my order— country ham, bacon, cheese grits, home-fried potatoes, Belgian waffles, and two large cups of orange juice.

9:37 a.m. I was helping Matt into my house to sleep off the rest of the absinthe stupor. Back to my truck, I barely heard what Toomey was saying to me because I was thinking about the woman that I was going to make mine again.

(48 hours with no sleep, and just thinking about her keeps me awake and stirred up. That woman has all kinds of control over me...damn!).

Excitement was about to bounce out of my chest, but when I opened my room door at my father's place, baby girl was sleep.

It looked as if she was fighting something her dreams. Putting an end to that shit as fast as I could, I took a shower to get death off of me, sprayed on some smell good then slipped under the covers beside her. I laid my arm across her waist and move in close to her to let whatever demon she was battling with, know that it has to deal with me.

(Men...no lie, it wasn't even ten seconds that she settled down and leaned into me. My ego inflated. I felt like top dog and before I realized it, I was sleeping too).

Everything I'm Doing Is Still Bad

Ladies, when healing physically from a bruise, a black eye, or broken bones it is powerful because it says to the abuser, you tried to take me out, but I'm still here.

When healing from self-imposed deprecation it is harder, but more empowering because it speaks to our internal self. Thereby, in our recovery process, we can create the person we wish to see in our self.

Pain waking me up telling me it's time to take a pill. Then feeling Danny's arm and body heat permeating through me made everything seem better. I not only felt like I had slept for thirty-six hours, I also felt alive. In spite of being all hurt up, nastiness got the better of me, and I lifted up the covers.

That fine thang was naked as a jay-bird. I got nervous and released the material from my fingers letting it drop back down like a hot potato, as I sautéed in the excitement that I felt between my legs.

Lying in the bed with my eyes closed while waiting for the pills to take effect I found myself getting mad at myself because I thought I could have fought harder, done more, and should have been braver. I really thought I was stronger than I was in that situation.

When I felt tears welling up in my sinuses, I got even hotter, and decided that I'M NOT LETTING THIS IMPEEDE ANY PART OF MY RECOVERY. I'M GOING TO FIX MYSELF AND MOVE FORWARD.

I began affirming, in a small voice, as not to wake Danny up.

"I am healing. I am whole. I am well. I am safe. I am fearless. I am moving forward with my life."

Ladies, even though we are hurting, feeling broken, scared, and violated, we have to initiate the self-talk to create our repair process. Even if you don't believe it...trick your mind and do it anyway, and eventually you will feel the seed of healthy recovery growing, or already be in place without you knowing when or how it began.

Turning towards Danny, waiting until my pupils adjusted so that I was able to make out my sleeping guardian's facial features, I felt protected, loved, and cared for.

Ladies, you know when your man is sleeping and looking like that four year old little boy who radiates innocence and perfect-ness that is wrap up in grandness?

But I know it was only a temporary jaunt because of silly-bag what's her name that Danny was dealing with, and the longer I lay there, the cloudier my emotions would get and eventually end up hurting me. So, I decided it was time to go home, bad ribs, bruises and all.

Although I was bumping around being loud, (*unintentionally I would like to think!*), I didn't even see a stir coming from the sheets. Dressed and with all of my belongings, I just couldn't bring myself to disturb Danny's flawless rest, so I sat down and wrote a note:

To: You Know Who

You looked like you were having a healing sleep, and I wanted you to continue the sleep of a Resting King. Call me when you get up…with your fine ass!

From: You Know Me

By the time I finished writing my message, my brother-in-law Rico was calling my phone, informing me that he was two blocks away, and that I could head downstairs. Rico was the only person who I thought of to come to my aid.

He is a dark chocolate cutie who stands about 5'7". He has a striking resemblance to 50 Cent, the rapper. It's funny because whenever I hang out with him and my sister, he always have woman running up on him asking for his autograph. He is a humble man, a provider for his family, and a great father. He and Shannon have been together for over 17 years, and they have two handsome, exceedingly intelligent sons who I know will grow up to be fine upstanding citizens under both of their tutelages.

On the way home, I asked Rico, "You didn't mention anything to Shannon or Ma, right?"

"Not a word. You know me better than that."

Feeling like a heel, I had to take up for myself, "I know. I just felt like I had to ask."

Putting his hand on my shoulder and giving it a squeeze, he replied "It's okay Sissy, I understand." Turning to me with a protective expression and an authoritative tone, he inquired "Is there anything that needs to be taken care of?"

"I can't say absolutely, but my gut tells me that things have definitely been dealt with." I saw the concern on his face, but he said nothing more.

Rico is the brother that any sibling would be lucky to have; the son that my mother loves as one of her own children, (*sometimes treating him better than Shannon and I*), and I love him and trust him explicitly.

When I arrived home, I got straight into bed. I kept up the charade that I was with Danny, making at least one check-in call per day to my mother and the twins. It was a blessing that the girls were with my mother and sister, six floors below on the 29th floor. From Sunday to Wednesday, I was popping pills like clockwork for the pain, and I was still bruised up pretty bad. I didn't want my children to see me like that. Plus, I just needed time for myself.

By Friday, I hadn't had a headache in two days, the dizziness and the ringing in my ears were completely gone, (*Thank You God*). I wasn't feeling fatigue, probably because I slept through the entire night for the first time.

I called downstairs.

"Hey Ma."

"Hello Quincee-Jane."

"Just want to let you know that I'm home now. I fell and decided to cancel my business trip."

"Are you alright?"

"Yes, I'm fine." I felt awful lying to her.

"I'll be up with the girls when they come in from school."

Three weeks later when I was feeling back to my normal self, my mother informed me that she called Danny on that first Monday, wanting to know why I had a black eye and was taking Vicodin. And after hearing the entire story, and being satisfied it was the truth, she made that fine thang swear to secrecy, so that I could heal properly without additional emotional interference.

Ladies, who would you be mad at; your mother or your man?

All was going well with Danny and me although I was chastised for the thousandth time for leaving unannounced. We spoke every day and several times a day. I was feeling exceptionally confident and ready to up my game.

The same evening that I found out about my mother and Danny's secret, I put in my regular nightly call.

"Hey There Handsome."

"Hello Sexy."

"I was thinking I owe you a home-cooked meal.
 What are you doing tomorrow night?"

"I…umm…well…I have a lot of work to catch up on, so I'm going to be working late for the rest of the week."

Immediately I caught the change in tone, attitude, and energy in the reply. I was so repulsed by the fake-ass response that I interjected, "You know what Danny, don't worry about it. I won't bother you anymore" and I hung up the phone.

My disdain was so great that I didn't even care about being rejected. I was actually surprised at my un-sought strength, and the 'I don't have time for this shit' attitude that I felt within. That moment forward, I went on about my business—taking no more of Danny's calls.

"Ring…Ring…Ring" the phone interrupted my thoughts—much to my pleasure because I wanted to put Danny entirely out of my mind.

"Hello. May I speak to QJ."

"This is She."

"Hey Girl, its Twink. We met at Tina's Labor Day party."

"Lana?"

"Yep, that's me."

 Hey there yourself. What a nice surprise." I lied.

She went on sounding bubbly as a dumb blonde, "Call me Twink. Oh I can't talk long; I've just finishing shopping for an outfit. I'm late for my manicure and pedicure appointment. I still have to get my hair done. You know how it is? Oh…I almost forgot why I called. I want to invite you out Saturday night to a mid-night cruise to no-where. Don't say no because I really want you to come." She cackled out, all in one sentence.

Ladies, always listen to your inner voice. If it warns you with bad vibes, remove yourself from that situation as fast as you can because if you don't, you will get bitten in the ass and have no one to blame… but yourself.

Shrugging off the feeling of darkness and wanting to play 'get back' at Danny, without hesitation, I agreed.

"Why not? It sounds like fun."

"Ooh goodie, the boat pulls out at midnight, so I'll pick you up around 10:30. I'll call you before I'm leaving out to get directions to you. See ya then."

After placing the phone on the receiver, a tickle of excitement ran down my spine as I proposed in my mind's eye Danny's reaction to me and Twink hanging out together, (*but never questioning myself, how did she get my home phone number?*).

Saturday night, 9:45 p.m. I was standing in front of my full length mirror admiring how I had put myself together. I had on my yellowish-green mid-rise boot cut suede pants and a strapless liquid silver corset that oozed off of my chocolate skin. Its deep-cut harmonized with the hanging teardrop choker that lay perfectly in between my cleavage. I had two different coordinating earrings that dangled on the top of my shoulders as they sparkled through my down swept braids. The matching suede crop jacket was the right length to show a sliver of skin in the back between my corset and my pants that hollered out 'sex appeal.' The chain link belt accented the silver chain loops on my silver-toe and heel sling-back shoes.

Topping the outfit off was my teal crocheted purse that was lined in silver taffeta. Hand crafted by Jacqueline of Style and Pride. That particular line is called "Hoe To Go", she includes a condom, a sample size lubricant, a cab service business card, and a shot size bottle of alcohol spirits.

Staying true to her word, at 10:02 p.m., Twink called and by 10:29 I was walking out of my building and saw her fiddling with something in the trunk of her black BMW. The coffee brown micro-mini that she wore exposed her butt checks, which didn't seem to bother her in the least, nor that she was in the hood, and the wolves were licking their lips for her, as their prey.

She wore a beautiful slinky iridescent red halter top that had less material than her skirt. Her brown leather boots made her legs look long and luxurious. Red earrings and bracelets capped the outfit perfectly.

I felt a tinge of something. I gave myself until the time that I walked up to her, to feel whatever then I was going to let it go…for good.

All my Overweight Sisters, I'm still carrying about 35+ extra pounds. On the norm, I am not intimidated by smaller woman because I am blessed with a sense of style and I know how to dress for my body type.

Walking up behind her and tapping her on her shoulder; as she turned around the wind was blowing her Shirley Temple curls all over her head.

Fighting her mane to get her face free, the shades that she wore made her appear that she was hiding something rather than going for a mysterious sexy look. I paid no mind to my thought because I always wear shades when I go out, (*Ooh ladies, don't let the boys see you steering at them*).

Before greeting me, the bitch gave off the expression as if she was surprised to be impressed by the way that I looked, (....*Oh the game had begun!*).

Trying to cover up, she cheerfully said "Hey girl...ooh you look hot! Oh yeah, WE'RE GOING TO HAVE FUN 2-NIGHT!"

In a serious tone, I responded "I plan to."

Once inside the car, our girly connection formed.

"Twink, stop playing, this is nice", as I caressed the smoke gray leather interior. There were all kinds of gadgets.

Bubbling at my excitement she began catering my delight. "Here let me adjust your seat. Ooh check this out", as she turned on the massager and my seat began to vibrate. "Do you drink Amaretto?" she asked as she produced two Dunkin Donuts foam cups and was pouring some into her cup.

Marveling, I answered "I sure do."

Although there was something about her that I did not like — outside of her dealings with Danny, there were similarities that continually flooded through as I was spending time with her.

Ladies, in situations such as these, it is integral to stay honed into your woman's intuition, and pay attention to that little voice in your head because that is what will keep you out of trouble and away from danger.

After filling both cups with the spirit, lemon juice, and ice, Twink returned the items to the cooler in the trunk, and we were off.

11:18 p.m., we were parked across the street from pier 16, in Manhattan. Twink was cheerfully chatting about everything under the sun except for what I really was interested in hearing about, (*you know who*).

No soon as that thought left my mind she began "Ooh girl, there are going to be so many fine men here tonight, I can't wait to get up in there."

As nonchalant as I could muster, I queried "I thought you and Danny are an item?"

"When the cat's away…the mouse will play", she snippily retorted as she attempted to conceal the venom that was glaring from her eyes. I could not have been more satisfied at her deception. Thinking to myself, (*Serves you right Danny. You're getting your dumb ass played*).

I had been checking my watch every ten minutes or so as we chitchatted, concerned that by the time we board there would be no seats available.

"Shouldn't we be heading to the pier because that line is getting longer by the second?"

"Not to worry. I have VIP seats reserved for us" she responded as she went into her purse produced two tickets, dangling them in the air, and continue "I wait on… NO LINE!"

"I like the way you play, Miss Twink" slapping her high-five.

She did not lie, we sauntered to the pier, bypassing that long line, and boarded the yacht. We were seated on the main deck. I watched eye candy as I sat at the table waiting for Twink to return with our drinks. There were all sorts of handsome men--chocolate, mocha, brown, yellow, short, tall, extra tall, bald, medium curly locks, long flowing manicured dreds, diesel-muscular, slim with just right everything…you name it, I saw it and my eyes were having a lip-licking, yum yummy good time.

Twink returned with two glasses, but only mine was full.

"Twink, where is your drink?"

"Oh girl, that shit been gone, I'm going back for a refill."

"Alright, I'm going to take a stroll." I was enjoying myself immensely—going from deck to deck to deck, dancing, sipping my drink, star gazing, and flashing my best girly flirtatious smile, so when I did look down at my watch, I was surprised to see that it was 12:50 a.m.

I hadn't seen Twink since she said that she was going to get herself another drink then remembering that I told her that I had the second round. I gave her all the money that I had in my purse—a hundred dollar bill.

I called her, and the phone went into voice mail "Hey girl where are you. Call me when you see my number, Chow." I didn't think anything of it; I just assumed that she couldn't hear her phone over the loud music.

Trying to remember when I last seen her. I walked all three decks of that yacht four times looking for her ass. When I made my last ascend to the main deck, steam was shooting out of my ears because this bitch was not only nowhere to be found, but she wasn't answering her phone.

Spotting two security staff members that were covering the gangway, I headed towards them. "Excuse me gentlemen, I know you've seen hundreds of faces this evening, but do either of you remember seeing a lady that....." I went on to describe Twink's attire.

The tall skinny brown-skinned one wearing all black from head to foot looked at me like he didn't want to waste his time talking to me. I thought it strange and just turned my attention to the one who looked like a light-skinned twin of Ving Rhames, wearing an olive green suit with a black button down shirt, smelling real good, and spoke in a sexy baritone voice as he offered.

"Yeah, Legs. I remember her. She left about fifteen minutes ago."

"Excuse me?" I felt another layer of anger drape down my body. Straightening my spine flat as a board, placing my hands on my hips, I inquired further.

"What Do You Mean By "Left" Left as in going to get something from her car and returning?"

"NO. Left as in "leaving" and NOT returning...Sorry pretty lady."

I took a few steps away from them and called her ass again. "Twink, this is Quincee-Jane. YOU NEED TO CALL ME!" *(WHAT!....The Bitch Was GONE!)*

Pulling myself together, as to not misguide my indignation, I walked back over to my informant and continued my discovery, "Excuse me again, what makes you sure that she is not coming back?"

Looking like he was trying not to be agitated by my investigation, he pacified me.

"Well she came out here about three or four times to ask about the departure time. Once she found out that we might not be pulling out for another half hour or so, she went back in for a few minutes, came back out and said that she wasn't going to wait. She flirted a bit, said goodnight and...left."

I was nonplussed by his response. Abhorrence attacked all of my senses. I wanted to fuck her up so bad that blood-fire tightened my chest. (*If I had of gotten my hands on her right then, I do believe that I would have went to jail that night*).

Incensed, I continued "Did she mention anything about coming with a friend, or somebody?"

"N-o-o-o. Let me guess…you're the friend and the somebody?"

I wanted to put my hands on her so bad that my stomach began hurting. Containing my anger and its physical manifestations, I responded "Yes, I am…That Person." I extended my hand out in genuine gratitude for the assistance up to that point.

"Hello, I am Quincee-Jane. It is a pleasure to meet you."

"Johnny Lee, the pleasure is all mine pretty lady."

Letting a smile escape from my lips, I thanked him for the compliment.

"Johnny Lee I promise this is my last question, what time do you think the boat is going to get underway?"

"Honestly, I don't know. This might be a DOCKED cruise to nowhere." He tried to halt his chuckle when he saw the lost expression on my face. The big man took a step towards me, grabbed my hand and in a compassionate tone stated.

"You are too fine to be looking this stressed out. Your blood pressure is touching the stars right now. Just breathe girl." He patted my hand and in a fatherly tone asked, "What can I do for you?" I abruptly removed my hand from his when I remembered that I had left my jacket on the seat of my chair—just my luck, the boat would pull off with it.

By the time Johnny Lee got out "Where you going?" I was up the ramp and crossing the gangway.

Headed towards my seat, I noticed that the table was occupied with four women, and I use the term loosely. The one on the far side of me was light yellow with short spiky hair. She had a bug's bunny overbite, and looked sickly thin in her loose fitting red halter top.

Next to her sat a pretty black complexioned girl with a nice body, but when she opened her mouth the top and bottom grills she wore made her look like she had do-do on her teeth. Topping that was her hot pink weave that went with her claw shaped hot pink nails that absolutely contradicted the "SEXY" that was written in beads across the chest of her hot pink short-sleeve blouse.

Sitting to the left of her was a light brown skinned stumpy build woman. She had long flowing black hair. She was thick and wore an apple green spaghetti string blouse that looked to be two sizes too small. Her boobs hung out both sides of her blouse and they were smashed down in the front. Plus she had sparkles on her body that made her look like a glow-worm.

Seated closest to me was the scrawny dark chocolate one with too much make-up on, which did not conceal the dark splotches on her face and chin. I was actually fixated, for a moment, on why she didn't cover the marks on her neck. She looked like she had a boob job because they weren't proportionate with the rest of her body's frame. She had on a white tube top that exposed her wide ass nipples--*(Eew!)*

Befitting with the evening's events, I also notice that I didn't see my jacket. Wanting a rational conversation and looking at them looking like third-class whores, I silently questioned the universe (*why me?*), took a deep breath, and walked up to the group.

Asking nipples, who was closest to me, "Excuse me, did you see a yellow/greenish suede jacket on that seat?" pointing to where I had been sitting.

She looked at me; as if I were dirt under her feet and said; "Excuse You", while the other three jumped to attention like they were ready for a fight. Thinking to myself, (*Give me a break!*).

Noticing out of the corner of my left peripheral vision, I saw a tall dark-skinned, extra heavy set security person heading towards us. Aware that the situation was spiraling downhill—fast, I informed the group that was my table, but I had left.

They looked at each other and simultaneously began laughing at me. By this time, Joe Security was asking skinny light-skin, whose blouse was so loose that her tiny tit was exposed, if everything was ok. The one that I initially spoke with yapped out.

"Naw, this bitch right here says we took her table cause she had a VIP ticket!"

(*Ladies, you know I was not going to let her get away with that.*)

"You chocolate covered bumpy troll …what Did You Say?"

With an 'I'm going to throw this bitch outta here' demeanor, blubber-butt security snarled loudly at me causing other party-goers to turn in our direction; looking at me questioningly.

"Where's your ticket stub?"

Instant reflex made me go for my purse, then it hit me, Twink have my stub, my coat, and my money. I went deaf to everything around me. I heard nothing as I saw the gruesome crew talking shit; whaling their arms, pointing their fingers, and looking at me as if they smelled something rank.

Honing back to reality, I paid no attention to the whore quartet. I turned to the security guard and informed him that "I am leaving." I did a perfect military about-face, scurried my ass off the yacht, and ran straight into Johnny Lee.

"Pretty Girl, you need to slow down!"

On the verge of tears from humiliation, embarrassment of my stupidity, and through anger I told him my story. It was his turn to be dumbfounded.

"Damn! and you say she is your friend?"

"Not at all, but that's another can of worms that I'm not about to touch!"

Johnny Lee informed me, "Gwenasia is Bobby's girlfriend."

"Oh really? So, nipples and the security guard are a couple. That's no solace for me being told off by Skeletor, Yuck Mouth, Stumpy, and Crater Face."

He laughed at my comment, but I saw more on his face.

"What?" I inquired sternly.

With the disposition of wanting to negate anymore on my plate of events, he solemnly added. "Let me start off by saying, I'm going to make sure you get home safely."

"Johnny-Lee, what is it?"

He paused.

I snapped out, "Tell me!"

"Your friend...Sparkle, Twinkle..."

I interrupted him, "TWINK"

"Yeah, that's it. Well she hangs out with Gwenasia and that bunch."

"WHAT...YOU MEAN TO TELL ME THAT SHE SET ME UP?"

My blood went cold. The next thing I remember was feeling my heartbeat hurt my chest because it was beating so fast and hard, while waiting for Danny to pick up my call. Instead I heard "You've reached Danny..."

Interrupting the pre-recording and growling into my phone, "This is Quincee, I should have known, when I need you, you're not around!" and I slammed my phone shut.

I was so mad that my hands were shaking and it took three attempts before I was able to dial Toomey's number.

"I don't believe it. What up girl?"

Relieved that help was in sight, I went full throttle with my story to Toomey without taking a breath of air.

"Woa, hey... slow down, I didn't understand a word you just said."

"Toomey, Danny's girlfriend, that got-damn Twink invited me out then left me and she took my money with her, and now I'm stranded out here at the Pier off of the FDR Drive and 23rd street, and I have no way of getting home. Can you please come and pick me up...Please!"

That uncompassionate fuck started laughing at me. I spewed, "You Think This Is Funny? You Know What? Fuck You. I Don't Know Why I Bothered Calling You...."

Interrupting my tirade, I had to hear a lecture.

"Hold up. This is the first time that you've ever called my phone. Then you tell me that you went out with bubble-head, of all people. She took your shit and left you stranded...And you expect me not to have a reaction. You know my black ass better than that!

First of all, why would you even fuck with Squeaky Dumb-Dumber, especially after what you went through at Dre's place?...Cuz you were on that bull-shit trying to get back at Dan."

I was speechless at having the truth thrown in my face so callously. There was no way that I was going to give away my womanly motives, or acquiesce to Toomey's analysis. And I was, for damn sure not going to let go of my anger because of my role in the madness that I got caught up in. The only come-back I had was, "I hate you!"

"I'll be there within twenty minutes. Just hold tight." and the phone went dead.

Before I could get my phone into my purse, it rang. Coming up short and late once again...it was Danny. I flipped the phone open and shut in one motion—I had no time to deal with too little...too late, (*Fuck Danny!*).

Although I was pissed off at Toomey's histrionics, insensitivity and ego crushing honesty, I felt relieved, rescued, and back in control of my predicament.

Immediately, my dulled senses shot back into focus. It was freezing cold outside in the early morning air. Goose pimples raided my body and I began shivering. By the time I walked back to the dock, my toes were frozen and my nipples were rock-hard to the point of aching.

Before reaching Johnny Lee, he saw me and interrupted his conversation with two other men. Walking up to me and with concern and asking, "Are you alright, Miss Quincee?" in a sexy southern drawl.

Ladies, I don't know what it is about them county boys, in how I am affected by the mere sound of their accent.

I had not realized how fine he was before that point. Suppressing my thoughts, I opened up my mouth to respond, "I...I...I'm f...f...f...i...n...e."

Taking off his jacket, he said "Oh no, that'll never do", escorting me into it. Smelling the scent of Logerfeld and feeling the warmth of his body heat reverberating from his jacket melted my erogenous zones.

"Let's try this again. Are you alright because I saw you having an intense conversation with someone. Did you finally get through to Twinkle?"

"No that was a friend of mine who is coming to pick me up."

Raising one eyebrow, he came back with "Mmm, you definitely have a way with friends."

Rolling my eyes, I shunned off his comment. He put his arm around my shoulder and we rejoined his friends.

Paco's about 5'8", a yellow complexioned Puerto Rican with a sexy thin beard-line that complimented his freshly cut Ceasar. He had reddish-auburn hair and the most striking grey eyes. His gray double-breasted suit and pastel lime green shirt was capped off sleekly with gray hushpuppies.

As he was being introduced to me, he grabbed my hand, kissed it and said, "Es un placer en condocer una mujer tan bella como tu."

Wanting to show-off my Spanish or the lack thereof, I offered "No intiendo (I don't understand), pero porfavor dime (but please tell me)."

"Ahh, you speak Es spanol"

"Un poquito" (a little).

"Tabien. I said it's a pleasure to meet a woman as beautiful as you."

My ego chimed with delight at the compliment. Next was his cousin Jose, who was fair-skinned and had that thick black wavy Ricky Ricardo hair. He was the younger of the two and just as handsome wearing navy blue slacks, a rust, white and navy argyle sweater that was zipped up to the bottom of his chin. His cashmere sports coat matched the rust in his sweater and his boots perfectly. Jose took my hand, kissed my palm and said "Milk chocolate after midnight has always been a favorite of mine."

The flirt monster in me appeared and I countered, as the inside of my hand was still tingling from his soft lips, "Such sweet words…from such a hombre guapo (handsome man)", and I bowed my head in a queenly nod to him.

"Muchas gracias señora bonita (Thank you very much pretty lady)"

"That wasn't a compliment, I was stating a fact," my flirt mode was at full force.

His face flooded blood red, and I marveled at the fertility of my charm-lexis. The four of us stood on the pier and talked for what seemed like a few minutes before, Johnny Lee nudge me saying, I think your ride is here.

I remembered hearing a horn blowing in the distance, but paid no attention because I was so engrossed in conversation.

Turning around, my jaw dropped at seeing Danny walking towards me. When the unwanted pretend-broker approached me, heat shot through my collar.

Sneeringly I shot out "Thank you for coming. Where is Toomey?"

Not waiting for an answer, I turned around and began walking back towards the handsome trio. The nasty in me, took my time. I exchanged business cards with the Paco because we have a common interest--real estate. Then I gave the Latin duo some cheek-sugar.

Turning to Johnny Lee and returning his jacket with abject sincerity I offered, "Thank you for taking good care of me. You don't know how much this means to me," (*I had actually gotten choked up at the thought of his kindness*).

He gently responded, "My momma always told me to look after a damsel in distress."

"Your momma would be very proud of you right now."

"Why…Thank you ma'am."

Grabbing me up in a bear hug with my feet dangling in the air was a big turn-on. Whispering in my ear, "I look forward to seeing you again Miss Quincee-Jane. When you get to the Bronx, make sure you call me, so I know that you've gotten home safely." Placing me back down on the ground and handing me his business card.

Endeared and intrigued by the southern gentleman, I gave him a kiss, ever so close to his lips then I walked away smiling knowing that that would not be the last time I see Johnny Lee.

Just like an on-off switch, I was fuming with rage. I don't know which had more potency-- Twink's bullshit, or Danny's blatant appearance.

Halfway to the truck, Danny met up to me with outstretched arms holding a jacket, ready for me to slide into it. Wanting to evade any and everything that the bastard had to offer (*except a ride home…of course*), I attempted to shun off the gesture, but there was something in those gorgeous eyes that made me follow the silent instructions, so I arrogantly put the damn coat on.

I said nothing until I got to the vehicle, where I saw Toomey standing like a chauffeur beckoning me into the front seat with a chauvinistic smirk plastered across the clod's face. To add salt to my wounds, the agitator-invoker had the nerve to tap me on the shoulder and laugh at me before closing the door. I was so mad that I went deaf for the second time that night.

Turning around to face the back seat, I went off "What the fuck are you laughing at, you horrid imbecile? I called You! I asked You for help, not your side-fucking-kick."

"Yo…hold up on that. Dan got your message, as I was leaving out of the house to come and pick your "left" ass up. So don't go jumping down my throat" then the bastard starting laughing at me again.

Still cackling at Toomey by the time, Danny retrieved a sweatshirt from the trunk, had put in on, and was back in the driver's seat. We hadn't even gotten on the highway before I accosted the handsome-deserter with my fury.

"That bitch of yours set me up!" Retelling my plight in an inarticulate fashion, I swore ever other syllable until I finished. "You need to call that fuckin cluck of yours and tell her that I want my jacket back, AND MY FUCKIN MONEY...All Of It! Just because she's your girl doesn't mean a got-damn thing to me. The dumb-fucking bunny doesn't even realize when she's in danger. I'm not one of those women who get pissed-off for a minute and want to pull hair and scratch.

I'm telling you now, if I don't get my shit back; you tell that pea-brain whore monster that I will find out where she lives, have EVERY fucking charge that I can think of pressed against her ass.

I don't believe this bull shit. How the fuck you're going to invite someone out then turn around and pre-fuckin-meditated-ly, leave them? Who does shit like that? Who the fuck do she think she is? Ooh, I could knock her the fuck out right about now...The mutant no-brain perverted twit."

Toomey was in the back cracking up, and commented "That's some funny shit."

Danny and I simultaneously yelled out "SHUT UP!"

"My bad...Damn this is a rough crowd", while throwing up those lanky ass arms in the air.

Turning my wrath back on Danny, "Why are you here? If I remember correctly, you didn't answer your phone."

Looking morose, "Quincee, I was in the bathroom when you called. Baby, I'm sorry that I wasn't there to pick up."

On fire, shooting back, "Firstly, I am not your baby. That's what you have twinkle-fuckin-toes for. Secondly, your apology means jack-nothing to me, so you can take it back and shove it up your lying ass.

Ladies, I know I was over the top, but I couldn't help myself by that point.

Taking the full brunt of my tongue lashing, the sorry sac-of-nothing made an effort to say something, "Quincee, Twink is...."

"I DON'T WANT TO HEAR SHIT ABOUT THAT SKIRVEY DING-BAT OTHER THAN WHEN I'M GOING TO GET MY SHIT BACK. FUCK HER, FUCK YOU, FUCK YOU AND HER, AND FUCK THIS WHOLE NIGHT!!!!!.

And what makes you think that I give a damn about you and gaa-gaa head? It's perfectly clear why you spurned all of my attempts of trying to get back with you.

You know Danny, I wouldn't have had a problem with you not being interested in us, shit I'm a big girl I can take it, but you could have at least grabbed your balls and told me straight-up. I would have walked away respecting you for it, if nothing else."

Having had enough, I said aloud to myself, "You know what QJ, none of this shit even matters." Glaring at the fine-as-wine pretender and daring any words to pass through those lying ass lips, and then I closed my mouth.

At the light turning into my complex, Toomey announced, "I have to take a leak, Q can I use your toilet?"

"Sure" I responded, and got out of the car, never looking back. It wasn't until I arrived in the lobby that I saw Danny accompanying Toomey.

Relieved to be back on my stomping grounds, I paid no mind to the straggler. Toomey was in and out of the bathroom in less than two minutes; all I had time to do was take off my shoes and put my hair into two ponytails.

Danny stood by the front door the entire time not moving or uttering a word, and was opening it as soon as Toomey appeared around the corner to my hallway entrance.

I headed out the door behind them because I realized that I hadn't thanked Toomey—in spite of how I got home.

"Toom...I appreciate you being there for me. I was caught in a bad situation, and I just want to say thank you."

"Oh...now I get gratitude."

Flaring up again, hissing "You just can't let shit go smooth, can you?"

"No because you have a foul mouth and you're a smart ass."

"At least I'm not a dumb ass."

Appearing to be bothered by my retorts the obnoxious vilify-er took the conversation to another level.

"You're acting like a...", and then the elevator door opened.

After Pip and Dip got on, I blocked the elevator sensor and asked the three young men already inside if I could hold them up for 20 seconds-- they concurred.

Directing my attention to Toomey, "Finish what you were saying. I'm acting like a what?"--seeing apprehension crawl on the egotistical bastard face.

"You're acting like a bitch."

Ready for the comment, I reviled "Yeah, and if I had my ass backed up in the air like a kitty in heat—you would want to be behind my bitch! Wouldn't you—you unremitting ass!"

One of the passengers commented "O.o.o.h shit", and smirked.

The other one said "DAMN!" and covered his month.

The last one was speechless with an, I wouldn't want to be your shoes look on his face.

Fuming, Toomey shot back with venom "You smell like you need some."

I snarled "You act like you want some."

"If you were mine…"

"I'm not yours."

Softening up my voice to a daddy's little girl demeanor and walking up on the opinionated pig ever so erotically, whispering loud enough for all to hear, "You want to pull my ponytail… don't you?" while twirling my right ponytail with my index finger, and looking like just-take-me sexy.

Visibly appearing awkward at my closeness, the battle-loser stammered out, "Yo D, talk to your girl."

In full bitch arrogance, I turned my intention to Danny and sternly inquired, "WHAT? You know what I'm talking about. Oh yeah, that's right…you DON'T!"

Ladies, I was writhing in afterglow because Danny and I hadn't had sex. It was a very powerful moment for me.

Before exiting the elevator, I turned around and inquired "By the way, how is Ma'Handra?"

Stepping out, letting the door close, I got off hearing Toomey chastise Danny "See that's your problem you let her…."

I thought to myself, (*good riddance, I don't have to worry about seeing Toomey or that bastard EVER AGAIN!*)

Revelations

Ladies, I didn't know!

October 6, 2005
Home
7:30 p.m.

The following Thursday night, in my room with research papers, my laptop, and books spread across my bed, working on a project due the next week. I was sipping on a Tequila Rose cocktail.

Ooh ladies, you should try it. It's a girly drink that is a Mexican cream liqueur made from a blend of strawberry cream liqueur and tequila.

Listening to the raindrops crash on my windowpane, and in deep thought… the phone rings interrupting my concentration. Perturbed by the disturbance, I slightly barked out my salutation.

"Hello, this is Quincee-Jane."

"This is Danny."

My heart skipped a beat at the shear sound of that missed voice. Unintentionally, responding in a sweet tone, "Hey."

"Hello Quincee. I know I'm the last person you want to hear from, but please, can I visit you…even if it's just for ten minutes of your time."

The request was so heartfelt that I forgotten all about the harbored resentment and ill-will that I previously felt. I simply answered "Yes you may."

All I heard was thank you, and then silence. Preparing, but not totally for my ambiguously wanted visitor, I called downstairs to my mother.

"Ma, can Hope and Harmony come down for a little while, I have company coming."

"Sure, send them down."

After confirming they were with their grandmother, I went scurrying to the mirror. I had to slow myself down because my insides were bursting with life. I decided that I wouldn't change my clothes. My oversized white T-shirt and fluffy pink socks would do just fine. My two pigtails coupled with my glasses gave off a look of studiousness.

Knowing that I had at least forty minutes, I took my time in straightening up the mess on my bed. Fifteen minutes had passed and I was laying back down thinking (*Am I going to yell; emit sheets of coldness; or maybe reign arrogant*); yet within those thoughts, an excited anxious energy was brewing in the bottom of my belly.

My mind went back to the prior week after I left Danny and Toomey at the elevator. I was pissed off to high heaven at both of them. Walking in my kitchen, why did I see two crisp one hundred bills on my kitchen counter?

Without my knowledge, Danny had put me in a better financial position than Twink left me in; then sequentially endured being humiliated by me, all in attempts to make up for Twink's egregious conduct.

My mouth, my heart, and my spirit smiled because ladies, deep down I know that Danny is a good seed.

As I was basking in the sweet sensations of what I was feeling, the doorbell rings. I damn near broke my neck trying to get off my bed, (*It didn't make any kind of sense!*).

Swinging the door opened to see Jay-Jay—my next door neighbor/Dominican nephew standing in front of me.

"Mez Quincee, my mom wants to know if you have milk."

Trying not to show chagrin in my demeanor, I walked to the refrigerator and returned with the entire gallon.

"Just bring it back when you're finished."

"Thank you Mez Quincee."

Closing my door, I chastised myself because I knew damn well that Danny would not have gotten to me that fast and because I had no business having those school girl flutters in my woman-person.

Less than five minutes had passed and Jay-Jay was ringing my bell returning the milk. Making up for my curtness, I had graciousness written on my face.

I opened the door to see Danny standing at my threshold— soaking wet, shivering, and looking like a little boy in dire need of some TLC, (*a.k.a. Quincee*).

Happy, yet horrified, I soothed out "Oh poor baby, look at you."

"ACK-CHOO" was the response that I received, and like a mother bear, I gently pulled the sickly-looking cub into my house, instructing, "Let's get you out of these clothes."

Stopping me in my tracks, "No Quincee, I don't want to wet your floor."

Warmed at the thought, I tugged until we were standing in front of my stove. It was already on, so the house was nice and toasty. I got the jacket off and tossed it on the counter, but I back off when I reached for the top button of the drenched burnt rust colored Polo long-sleeved shirt.

"I'm going to get you a towel"

"Thank you Quincee."

Walking away and trying not to feel myself cream in my red thong, I dashed into the bathroom to clean off the oozing energy manifesting between my legs. Grabbing a towel from the closet, I walked in the kitchen to see a naked muscular back, and the tightest ass facing me, *(It is ridiculous. Danny has the type of ass that women dream of having and work countless hours at the gym to attain).*

Attempting not to get caught looking, I turned my head, passed the towel over, and began collecting the wet clothes off the countertop. Looking down, I noticed that my loose key had been added to my key ring. I paused and smiled because I had been fighting with that damn thing for weeks.

Ladies, it's the little things that make me happy. The forces were stacking the chips in Danny's favor.

By the time I finished putting the articles of clothing in the washing machine; Danny was in the living room looking out of my picture window—towel around waist, and drying off those long wavy locks with a piece of paper towel.

Looking 10 levels above sexy, I thought I was going to pass out from feel-good just staring at the epitome of an Adonis standing feet away from me. Walking my flustered ass back to my room; I pulled a sweatshirt and oversized gym-shorts from the dresser drawer.

Returning to the living room and instructing, "Here put these on. I don't want you to get sick.", and as if on cue, a succession of sneezes filled the room, "ACK-CHOO...ACK-CHOO...ACK-CHOO."

Countering with, "I'll be right back. I have something for that."
Towing in hand Nyquil and Tylenol PM, calling out more
instructions, "Take this, now a swig of this."

The compliant sneezer ingested the drugs then led me to the
couch where we both sat down. Taking my hands and looking into
my eyes.

"Quincee, there are some things that I need to tell you, and I
want you to hear me out before saying anything…Please."

Waiting for my reply, I was perplex, but complied, "Okay."

"Baby, everything isn't always as it seems. Remember that night
at Cheryl's house when I kept moving away from you?"

My blood bagan to rise, and seeing my reaction, the explaining
prince continued. "Quincee, I know you don't want to relive that
night and I don't want to put you through any unnecessary pain, nor
hurt that I've already caused you, but please… let me speak my
piece.

I want to clear up the misconceptions and all the bad-blood that
have passed between us."

The mild mannered; yet, determined truth un-folder talked well
over a half hour with no interruptions from me, which was an
absolute first because I always have something to say— a question
to ask, a comment to make, or food for thought to offer.

Feeling complimented at being wanted and even more so
empowered when it came to the blue-balls admission. I winced with
agitation and gall as I listened about Ma'Haundra.

"Quincee, even though I've felt that I've had legitimate outside
influences nipping at me, there was, and still is no excuse for me to
have treated you the way that I did. I hope you can find it in your
heart to forgive me."

I had no intentions on doing any such thing.

Fuck that! My sistahs, do you feel me?

After maybe five seconds, the quiet was broken with "I hear you
loud and clear, but if you let me, Quincee-Jane Catfire I will spend
the rest of my life making up that mistake to you."

A tinge of the emotional scab on my heart was abraded by those
intensely sincere words.

The next discovery was about Twink, but before it got underway,
Danny got up and retrieved the wet plastic bag that was still resting
on the hallway floor.

"Here you go baby."

It was my jacket that Cruella De Twinkle-Not had taken from me. Overwhelmingly pleased, I reached over and gave some happy-innocent cheek sugar to my coat retriever.

"I went straight to her house after leaving here Sunday morning."

Earnestly appreciative, I softly said "Thank you Danny."

"No thanks necessary. It was my intent to get your property back to you."

With a bowed head, looking as if to be feeling all of my hurt and humiliation of the Twink episode, my sick prince, offered.

"Quincee, I apologize for what Twink put you through. You have to know that I had no idea she would pull any shit like that. She probably was pissed at me when I bought her home from Tina's spot…Friday Night!"

Wanting to get all the juicy details; but, asking the more pertinent question instead. "Danny, why didn't you tell me about Lana the weekend that I was at you father's place?"

Now coughing and sneezing, but unashamed of the streaming tears, I listened to and believed.

"I didn't tell you because I was enjoying….no it was deeper than that. Quincee, you don't know what it means to me having you in my world. I was afraid of bringing up anything. I didn't want to chance, you not ever speaking to me again.

If I had the slightest clue about Twink, I would have stopped her dead in her tracks.

I'm sorry for everything; for Twink, for trying to avoid you, for Ma'Haundra…"

Taking my hands and looking into my eyes, "Quincee, if you don't believe anything that I've said, know this. I feel NOTHING for Ma'Haundra. That night at the club was the first time I'd seen her after I walked out of her life."

Hearing the story of their breakup doused the Ma'Haundra anxieties that I had. I went back to listening intently.

"The conversation with her wasn't even two minutes. Truth be told, I was wishing you were there by my side, so that she could see for herself how much I was…and still am feeling you."

Looking weak and peaked; but, still communicating and steering my soul, "My heart was stolen from me seven months ago. And You are the thief Quincee-Jane Catfire."

Ladies, I was free-falling.

After wiping the tears that were shed for me by the crumbling puppy, I went on to find out all about Miss Twink and what role she plays in Danny's life. What nagged at me most was the extent of their relationship. There was family history and it sounded like she has psychological and social emotional issues. Personally, I believe the evil hef-fah is missing a few stars, and the remaining ones are about to implode.

Knowing that there was no way I would ever tell Danny not to speak or see Twink, I had to halt my reeling mind because I was acting as if Danny and I were together, or would soon be. Cognizant again of the words that were exiting the venting implorer's mouth, the conversation had gone to another topic.

"The night when Dre's cousin was protecting you from me was the second worse hurt I've experienced, up to that point in my life."

Ladies, I felt like a heel because… I did go a bit overboard that night in Dre's kitchen.

Not waiting for a response, the injured beneficiary went right into the next clarification narrative.

"As for the night that you hung up on me, baby…please believe… that me not wanting to be with you, is the furthest thing from the truth."

The last discovery emission was about Jimmy—the TooGood's wayward wild-child. My mouth was agape and my mind was crawling with questions, but more importantly with concerns for both their well-being and mine.

Suddenly, panic attacked my chest.

"Is that situation resolved?"

"Everything's okay and I don't want you to worry about any of it. I shared that part of my life with you because that's what I've been dealing with since a few days prior to Tina's party.

Quincee, I want you to know that when I didn't accept your invitation to dinner, that same day I received a text from one of the thugs that Jimmy was dealing with. I didn't know what would be going down with any of that bullshit, and I needed to keep you as far away from me as possible in order to protect you. Your safety means everything me. Do you understand what I'm saying?"

Feeling protected, and so moved I just barely got out "Yes."

Like a ray of lucidity, all the pieces of the puzzle came together. The Dark Knight was actually my Knight in Shining Armor.

Holding my hand a bit tighter, I listened, "As far as Twink goes, there has never been, and will never be anything sexual between her and me...Period!

"Danny, I had no idea, I..."

Cutting me off by lifting my right hand and kissing the inside of my wrist, the exonerated love recipient whispered, "You don't have to apologize to me for anything. I love you Quincee, and I have been in love with you ever since that night I kissed you in front of your door."

My heart was so full that joy tears poured down my face.

Still gazing into my eyes, the love declarer went on, "I know that you've hated me for a minute, but now that you know all of my truths, I also want you to know my intentions."

Scooting closer to me, gripping my hand a little tighter, and looking deeper into my eyes.

"Quincee, I want you to be my wife. I want to grow old together with you. I want to spend the rest of my days loving you and making you happy. But first.....I need to know; do I have a chance? Are you seeing—are you with Dre's cousin?"

Caught up with love butterflies dancing in the bottom of my belly, feeling absolute goodness in my heart, and my chest about to explode with glad tiding palpitations, looking deeply into Danny's eyes, I informed "There is no Me and Stormy. Do you understand what I am saying?"

Gazing at me and perceiving me fully, as I am receiving unadulterated alpha male energy, I was surprised and endeared at what happened next.

Dawdling about for a few seconds then sounding and looking like an eleven year boy, "... Quincee, can I... uh...Will you umh...will you be my girlfriend...I mean will you be my lady?"

We were sitting adult-close; but, my heart was pounding happy beats, like and an eleven year old girl who just got her first boyfriend proposal.

The Commitment Intender began rubbing the side of my face, and before I knew anything, had cupped my chin, and kissed me....nice and soft and full and slowly, (*which I was more than ready for*).

First, I felt my top lip being kissed then my bottom lip. Next, I felt the cream-inducer's tongue penetrate the right crease of my mouth; sliding it back and forth on my tongue. Twirling it, teasing it, poking it, and making love to it. The wave of pleasure was so deep that I tried to defog my brain from the manic eroticism that was making me dizzy.

All I wanted to do was lift up my tee-shirt, slide my thong to the side, spread eagle, and get did.

Fortunately, my virtue was saved by the washing machine's timer. I hurriedly announced, "Ooh, your clothes are dry", and I jumped my happy hot ass up and out of danger's way.

Safely standing next to the utility closet, pulling the clothes out of the dryer, Danny walked up behind me sensing my apprehension and continued on to say in a tender manner, "I know I've given you a lot to think about. I'm not expecting you to give me an answer right now."

When I turned around to make a comment, I was standing by myself.

Scared shitless, I managed to find something to do in every room except the living room for the next half hour. When I summoned up the courage to peek around the corner, Danny was fast asleep, head nodded back on the couch, mouth wide open, and looking... at peace.

Around 10:45 p.m. my house was settled down for the night— I turned the television off that was watching the twins, and Danny was hard asleep in my bed --that Tylenol PM and Nyquill did some serious damage. Baby woke up only to walk from the living room to my bedroom.

Soon as I got in the bed, my mind began battling with my emotions.

Ladies, you know when you're at that fork in the road where your heart has been won over by his apologies and his tears, and hearing him tell you all the right things, but then your mind remembers the pain that he's inflicted and you're just stuck on what to do.

That's how I went to sleep.

4:15 a.m. rolls around, and I've always been a fan of early morning smerties. That-- give me what I need to start my day off right--sex. I don't know what came over me, but in my sleep, I rolled on top of Danny and began bumping and grinding.

Feeling hands on the lower part of my back pushing me into the crouch-of-no-return, I woke up startled at my predicament.

Rolling my ass off, and over to my side of the bed, Danny observed my expression, turned to me commanding.

"Open your legs."

Flustered, disgusted, and bouncing up, I barked "WHAT?"

"I said, Open Your Legs."

Sounding sexier than sex itself, and before I could retort a snippy come-back, I felt my legs being pulled apart with one hand, my chest being guided back onto the bed with the other hand, and the weight of a rock hard, sexy, body on top of me.

The Sex Reciprocator begin to grind me so slow that I felt pleasure enter in to my wetness, rush up my entire body, and exited out my mouth with a sigh from Danny's love-power.

Pumping me again and whispering in my ear "How you just gonna jump on top of me then roll off...huh? And you can't take that shit back because I felt what need."

I was so pissed off at myself, but it didn't last long because I had my left leg slid up and opened with the Orgasm-Seeker grinding deeper into my 'She' with a slow firm steady motion.

Rolling off me, looking me square in my eyes and commanding, "Open your legs and touch my pussy for me."

Ooh Ladies, I couldn't help but be an obedient sex participant.

When I slid my hand into my thong, my slit was nice-nasty wet. I moaned at the first stoke. Paining my sex agony with more pillow talk, "Let Daddy talk you through your release."

My legs where spread about shoulder length apart, and I eagerly followed my orgasm facilitator's instructions.

"I want you to tighten up the muscles in your feet. Now bring it up into your legs. Keep stroking her for me. Let the tension move up to your thighs...mmm. Is she still juicy?"

I could barely get out "Yes" because my body was so tense with an unfamiliar energy churning in a new level of my core.

"Now bring it up here." touching me on the crease between my belly pouch and the tip of my mound.

Keep your legs tight; stroke her until she begins to heat up, (*which actually happened*). Now push your pelvis upward, and think about, when I put my hands on you, how I'm going to make you and 'She' mine.

The Climax Coaxer kissed me on my shoulder blade and instructed, "Keep rubbing her until she burns."

Between Danny whispering sex-sweetness into my ear, my own thoughts, coupled with the heat of the onslaught of my climax--all ignited a pressure that sent me to a parallel state of being.

My precipitator of pleasure calmly said "Let that cat cum for me."

I orgasm'd real hard and extraordinarily long. The energy that it took for me to keep quite because the girls where in the next room, plus hearing the Love-Instructor cuming with me, sent me to a universe that I had not known of before.

Ladies, what made the entire event even more special for me was that I was covered up by the sheet the entire time, so Danny didn't see nor feel my flesh...the mystery of me, was still intact?

It took damn near a complete minute for my breathing to calm down, and that in turned, brought on a quenching sleep.

When I regained consciousness, it was 5:35 a.m. and I felt Danny stroking the side of my face, smelling really good, and saying.

"Baby, come lock the door."

"Huh?"

"I'm going to head out because I don't want your girls to see me here."

Cobwebs still in my brain and sleep still in my eyes, I concurred and made my way out the bed. At the door, I received a warm, soft kiss on the lips.

Opening my eyes and seeing love staring in my face, I said, "And...yes."

Now looking at me ambiguously, "Umh?"

"Yes, I will be your girlfriend."

Viewing joy then seeing that eleven year grin on Danny's face, but I was swooped up and kissed like a woman who is loved.

"I'm going to be calling you all throughout the day. Girl, don't play with me and not pick up your phone!"

In a submissive tone, I responded "Yes Danny."

I locked the door and went back to bed.

Should I... Shouldn't I

Ladies, it's a beautiful thing when he does exactly what he says he's going to do? But when the 'Remember' in you, is standing firm and not wanting take any shorts, do you ignore it and roll over like a kitten, or do you stand defiant like a Wild-Cat?

The entire day, I received calls from my boyfriend.

Call one, "Hey sexy lady, I left my phone at your house, is it alright if I stop by tomorrow and get it?"

"You can stop by any time…sexy right back at you."

Call two, "Hey, just calling to check in." Call three, "Are you going to be home tomorrow around 2 o'clock…I'm having something delivered to you? I'm going to call you right back." Call five, "I'm heading into a meeting, I just want to tell you I Love You."

Call six, seeing the caller ID, I was amazed because I really didn't believe that I would be receiving that many calls.

Come on Ladies, you know how it is when they say, "I'm going to call you." And you get one call late in the day, or you have to call him."

But not with Danny, "Why do you sound so surprised? When I tell you that I'm going to do something, Believe it. End of story!"

My heart coo'd at the thought, the intention, and the attention.

And the last call, "How was your day? Do you need anything? Keep 'Her' warm for me. Have sweet dreams, baby."

I couldn't wait for Saturday to come. I didn't know if I was more excited about seeing Danny, or looking forward to my friend Cree coming from California visiting for the weekend.

I met Cree while I was a consultant for a beauty, nutrition, and health company. She worked at their corporate office in Orange County, California, and was instrumental in my knowledge of the business. I don't know how we began our friendship, but it has definitely developed into a sister-ship.

Cree is 31 years old. She's light caramel, about 5'2", 113 pounds, and has a Beyounce/J-Lo booty. She has striking eyes, but it is her personality, her faith in God, her gangstah, and her loyalty to her friends that makes her more than likeable.

Saturday morning a little past eight o'clock, my door bell was ringing off the hook. To my surprise, she was not alone, so all the girl time I had previously planned for us was out the window.

The tête-à-tête interrupter was her boy toy—Vance. Cree was a bit freaked out because baby-boy was 24 years old. Being that young, Cree felt that she was robbing the cradle. Personally, I thought it was good fit for her because her motus operandi is much older men than herself. The little chocolate cutie was manner-able, charming, kept me laughing, and was a puppy-in-heat for Cree.

Time was literally flying by because we were having just that much fun laughing, talking, and listening to music, in addition to Cree and I dancing about, in the living room.

Saturday afternoon around half pass four, I get a call from Danny.

"Hey sexy"

"Ooh, are you okay?"

"I'm alright."

"You sound awful."

"I've got a headache—I'll be fine. Practice will be over soon, I'll be to you around 6:15, 6:30."

"Mmm, goodie, I look forward to seeing you."

"Toomey is with me, is that okay?"

I was trying to think of some kind of excuse because that idiot was the last person that I wanted to see; let alone come to my home. Not quick enough on my feet, Toomey yelled into the phone.

"Thanks Q for letting me come and visit."

I was stuck, and felt it inappropriate to say anything otherwise. Besides I was going to see my baby.

"Do you need anything? Okay, then I'll see you soon sexy."

At that point, Cree and I had been drinking Chi-Chi's --a blended drink made with pineapple juice, cream de coco, ice, and vodka. Vance was downing Heinekens and watching us. By the time Danny and Toomey arrived, I had finished two glasses and was nursing the third --needless to say...I was feeling pretty damn good!

When I swung the door opened, Danny scooped me up with one arm, drew me close, said "How's my baby doing?", and then authoritatively bit me on my neck. The gesture was so unexpected, fast, and full that my mind cooed at the surprise and pleasure, (*It felt like Danny was telling me...Daddy's home, but I can only give you a little bit because we have company*).

My mouth wanted to be invaded and my body wanted more of everything. I was pissed off because I leaned in to get some sugar; instead, all I got was a corny but nice kiss on my forehead, as that knowing-bastard walked into my house.

Ladies, the rejected she-monster in me instantly surfaced, with fangs out-- ready to draw blood!

My mind was reeling as Toomey walked through the door, greeting me.

"Hello Ugly, how you doing?"

"Exceptionally well—liver lips, thank you for asking. How's life on the turkey buzzard farm?"

I hadn't forgotten about our last exchange, I instantly acknowledged the loser's previous status, and I was more than ready for round two.

Danny turned around, looking at us both and chastised, "Don't Start!"

Toomey and I simultaneously pointed at each other as the initiating culprit, as we were going back and forth.

"She started it."

"No you started with me first."

Danny grabbed my hand, directed me towards my bedroom, shut the door behind us, pulled me extremely close and said, "Hey Sexy Lady. I've been looking forward to this moment ever since I left here the other day."

Ladies, I was purring and tingling on the inside, yet I was also scheming at how to get payback for being rejected.

Behind closed doors looking up into Danny's eyes and realizing just how sick my baby was feeling. The she-bitch in me melted down into the floor.

"Baby, Oh God, you looked terrible. Bend down…let me feel your forehead. You have a fever" then it hit me. It was from Danny's getting caught out in the rain…coming to see me, and I honestly felt bad.

As I was sharing my thoughts, I was interrupted.

"Stop! It could have been seventeen inches of snow on the ground and blizzard conditions; I would have walked the same distance even longer if I had to."

Puzzled I asked…same distance? "Didn't you park in the garage?"

"No baby. I forgot to tell you…there was police activity in your complex that night; about fifteen cop cars, a patty wagon, and a police unit command post set up by the school.

When I called you, I was by the Fire House on Sedgwick Avenue. It wasn't until after I hung up with you that I found out that the River Park Towers was blocked completely off. The closest parking space I could find was over there by Bronx Community College."

I was floored because that was about fifteen to twenty minutes walking distance.

"To have what I have now… the rain, this cold…means nothing to me. Ever since Thursday night, I've been able to breath. That's what you do to me Quincee-Jane Catfire."

My heart pounding and speechless, I pulled myself together real quick and said "I want you to get better."

"I will. I'm not going into the office until Wednesday or Thursday, so that I can shake this bug off completely. And sexy lady, that's why I didn't kiss you when I came through the door; I don't want you getting sick."

I felt like pure baby do-do after thinking all those negative thoughts because I didn't get my way.

"I'll bring you some homemade chicken noodle soup while you're recuperating in bed."

"You would do that for me?"

"You've been such a good boy, you have no idea what I have planned for you", I said as my eyes seared through to the soul of the eyes that I was looking into mine.

The gaze I received in return heated my ass up all over again. I stood up on my tippy toes getting ready to do something erotic to Danny, but was interrupted by the creep mongrel.

"Yo Q, can I get something to drink in this house? What kind of hostess are you anyway? You have company out here and you in the bedroom doing God only knows what with Dan?"

The barrage of questions was asked, while banging way too loud on my bedroom door.

Dropping my head shaking it from side to side wanting to scream, I looked into Danny's eyes, and announced, "That's YOUR friend!"

"Quincee, be good!"

Snapping at the one I cared for, "I'm always good," then snatching myself away from being held, turning to the door, and flinging it open inquiring "Jealous because you don't have a woman up close, invading YOUR personal space?"

Towering in front of me, the pain in my ass continued in on me, "Damn woman...get on your game. You're always bragging about what you're good at. What happened?"

Steam spewing out of me ears.

"I have water, milk, coffee, tea, soda, or liquor. WHAT DO YOU WANT?"

Acting like nothing was said to offend me, "We're a little testy....aren't we?"

"Fuck you Toomey" I growled as I pushed my way passed the insolent ass and headed for the kitchen. Refusing to give anything more than I had to, I reached in the cupboard to grab a foam cup then moved to the freezer.

By that time, I saw and heard Danny in the living room talking to Cree and Vance.

"Nice to meet you; how long will you be in City?"

After answering, Cree commented "I finally get to meet Sir Danny. I've heard a lot about you!"

"I hope it was all good."

"Let's just say, you make my friend very, very happy. Thank you for that."

Smiling shyly and appreciatively, my baby responded "It's my responsibility to keep her happy. It's nice to know that I'm on my job."

Later that evening when Cree and I had a chance to talk, she threatened me, "Bitch, if you fuck shit up with that fine mother fuckah, I'm flying back to New York and personally kicking your ass!

Still feeling hate and discontent, I snarled "HERE!" shoving the cup so hard towards Toomey that ice chips and water fell on the both of us, the countertop, and the floor.

"What the fu...? There is something wrong with you. You're just an ornery hag!"

"What did you call me?"

"You heard me!"

"How dare you try to insult me, in my own house, you cantankerous ass-lick!"

I don't know how Danny just appeared in between the two of us. Looking directly into my eyes with a stern frown and commanding Toomey "Get your shit, we're leaving."

Toomey shot back "With pleasure!" then headed toward the door.

Danny went into the living room and said good-by to Cree and Vance. Kissing Cree's hand and shaking Vance's.

"When Quincee and I get out to California, we'll definitely get together with you two. Have a safe flight home."

Back in the kitchen and looking down at me, but with a much softer expression and in a calm tone, my aggravated sick prince said while holding me close, "You need to calm your fire. I'll call you when I get in the house", then giving me another fatherly kiss on my forehead, and exited my apartment.

Feeling hurt, sad, and told-off…there was nothing left for me to do; but, follow their asses out into the hallway, (*I know…I know…I know. I should have kept my ass in the house!*).

I was ecstatic that they were still waiting for an elevator. Walking up to the both of them, I started out nice.

"Did you have to wait long coming up?"

"What's it to you? Aren't you supposed to be in the house hosting with the most-ing?"

I ignored the jerk, but obviously big-foot was also in the mood for a toe-to-toe verbal throw down.

"Oh, now you're deaf and dumb, but a few minutes ago you were full of lip. I guess you were just showing off for your friends."

Still looking at the dipstick with a blank expression on my face, I remained silent.

"You're standing there acting holier than thou, but you're not. You're no better than I am!"

At that point, I had heard enough and terminated the harangue onslaught. Cognizant as to not make a scene on my floor because I am the floor captain, I walked up on Toomey and unloaded my chest.

"I am nothing like you. You are an unwanted lonely miserable individual. I don't know who did what to damage you, but your psyche is scarred and you are unkind, unlikable, and un-liked.

Your malfeasant nature is directly opposite of me, my spirit, my like of people, my concern for humanity…I could go on and on. So don't compare me to the likes of you.

You are so busy being nasty to people that you don't even know when someone has you back."

Coldly retorting, "Oh, so now you're my saving grace, my guardian angel...yeah right!" and then the skinny bastard laughed in my face.

Adamant to get my point across, I juicily gutted out "Remember Tywanna?"...then the elevator door opened.

As Danny was about to get on, Toomey commanded "Let that shit go." Coldness was replaced with borderline curiosity "What about her?"

Still incensed, but marveling at the taste of Toomey's interest, I revealed "Do you remember the Saturday that all of us went to eat, and she got pissed off at you because you, Danny, and Matt cut the night short to watch a game, a fight, whatever it was, and you snap at her then she went to the bathroom?"

"Yeah...and?"

"Well, what you don't know is that when I went into the ladies room, I was in the stall next to her. I overheard her talking on the phone telling someone how you mistreated her.

"That ass whole think it's all about The Toom. The Toom don't play that. You should be happy that you get the chance to hang out with The Toom.

Let's see who's zooming who now. Girl I got the dumb mother fucker's wallet. Put your shit on bitch cuz we goin shoppin...to--night. I'm gonna lock down all these mother fuckin credit cards. The Toom can eat out the crack of my ass. We gonna eat hell-ah good for a while."

"Then I heard them both laughing at you."

Normally, I am not a fan of seeing anyone's feeling get crushed, but that day, I almost came, watching Toomey's chest implode. I continued my story.

"Then she said "Does Quanesha still work at Macy's? Find out if the bitch is working tonight. Cuz if she is, that's our hook-up. All I got to do is throw that hoe a hundred dollars, and we can buy gift cards. I'm going to drain this mother fucker drip dry...word to mother! Alright bitch, I'll call you when I get around the way."

Infuriated at remembering what went down, and at Toomey's contempt towards me, I went on.

"Then she was planning to have your ass setup by somebody named Jugger." I know I struck a truth nerve because Toomey's face went colorless and Danny even responded to the name.

Not caring about their reaction and still looking into Toomey's eyes.

"It was me who stood up in your defense and confronted that bitch. I waited until she came out the stall.

"Umm, you have Toomey's wallet?"

"Girl, you trippin" and she tried to play it off. When she saw that I wasn't backing down, she tried to jump bad.

"I know YOU BETTER GET OUT OF MY FACE WITH THAT SHIT."

"Before the bitch could blink an eye; I had her larynx between my thumb and forefingers. By that time, Cheryl was coming out the stall, I told her to go through Tywanna's bag.

Cheryl turned her pocketbook upside down on the counter, and low and behold there was your wallet AND your pager. Cheryl also pulled out Tywanna's driver's license and called out her address.

Cheryl wrote down all her information. I warned the bitch that, if anything happened to You, Cheryl, or myself that I was sending someone to see her monkey ass. But if everything was cool, she would never hear from me again."

Stumped by Toomey's expression, I felt compelled to say, "If you don't believe me, the next time you see Cheryl; I pray that she makes it out of the hell that she's going through right now; but, you ask her.

I was ready to knock that bitch's lights out for what she had planned for you. Yeah, I know that you and I have a rocky rapport and we're always fighting and shit—but I wasn't going to let you go out like that."

Taking a step closer to that mental-cripple's face and authenticating,

"There was no fucking way I was going to stand by and let some rag-a-fucking-muffin from the street—do you.

I know my job as a friend. It was me who stepped in for you when you didn't have eyes, ears, and knowing on your fuck'n side. And no, I didn't do it because I am your guardian angel; I did it because it was the right fuck'n thing to do, and that's just who I am. I'm loyal to my friends Toomey, and I don't have to go around bragging about how I protect, or stand up for them."

Failing to prevent hurt from poking through, my voice rancor out, "But you don't have to worry about me making that mistake again because have you tell it, I'm just a loud mouth show-off good for nothing liar who deserves only to be disdained by you."

Stunned at my reveal, perplexed by my hurt "Quincee-Jane, I...I didn't...."

Chopping the jack-ass's sentence off, "I know you didn't, and you weren't supposed to. That's how I take care of my business. So FUCK YOU!"

Ready for Toomey to be gone from my sight, I pushed the elevator button, I could tell that the ambiguous weeble-wod wanted to say something, but was hesitant, which was a good thing because right then, I saw myself punching that giant geri-curl beanie-baby dead in the face.

Danny walked to me, hugged and kissed me on the forehead...yet again, which pissed me off yet again, then said "Are you better? I'll call you after I drop Toomey off."

"I'm good; call me when you get home" then the elevator door opened.

Toomey still looking like fig-mo walked passed me, entered the elevator car, waited until Danny was in and commented.

"You need to get in the house because you are showing too much skin."

Even though it was said in an apologetic manner, it wasn't the right time or the right thing to say to me. I was wearing sky-blue patent leather flip-flops, baggy acid washed blue jeans, and a white square-neck daisy duke blouse that had snaps down the front instead of buttons.

The elevator was full of people--mostly men-- and before I realized what I was doing, I grabbed the top edges of my blouse and unsnapped it completely open in one motion, exposing my sky-blue deep cut bra, and cleavage of life.

Hissing out to Toomey "No, this is showing too much skin...Mother Fuckah!!!!" as the elevator door was closing. I was so heated, that I saw myself punching Toomey in the mouth.

Before reaching my apartment, Danny was coming out of the staircase exit. Meeting up with me, grabbing me by my wrist and not letting go until we were back in my bedroom.

I was pinned up on the wall by the door. In a voice that was overflowing with authority, that Fine Dictator said.

"You just can't stop playing me… can you? This is for that bitch in you. Tell her that I'm waiting on her and I have something for her when I see her."

All I could feel was a strong hand pressing down on my chest that was way too close to my throat with enough force that made me not want to move. An even powerful palm lifted up my left thigh, as far as it could go.

Alright ladies, I admit I felt a tiny bit of fear. I'm lying... my ass was scared shitless; but also turned on.

I was messed up because I was being intoxicated by the aroma of cologne, pure alpha maleness, and a growing orgasm churning at the core of my energy, as my crotch was being pumped…ever slow, slow, slowly.

It was so intense-- it seemed like I felt Danny's sexual ambush on my bare pubic flesh. The sensation was so overwhelming that I couldn't even put my thoughts together in linear form. I was trying not to murmur, moan, make no kind of sound at all.

The next thing I heard in my ear was, "Let It Grow!", and when I purred out an "Mmm" that sowing fuckah menacingly whispered in my ear.

"You better not EVER pull that shit again to anybody, anymore, or your ass is mine," while my crotch was still being pumped with a rhythmic torture. My one leg that was still on the floor was wobbly. Sound and words were failing me…I couldn't speak.

Then I heard "Do I make myself clear", being entrenched in my ear.

Just as I began to feel the commencement of my climax, that Orgasm Arouser planted a seed inside me; illuminating in my mind's eye.

"This nut is mine, and it won't be popped until I ease my hard-on in you," then backing away from me, the bastard walked away, and left my house, never looking back at me.

Don't you just hate it when he has full control of your womanliness, and to add insult to injury your body forlorn you for the thought of his touch.

But Ladies, I had something for that fucker….My wildfire. I wasn't' going out like a punk.

The Final Straw

(Men, what is it with them. They bitch and moan when they don't get what they want from us. "You don't talk to me. You don't share your feelings with me." Yet, when we do open up, they take that as a sign of weakness and then they want to show their natural asses. The woman that I love is no exception).

Despite Quincee being sexy, classy, articulate, intelligent and gorgeous, the woman has a vernacular that is every bit of the sailor that she states she will always be. I've had my share of being on the receiving end of her alter ego's tongue annihilation.

Prime example, one night, while there was no communication between us, Twink did some foul shit to her. Toomey and I went to her rescue.

All my efforts meant nothing to Quincee. She cursed me out…in my own got-damn vehicle, while I was driving her ass home to from being stranded in Manhattan, but that wasn't the worst part of her ass being rescued.

Toomey and I ended up going upstairs to her apartment. Everything was going as tense as the entire situation. In and out of her house, and back waiting for the elevator, I thought I was home safe, (*HELL NO! I WASN'T*).

She and Toomey got into a heated exchange, and I was staying out of it because she's a gown ass woman, and the way she'd chopped my ass up; she was on her own!

They had been going at it for a minute. We were on the elevator when she held it up. The both of them up'd their nastiness to street-level—the next thing I know, Quincee rushed Toomey. She was all up in the poor cat's face. I saw my buddy get nervous then did the dumbest thing by putting me in it, "Yo Dan, talk to your girl."

She turned to me… and said some low-blow shit. She didn't curse, she didn't raise her voice, and what stung the most was that she didn't lie about what she was saying.

Before the elevator door was closed, Toomey jump in on my ass.

"See that's your problem you let her get away with bull shit like that. She just Bitch'd the both of our dumb asses. Did you see what she did to me…walking up on me like that. I felt all type of shit running through me."

Right then I knew Quincee threw some of her energy thing on my friend.

"And you standing there, not saying a fucking word."

I was tight but I was going to deal with the situation straight on. "You finished?" even though I knew the answer because Toomey always have something else to say.

"Naw"

"Speak you piece."

"Another problem you have is….her ass is HOT! You know what I'm talking about. And it needs to be tamed.

You're going to fuck around, and somebody else is going to take her right from under your slow ass. You and I both know, you're nose is wide open for her. Too bad I'm your friend because that keeps me out the game from talking to her."

Looking straight into enemy eyes, I let the bastard know "MURDER AND BURY THAT FUCKING THOUGHT!"

(If I had my gun on me, Toomey would have been sucking on metal).

With hands thrown up in the air, like I was a cop or something, "Dan…I'm just saying. You need to check that shit. She's made both of us look like fools and feel like assholes."

I couldn't deny it, my comrade was right. Determined to resolve the estrangement between Quincee and I, what do I go and do? I confess my undying love for her, to her, and I really expected her to behave.

(Men, don't say it because I know how it sounds and I know what you all are thinking. But, come on…You all know how it is, when they have that wild fire in their blood. It's who they are, and we love them more, for it).

That same night driving home after I dropped Toomey's ass off, it hit me, Quincee was just like my mother, and I was going to step into shoes like my father, and tame that cat, in her. Ready for battle with Quincee-Jane Catfire, it didn't take her defiance long to rear its ugly head again.

On top of her game in full bitch mode, the next incident occurred not even 48 hours after she and I mended our broken pieces.

I had gone to pick up my phone that I had left at her place. Toomey was with me and from the sound of her voice; she didn't want my assistant basketball coach tagging along with me. I don't know what it is with them two, when they get together. They act like a 6 and 8 year brother and sister, and this day was no exception. It was so bad that I left her house sooner than I expected or wanted to.

Out waiting for the elevator again, like De'Javo she and Toomey were still going at it. The door opens, Toomey says something smart. Tell me why my girl decides that she's going to open up her blouse.

The move itself—how she did it, was a turn-on. Those titties and cleavage looked sexy as three orgasms that I've been waiting to have from her, (*but you don't do no shit like that*).

Walking up on her ass before she reached her apartment, (*Let's just say...I took care of it. She won't be doing any bullshit like that again!*).

I thought I sat down that cat-bitch in Quincee because we had an understanding of what I wasn't going to accept anymore, but that feline wasn't asleep yet.

Paying a high cost of public humiliation from those who are close to me; I'd put myself in a position to be called a pussy, punk, whipped, sucker, and Toomey's favorite...The Castrated One. The worst part is that all the adjectives fitted my dumb ass. Quincee had let her defiance take hold of her, and she ran with it like a cat in too much heat.

One Friday night around 11:30, Toomey and I had just picked Matt up from the airport and we were back in the city headed to get something to eat.

I was thinking how good it is having my boy home, when Toomey called out "Yo Dan, ain't that Quincee?"

By the time the statement registered, I was out of eyesight of the person, and when I looked in my rearview mirror, all I saw were men who looked like security, standing in the middle of the sidewalk.

I made it my business to find out because up to that point, ever since I put her ass in check, she hadn't taken or returned any of my calls. Halfway through week one, I'd stop calling her because I was tired of chasing her ass, (*she wasn't going anywhere*). As long as I spoke to her at least once a week I was good.

This night was in week three and I admit it, I was anxious, but I hid it from the fellas because I was already a bitch in their eyes, when it comes to Quincee.

I dialed her phone, and got her voicemail. Then I tried my old cell number. I never got back my phone from her; the night she left my ass at the club; but, I've continued to pay the bill.

(Fuck that. I don't want to hear what you got to say. I was trying to make her mine again....so be it!).

She picked up on the third ring.

"Hi"

I love the way she answers the phone…it turns me on every time I hear her.

"Hey, it's me Danny."

"I still know your voice."

"That's good to know. What are you doing sexy lady?"

She went on to tell me that she was at a club, and that she was outside because it was hot inside.

Good, then it was her. I translated her comment to mean that the men were on her ass.

"How are you planning to get home?"

"I'm up for options. Do you have any suggestions?"

She was feeling herself and fucking with me, and I have to admit, I was feeling her response.

By time the conversation ended, I was parked and getting out of my truck. Walking over to her, two out of three men were standing in front of her, actually blocking me from her.

As if on cue, I heard and saw out of the corner of my right eye, my boys were out the truck…and ready for…whatever.

I thought (*WHAT THE FUCK…she has lost her got-damn mind. Now you're pulling my boys into your shit*).

That was the final straw. Something in me just snapped. I felt a calm take over me, and the voice in my head said (*NOW!*).

The one thing she did right though was to set their asses straight.

"That's my baby", and they backed the fuck up off me.

Looking at my expression, walking up to me, and kissing me on the cheek, she offered, "I'm sorry about that baby."

Grabbing her by her damn wrist and never acknowledging her apology, I told her ass "Let's go".

"Just a minute baby, I'm here with a friend, and I have to make sure that she gets into a cab before I leave."

Watching her ass disappear back in the club, bouncer number one approaches me.

"Man, I apologize. I was just looking out for her. When she first walked outside, she had heads turning. Niggahs going in the club, coming out of the club, ones just passing by on the street where all up on yo shit."

By that time bouncer number two had ended his phone conversation, and joined in.

"I'm with my partner here."

"Man...no disrespect, but umm you got a wild one on your hands...and she's fine like that too...GOOD LUCK, BRAH!"

"I appreciate that...good looking out."

I shook their hands, gave them my card and fifty dollars apiece. They took my money with big ass smiles on their faces. Bouncer number two was quick to say "It was all my pleasure."

I ignored the fool's comment.

(Men, check this out. If Quincee goes back to that spot, or wherever they are bouncing at, they will watch her for me, and will have no problem snitching on her ass).

After waiting another fifteen minutes or so, Quincee and her friend came out the club. She introduced us.

Glo is about 5'5" with velvet dark chocolate skin and exceptionally white teeth. Her hair was in a tight ponytail that reached to her waist and she had bangs. The black jeans that were cut real low looked good with her gold halter top. She was carrying flat shoes in her hand, *(It looked strange to me because I thought when females go bare-footed it's because their shoes are too high...umh--what do I know?).*

I have to admit, Quincee's friend looked damn good, but I was ready for her to be on her way. While she was out in the street trying to hail a cab, I pulled Quincee to curbside to speak to her in private.

"Are you alright?"

Sarcastically responding, "Why wouldn't I be?"

She was adding more fuel to an already five alarm fire.

I manned up, and walked away from her. By the time I got back into my car, I watched Quincee walk over to bouncer number two, and give him the blazer she was wearing. When the jacket came off her back, the three of us, in the car, in perfect sync, howled out "D-A-M-N!!!"

This brick shit house had on hip-waist dark blue jeans, a mustard yellow see-all-the-way-through long sleeved top that showed off the bright bra she was wearing. The triple D's hugged the bra every which way but loose; and they were calling my name. I had to hold my composure to keep from licking my lips.

Picking up my bottom lip to meet the rest of my mouth, I got back out of my vehicle because she did not need to be standing there without me.

Watching me walk towards her she met me half way and we ended up standing by the hood of my truck. She stood there purring sex appeal. I struck up a conversation.

"How has life been treating you?"

Being downright conceited, with her hands on her hips, an elitist expression, and in a nasty low voice, she remarked.

"Life has been treating me very well, thank you for asking. So you want to be one of my options of getting me home tonight?"

I was caught off guard with the question, and pissed the fuck off by her attitude.

Reading my posture, and before I could speak, she retorted "You have something on your chest? Speak up....WHAT?"

She waited a millimeter of a second then egotistical added, "I thought not!?", and then she turned and walked away from me.

Once more, she had embarrassment my ass. The car windows were down and I know Matt and Toomey heard the entire conversation. Dumb-founded and a prisoner of my own thoughts (*Dad, I don't know whether to thank you or curse you for making me the gentleman that I am... because right about now, Quincee needs to have hands put on her*).

There was nothing left for me to do except get my yellow ass back into the car. Smoke steaming out both ears from my thoughts and not looking forward to facing my boys, I sat down in the driver's seat and didn't open my mouth.

I felt Matt's sympathy. My dog looked embarrassed for me, gave me an encouraging nod then turned and gazed out the window, (*I felt like raw shit*).

Toomey on the other hand, I could see—was ready to rip me a new asshole; going straight for the kill.

"What the fuck is wrong with you? How long are you going to let that she-monster make a complete punk out of you? Where the fuck are your balls?

It's time for you to tax that ass because it's well over hot, and set that bitch straight. She got you walking around like a got-damn puppy on a string. Naw, I take that back. You're acting like a fucking kitten.

Your shit is so whipped; if she tells you to jump, you don't even have to ask because your castrated ass already knows how high, where and when to jump... damn niggah!"

Little did either of my partners know that a plan had already been set in motion? Just then Quincee walked up to the car, waved to her friend as her cab was passing, and got into my truck.

(Men, The plan had commenced).

I decided that her ass would be staying at my place, instead of taking her home, but I had to make a quick stop first. I didn't say anything. I drove to Matt's place and parked the car. On cue my dawg was out and walking beside me, and we disappeared into the apartment building.

Ten minutes later we were walking back out and I handed Quincee a T-shirt from out of my bag in the trunk. I wanted her to say something smart; but she took it and put it on.

The next stop was my place. My mind everywhere; between the bouncers, what she was wearing, her stink ass attitude, and her absolute disrespect for me... all the makings of a perfect recipe for what was about to come.

I could tell that she was tipsy because she was the only one talking, and she wasn't aware of it, or that I had her ass was riding in the back seat.

We arrived at my spot; I parked the car, got out and went straight to open up the door where she was sitting. I grabbed her by her wrist, and yanked her ass out of my vehicle.

Stumbling out, "Baby wait, I have to put my shoe back on."

I didn't give a damn about anything she had to say and when she realized that I wasn't going to let her go, or give her time to do shit, she hobbled out the car.

Turning back and looking inside, she asked Toomey, "Bring my pocketbook, please."

Before she could get her request in, I already had her ass on the curb, walking toward the house, bypassing the group of college students that were walking pass us.

From her response, I could tell that she was coming back to sober-land. I heard embarrassment in her voice because all eyes were on her being dragged up my walkway.

"Baby, I only have one shoe on. You're keeping me off balance."

Ignoring her complaints; never missing a step, and keeping her in tow, my thoughts were spewing. Walking us in the house, and up the stairs, I didn't even wait for Matt and Toomey to come in behind us, in order to close the door...I left the mother fucka opened. They were only about six steps behind us, so, if Quincee happened to tripped and fall, they would be there to catch her ass.

At the top of the stairs, I headed straight to the living room. Putting my bag down on the side table, I began feeling for the object that I wanted. By that time, Matt and Toomey were in the room with us, Quincee looked nervous as shit, (and rightfully so).

After I had what I needed in my hand, I let her arm go, turned around, and pulled her to meet my face and said "You have mother fucka's protecting you from ME!"

Grabbing her by the arm again as I was sitting down in the chair, I pulled her across my lap.

She called herself, yelling at me "WHAT ARE YOU DOING?"

With all the force that I had, I POPPED that ass with my paddle.

Toomey jumped up and down like a got-damn fool, "Oh Shit!...a-a-a-a-ah" , and started laughing and clapping. Matt just stood there looking shocked.

Quincee screamed out in pain, as she tried to lift her torso up, but I pushed her back down, and popped her ass again. She attempted covering her ass with her hand.

"Move your hand." She didn't.

"Move your hand or either your hand or some fingers are going to get hurt."

When she moved her hand, I popped that ass a couple of times more. "This is for all the shit that I've been putting up with, from you"....POP...POP.

"Who the fuck do you think you are?"...POP...POP...POP.

She was hollering and crying. "SHUT THE FUCK UP! I hope you got your shit off because AS OF NOW...Your Party Is Officially, the fuck OVER!"...POP...POP...**POP!**

That's when Matt came over and grabbed hold of the paddle, as my arm was extended in the air ready to connect with Quincee's ass, again.

(Men, I was seeing red. That cat was all mines, and it was in the process of being tamed).

Standing up, I let her fall to the floor. Taking a deep breath, turning around and picking her ass up by the back of my shirt she was wearing. Standing in front of me, I grabbed her by the neck of the shirt, and twisted my hand around until there was no slack between my hand and her neck. Bending down nose to nose with her, I barked at her.

"Do you want to leave out of my life… because you can get the fuck out right now! No harm. No foul!" while pointing in the direction of the doorway, with my free hand, not giving a good got-damn if she wanted to head for the hills.

Sniffling with big bubba tears streaming down her face, and snot dripping down to her top lip, I just barely heard.

"N…N…No."

I twisted the shirt a little tighter around her neck, and brought her to my eye level, to the point that she was on her tip toes, and I unpleasantly informed her, "YOU WILL RESPECT ME!"

Seeing fear and defeat in her eyes, she replied.

"Y…Y…Yes."

I let her go, and instructed the fallen cat, "Take your ass in the room."

After she was out of my grip, she turned to walk toward the bedroom, and shouted back "I'M NOT YOUR FRIEND",

"I don't give a damn. Right about now…I'm not liking you either", while walking behind her, but heading to the bathroom in the opposite direction.

Splashing some water on my face, and regaining my composure from the battle that needed to be had, the weight of the world was lifted of my shoulders.

(Men, I felt my pride rising from the ashes like a phoenix, my self-esteem stiffening my backbone, and my masculinity rebounding from the Defiant She-Bitch's crippling grip. It felt good to have me back. All my brothers in stupid love right now, make it happen for yourself).

She needed some time to sulk from embarrassment; nurse a sore ass, plus she needed to think about how she will be treating me from that point forward.

Feeling brand new, I remembered my earlier plans, and decided to head out despite the hour, and leaving Quincee in the house alone.

Looking in the mirror, realizing that I had to change my shirt because Quincee wrinkled it while on my lap; I put on a black Brooks Brother shirt to match my black slacks, and suede loafers. I splashed on some more Sung. Shit always happens whenever I wear that cologne, but I was feeling myself, and I was ready for anything.

Making a quick stop in the dining room, I got the bottle of Karpatske Brandy Special from the liquor cabinet. It is a Slovak brandy that is aged in two phases for eight years, in oak wood. I also picked out three El Rey Del Mundo 1848 Cuban cigars from their holding case (*Thanks Pop for turning me on to the finer things in life*).

Standing in the living room holding the items up in my hands, before asking my boys to join me for a drink and cigar, Toomey walked up on me, patting me on my back—lauding and grinning like a proud father, "Welcome back, my niggah!"

Matt just looked at me, and gave a nod of approval, (*I was feeling damn good*).

I held up the items in my hands, no more was needed to be said. After our brandy sniffers were filled, and cigars lit; Toomey, of course had something to say.

"Yo Dan, I know I said some rough shit back in the car... that's only because I felt so bad for your pitiful ass. But right now... I'm so happy that I could almost cry. I had given up all hope on you, but the way you waxed that ass in here tonight...You The Head Niggah In Charge."

With a somber expression, and tone of a southern Baptist Preacher presiding over a funeral, that crazy ass fool eulogized.

"We are gathered here t-o-n-i-g-h-t... to say good,b-y-e to an un-w...a...n...t.ed; yet be...l...o...v...ed friend—The Castrated One. Let that mother fuckah rest in peace and never to return...here here!"

"Here, here" with a big ass smile on my face, I agreed.

Sitting for a bit talking, drinking, smoking and relishing my rebirth, I asked the fellas "Yall ready to go?"

Both of them looking puzzled. It dawned on me that they probably thought that I wanted them to leave. Then I rephrased the question.

"Do yall still want to go out because I'm starving?"

Toomey was the first to speak, "Shit yeah." The second time that night, I caught my boy off-guard. Matt asked, "What about Quincee-Jane?"

"What about her?"

"Enough said."

Before rolling out the house, I did go back to my room to let Quincee know that I was heading out. I turned the doorknob, and it was locked. I had to talk through the door.

"Quince, I'm leaving out. If you need me, just call me."

I placed my hand on the door because I really wanted to touch her, to let her know that everything was alright with us.

(No men, that's not the punk resurfacing—it's my raw love that I'm not afraid to show).

I turned and headed to meet my boys downstairs.

Tying Up Loose Ends

*(Men, you know the old adage, "When it rains, it pours."
Normally the beneficiary of that saying is a victim of some sort. For
me, I was in resurrection mode and was ready for hurricane winds
to blow...and they did!).*

Saturday
October 29, 2005
Manhattan, 1:40 a.m.

Walking out my front door, the early morning air had a chill to it,
but I didn't care. The three of us laughed and talked all through
diner. Filling our stomachs with steak, potatoes, and salad—me;
shrimp and rice pilaf—Matt; and eggs benedict and grits—Toomey.

I was in the mood to keep my flow going and I put the
suggestion on the table.

Toomey recommended, "How about hitting up a club?"

I offered my opinion, "Anywhere but Snoozes. Look what
happen to my ass the last time I was there."

Toomey look baffled, and said "What? I had a damn good time
that night—Miss Talaya, Miss Talaya—the yellow cutie. Truth be
told, I ain't never had a woman who put me in my place before;
making me want to change my game."

Trying hard not to feel an impact from that night, I looked at my
friend and said, "That's right...you did do a disappearing act that
night." Then I told the Ma'Haundra story.

"Shit man, that's fucked up...No wonder why Quincee was
acting like a bitch. I'd been mad at your ass too."

Matt shot Toomey a grimace.

Toomey shot back an 'I-don't-care' look, saying "What?"

Feeling good that Matt, now considers Quincee a friend, after
the Cheryl incident. That's why I wasn't surprised when my boy
grabbed the paddle out of my hand when I was wailing on Quincee's
backside.

Changing the subject, Toomey suggested an after hour spot, up
in Harlem. We all agreed, finished our meals, and headed out.

The club had a good size crowd at 3:20 in the morning. Walking in, the bar is on the left side with a mirror along the entire length of the bar. The right side of the space is one long cushioned bench. Forward of there is the table and chair section, and forward of that is an opened room dance area. The DJ's booth was suspended on a platform at the far side of the room, and the speakers were positioned in all four corners of the dance floor.

The music was jumping to Lil John was screaming, "*Get Low...Get Low...Get Low.*" It seemed like all the hot good looking asses were out that night (*minus one – My baby)*.

We ordered drinks and walked around a bit. Toomey disappeared on us as usual. Matt and I decided to check out the lower level. Downstairs had the coat check room, restrooms, a game room that had an impressive pool table and a hidden nook where we saw couples slipping into, to do their thing.

Matt and I decided to wait for a game of pool. In the meantime, my eyes had a very good time, just looking at the scenery. There were some of every color, shape, size and race—yellow, dark chocolate, Black, Spanish, Jamaican, Asian. Six honies had offered Matt and I conversation, drinks, and phone numbers.

While I was playing a shot on the pool table female number seven approached Matt. She was light skin and stacked in all the right places. Stating her position up front with her hand on her hip, looking like she was undressing my brother in her mind, "You have the look that I want to know better, and you look like you can handle two."

Matt shot them that smile that girls and women have been cooing over for decades then went on to say.

"Thank you for the compliment, I am truly honored that two beautiful women such as yourselves would even consider having me."

They were both blushing and gawking, and probably cumming on themselves. Watching them get their panties charmed, (*if they were wearing any*), Slick continued "But I have to decline your offer because I'm spoken for."

All I could do was laugh on the inside when they began to pout, and female number one said, "Well if she ever decides not to give you what you want or need—give me a call", and handed Matt a slip of paper.

Female number two—a Spanish cookie, with over-size breast, too little material covering them, and an attitude that said she was ready to get her freak on. She looked Matt up and down and asked, "Are you sure you're not single—even just for tonight?"

"Yes, I'm sure."

"Damn!"

She placed her business card on the pool table, licked her lips then they both walked away.

Matt picked up the card while she was still standing there, and when they were out of sight, handed the card to me. That's something we've been doing for years.

It all started when we were in our middle twenties, and I called myself being in love with a woman named Tameka. It was also back in the day when I didn't turn down any offered ass. One particular incident when she busted me with several numbers in my wallet, which happen more often than I care to think about.

You see, Tameka is one of those female's that searched through all my shit—my house phone, my car, my pockets, my cell phone, (*It was unbelievable how she could always find out my code to unlock my phone*). Usually when she confronted me, I would make up some lame ass lie, we'd fight, I'd let her get as nasty as she wanted with me in make-up sex, and everything would be fine, until the next time I got busted.

But the last time it happened, she just up and left my ass. It wasn't until then that I realized that I loved her, but by then it was too late. So, I went to Matt sulking about what had happen. That's when my brother came up with the perfect idea.

"Okay Dan, here's what you do from now on, when you get numbers, make sure that the female sees you taking it, but then you give it to you me. I'll hold on to it for you, or get rid of it for you. Either way your hands are clean because on one hand whoever you're with won't find the number and bust your dumb ass, and if you meet up with a female that has given you her number, you can honestly tell her that you have it in a safe place, (*My boy is a genius*).

(Men, if you plan to do this, you have to be able to trust your partner in crime because it has the potential to go all the way wrong. Like your partner ends up liking your girl and you get assed out, or he may even want to check out the phone number for himself. Be careful to know your people).

The plan has been in motion ever since. But this time, Matt handed me ripped up paper. After we finished our game, we went back upstairs.

As soon as we got to the top of the stairs, we saw Toomey talking with a woman, who actually looked to be interested in the conversation, (*It's about damn time*). To be frankly honest, I was "Oh shit" surprised, but genuinely happy for my friend.

There must have been something in the air that night because when Toomey joined us at the bar, there were no comments, or sarcastic remarks about how females are just to be fucked, or how stupid they all are. I was impressed because "The Toom" was actually giving off the impression of a smooth operator.

We had been sitting and drinking for about half hour or so, and in between that time we had several offers to dance, I wasn't in the mood; Matt isn't a dancer; but Toomey was all over the dance floor, and the cat can move.

Toomey came back from dancing the last time, and the three of us were sitting, chilling and enjoying ourselves, but decided that we would finish our drinks and head home, when all of a sudden I heard a voice.

"Hello Danny."

Matt was to my right, and Toomey was on the left. When I turned around, I saw Ma'Haundra standing behind me with a smug grin on her face like 'okay, I'm here now.'

She looked at Matt and knew better than to say anything. Matt despised her, for all the pain she had put me through, and for trying to break up the bond between the two of us, while she and I were together.

She moved to stand on the other side of me. The entire fool in Toomey came out, "Don't even think about it. I'm not giving up my seat for you", and looked in her face, as if to say 'you crazy bitch.'

Seeing that neither one of them were going to cut her any slack, I turned around on the barstool to face her.

She started the conversation.

"So how are you doing? You are looking good…as usual."

"Thank you, and you are looking well also." I said.

"So tell me Danny, what are you up these days? And why haven't you returned any of my calls?"

I was not feeling her, or her questions, but I replied, "Well, the last time I saw you, you introduced me to your "new love" if I remember your words correctly. So there's really no need for me to call you, or interrupt what you have going."

She smiled, bit her lip and said, "Yes, you're right, but ever since I saw you that night, you have been on my mind. Anyway it didn't work out, I'm single again."

I picked up the bottle of Heineken that I had been nursing, by my two forefingers, and took a swig, as she went on.

"So when am I going to see you?", and placed her right hand on my upper thigh.

Matt kept looking forward into the mirror, Toomey looked down at her hand on my leg like she had lost her mind then turned to look towards the door.

I let her hand rest on my leg for about ten seconds then I removed it and told her "I'm seeing somebody."

She stepped back. I could see that she was startled, but I didn't know if it was because I removed her hand from my leg, or because I told her that I was seeing someone.

Ma'Haundra was not use to not getting her way with me. That was one of the problems with our relationship. I could never say no to her, and she never had any limits on what she asked of me, or wanted from me.

"Oh, is it that little dark skinned female that was totally intimidated by me the last time I saw you?"

I was heated like a mother fucka, at her condescension. I felt the same heat rise in my blood as did earlier with Quincee's antics. I replied.

"Yes, as a matter of fact it is" then I turned back around to face the bar.

Filled with disgust, she said, "Oh really, well where is she? I don't see her."

Never turning around to face her, I just tilted my head in her direction and calmly informed my ex.

"She's at home, where she belongs…in my bed… waiting for me!"

Ma'Haundra was noticeably taken aback, and did not recover as quickly as she normally does.

Matt just smiled while still looking forward and Toomey burst out laughing.

By that time Ma'Haundra was livid, and spewed "That bitch doesn't have anything on m…" She tried to stop herself, but it was too late.

Quincee was on my brain, and I swear to God the scent of her deflated defiance was all in my nostrils, my throat, and working its way down. It was at that moment I knew that Ma'Haundra will never have any place in my life….ever!

Through the mirror behind the bar I saw her step back and try to recover from her oops, and collect her thoughts. She smoothed out her eyebrows, and the make-believe wrinkles on her pant legs. She took a deep breath and walked up to me, placed her hands on my upper back.

She always had a thing for my back. I was blessed with a good body structure, and the gym does the rest.

Attempting to vindicate her slipup, "Look Danny, I apologize about my outburst", moving close enough to me to feel her nipples leaning on my back, and whispering in my ear.

"Do you accept my apology?"

Finishing the last sip of my beer, feeling indifferent at her presence and wanting to be all up in Quincee's everything, I let Ma'Haundra know.

"Your apology is not accepted and lean back up off me."

She stammered back in disbelief, and murmured "Uh"

Turning towards her again, "There is nothing left between you and me. YOU made that decision when I found you in bed with dude. Now I'm solidifying that for you. I'm in love with someone else. One thing that you can count on lacking the rest of your life…is me."

Turning to my boys, asking if they were ready to go, "Toomey said let's roll, and Matt was already off the barstool.

In the car, the mood was good. Toomey wanted to get dropped off at Grant Projects that was just a few blocks away and re-lived the whole Ma'Haundra scene the entire ride.

In the car by ourelves, Matt asked if I was okay.

"Yeah man, I'm good—actually… real good!"

"Are you sure", looking at me trying to read if I was telling the truth.

"Yeah, I'm positive."

The rest of the way downtown, I brought Matt up to date with what's been going on with the business, with Quincee and me, and Matt filling me in on Cheryl's progress. Pulling up to the front of Matt's building both of us just sat in silence. My brother opened up the car door turned to me and said "If you need to talk, just call me. If you can't get into your room, I guess you will be sleeping your women-paddling ass on the couch."

I laughed and said "Really man, I'm fine. But I will, if I do" and "I'm Not Sleeping On the Got-Damn Couch Tonight!"

Starting my truck, I was on my way home, heading to see the woman who had both my heads attention.

When I first got in the house, I sat down in the living room, in the dark to digest the past several hours. I was reeling in what seemed to be a surreal evening.

First seeing Matt, then what had taken place with Quincee, and last with Ma'Haundra. All in all, everything was right; my life had come back to me. I sat in my lazy-boy chair and relished for a little while longer. I looked at my watch and realized the time – it was ten minutes to six.

It was late, I was tired, and I wanted to feel Quincee's body next to me, so I headed to the bedroom. Just as my room door came into view, I remembered that she had locked me out.

Thinking out loud, "Damn where the hell did I put the key?" Calming down from being pissed off with myself because…shit I'd never been locked out of my own got-damn room before.

(*Women have always tried to get me to bring them into my room; yet, this woman gets in, and locks my ass out*).

I turned the knob, "Yes!" It was open", I smiled to myself.

Walking in and seeing her in my bed with only a thong on made my heart feel damn good. She was lying in the "H" position with a makeshift compress on her behind. It was a plastic bag with water in it. I assumed that the heat from her ass had melted the ice.

I tip-toed a little closer; I could see that her eyes were still puffy from crying. She was sleeping peacefully looking bruised and hurt and beautiful.

Watching her, I thought to myself (*All I want to do is take care of her*). So I tiptoed toward the bathroom.

(*Men, I tell you, I was on some new shit. I have never tiptoed in my own house before…but, it's all good*).

I ran warm water, making sure not to have it too hot to irritate0 her behind. I bordered the entire room with lavender candles to soothe her senses. I lined the Egyptian marble floor with white rose pedals, from the arrangement on the dining room table, as a symbol of peace and to soothe her heart because I know she still had to be pissed off at me. I pulled a new robe out of the linen closet, and placed it beside mine on the wall hook. Turning the Jacuzzi off after it was filled up half way; I inspected the room to make sure everything was to my liking. I stripped down to my fitted boxes then headed back into the bedroom.

As soon as I leaned down on the bed, she stirred.

"Mmmm!"

It sounded like music to my ears. I gently took her hand in mine and whispered *"Quincee,"* as I kissed the inside of her fingers that I had threaten just hours before.

Turning her head towards me, and in the sexiest, yet small voice she said "Hi"

I whispered, "Come with me", and she did, without hesitation.

I helped her off the bed, and as we were walking across the threshold of the bathroom, I saw her wince in pain—my heart skipped a beat of pleasure, but she didn't make any complaints. In the bathroom, she stopped to soak in the sights and smells that I had set up for her. She looked up at me asking "This is for me?"

"From now on, everything I do…is for you."

Taking her by the hand, I walked her to the Jacuzzi. Out of my boxers, I got in first, and then escorted her, still with her thong on, in with me.

Sitting down at the same time, Quincee waited until I settled in then she laid down in the water on top of me (*I had to talk to myself. Down boy, down!*).

Laying her head on my chest, I began stroking her forehead then working my way lower, to caressing her back. While her face was still on my chest, and in a little girl pouting voice, she informed me. "I'm not your friend."

Sympathetically responding, "I know."

Looking up at me, with tears welling in her eyes she said "I can't believe you spanked me. And my butt is hurting really- really bad."

Just then another set of tears rolled down her cheeks that glistened on her face from the candle light (*God, she was beautiful*).

Raising her chin, until her eyes met mine, I commented "I had to get your attention. You won't be disrespecting or embarrassing me anymore...now will you?"

Looking at me with a soft expression and lowering her head back down on my chest; a few seconds later, she whispered "I'm sorry."

As far as I was concerned, our connection was equally re-solidified and a commitment formed between us that no man or woman could ever touch. We stayed in the water long time. Comfortably lost in my own thoughts, she fell asleep.

When I felt her shivering, I woke her up, "Come on baby, let's get you out the water."

Stepping towards her, to place the robe around her shoulders, I felt that same rush of energy that I had felt the night when I kiss her in front of her apartment. The shit took my breath away, (*I swear, we weren't even touching, but we had to step further apart from each other to regain our normal breathing*).

Turned around while she slipped out of the wet thong and put on the robe, I then cautiously grabbed her hand and lead her into the dressing room area that is connected to my bathroom, while trying to understand the feeling that she hit me with. Drying her off and then oiling her down with Body Oil, (*Woman like that stuff. I always keep things like that on hand; to make them happy*). I watched her body fall in love with me; by the way she reacted to my pampering.

Looking at the clock, it was 7:45 in the morning, and I needed to get some sleep because there was a list of things I needed to do before Toomey arrived. Plus I was going to throw some steak and shrimp on the grill after the meeting, catch a few ball games, and then watch the fight later on that night.

Soon as we got in the bed, my baby laid her head on my chest and was asleep within minutes.

Waking up to the alarm ringing at 11:30, I felt like I had slept for four days. Life felt good again.

Stretching to get the kinks out, the answering machine light caught my eye. The first message was from Jimmy.

"Yo Dan, pick up the phone. It's me Jimmy. Pick up the phone. When you get this message, call me back. It's important....DAMN!", and the recording cut off.

Calling all of his numbers—home phone, cell and beeper, I didn't reach him, so I just left messages. I didn't know what to think, when it came to Jimmy. He's probably calling because he needs more money. I'm DONE worrying about my brother.

My father is literally through with him, but is broke up and blames himself for Jimmy's fucked-up-ness. He feels that he should not have worked so hard, and should have spent more time with us, especially after our mother died.

My father disinherited Jimmy from his will and the business, after Jimmy had my father's office manager robbed at gunpoint. On another occasion he sent some criminals to the office to demand payment for Jimmy's outstanding debt. The final straw was when Jimmy stole $75,000 from one of my father's clients' account.

(How much would you put up with, if it was your sibling? If any of you out there are like Jimmy, know that your ass is on borrowed time).

I have to love my brother from a distance and pray for him. That's all I'm prepared to do now because I've enabled his ass and have been feeling stupid and used by him for years. But more important, now I have Quincee and the twins to think about and keep safe.

I put the scam artist out of my mind because thinking about him was fucking with my joy. Just then, I heard and felt Quincee move. Turning and facing her I saw that her eyes were still swollen--she looked more beautiful than ever, to me.

I made a mental note to pick up some chamomile tea for her. I use to date a model who loved the fast lane. She always had bloodshot and puffy eyes after a wild night of drinking and drugs. Tai was her name. Chamomille tea was her cure-all for her eyes to get them back to normal before a shoot. She said that alcohol lowers the anti-diuretic hormone (ADH), and that ADH increases and assists the body in retaining fluid. By heating up the tea bag and placing it on the eye, the tea has tannins, which act as an astringent.

(Men, I tell you, the things that I have learned from women).

I threw on some sweats and headed down to the basement where my treadmill is and put in five miles. Back upstairs and showered, I threw on some jeans, a turtleneck, a pair of loafers; grabbed a suede blazer then headed out to the bank.

I had to withdraw money out of my personal account to replace what I took from the office, in order to bail Jimmy's ass out of trouble.

I had forgotten until Pop's Assistant, Lynne HappyRoc, (*no kidding, that's her last name*), reminded me. She's my father's right hand and he trusts her explicitly. She's a retired Senior Chief from the Navy and she has no problem putting any one in their place. Friday, before leaving work, she walks in my office and says.

"You waiting on a personal invitation to replace the funds you took from petty cash? Let's Get It Poppin!" Then she turned around and walked out the door.

Even though my father doesn't check the petty cash on a regular basis, I wasn't about to chance Senior Chief bringing him up to date. And I'm for damn sure not going to put myself in a position to have to explain shit about Jimmy to Pops. When it comes to those two, I stay completely out of it.

It was a perfect fall Saturday afternoon. The temperature was in the high sixties. The sun was shining bright, not a cloud in the sky. The air was crisp with a nice breeze—strong enough to wake up my senses, but not enough offend my breathing.

The streets were full of people out, enjoying the day. I watched a Chinese mother trying to negotiate with her toddler, while the infant she was strolling, slept; two Jewish elderly women walking arm and arm smiling and talking. Across the street there was a Caucasian tourist group wide-eyed with New York excitement on their faces, dressed in shorts and hooded sweatshirts; and three twenty-something year olds Ghetto Fabulous African Americans. You know the ones with the multi-colored hair weaves, abnormally long nail in bright colors. Plus wearing clothes that really don't suit their body proportions—I love New York.

Taking in the sight and smells of the city; although I do not eat food from outside carts, everything smelled damn good.

My thoughts then turned to my future. I'm in my late thirties; it is high time for me to be thinking about settling down. Seeing Quincee at my side, a smile broke out on my face. She is the woman that I want to spend the rest of my life with. I've known her for less than a year, but within that time she has turned my life upside down, around, and right. She's taught me all kinds of lessons, and I have grown personally, from knowing and loving her.

She's held me at bay because I've never waited longer than week before getting some ass from a woman. Unpredictably, she's won my father over the first time he met her. So much so that he asks about her frequently. I didn't have the guts to tell him that she wasn't speaking to me for a time.

I would have never thought in a million years that I would get over the hurt that Ma'Haundra put on me, but Quincee has wiped all of that shit away. The feeling of wanting to go through life as a bachelor is gone. The writing is on the wall, I won't let that woman get away from me ever again.

All caught up in my thoughts, feeling the gnats twirl around in my stomach about how and when I would eventually propose to Quincee, my phone rings.

It was Matt, and it didn't sound like it was going to be good.

"Dan, I drove over to your place to see if you want to get a game in, and I see Twink walking up the block, I figured I'd give you a heads up."

"SHIT! Where is she now?"

"She's getting ready to ring your doorbell, in about thirty to forty seconds. I take it, you're not home."

"No, I'm about 4 blocks away."

"Don't worry, I'll handle it." Then the phone clicked off.

I picked up my stride to get my ass home even though I had complete confidence in Matt.

Thinking to myself (*What are the odds of having Quincee and Twink at my house, at the same time*).

Turning onto the corner of 19th street, relieved at seeing nothing out of the ordinary. About halfway to my house, I spotted Matt's truck. Twink was in the passenger's seat. I saw her detect me through the side-view mirror. She sprang out of Matt's vehicle like a leopard about to pounce me. I was prepared for whatever she had to say or wanted to do.

I hadn't seen her since the night I left her house with Quincee's jacket. Standing on her door step, ringing her phone off the got-damn hook and yelling "Open your door!"

She did.

"All I want is Quincee's jacket."

When she returned to the door looking all sad and shit, she tried to say something.

"But Dan…"

I cut her ass off, "You can't say jack shit to me right about now." I turned around and went on about my business, and avoided all of her attempts to get in contact with me. She was not use to that type of treatment from me...ever.

So, I know when she saw me that day, that ass was antsy. The only word I allowed her to get out of her mouth was my name before I grabbed her by the wrist and lead her towards my door.

She didn't fight or flinch.

Unmoved by her compliance, I was going to have her obedience one way or another. I was pissed off at Twink for everything it seemed like she'd ever done to me.

I dialed Quincee number.

"Hey, how's my baby feeling? Good. I'm outside and I have Twink with me. Meet me in the downstairs living room." I hung up the phone.

(I had to give her prescience—to let her know what was about to happen. In case she put me in the dog house later, I could win some points for it. Men always try to position yourself on their better side).

I turned to Matt, "Thanks man!"

Looking into a blank face, "Not a problem, I'll be up...in a minute."

I know I was walking on thin ice, especially with how Quincee felt about Twink and not knowing how she would react. But I wasn't worried because I was running this show. Shit was going to be resolved...end of story.

By the time I got in the house and had flung Twink towards the sofa and told her to "Sit down and don't move", Quincee was coming down the stairs.

Watching her, she looked absolutely beautiful. Her hair was pulled back in a ponytail. She had on a white tee-shirt and grey sweat pants of mine, and a pair of white socks.

Walking over to her making sure that she was alright, and after being satisfied with her response, I gave her a nice kiss on the lips. Before leaving her mouth, I bit her tongue to make her wince just a little bit for me.

(Brothers out there, always remember, women love it when you make it all about them in front of their enemies).

Looking down into her face, she still had a little puffiness around her eyes, and my heart skipped a beat for her, but I didn't let on. Whispering in her ear,

"This forum is for you; but, baby I don't know if she can withstand all of your fire."

I refused to take the time to read Quincee's face; I turned to Twink and started in.

"Lana, what the fuck is going on with you?"

My childhood friend/sister went ghostly white. I hadn't called her by her given name since we were in grade school. My intention was to get her attention, but I had no idea that it would alter the course of the meeting.

She fell back on the couch throwing her hand up to her chest like I struck her in it. She started wailing and talking at the same damn time. I had no idea what the hell she was trying to say. She looked pretty pathetic—actually. It was like Quincee looked the night before.

Unaffected by her tears, I was ready to move on. I told her straight up, "You need to calm down. I don't understand a word that's coming from between your lips. But let me make my position perfectly clear. Either you respect Quincee, or stay away from me...altogether!"

By that point, her eyes were swelling, her nose was red, and snot was mixed in with her tears. She turned to Quincee, "I...I...am so...so...sorry....for...the...the way...I...I...I trea....treated...yu...you. I know how Danny feels about both of us. I was hurt abou...about someth...something else."

She went into detail, which I only caught part of, but my Quincee was there listening surprisingly attentively to all what Twink was confessing. Winding down Twink finished up with, "I...I... was so wrong. ...and I...I am so... a...ashamed of my...myself. I... love Dan...Danny, and I don't want to be part of making you two unhappy any...anymore. Ple...plea...please can you for...forgive...m...me."

Quincee took Twink's right hand, looked my friend square in the eyes and said, "All is forgiven. It's over." She walks over to me and says, "I'll see you when you get upstairs." She kissed me on the cheek and left the room.

I was fucked up. I asked myself (*what just happen here?*). I just knew that Quincee was going to take Twink's head off.

No soon as Quincee was out of the room heading for the steps, I heard Matt coming through the front door. Baffled at the expression on my face and not sure what to make of the whole scene, my brother cautiously asked me with one eyebrow arched "Everything alright?"

"Everything's good."

Twink timidly interrupted, "Matt, I have a favor t…to ask. Would you drive me to my mom's house, please?"

"Sure. You Ready?"

"Yes."

Standing up, putting on her coat, and walking towards the door, she stopped in front of me. Looking too embarrassed to look me in the eyes; she said "Danny, I apologize. I wish you and QJ happiness and the best of everything."

My broken friend glanced at me, appearing the same way she did that long ago day when I protected her from that group of bully bitches. She requested, "Please don't stop being my big brother." Not waiting for a response from me, she walked to the door.

Needing to release some steam, tension, aggravation, and sexual frustration, I told Matt "Let me know when you're headed back this way. I do want to get a game in."

After locking the door, I skipped two steps each trying to get up to Quincee.

She was in the kitchen. I stood quiet in the doorway just watching her every move. Liking how she made her way around my house; like she belongs here.

Cringing when I saw her flinch in pain when she bumped her behind on the corner of the countertop, it also made my dick hard to know that I had finally tamed that ass, or what Quincee calls "The Defiance in her." I watched her for a while before she realized that I was there.

"Hey you! How long have you been standing there? I'm going to cook, so I'm rummaging through your cabinets to see what I'll be working with. I hope you don't mind?"

I just stood there gawking at her—for one because she was so beautiful. Two, I couldn't believe that she was actually in my house because not even a week ago she thought I was pure shit. Three, I was still in shocked at her response to Twink. And four, she was looking so sexy; I had to calm my throbbing down.

She kept asking me, "What……………What.?"

Walking to her and pulling her close, I made an effort to be as casual as possible,

"You know I would have lost all of my money if I had bet on your response to Twink?"

"I'm sorry baby, but yes you would have."

Even more perplexed at her calmness, I had to ask, "Why? I don't get it. You cussed my yellow ass out. You ate Toomey's ass for a midnight snack, yet when the guilty party comes around; you accept her apology, with not so much as a negative word parting from those sexi-licious lips of yours…I don't get it."

Matching my tone, she shared her explanation with me.

"Did you see her? She looked like a withering flower, imploding from self-demise. She is hurt, she's tormented, she's lonely, and she is unloved the way that she wants and feels that she should be loved. Between the two of us, I am blessed; I have my self-worth, my family. I Have You! It would have been cruel of me, and I would be mocking God, if I had said anything other than what I did. Your friend is in pain, much more so than any anger I felt when she did what she did to me. I wish her strength."

I was in awe of the woman standing in front of me. Her compassion reminded me of my mother's heart, and for a split second I thought I heard my mother's voice whisper in my ear, "She's the one." I fought back tears, and let myself fall deeper in love with Quincee-Jane Catfire.

Drama ...It Just Keeps Coming

Ladies, you know how it is when you test your man to see how much you can get away with, and he responds by exuding his alpha potency?

Everything is in balance with Danny and me. All areas in my life are at peace; oh but not for long because unfortunately life has this element in it called...Drama.

October 29, 2005
Danny's House
The morning after...

A series of unexpected events unfolded (*what happened...I will never tell*), that left me in a critical decision making position. Although I felt my back was up against a wall, I know that my feelings for Danny are true, unwavering, and love-secured.

Waking up Saturday was a bitter-sweet contrast of throbbing soreness; along with feeling the elation of knowing that the love Danny and I shared is reciprocity at is finest.

Realizing that I was in the bed alone, a little bit of "DAMN" hit me along with a spasm of pain. Just then, my cell phone rings. I opened the receiver.

"How's daddy's girl?"

Ladies, all I wanted to do was play with myself. It didn't make any kind of sense...but I'm alright with it.

I've never had the opportunity to hold that title because I didn't meet my father until I was 21 years old. There are no fatherly mental or emotional connections. So for me, I am Danny's Daddy's Little Girl!

"I hope I didn't wake you?"

"No. you didn't," unable to prevent myself from cooing into the phone.

"I just want to let you know that Toomey's coming over this afternoon so we can strategize some plans for the team, and I don't what that crazy ass to ring the bell like a lunatic and scare you."

"That's YOUR friend!"

"Quincee...Be nice."

"I don't want to be nice", I said sounding arrogant, yet pout-ty.

"Baby, if that's not how you want to be, then go right ahead."

"Do you need anything? Do you want anything?

"No, I'm good. The only thing I want is, you."

"Mmm! Keep her warm for me. I'll call you when I'm close to home. I Love you", then the phone went dead.

My Sis-ters, what do you do when he gives you your way, even though you know that your way is NOT right? On top of that, he's not afraid to tell you that he loves you. I was falling into love's swimming pool; and it felt exceptionally good floating atop its warm waters.

Although I was sore and a bit hung over, I had agility in my movement, as I sprang out of bed. My plan was to cook a nice brunch for them and head home so that they can be alone to do their business thing.

Spryly making my way to the bathroom, mentally contriving my menu; (*eggs, bacon, sausage, applesauce, griddle-cakes, orange juice, coffee- for me; hot chocolate and cool whip for Danny*). Stopping dead in my track and becoming horrified when I saw my reflection in the mirror.

My eyelids were swollen like four mini half-balloons. I had dried tear stains running down both sides of my face. Moving in closer to inspect my face…damn, damn, damn! I had a line of dry drool extending from the corner of my mouth to under my chin, and well down my neck.

Pleading to the universe that I wasn't seen in that capacity, I headed to the shower and luxuriated in the hot soothing water as I bathe in my thoughts of Danny.

Out of the shower, finding some clothes of Danny's that I could fit into. I felt good. Everything was in accord. That was about quarter pass 1PM.

Turning on the radio, I instantly began rocking my head to Bobby Womack and Patty Labelle's "*Love Has Finally Come At Last*" I hadn't heard that song in years, *(I took it as a sign)*.

Sashaying and singing my way over to the window so that I could inhale the crisp fall breeze that was infiltrating the room. Standing there with my eyes closed, letting the emanating sunrays soak into my pores; swimming in my thoughts that conjured up dancing Danny butterflies in bottom of my belly, when my cell phone began ringing again.

Racing back to the bedroom because…I just knew…it was my baby. I didn't even get a chance to say anything, I opened my phone and all heard was, "Twink is with me" and "Meet me downstairs."

The command was so imposing that it subdued my refusal and I obeyed like a seaman recruit taking orders from the Captain. All the soft and ku-fuffle feelings I was just experiencing, flashed into blood rage, and warrior mode. I had no time to think because no soon as I closed my phone, I heard keys unlocking the door.

All My Warriors, it is during times such as these that you must put your game face on. No one needs to know what you're thinking or feeling. This way, if you plan on doing something—on the low, you want to position yourself to be either last or nowhere on the suspect list.

Walking down the stairs with inner attitude and feeling the same pressure that had tightened my chest the night that Daisy-dumbbell set me up, I was ready to charge her when I entered the living room.

Instead, I slowed my pace and immediately began assessing the state of affairs. The first thing that came to mind was (*why is she wearing a halter top and hip-huggers in this weather?*). The bitch was pulling out all her resources in an effort to get her love-claws into Danny.

What happened next, I would have never imagined in a thousand years. What was supposed to be a reckoning? The justice assembly for my indignation was actually transcended into a surreal forum.

First, there was Danny's attitude. In the midst of standing no more than three feet from my enemy, thirsting to punch her in the face; knocking her lights out, and then sending her ass to the hospital; my commander-in-chief invaded my personal space.

Searing my eyes with honesty, loyalty and concern, then inquiring if I was alright; informing me that I could get all the infested shit off my chest then bending down and kissing me real…real nice.

Ladies, has your man ever made you feel like a rare flower, like pure love; like you are the only one that has his heart, mind, and his dick…and doing it in front of your arch rival?

All of it being done, not in a nah-nah demeaning way towards Twink; but in an, I love you Quincee way. The way I saw it; it had to be cold-hearted from Twink's position, and I lapped up her losses like a kitten with a bowl of warm milk.

My Resolve Coordinator turned toward Twink, asked her one question, consisting of nine words, and the dweeb emotionally imploded.

Basically, she was told that it was all about me…not her, and if she didn't get her act together, she might as well walk away…for good!"

She appeared to have a lethal fear of being oust from Danny's heart and life. She looked crumbled, lost, lonely, and dejected. I was taken aback by Danny's lack of concern for Twink's despair.

At one point she was telling us how her mother isn't around as much because she thinks her mother has a man in her life.

"Don't get me wrong, my mother has been through hell and back, and I am happy for her because she deserves love and to be loved. I just feel like—what about me?"

When she uttered those words, I was messed up on the inside because I too had been in that same very dark place before, and I wouldn't wish that on my worst enemy.

Then my mother's words chimed in both of my ears "You don't knock a man when he's already down." I took that to include women as well. That was the second event that transformed the meeting into something bigger than my lust for retribution, which impelled me instantly into the third.

Looking at the broken spirit in front of me, and feeling her pain— yes, even after all she had done to me. Watching her in that pitiful state, I became washed in gratitude, as all of the people who I am loved by, blazed before my mind opening up my heart and my eyes. By the time she had finished sniffling out her apology to me, she had already been forgiven.

Lastly, the Good Book popped into my head (*God said "When you help the least of My brethren, you help Me"*).

I do not have anything in me to assist Lana in her plight, but the desire for revenge is no longer palpable. There was nothing left to be said.

1:50 p.m. I was back upstairs rummaging through Danny's kitchen cabinets and planning my grocery list and reliving the past ½ hour.

I was astonished at the irony's turn of events. Exhaustion began to creep up on me and I wish that time would speed up, so that I could be home in my bed, in the serenity of my own familiarity to nurse my physical wounds.

A few minutes later Danny was in the kitchen with me.

Ladies the power feels intoxicating when you know he wants to ask you something, but not quite sure how to go about it. His fear is your victory.

I felt those fine ass eyes searing the back of my head as I nonchalantly continued on about my business. Not in the mood of being a dissident of any kind, and never ceasing my inventory check, I allowed myself to be put through a TooGood Inquisition.

I was straight forward with Danny about my thoughts regarding Twink. The exchange was non-eventful (*thank God*), and one of my last comments was, "I'm not trying to be funny…but you should really try to convince her to seek out therapy because her hurt goes so deep that she's knocking on unstable's door…at lightning speed. And I think that her irrational behavior is only going to become more volatile."

When I saw the 'I can't believe you're on her side' expression on Danny's face, I verbally replied, "I wish her strength," and I terminated the conversation.

Danny pulled me close and hugged me. It was that safe, warm, feeling loved type of holding me, when the doorbell rang.

The one person that I least wanted to see; it was Toomey. I looked at Danny and informed "That's your friend", and I vacated the kitchen.

Standing in the middle of the bedroom and deciding if I was going to change into my jeans and shoes, or just find the sneakers that Danny had bought me, my phone rings; it's Harmony.

Being the diva that she is, all I heard was her yelling at someone to shut up, then her screaming "Mommy" to me. There was all kind of commotion in the background, and I heard Eli's voice. Alarmed for her safety and annoyed with her theatrics, I commanded into the phone, "Slow Down, And Just Speak To Me!"

"Amah, be quiet, I can't hear Mommy."

She returned back to the phone, in full drama gear, sputtering out her performance, but all I heard was "Daddy's girlfriend pushed me and called me the B word, and daddy didn't do anything."

In full metal maternal mode, "Where are you?"

"In grandma's house, but she's sleep and I don't want to wake her up."

"Where Is Auntie Theresa?"

"Home."

"You go to Therese's house. Leave right now. Where's that woman at?"

"She left because Amah was cussing her out."

"Alright, don't say anything to your father, even if he says stupid shit out of his mouth. Do you understand me?"

"But Mom..."

"DO YOU UNDERSTAND ME??"

"Yes Mom."

"I know Amah is with you because I can hear her damn mouth. I'm downtown right now, but, I'm on my way. I'll call you when I'm getting in a cab. What are you not going to do?"

My daughter slowly replied "Don't say anything back to daddy."

"What are you going to do?"

"I'm going to Aunty Theresa's house."

"Very Good! I love you, and I'll see you in a few." I felt the blood bubbles popping through my veins.

How dare that mother fucker let another woman touch his child...my child...our child? I was going over there to fight. Mothers out there...do you feel me?

Checking my watch; it was 2:20 p.m. My plan was to be in the Bronx by three o'clock. I lost track of time because the next thing I remember was opening up the sneaker box and impatiently removing all the dag-gone tissue paper then losing it when I found out that I had to lace the damn things.

It was all becoming too much. My plan kept being re-routed. Initially, I was going to be fully dressed and walking out the door letting Danny think that I was going food shopping, but noooooo. The forces were messing with me.

I don't know anything about sneakers, I didn't see holes in the normal place where they were supposed to be, which meant I had to go and get help. Accessing, adjusting, and adapting to the situation, I gathered poise and headed to Danny.

I had forgotten that Toomey was in the house, so when I found them in the dining room, Matt had joined the group, and they were all bent over the table viewing materials, and in a concentrated discussion.

New plan...keep your game face on, don't let Toomey fuck with you, get my sneakers laced, get the hell out of the room, then back to plan C.

When I looked up, why were all of them looking in my face? I paid that no mind, spoke to Matt, and went straight into my strategy.

"Danny, can you lace these sneakers for me? I don't know what's going on...I don't know where they go."

Looking at me incredulously because everyone who knows me, know that I do not wear sneakers, but responding "Sure baby", while taking the box out of my hand.

Danny was at the head of the table, Matt on the right side, and Toomey the furthest from me on the left. Matt got up, held the chair as I seated myself, then sat in the chair next to me.

Before I could sit down good; just like perfect bad timing, Toomey condescendingly greeted me.

"How you feeling?"

Making another smart ass comment and gesturing, then laughing at me.

Holding my attitude down and my dignity in check, I ignored the dumb-cluck; besides my baby stood up for me, telling Toomey to "Nip that shit!" in an unyielding tone.

All was well for about twenty seconds then my phone rings again. The ID display said it was Harmony again.

"Hi baby. Are you at Auntie Therese's?"

"Hello, to you too, I knew you still wanted me. Come and give me some!"

It was Eli. I was completely disgusted.

Plan E: Adjustments...maintain situation anonymity. I had to dig real deep in order to summon civility in my voice.

"Where's Harmony"

"You need to talk to your daughter. She's acting like all the rest of these fucking females over here."

Hatred punched me square in the chest. Fuck hiding an attitude or anything at that point!

"Wait a minute. Do you really think that I'm just going to let you talk about Harmony while you're on... her phone... that I pay for?"

When I opened my mouth again, I was ice smooth because I wanted him bad and I didn't want him to hang up on me like he usually does when I set his ass straight.

"How are you going to side with a piece of ass over your own daughter?"

He came back with, "That's right, your daughter, she's uppity just like you. You should-da heard the things she was saying to Lola."

"Personally, I don't give a fuck about Lola, Bola, Bamby, you, or Lulu's kids!"

Then he wanted to buck up his chest and get loud, "Who the fuck you think you talking to?"

I ignored the question. In my mind I'm thinking (*That's 1*) and I responded.

"Oh, you want to cuss?"

Simultaneously, I grabbed the second sneaker and watched Danny, so I could get the shit done faster and be out the door sooner.

Back to the fool on the other end of the receiver, I coldly asked "Where is Harmony?"

"Why you asking? SHE'S HERE WITH ME."

"No, she went to visit her grandmother and aunt, you just happened to show up. Get it straight."

"YOUR DAUGHTER IS A FUCKING MEANY!"

I thought to myself (*Number two*).

I countered "Eli, lower your voice. I'm not yelling at you. And stop talking about my child."

By then, I had the room's attention, but I didn't care about them, or that my business was being exposed.

"She's my daughter too. And you're right; Lola is just a piece of pussy. I love you Quincee, and I always will. I want my family back, I want to come home."

Removing the phone from my ear, and looking at it utter disbelief; I was repulsed. Before I could respond, he went into a bitch-fest.

"All of this is your fucking fault because you put me out. Fuck you Quincee!"

Ladies that was the third strike....and...His Ass Was Out.

With all the base, thug, bitch, nasty, protective-mother, and I'm coming to put my hands on you—in my voice, I stormed.

"YOU SORRY PIECE OF WALKING CONSEQUENCE OF SPERM. This conversation is not about you, or what you feel, nor what you want. This is about my daughter and how once again, you've fallen short of being a father—you're supposed to be there supporting her and giving her unconditional love when she needs you; but instead you're treating her with malice aforethought.

You're her judge, jury, and executioner, and you're willing to sell her down the river.

That's the shit that makes my heart hurt, and makes me hate you. Then you want to talk that dumb shit about how you love me and the girls. You love no one but Eli.

Let me ask you--where was your love when I had to choose between paying rent or buying food to feed our babies?"

"They would have been better off with me. I should have took them with me."

I couldn't believe my ears. I had to chuckle at that one. I turned the phone to my mouth because I wanted to be loud in his ear.

"Are you trying to make me feel bad? You Sorry Sac of Pus Shit! How dare you mention a title that you as a man couldn't live up to even if you worthless ass life depended on it.

What about the year you told them that you were going to take them for the summer. For two months, all I heard were stories of how daddy has a new house. We have our own room, with a computer, play station, and toys. Daddy got a back yard and it has a swing set that daddy got for us.

I was jealous as fuck because I could barely provide the necessities for them let alone those things for them at the time, but I sucked it up as I watched their faces light up with anticipation at being with you.

And when school got out, where were you? Your punk ass was nowhere to be found, leaving me to pick up your fake lying ass pieces.

And I did. I lied my ass off for you because I'd rather glorify you in their eyes than have them think that you don't give a fuck about them.

And another thing, where is your loving them when it comes to paying your $25 a month child support. You got off easy—that's only twelve dollars and fifty cents per child; but your love hasn't paid me not one cent for them; yet you can ask them for money to buy your cigarettes and beer?

Walk behind me and eat my maternal dirt. You're trying to make me feel bad? Man—fuck you!"

There was silence on the phone. I continued "Yeah, I thought so."

Having a hard time balancing the phone and working with the damn shoe lace, I snapped out to no one in particular, "How do you I get the damn speaker phone on?"

Matt took my phone and appeased me. Now the phone is on the table, the sneaker in between my knees, and the shoestring in my hand.

Eli came back again with everything being my fault.

"None of this would be happening if I was home with you and my daughters. You broke up our family."

"I Didn't Break Up Shit! You told me, Quincee-Jane PLEASE kick me out because I don't want to be in this mother fucker no more—the day you put your hands on me, and did the shit in front of my girls. So mother fucker, let me tell you this one last time. There is nothing between us—not now, it hasn't been for twelve years, and there will never be. Entrench that into your brain, and don't come back at me with that bull shit anymore. Where's my daughter?"

"Don't worry about it. She's with me."

"Put Harmony on the phone Eli!"

"No"

"It's all good because... I'm Coming To See You!"

"Oh... so you're playing on that shit. You don't have no brothers. You ain't got no people, but you coming to see me. What you going do, what you got?"

I saw myself punching the bitch dead in the mouth. I was seeing red. Indignantly as I could muster, "I DON'T NEED ANY FUCKING BODY WHEN IT COMES TO PROTECTING MY BABIES....I'M A STONE WALL BY MY MOTHER FUCKING SELF, so you say that to say what mother fuckah? Oh yeah, I'm coming to see you son!"

"Just calm down! Look Quincee, I apologize. I..."

I cut that yellow ass off. "Naw, don't bitch up now. Stand up to your convictions. I'll be there soon. I want you to say what's on your mind, and I want to be face to face with your ass, so you can hear what's on mine."

When he realized that I wasn't backing down, he had to up his testosterone egoism "Oh it's like that? Then come on. I..."

Another call was coming in and I click over.

"Hello, love-muffin."

It was Hope.

"I just called to Auntie Theresa's house, and Amah was saying something about a fight, with daddy, Harmony and somebody else.

Mommy....Mommy are you there?"

Jumbo crocodile tears starting dropping from my face onto my lap. I was fighting hard to prevent my voice from cracking before I spoke because I was about to lie to my daughter on behalf of her father.

"Hello my love-child, I'm here."

"Mommy, what's wrong?"

"Nothing's wrong. You know how you get that funny feeling in your nose when you have to sneeze, but the sneeze won't come?"

I thought saying that would give me a few more seconds for recovery. Out of nowhere, Toomey authentically fake sneezed three consecutive times in the direction of my phone.

I was so moved by the unsought supportive gesture that more tears came pouring out of my eyes, as I mouthed a thank you to my collaborator.

I got thumbs up and a don't-mention-it wave off.

Collected, I rejoined the conversation.

"Baby, I haven't heard anything. Are you sure Amah isn't joking with you because the last time you were over there, she called you and had you believing that she was kidnapped and in the trunk of somebody's car—remember?"

Breaking her concentration from my emotional state, she started laughing, thereby enabling me to let down her guard, and lead her into a deeper lie.

I'm not proud of the act itself, but I promised God 12 years ago that I would never argue with Eli in front of my babies. And I'm proud to say... I've kept my word. So whatever it takes to keep my girls out of Eli's and my ugliness, I will do it unwaveringly.

"I tell you what; I'll call over there to see what's going on. It's probably just your father drinking and acting a fool."

"Okay, but you'll let me know if I need to go over there. I bet its Harmony's fault because she talks mean to daddy."

"Hold up on that. Because you and I both know that your father treats you better than he does Harmony. Don't you think that hurts her feelings, and just maybe she is effected by his relationship with you?"

Feeling her, feeling her sister's pain, "I never thought about it like that before Mommy. I'm sorry."

"Give Harmony a break. Are you having a good time at Miss Debbie's house?"

"Ooh yeah, we're getting ready to go to City Island and then to the movies."

My daughter was all happy again. I ended our conversation and was relieved that I didn't have to worry about her becoming involved in the impending mêlée.

Tell me why, when I clicked off from Hope, Eli was still on the other line.

"Quincee, put your draws back on. I didn't call you for all this. All I want to do is talk to you."

"I don't care what you want. My position is…you have never laid a hand on Hope and Harmony, but you're going to allow some bitch from the street do that to my child.

You're going to get your chance to talk to me because Poppi, I'm coming to see you."

"Oh, so you still talking that bullshit. You aint got no skills. You aint got no backup"

"Well then Eli, I guess this is your lucky fuck'n day. This conversation is over until I see you." I hung up the phone.

By that time I had the damn sneakers on and before I could exit the room, Danny said "I'll meet you down stairs in the car."

Falling deeper in love, but adamant with my position, I kindly responded, "I love you so much. I don't think you even know, but this is something that I have to do alone. I've never brought my baggage into our relationship before; I'm not going to start now."

I couldn't believe I was standing strong, as I looked into the eyes that were loving me back, and I felt every ounce of the protector in Danny.

Stating my plans "I will call you when I get there, I'll call you when I'm heading home, and I'll call when I get in the house."

I said good-bye to Matt and Toomey, got my things, and I was walking out the door at 2:55 p.m.

Ladies, don't you love it when he listens and obeys your wishes!

The Protector

(Men, I'm in love, I know that she is the one, and I have finally tamed the bitch-beast inside of her.
Why now, the ex wants to rear his head and impede on my lady's happiness.
Although this baby daddy drama is new territory for me, I am not intimidated by any means... I know how to take care of mine).

My mind hadn't settled down from the Twink incident, let alone all the events of the past week. (*That should have told me something*).

I was in the dining room with Matt and Toomey refining my strategy for the next practice with the T-Byrds; my junior female basketball team, when Quincee came in asking me to lace the sneakers that she previously made known to me that she would never wear.

Even before that, I knew something was wrong from the moment that I saw her face and it didn't take long for me to find out what the problem was.

Toomey, Matt, and I listened as her past unfolded to us. It pained me bad to see the hurt she was in. I was pissed off at that punk-ass Eli for being an ass-hole to her, and I was itching to meet the fool who let her go because I was going to make it clear to him that from that point on, he had to deal with me.

By the time she hung up the phone with him, I knew it was going to get bad between me and him. She left the room, but I didn't say anything to her.

My pretty girl came back looking like a little tomboy, with enough attitude to cram the room and make all of us want to follow her lead. She chopped my plan when she found out that I had attentions on going with her. I would have stood there arguing and debating with her, if it wasn't for Matt.

"Let her go."

The trust between us is so tight that I gave into her without a fight. I kissed her on the forehead, and let her walk away from me.

Turning around, seeing Matt wink at me, while holding Toomey back by the shoulder.

"You're just going to let your woman walk out; on her own like that. What the fuck is wrong with you?"

I looked at the individual that I call my friend, (*sometimes I wonder why*) and replied, "I'm not" and "Y'all ready to roll?"

Always more than ready to get into some shit that fool wigwagged and said "Ahhhhh. Now that's what I'm talking about!"

Before my outside door had closed, the three of us were standing at the upstairs banister peeping over it, looking like eight year olds trying not to get caught. Once the door shut, we flew down stairs, taking 3 steps at a time.

Toomey was out the house first as the point man, making sure that Quincee didn't spot us and to determine which direction we would be headed. Matt was next—running to the truck to have it started by the time Toomey and I get in. I came out last, making my way to the moving vehicle and trying to calm the hate that was burning my chest for that punk-bitch that I was about to face.

Toomey was a little ways down the block pointing towards Quincee rushing ahead. By the time Matt backed up to the corner, Quincee was getting into a cab. Toomey and I jumped in as Matt backed onto 1st Avenue, heading uptown.

About a half a block further up, my phone rings; its Quincee.

She sounded suspicious "Where Are You? I called the house and you didn't pick up?"

"Baby I'm headed for the gym."

"Oh that's right, I forgot. Just checking in—I'm in a cab now."

"I like that you called to check in."

" Ooh good because...I like you!"

In the middle of all that was going on, she's making me blush and making my shit throb.

To play the game up, I asked her "Do you need me to be there with you?"

"No baby, I'm good. I'll call you when I get there. I'm loving you."

Then she hung up.

I tell you...I had a warm feeling in a place that I never felt before. It was scary, but I wasn't afraid.

Matt had no problem following the yellow cab to 23rd Street, onto the FDR Drive then the Willis Avenue Bridge exit. It wasn't until we were well into the bowls of the Bronx that we got caught at a red light.

Toomey hopped out the truck and ran to the corner of Boston Road and a hundred sixty something street. By the time we drove into the block, Toomey was at the next corner beckoning us to turn onto the avenue.

Looking down that long ass street I could see there was something going on. I told Matt "Step on the fucking gas."

In less than the seven seconds it took to reach her, I saw her leap on somebody's back, which I assumed to be Eli, and grab him around the neck, in an effort to get him off of a female that he had in a choke hold.

Getting out the truck before it came to a complete stop, I watched Eli back up and slamm Quincee a couple of times against the side of the house. By the time I got to her, she had slide down the brick face and hit the ground with a hard thump.

While that was happening, the short heavy set female pulled away from Eli's grip, turned around and cold cocked him in the face, knocking him to the pavement.

Kneeling down to check on Quincee, I managed to get out "Baby?", when a boisterous voice yelled out from the second story window.

"WHAT THE FUCK IS GOING ON OUTSIDE MY HOUSE."

I couldn't tell if it was a male or female, but everybody froze and looked up.

"Theresa What the Fuck Did You do to My Son?"

"I knocked the shit out of him because YOUR SON was trying to take me out. It's not my fault that he wanted to be The Man, and hurt his already hurt hip."

"Bitch You Better Hope That He Doesn't Have To Go To the Hospital Because If He Does, You Will Be Taking His Ass."

She instructed a mid-fifty year old brown skinned cat with a post office uniform shirt on to help Eli up into the house and to get his ass some pain pills.

I smiled when I saw his bitch ass wincing in pain as he was being help into the next building.

The big voice woman surveyed the immediate area and commanded, "DABNERS....UPSTAIRS...NOW!"

They came from all directions; tall ones, thin ones, fat ones, light skinned, light bright, and bright- bright ones, looking like mindless laborers walking towards their dictator.

She faced Matt, Toomey and me and D'd us up.

"Who are you?"

Quickly responding on our behalf, Quincee informed her. "They're with me E-U" grabbing my hand and stepping in close to me. There was no way in hell that I was going to let her step foot in that house without me. When she made a move towards the steps, so did I and Toomey, while Matt stayed outside.

It was almost comical because we were lined up on the staircase in single file like pre-schoolers, while she towered over everyone at the top of the second floor landing, pointing individually and directing "You, you, you, and you" the younger clan—10 of them ranging from 6 years old to early 20's on the first floor. "You, you, you, and you… in here," which ended up being Quincee, myself, Theresa, and Toomey.

Walking past her to get to the sitting room, I thought to myself (*Damn that's a big woman. She would have eaten my mother alive for breakfast*).

The woman was my height, and she had me by 75 pounds. She has a big face. She's brown skinned with a black, brown, and silver ponytail. She had on a red flowered house dress and house-shoes. Although her walk was defective and she used a cane, it did not seem to slow her down one bit.

She barked out, "What the fuck is going on?"

Quincee started with the phone call from Harmony, and she finished up by saying "I came over here to get my baby, also to confront Eli because I hold him personally responsible for all of this."

The big woman called Harmony's cell, put her on speaker, got her input then hung up the phone.

Quincee commented, "E-U I can't let Harmony be exposed to this, that's why I'm going to keep them both on my side of town for a while."

I didn't think it was possible to see smoke come out of someone's ears, but that big woman was mad as fuck. She then called for Eli. I thought my ears were lying to me earlier, but they weren't.

Paying no attention to the knot on his forehead, the bruising around his eye, and the blood in the corner of his mouth-- she went off on him.

"WHAT THE FUCK IS YOUR PROBLEM. YOU LET THAT STINKING HOE COME INTO MY HOUSE AND PUT HER HANDS ON MY GRANDBABY. YOU STUPID ASSHOLE...I DON'T WANT THAT FUNKY SKANK IN MY HOUSE NO MORE. AND YOU TELL THAT GREASY BITCH, WHEN I SEE HER, I'M GOING TO PUT MY FOOT ALL UP IN HER BLACK ASS."

"But Ma, you don't know what happen."

"Yes the fuck I do know, you let some grimy bitch put hands on your own flesh and blood, and now Quincee might keep them away from me. That's what the fuck happened."

Turning to Quincee, he spitted out, "You can't stop me from seeing my kids. Who you think you are? You ain't nobody."

My body went tight; I wanted his head... bad.

Responding to my tension, Quincee began stroking my thigh until I calmed down. Then baby removed her hand from my leg, stood up, and said her piece.

"I've known for a long time that you're dumber than a baboon's ass, but now let me tell you why.

Eli, I can get your dumb ass arrested at any time for non-payment of your child support order. I can get an order of protection against you today, with all the lumps, bumps and bruises I have on my body right now, but more importantly, I can stop the twins from coming over here because their minors and I have full custody of them. So Walk With Me Mother Fucker Because I'm The Head Bitch in Charge!"

I swear I got a hard-on watching my baby in action. She had his balls in the palm of her hand and she was squeezing them into mincemeat.

His mother jumped in again and read his ass for another five minutes or so.

"You're my son and I love you, but you're a fuck up, a dead-beat father, and a fucking idiot."

Pointing at Quincee-Jane, "You know this girl has done a damn good job and is doing the best she can, raising your children. Why do you keep fucking with her? Keep your yellow ass away from her."

"Ma, all I want to do is...."

She cut his shit short, "Shut the fuck up, I know what you want to do. You want Quincee to take you back, so you beat her ass. Boy, I Didn't Raise You Like That."

At that point, he saw me laughing at him. If he was any kind of a man, he would have confronted me, but instead like a whinnying bitch, he turned on his mother.

"How the fuck you going to take her side over me? Then your daughter tries to paralyze me, and you don't say a got-damn thing to her."

I was baffled because the big woman did shout his sister out, which meant his ass must have been knocked out cold. I was cracking up in my mind.

Theresa butted in, "Yeah and I'll do it again if you come at me again the wrong way. Cause you're wrong now!"

They went back and forth a few times and then he went into bitch-mode again.

"All you fucking women in here stick together. A niggah don't stand and chance in this fucking house… Fuck all y'all."

E-U took a step towards him, "That's it; get the fuck out my house."

"I aint going nowhere!"

She limped towards him, "Oh you want to try and break bad? Mother fucker you came out of my twat, and so help me I'll crack this cane across your fucking skull, and bury your dead monkey-ass in the backyard myself. And you won't be missed because nobody likes you except for me, your aunt, and the twins."

The pathetic fuck's defeat was Quincee's victory and my consolation prize. His mother was all up in his mug-piece looking down at him, when she ordered "You leave Quincee-Jane the fuck alone. You give that bitch of yours my message. Go and make it right between you and Harmony. Now get the fuck out of my face, and get the fuck out of my house…go…GO!" And just like that…he was gone and situation was over.

The enforcer then turned to me and Toomey and apologized for the scene and introduced herself. Squaring off at me, eye to eye, "Are we straight? Everything's good?"

I responded "Yes ma'am, we're straight. Everything's all good."

She was reassuring herself by qualifying her son's safety from my potential input. That's when I realized Eli was no threat to Quincee…at all.

The Provider

(There's nothing worse than a man not taking care of his own seed. As far as supporting women goes, my motto had always been 'If you share your ass with me, I'm going to share some of my money with you' and I've never been cheap with my wallet).

The other side of the Bronx
Enemy territory

When big momma left the room, I called Matt and gave an update.

"Everything is cool. You're not going to believe the shit that went on up here. He's a fucking punk."

"Yeah, I can believe it. The pussy is out here with a forty ounce in his hand, limping up the block talking to his-self. He almost walked into my truck. You want me to shoot him?"

"Naw man…at least not today. I'll be up here for another fifteen minutes or so."

"Not a problem, I'm on the phone with Cheryl."

"Hey… Tell her I said hello."

"Will do."

I was on the phone with Matt less than two minutes, and within that time the small room had filled up with Dabners chatting, laughing, and by the time I hung up the phone—the music was blasting and they were dancing.

Theresa strolled over to the couch where Toomey, Quincee, and I were sitting. She's about 5'2" and light-bright damn near white complexioned. Her hair is red and she has clear gray eyes. She's on the wide side, and her personality is even bigger. I like her because she seems real, but more so, because she took up for Quincee.

The round face happy woman introduced herself to me and flirted with Toomey. Grinning and holding her hand up for a high-five, she stood in front of Quincee.

"Hey bitch, gimme some. When I saw your ass jump out the cab looking like Rambo's half-sister, I knew it was on then!"

Responding with her half of the five, and her position, "I didn't do a damn thing. You saw how he was flinging my ass around like I was a wet noodle. I was pissed because I was trying to choke the life out of his got-damn neck, and he didn't feel a thing. How many times did he bang me around and I hit either the side of the house or the ground?"

"Ooh bitch, thanks for cushioning my big ass from the street. I know you hurt something somewhere because I felt no concrete."

I looked at Quincee, but she refused to turn to me, and I realized that there was a lot that I had missed.

Theresa turned to me and Toomey.

"Sorry about the madness. My brother is a 100% bona fide fuck-up. But hey, everybody got one in their family."

She was so right because I instantly thought of Jimmy, and I replied "No problem, I'm here because I want to keep my woman safe."

"Well alright now, that makes me happy; cause this is my girl and I love her like she's my own sister. She deserves to be looked after. You treat her good or I'm coming after you."

Throwing my hands up in compliance, "You got it. I'm not trying to go up against that right hook of yours", and we all started laughing.

Walking towards Quincee and grabbing her hand was a young female with a brown/red complexion, about an inch taller and thirty pounds heavier than Quincee. She sported a long ponytail and bangs. The light blue headband matched her baby phat sweat suit. She has thick manicured eyebrows, fat cheeks and a bright smile.

Pulling Quincee to her feet, the young girl hugged Quincee and said, "I love you mom."

I was surprised because she looked nothing like her mother.

Quincee introduced her to Toomey and me. Harmony is pleasant, very respectful, and soft spoken.

"It's very nice to meet you both."

She's a charmer. I saw Quincee-Jane all up in her personality. She told her story again.

What started it all was, Eli calling Harmony a skeezer and she retorted by calling him a Mc Nasty Nugget. I was trying to hide mine, but Toomey burst out in a loud laugh, and the rest of the room followed.

Quincee got serious, "Harmony, go and get your things, we're leaving." The child's face broke out in disappointment.

"Hold up. You're wrong now. We're going to the hotel upstate tonight. Why she can't go? Dick-face won't be coming around for a while. You know damn well he aint nothing but a momma's boy, and can't stand for my mother to be mad at him. Child please…let my niece stay. After what she went through, she deserves to go out and have a good time."

Harmony was standing behind her aunt begging.

"Mom please…pleeeese…pleeeeeeese!"

After the fourth please, Toomey advocated for Harmony. "Go on and let her stay. Don't be a hater and cramp the child's fun."

"FINE! You Can Stay."

I don't know who was happier—Harmony or Theresa. They started jumping up and down, doing the happy dance, and started kissing Quincee all over her face.

Watching my lady giggle like a little girl was satisfying to see, but even more so to have the situation end the way that it did because there was potential for shit to go Real Bad!

Harmony ran up and hugged and kissed Toomey on the cheek, saying "Thank you Mr. Toomey."

It was funny watching my boy get caught off guard, blush, and speak out in a fatherly tone. "You just make sure you have a good time."

"I will, and thank you again."

She walked back over to Quincee and asked, "Mom can I have some money?"

Bending down pulling cash out of her sock, "Here, this is all I have on me."

It was $27. Harmony was disrespectful by no means, but she stated her case.

"Mommy I don't think this is going to be enough because we're going to the movies tonight and I have to pay for my food."

"When I get home, I'll send you some money in a cab with Fred."

Looking like she was ready to cry, Harmony said "But mommy that's going to be too late."

I could tell that if Toomey and I weren't around Quincee would have read Harmony; instead, she conceded not to embarrass her daughter. She asked Theresa when she was leaving.

"As soon as I take a shower and get dress."

Turning back to Harmony, "Well I guess you're outta luck because that's your only option."

(To all you men out there that's taking care of another man's seed, this is how I fell deep into it).

Harmony just stood there with tears in her eyes and said "Yes Mom."

I felt bad for the teen because Quincee was adamant about her position and had no sympathy for her daughter's predicament.

I couldn't remember the last time I had seen a fourteen year old showing that much self-control and respect while disagreeing with their parent. I also thought back to Quincee's conversation with Hope. I like her girl's character. I think Quincee have good kids.

Not asking Quincee, I called Harmony over to me and handed her a $100 bill. Quincee's eyes damn near popped out of her head.

"Baby, I can't accept you doing that for my baby, but thank you so much."

No plan to compromise, I questioned "Why?"

Seeing embarrassment in her gratitude, she answered, "Because she's my responsibility."

I couldn't let my woman go any further. Pulling her to the side where it was just the two of us. Looking down into her sexy eyes, placing my index finger over her lips, so that all she could do was listen, hear, and feel me.

"From this moment on...whatever you can't do for yourself or the girls, or whenever you don't have... I'm here for you and them. I love you, and I'm not going to see you all go without. End of story!"

Staring up at me, she tried to fight back her tears; instead she just dug her head into my chest and positioned her body to be flush with mine. I was blown away because I could feel all of her gratefulness as it passed through me.

(Men, love was showing me some new shit, and it was making me feel damn good).

While I had her in the corner, I saw Toomey slip Harmony some money too, and made a gesture to keep it quiet from Quincee. Ole boy was softening up.

Quincee pulled back a bit and told me "Things seem to be back to normal, I'm ready to go home."

We said our goodbyes and were walking out of the house within the next five minutes.

Before getting into Matt's truck, Harmony came running out the house and bum-rushed Quincee "Mom, how you gonna leave and not say good-bye?"

"Baby, I thought you had left to Theresa house."

"No, I was in E-U's room. Come here."

She jerked Quincee towards her, planted a big long kissed on her cheek, and said "I Love Mom." Then she hugged me and Toomey, and the both of us stood there looking like awkward proud uncles.

The day kept spinning out surprises, and it was 3 for 3 in the positive, *(Who knew that there was more to come?).*

The Gatekeeper

(The woman that I love, with all our cards on the table, and feeling her feel me, all of that in place, I'm still walking around with purple/blue-balls from wanting to touch her, taste her, satisfy her, and give her what her body has been asking for...me).

It was ten to five when we were heading across town to Quincee's house. My lady looked hurt, angry, stressed, and exhausted. I turned to her and asked "Baby talk to me!"

"I have a headache, and my neck, my back, my arms, my chest, my ass, my mind...everything hurts."

A pain shot straight through my heart listening to her.

"I just want to soak in my tub."

Toomey being Toomey said "Yo Dan, what about the game, we're going to miss part of it."

Matt shoot Toomey a sneer.

Toomey sincerely asked, "What...what I do? What I say wrong? Yo Q, can I check out the game at your house?"

"You most certainly can."

Toomey gawked at Matt with vindication then turning back around to me and announced

"Yah can do what yah want; I know where I'm going to be."

Inspecting my face through the rear view mirror Matt ask, "You good with that?"

"Yeah partner, I'm good."

The decision was made and we drove to Quincee's apartment complex, and park in the garage. While waiting for the garage elevator to come, she ordered,

"When you get into the elevator, don't touch anything, don't lean on the walls and look down to make sure you're not stepping in anything."

Matt and I just looked at each other, and didn't say a word, and Lord knows I was praying that Toomey didn't say anything either-- my prayer was answered.

(You should have seen the four of us looking like stuff sardines standing in the middle of the elevator cabin).

Toomey broke the silence, "Oh shit--look" and low and behold someone had scribbled on the elevator door, "RIDE AT YOUR OWN RISK."

Walking on the street level of the development, which is called the plaza, Toomey commented, "Q, no disrespect, but it looks like a fucking jungle over here. Is it always like this?"

Taking no offense, she replied "Yes. It's the straight up 'Hood.' I know it; but, it's also my home, and there's beauty here too." (*She did not lie*).

In the building now, the three of us were waiting in the main lobby while Quincee went to check her mailbox.

Walking in the building, who do I see, but that B-Pong Negro. Strolling in her direction, I watched him undressing her with his eyes, and licking those big ass lips of his. When he got close to her, I heard him say to Quincee, "Mmm girl you look so good, you make my teeth hurt."

Locking her box, she walked by him shunning his ass off like a big sister would do, which made me very happy.

Matt paid no attention, but Toomey was looking at me like 'Aren't you going to say something to his ass?'

I had more than enough confrontations in the past 24 hours besides, Quincee didn't need that nonsense.

Up at her apartment, as soon as all of us were inside, she gave a quick directional tour of the layout then said, "Make yourselves at home. You'll are welcomed to everything in the cabinets and the refrigerator, and the remote is on the table by the TV." Then she went to her room.

After making sure that my partners were cool, I headed to the back to her.

She opened the door for me, she looked broken from fatigue. I lead her to the dresser, where I sat on top it then move in between her legs and let her rest her head on my shoulder.

"Thank you for following me to Eli's house."

I wanted to kiss her so bad right then, but that wasn't what she needed. Instead I hugged her, and she winced.

Starting my physical investigation, "Let's see what's going on," while pulling my sweatshirt over top of her head. I got pissed off all over again—my baby had black and blue bruises all over her back, and when I looked closer, she had hand prints around her neck.

Comprehending my rage and directing my face towards hers with her hands.

"Baby, it's over. There's no need for any retaliation. Harmony is fine, I'm fine—the bruises will heal and all the marks will go away."

I wanted to take the conversation further, but going with her flow, I saw that I would be putting her through more bull shit that she didn't need or deserve, so I let it go.

"Whatever you want baby, you got it."

"Can I have a kiss?"

It fucked me up because that was the last thing I expected to come out of her mouth. Before I could slide my tongue in her mouth, she was all up in mine. I knew I wanted her bad, but the way she was kissing me, I think she may have wanted me just as much-- my shit was jumping summer-salts.

She started moaning placing one hand on the side of my face, and the other inside the back of my pants then she pressed those triple D's against my chest. I don't know which felt better, her hard nipples or the heat from her hand that was lighting my ass up.

Still following her flow, I scooted her closer to the edge of the dresser, guiding her by the small of her back into me; leaning in to plant a TooGood kiss on her.

Then "KNOCK...KNOCK...KNOCK". It was that got-damn Toomey.

"Pardon for the interruption; but Q, can I throw that frozen pizza in the oven?"

Smiling at my aggravation with Toomey before responding, "You absolutely can. Mi casa es su casa (my house is your house", she commented while backing out of my grasp, jumping off the dresser then heading for the bathroom.

When I heard water running in the tub, I knew it was a wrap with what was going down before the knock on the door. All I wanted to do then was to pitch Toomey and the got-damn pizza out the front door.

It took me a minute before I was able to move from the dresser. My shit was throbbing so bad that I was in pain. If I had gotten my hands on her right then, my hard-on would have made her cry.

I was feeling Quincee so deep that I couldn't even past the bathroom without knocking on the door and going in. It smelt like berries and crème in there. I wanted to open my mouth and taste the scent that was opening up my nose, further than it already was.

Asking her through the closed beige laced shower curtain, "Is there anything I can do for you, or get you?"

"Would you mind just sitting in her with me? I really don't want to talk, but it would be nice just to have you in here with me."

"Yes baby, I can do that for you. I'll be quiet as a church mouse for you."

"I LOVE YOU."

I almost fell, my knees buckled so got-damn hard. I felt like the luckiest cat in the world. (*Shit…knowing that my baby loved me…WHAT!*)

"Miss Quincee-Jane Catfire, I love you too."

Sitting on the toilet seat, and minding my own business I looked down and saw her thong on the floor.

(You got-damn right; I picked them up and took a big sniff. Fellas, I was fucked up. Her scent was so soft, and sweet; I couldn't get enough. I kept on inhaling, holding my breath and then inhaling some more, trying to burn her scent into my brain).

I had to force myself back to reality, when I was ready to wash my face with her thong. As if she sensed me.

"Hey…you okay over there?"

"Yes baby, I am. But I'm going to go and check on the boys."

"Okay. Thank you for hanging out with me."

"Baby, you don't have to thank me, I'm here for you."

Taking one more sniff of her thong, standing up and opening up the door. Before I closed it, her phone rang. She asked me to pass it to her, which I did.

Walking to the living room, I saw Toomey in the kitchen playing bartender. "Yo Dan, here… I fixed you a shot of Tequila."

Reading my expression, Toomey added, "Q said to make myself welcomed to the cabinets. I found this in the cabinet…damn niggah. You need to lighten up!"

Giving in, I said "Thanks man," and took the shot straight to the head then walked into the living room and sat down next to Matt.

My ass hadn't even touch the couch, when Matt asked "Have you figured out what you're going to do with that fool?"

"Not completely."

"If you need me?"

"I know."

Toomey walk over to the window by the office area. "This is a sweet view. Is that Yankee Stadium over there?"

Matt and I got up to see, and in the midst of us all trying to look out the window at the same time, one of us pressed the speaker button on the phone.

We heard, "Pussy, you there?"

Quincee answered, "Diva, I'm here."

"Hold on, your boyfriend want to say hello."

The three of us looked at the phone.

Hate flashed across my chest, and I thought (*what the fuck is going on after all that I've been through for her*). Then we heard.

"Hello Auntie Q"

"Hello baby, how are you? Are you being a good boy for mommy?"

The three of us looked at each other with different forms of relief on our faces. The small voice answered honestly "I'm trying to, but mommy is real mad at me. Can you ask her to let me watch SpongeBob Square Pants?"

"I'll see what I can do."

"Thank you Auntie Q. How come you didn't come? You said that you was going to be here for my birthday weekend. I'm nine now."

"Wow, nine is a really good age. I'm sorry Junior, but something important came up."

"Can you come today?"

"No baby, I have company."

"At your house?"

"Yes"

"Are they going to be there for a long time?"

"Maybe"

"Are they going to spend the night?"

"Possibly"

"You're going to sleep in the bed by yourself right?"

Before Quincee could respond the mother began chastising the little Junior.

"Give me the phone. You need to mind your damn business and stay in a child's place. Go in the room and cut the damn TV on."

In the background we heard "Thanks Auntie Q!"

"My boy has it bad for you."

"That is so adorable."

I had enough listening to her conversation and I was looking for the button to turn the phone off.

Toomey was trying to stop me, so while we're whispering our conflict, and trying not to get caught, Quincee's friend asked,

"What's this I hear…someone's sleeping in your bed? Ooh girl, please say it's true—you finally going to get some. How long has it been since you did the nasty?

Time stood still for me, as the three of us once again zoned in to the phone.

"I swear, I don't know how you do it. It's been…what… three and a half years right?"

"Why are we talking about my sex life or the lack thereof of it?"

Matt's eyebrows arched up and eyes popped opened like— Damn!

Toomey's big ass mouth said "Oh shit", and I think Quincee heard it.

She asked the caller "Bellah did you hear that?"

The voice on the other end said "Hear what. I didn't hear anything. What…you're trying not to tell me who's in your house, possibly your bed.?"

"No that's not it! Just hold on for a minute, I'll be right back." Then the line went silent.

We knew she was headed into the living room. The three of us should have won an Academy Award that day. By the time we heard her bedroom door open, I clicked off the speaker phone.

Hearing her turning the corner towards us; we were looking out the window, discussing Bronx geography.

"Are you guys okay out here? Can I get you anything?"

Holding my arm out beckoning her to come to me; she walked right into my arms.

(Men, you can imagine how I was feeling at that moment).

Matt responded, "I'm good", and Toomey asked about a park that could be seen in a short distance—throwing her sweet ass completely off guard.

She stayed there drawn into the conversation until she remembered "Oh damn, I'm on the phone. Excuse me guys" and she darted out of the room.

As soon as I heard her door slam closed, I looked at my boys and said "Let's roll! I'm going to the house."

Matt gave me a fist pound, and Toomey said "I know that's right!"

"I'll meet you by the elevator after I let Quincee know we're heading out."

I walked them to the door then headed to the bedroom. She was off the phone, lying on her bed looking tired and too sexy to be in bed by herself. I thought (*Just hold on baby, daddy's coming!*)

I knelt down on the floor beside her.

"Baby, I'm going to ride downtown with Matt and Toomey, so I can get my car. I'll pick us up something to eat on the way back."

"That would be nice."

"You going to be alright?"

"Yes Danny."

"I'll call you when I get in the house", then I bent over and kissed her on the forehead.

I wasn't going to do it to myself, by kissing her on the lips. Shit I almost had a horny-stroke when she was standing beside me in the living room.

As soon as I walked into the hallway, I heard the elevator door close, and Toomey was complaining.

"Yo Dan, they talking about there's only two working, shit we could be waiting all night for another one."

I didn't give a damn because nothing, I mean, nothing could rain on my parade. Quincee is all in my brain and waddling around in my cum, with her name on my nut.

Just then, her door opened, and she ran out to meet us. She had on a long black velvet robe that had leopard print around the cuffs and neck, and a pair of those black fluffy high-heel slippers.

She walked up to me and said, "Here, take my keys just in case I'm sleep when you come back", catching me off guard.

Not giving me a chance to respond, she placed her keys in my hand, and then turned to Toomey. My stomach did a quick flip because the last two times they met in this spot...it was not good.

Walking up to Toomey and standing there a few seconds before saying anything. When I looked at her, I noticed that she was fighting back tears. Taking a step closer and bowing her head onto Toomey's chest then looking up saying "Th..Thank you for your sneezes……. Just prior to you do…doing so, I felt ah… I felt alone, but you helped me protect my child."

Her voice collapsed from Toomey's sentiment, and her tears poured down her face as she fought on, "Thank you for being my friend and coming to my rescue."

My friend was so dumbfound that the only response that fool could come up with was to shove Quincee on the shoulder, so hard that it jerked her backwards.

My baby just stood there and took it, then moved in even closer and hugged Toomey real tight. That was the second time I seen water in '*Dry Eyes*'. It was a moment to remember, because I doubt I will ever see anything like that again.

Matt and I just stood there looking solemn. Toomey poked her on the shoulder, and manage to choke out "As long as I am breathing, you have a brother in this fucking world, and you'll never have to fight alone again—now go on and get outta here", while pushing her away.

She turned to face Matt. Once again she was fighting through a cracking voice.

Matt grabbed and hugged her around her neck, then bent down to her ear and stated, "I would have killed that mother fucker for you. All you had to do was…say the word."

"I know….Thank you!"

Walking over to her, taking her by the hand, I led her back to her apartment. Bending down to give her a safe kiss, but she slipped her tongue in my mouth. She had my meat jumping again. The love that I was feeling from her was making my heart beat so fast that it felt like it was going to bust out of my chest cavity. Right then I caught a whiff of her scent from my top lip and my entire body pained for the woman.

I pulled away from her when I heard the elevator door open.

"I'll be right back to you girl."

"You better."

That shit sent another sensation down my third leg. I ran to catch up with Matt and Toomey to get on that crowed ass elevator. We rode downstairs in silence, and I damn sure needed that time to pull myself together.

In the basement of the garage, Matt pulled up to the parking attendant to pass him the ticket, and who was it...B fucking Pong. As soon as I recognized him, I was out the car walking around to him.

"Yo chief, can I holler at you for a minute?" I didn't give him the opportunity to say no.

"Quincee told me that you are family friends. I can respect that, but I have a problem watching you undress my lady in your mind, and your sly ass comments to her."

Self-assured and not bothered by my position, "No disrespect intended partner."

He fessed up, trying to sound innocent as ice cream. I ignored his remark and continued.

"That shit is dead. We clear." I waited for his response.

"We clear!"

Back in the truck and ready to roll out, so that I could get back up this way to Quincee.

We weren't out to the complex before Toomey questioned-- sounding genuine, "Yo Dan, you know sometime....shit...uh... all the time when I would fuck with Q, you know I didn't mean 90% of the shit that came out of my mouth? I would just be fucking with her."

"Toom, I know. You're good in her book."

"You think so?"

"No question about it."

"Dan, when that faggot told Q you aint got no brothers, I saw myself putting a bullet right between his two fucking front teeth."

"You'd have to wait in line for that one."

The mood was changed when Toomey called out "Three and a half years. That shit fucked me up, but it all makes sense now."

Matt decided to add to the applause and played the live version of Ushers' "Nice and Slow" slow-jam. When it got to the part "*I got plans to put my hands in places I've never seen, do you know what I mean*" Toomey leaned forward from the back seat, and was patting me on the back "Ahhhh, Go Dan! You the man! Got-Damn!"

We rode to Harlem having a damn good time, acting like way back in the day-- laughing, talking, singing, snapping and having my boy's big-me-up with regards to the night ahead of me.

At the corner of 118th and St. Nicholas Ave, Toomey got out of the truck, walked up beside me, leaned on the front door, looking disturbed.

"This is some bullshit—I got all envious and caught up in your shit—at not wanting to be the niggah that's not getting any tonight, so I made call.

S-h-i-i-t, shit, shit. I just now remembered…the bitch got five kids! I'm sick… oh got-damn…got damn… got damn, I'm sick!"

Matt and I were cracking up laughing, when a woman with rollers in her hair stuck her head out of the window and yelling as keys hit the pavement, "TOOMEY, TOOMEY, take the keys so you can let yourself in, but first I want you to go to the store for me. Call me and so I can give you the list."

Our friend looking pitiful and pissed off said, "That shit is not funny!" Tears were coming out my eyes I was laughing so hard.

When Matt drove off, Toomey yelled out "fuck yall" and flipped us the bird. I was laughing so hard I barely got out "Yeah, but who's getting ready to walk their ass to the store?" It took us damn near five minutes to recover from that fool.

I asked Matt about Cheryl, and a gigantic smile took over my brother's face.

"I'm flying back out to her on Wednesday night and I'm staying until after the holidays."

I said "Good!", but then my face dropped.

A tradition would be broken; it was going to be the first Thanksgiving that we didn't spend together; since we met well over twenty years ago. I wanted happiness for Matt and Cheryl, and I know that would unquestionably be a positive for both of their recovery. I smiled again and wished my brother well, (*I really felt happy and sad at the same time*).

By 7pm we were parked in front of my house, ready to exit as soon as the car stopped, but instead I asked "You gonna stop by before you leave?"

"Yeah, but I'll wait for you to call me, after you come up for air."

Giving me a dap, Matt toasted "Make IT Yours!"

"You Know!" I replied as that was my full intention to make the pussy all mine! Walking away, I heard "Don't go making a baby... even though I wouldn't mind being and uncle."

I stopped dead in my tracks at the unexpected comment, smiled at the thought, and then resume my pace to my front door.

In the house less than five minutes, I was butt ass naked and stepping in the shower. My mind could focus on nothing but Quincee and the cat that I was more than ready to meet.

Going back to when we first met; how my father fell for her at first sight, plain missing her when she walked out of my life. Remembering actually getting sick to the stomach when I thought I had lost her for good at Dre's crib. Then coming full circle when I met back up with her at the pier, having her back in my life, and now knowing that she loves me; I was so full from thankfulness that before I even realized it, I was on my knees.

"Dear God, I'm humbled before You tonight, not knowing if I truly deserve to be feeling this overabundance of joy in my heart. I thank You for everything. Thank You for my life and having me live it well.

Thank You for Your grace, thank You for Your mercy. Thank You for keeping my family and my friends safe. Thank You for love, thank You for giving me the thousandth second chance in my lifetime.

I pray that You always walk with Quincee, Hope and Harmony. May my love for them have Your blessings, guidance, and nurture. By Your grace, let no man separate nor put us under?

And thank You Father God for giving me my mother's soul everlasting life... Amen."

By the time I finished, I was wiping tears away that I knew wasn't shower water falling down my face. I felt light as a feather, and my heart was ready to love Quincee-Jane until the day I close my eyes to this the world.

Out of the shower and feeling brand new, the thought of her scent, picked up my pace. My hard-on remembered very well and started talking to me. *(I wonder what the pussy looks like. I can't wait to feel the pussy. Mmm, I wonder how the pussy tastes).* Just thinking about eating her, made my mouth water and had me double over in pain...again.

Focusing her out of my mind because all I keep thinking was (*how good I plan to make her body feel, and how I could hardly wait to be touched by her*).

Standing in front of my full length mirror I gave myself a quick once over. I had on Mochian brown Ralph Lauren corduroy pants, my army green shawl collar pullover sweater that went well with my espresso colored hush puppies. I put on a brown sculley-cap on because my hair was still wet then splashed on some Sung. I was set.

Downstairs, I grabbed my brown pea coat, my keys, my bag that I had packed, and I was back out the door in a little under an hour.

In the Bronx, I drove to Little Italy to a restaurant that Quincee mentioned. I ordered some shrimp scampi and angel hair pasta, Caesar salad and a small cheesecake to go. The bottle of Pinot Grigio wine that she likes should go good with the meal.

The closer I got to her, the more excitement almost caved my chest in. (*I was cumming in my mind just thinking about what I was going to do to her*).

Standing in front of her apartment with my bag across my shoulder, the bundle of two dozen long stem roses under my left arm, the food in my left hand, and I was getting ready to put the key in the cylinder with my right hand. Waiting for what's on the other side of the door...

(*Men, life doesn't get much better than this*).

The Introduction

(Making It MINE!).

Walking into the apartment, all the lights were out except a faint red glow coming from under her room door. I put the food on the counter. I placed the flowers in a pot of ice then headed towards the back of the apartment.

Knocking on the door before entering her room, "Hey there pretty lady."

Lying facing the wall and turning around to me, she replied "Hey back at you sexy gent."

By then I had knelt back down in the same position on the floor beside her, as before I left. Observing her cringe in pain from all her injuries gnawed at me, and she read my mind, "I'm okay" then she kissed my hand.

For the next thirty seconds, I just continued surveying her. She was perfect in all of her wounded perfect-ness.

"What?" she asked in a conciliatory tone.

I was so caught up with emotion that I had to mentally slap myself in the back of the neck to speak.

"Just star-gazing and enjoying the view."

Seeing her blush brought joy to my heart. "Are you hungry? I got some Italian food." and I called off the menu.

Remembering the roses, I got to my feet beckoning for her "Walk with me. There's something I have do."

Grabbing my outstretched hand, I helped her out the bed. Tell me why the only thing she had on was a sun-yellow thong that was tied on the sides. The animal in me wanted to rip the piece of material off of her with my teeth and commence to eating her until I was full, (but I didn't).

Instead, I moved my sight upward clearing my throat to take my focus off her holding those triple D's in her hands; I was disappointment at not getting even a glimpse of nipples. She had them fully covered. Truth be told it's the first time ever dealing that size before and I wanted to suck on them… real bad.

(She was not making it easy for me to be a gentleman, but I remembered my father's words to my uncle June-Bug years ago, "The more gentlemanliness you show a woman, the wider she will spread her legs for you).

So what did I do, I turned around until she got her robe from the foot of the bed and put it on.

She turned to me and said, "Chivalry still roams. Your mother would be very proud of you."

"Thank you Ma'am."

Taking her by the arm I lead her to the kitchen. Once she spotted the roses in the sink, her face lit up.

"These are for me?"

"Yes baby, there're for you."

She swung around and bent my face down to reach hers, and gave me a nice kiss.

To control my hard on, I scooped her up and sat her on the counter while I arranged the roses in a vase that I took from the top of her cabinets.

She snacked on the salad and pasta, fed me the pasta and shrimp, and we sipped wine from the same glass.

Laughing, talking and acting silly with Quincee, felt like I've known her all of my life. It felt good…it felt right just being there with her.

Finishing up my workmanship, we admired the arrangement that I had put together. Looking impressed, she asked me.

"Where did you learn to do that; it's beautiful."

"As punishment for stealing flowers, my mother made me work at a florist for an entire summer."

"How old were you?"

"Thirteen"

"I bet your friends laughed at you, didn't they."

"All of them, every day, but the girls didn't; especially when I brought them flowers."

"Good for you," she told me, sounding like a loyal wingman.

After a few moments, she poked me on the shoulder; I responded with an arched eyebrow as I positioned myself in front of her.

Countering, she pulls me close in between her legs.

"Don't worry, I won't hurt you…the water is just right."

Then she bit my bottom lip hard enough to make my dick twitch, pushed me to the side, jumped off the counter and headed to the hallway; saying, "I'll see you in a bit."

Checking out her sexy ass as she sashayed to the bathroom, I decided to make myself comfortable by stripping down to my boxers and wife-beater.

Returning to the kitchen, pouring two glasses of wine then I waited for her and our meeting in her bedroom.

The ambiance of Quincee's room matched my mood, and what I had planned for her. The majority of the walls where covered in a red suede textured fabric. The wall were her black antique dresser sits, is covered with gold silk fabric. I feel like I'm inside of a jewelry box, when I'm standing in front of it.

The two columned corners at diagonal ends of the room are painted metallic gold, which matched the stucco painted ceiling. The flooring is metallic bronze with black and red and gold running through it. When I look down, just inside the threshold of her room, Quincee-Jane was inscribed in floor. All I could do was smile, because that's my baby.

Her black leather sleigh bed stood high up off the floor that had a velvet patch-work spread of black metallic gold, green and red that covered the temperpedic mattress that I bought for her. She had all shapes and sizes of pillows that were giving me ideas of what to do to her with them!

The opened black vertical textured blinds hanging at the window were letting the lights of the city in. I was lost in thought and my attention was transfixed on the red lava lamp that was bubbling sexual shapes. Interrupting my preoccupation, Lady Quincee walked into the room with a smile on her face, saying "Hey you."

Staring at her, she had on a blood red baby doll nighty. It had spaghetti straps, and it came together at her cleavage with an orange ribbon, and the rest was made open down the front. She wore matching frilly panties, making her look like edible chocolate on the inside of a cherry.

The entire room smelt of her essence and of her sex.

Wasting no time; I walked over to her and guided her to the wall adjacent to the door then inquired.

"Can I ask you a question?"

Looking me square in my eyes and countering, "As long as you make it personal—yes you can."

She was making me work hard for my cool. I raised her hands above her head, and firmly held her wrists with my left hand. I stood straddled in front of her so that her legs were in between mine.

She remained in place, still staring into my eyes, while trying to catch her breath that was taken away by her excitement.

I bent down and whispered in her ear, "Are you ready for me?"

"In what way would that be?" The arrogance in her inquired while she attempted to maintain an even voice.

Moving closer on her, and pressing my body against hers so that she could feel more of my weight, I bent down and whispered in her ear again, "I'm here to collect my nut."

Her breathe lost its control, and I watched her effort to contain her heat, dissipate. Reiterating my question, "Are you ready for me?", and before she could respond I slide my tongue into her mouth while pressing my hardness on her.

Tasting her hurt, smelling her lust, feeling her want, and hearing her satisfaction…then I pulled out of her mouth.

She panted, and I acknowledged her response with an "Mmm hmm" and I pondered aloud, "Girl, why do you have to feel so good on me?"

"Because I'm your lady, your women, your whore and Your Queen… And as my King, you're supposed to feel like this with me up on you. Now come on boy and kiss me again like you mean it."

(Men, she had my heart and my shit jolting).

I covered her eyes with my right hand then slid my tongue in and out of her warm wet mouth like a skilled dick making slow love to a cum-ready virgin. Kissing her like that was sugar-dip sweet as I listened to her moaning in love-pain.

I witnessed her arousal jumped to another level of wanting me, when I told her "Don't move your arms." With them still suspended above her head without my assistance, I took off my wife-beater because I wanted to feel her bare flesh on me. I spread the nighty apart divulging her torso, and lean up against her.

Her skin was hot to the touch, wet from her panting, and softer than a newborn's cheeks. I laid on her for a minute longer, savoring the feel of her.

My baby said "I know you love me because I feel it radiating through you into me."

I press all my weight on her and came back with, "You keep on feeling it because it's not going anywhere."

Then I untied the ribbon to her top. I took in the sight of her triple D's. They reminded me of milk chocolate melons, and her nipples were like dark chocolate kisses ready for me to touch them.

Giving them what they needed by placing my palms on the outside fleshy part of the twins, I ran my face all over them. When her breathing became so shallow, to the point of craving, I tried to swallow her right ripe nipple; it swelled in my mouth like a flower opening in the sunlight.

She moaned, and I nibbled on it, she groaned and I bit it. Her body was calling for more, so I obliged the left nipple the same way. The hungrier I sucked, the more she arched her back to put more of her in my mouth.

When her passion noise turned into a distressed love cry for me, I stood up straight and bent down so that my lips where touching her ear, and I softly asked "What do you want?"

Barely audibly she pleaded "Please….Release me from my tournament."

I placed my hand back over her wrist; I began kissing her again as I guided her legs open with my foot. Got-damn she looked good with her arms in a love-slave position and her chest heaving from the TooGood-heat she was receiving from me. *(All of this.. for me? Thank You God).*

After taking in the sight of her a little longer, I kissed her again, but this time, I placed my hand on her stomach, just above the sheer thong.

The pouch at the bottom of her stomach even felt sexy to my hand. And I rubbed and caressed it to let her know that it was all good to me.

Her breathing increased again, and her body reacted. She went up on her tiptoes, thrusting her pelvis outward in an attempt to maneuver my hand to where she wanted it to go.

I drew my body back, looked at her and asked "What?"

She said nothing, so I asked for the second time looking deep into her eyes "*What?*" while sliding my hand down into her throng and making first contact with the pussy that I had been waiting to meet, (*What…she had on a crouch less thong….Got Damn!*).

Her 'She' was soft, bald, chunky-full and nice and wet. Her flesh and her juices felt like liquid silk between my fingers.

To slow down my hard-on, I pulled away and placed my attention and hand on the outside of her mound; cupping it as if to protect it from everything and everyone except me. Then I began rubbing the insides of both of her soft ass thighs with care. When her anticipation became too much for her, I slid my hand back into the open hole in her thong and started stroking her wet pussy again.

Out of nowhere she started talking shit, "I know you like what your feel mother fuckah." That defiant shit-talking monster in her was too arrogant for her own good, but she and it were turning me more the fuck on.

The more shit she talked to me, the softer I stroked the pussy, I needier caressed the pussy, and the more fun I had fondling the pussy. When I felt her ready to drop her load in my hand I zoned in on her clit, and massaged it like a master artist strumming a one of a kind viola. I was sending a message to the pussy, (*Hello, I'm Danny, a.k.a. your one and only doer*).

I found her nut because of the way it felt, and each time I glided my finger over it, she moaned out in ear-pleasing want for me. Her breathing turned into sighs and grunts that were blowing my mind. She looked up at me, and I informed her "I'm ready to eat."

I couldn't see the expression on her face, nor what she was thinking because I was in my own zone. I let her wrists go, took her by the hand, and lead her towards the dresser on the opposite side of the room.

I picked her up and sat her down gentle-like. Moving in close in between her legs, resting my hands on the insides of her thighs, I began kissing her for the eleventh time. Quincee is an expert kisser. Her lips are soft as fluff and her mouth taste like early morning sunshine. She bit me on the lip again and I reacted by jerking her thighs open wider.

As if it was there just for me, she had a chair at the base of her bed, which I slid toward me and took a seat. I raised her legs; so that the soles of her feet were flush with the top of the dresser then I spread her full eagle; widening the opening in her thong. I took my first peek at the pussy. My woman has a pretty, pretty pussy.

(In the back of my mind, I knew that it would be because come on men; they all DO NOT look alike. I can share some horror pussy looking stories, and I know you can too!).

I couldn't wait any longer, I bent forward and I inhaled her womanhood and her scent that had been driving me crazy ever since I sniffed her thong earlier. I let it soak up into all of my senses—to familiarize and fill my brain up with it. I welcomed the juices that were dabbing my lip, my nose, and wherever else I chose to touch her with.

Confirming in my mind that her women scent was welded in my brain, I blew on her, and she moaned out "Fuck You!" Satisfied with the comment because it informed me that she was ready for what I have to offer.

Sliding my tongue out of my mouth, I began slowly licking the top of her pubic mountain, working my way to the insides of her thighs.

She started wrenching and wiggling, so I started blowing on her clit.

My sex kitten was squirming with pleasure and pain of wanting more, but I was going to make her wait because I wasn't finishing acquainting myself with the pussy that I was making mine.

Lost in my own world of communicating with 'She', I didn't come up for air until I heard her call out to me.

"Baby my legs are sore."

"Mmm, but how is your pussy feeling?" I responded.

"I hate you."

"I love you too. Now watch me eat me you."

With the tip of my tongue, I started at the base of her opening and licked her all the way up to the head of her clit. She tasted like perfect love in my mouth.

Purring with satisfaction, her pleasure tasted cookie-candy sweet to my taste buds. I wanted more, so I spread her lips back to reveal that most sensitive area—her knob. Gently sucking on it, while simultaneously twirling my tongue around it, she was going crazy.

Her body began gyrating uncontrollably, and she grabbed me by the back of my head and was pushing my face deeper into her love-joy, (*I was fucking loving it*). I ate the pussy like it was melting ice cream, inside my mouth.

The more she wanted to give me, the more I wanted, and the more I took. The more I licked, the more she moaned, and the hotter the pussy got. Realizing that her clit was getting hard in my mouth (*I had not experienced that before... the shit was on then!*) I made love to the clit. I licked it, I lapped it, I sucked it, and I waved my tongue all around it.

While she was still in my mouth, I took her ass in my hands and pulled her towards me, so that her back could arch, and then I slide my middle finger right up in her (*Mmm mmm!*)

She received me so well that I was able to insert two of my fingers, less than two inches in from her opening; feeling for that almond shape bumpy surface embedded on the top of her female wall...BINGO! I found it, (*her G-spot*).

My baby's whole body spasm when I rubbed over it. I began massaging her spot with firm shallow strokes, while still sucking on her meat.

(Yeah, the pussy was being made mine. I love eating it and I intended to enjoy my meal. It was also my objective to let pussy know that can't nobody do it like me, and for Quincee not to want anyone else to touch the pussy, but me. I was making the pussy yearn for me).

Feeling her heading into her third level of frenzy, the more I sucked, the more sexual she became. The more I stroked the pussy, the nastier her body responded.

"Please, lick She some more. Mmm...mmm, don't stop...ooh, I hate you."

Complying with her request, I lifted her off the dresser, and carried her to the bed as she wrapped her legs around my waste. I undressed her first and then myself.

Laying her face down on the bed, and with my legs, I extended her legs to their widest position. The front part of my body felt like it melted into her when I lay down on her. As she was about to say something, I stuck her.

For the second time she said, "I hate you."

"Why baby?"

"I'm not telling" she just barely got out.

That led me to believe that I was giving it to her and the pussy just the way they both needed it. Since I could only stroke shallow thrust up in her, I made them worth it. I glided in and out of her, only working the head of my dick. It was my intent to take her for a slow ride on TooGood's Love Train.

She wanted to move faster and tried to do so, but I stopped her and maintained... my pace. It wasn't until I heard suffering in her voice that I turned her over onto her back. Her body and pussy were hot, wet, and ready for me.

Staring into her eyes, I told her what was on my mind.

"You are the most beautiful women in this world. Thank you for loving me and letting me love you."

She moaned and opened her legs wider for me.

(Men, I'm telling you, they like it when you speak to their hearts. Try that shit today and watch what it gets you tonight).

Bending down and kissing her just the way she likes me to, she started purring and grunting out "I really really hate you!"

"Why baby? Haven't I been a good boy?"

Rhetorically inquiring as I ask her with my lips on hers. Torturing her long enough, when she went to answer yes, I poked her mouth with my tongue and slid my dick all the way up inside her...real slow and steady.

As she lost her breath, it had nowhere to go but into me, and I inhaled it like it was my first breath after being submerge under water for too long.

Whispering to her, "Daddy knows how you need it."

(I don't know what she's doing to me because normally that Daddy shit had never been my style).

Responding by arching her back, clawing mine, she said *"Thank you Daddy."*

Her words had my head spinning with love, with happiness, and with a nut that had her name on it.

She was so tight that I felt her inside walls grazed over ever vein in my dick. I pulled out of her. Her 'She' was so wet that I was able use my fingers to go in, down, under, and then up, to pop the explosion that was about to happen.

My dick back inside of her, I arched my back with every stroke that I gave her to intensify the sensation that I was slowing pumping into her. That thing between her legs was virgin-like tight to the point that I felt her even after I pulled out of her.

"Girl, my sex doesn't want anyone but you."

"It's not supposed to because... I'm Your Queen."

I could sense her load was in overdrive aching for me, "m-m-m-m-m....Danny, please don't stop...don't stop...s-s-s-s-s-s-s...a-a-a-a-a-h...m-m-m-m-m...y-e-e-e-a-a-a-h!"

The more she called out my name, the more I stroked, and I stroked, and I stroked her insides; filling her socket with my extension; matching the rhythm of her sweet cavity that was receiving me.

Our bodies where covered with sweat. The flavor of our make-love in the air and her raw flesh that she wanted to give me was making me feel like a got-damn giant.

Lifting up, looking down, and seeing her clear liquid creaming on my dick, and hearing her distressed moans; I was on the brink of explosion and she was ready to pop too.

She commanded to me "You're My King?"

"Yes Quincee, I Am Your King"

Then tell my dick to CUM WITH ME!"

"A-A-A-A-A-A-A-A-A-H-H-H-H-H-H. S..H..I..T! S-S-S-S-S-S-S-S-S-S...M-M-M-M-M-M. U-U-U-U-U-U- U-U-U-H-H-H-H-H-H!"

We shouted out our release as we came together, for so long that both of us tried to kept hold of the feeling (*the one that you feel right now....Hold it!*).

She asked me, "Can you see the colors?"

What fucked me up was...I did. I saw what she was seeing.

(*At that moment, I knew what the meaning of oneness was, and the description of what love feels like, and I'm for damn sure not ashamed to admit it*).

"Yes baby, I see the colors."

I saw red, crimson, yellows, golds, greens, blues, and colors that I had never seen before in this world that was glowing in my mind.

Sliding down beside her and guiding her into my arms, as our bodies were still heaving down to normal. Quincee began rubbing up on the side of me, alerting me that another seed is forming for me.

Responding to her love-call, "Baby, I want you to get some rest because I'm going to be TAKING that thing of mine that's between your legs...all weekend."

Then I lifted her chin up and asked "Who is protector of your safety?"

She cadence out, sounding like she was back in the Navy, "You Danny... Are...My...Master-At-Arms!"

"Who's the provider for you and the girls?" I asked her.

Openly admitting and it sounding like new money in my ears, "TooGoode...You are...My bringer of good will."

"And who is the gatekeeper to 'She'," placing my hand on the top of her mound that is going to keep my nose open for the rest of my life.

"You are...Danny"

"WHO...Say My Name Girl!"

"You are...Daniella Marie TooGood!"

"And, Whose Woman Am I?"

Arrogant, but turning me the fuck on; "You Are My Woman, Danny...Mine and only mine."

Smiling and giving her a quick kiss on the lips, I let her know.

"I'll see you in an hour."

Looking at her lay, exhausted from the trials of last night, today and our meeting in the bedroom, well within the protection of my arms, she fell off to sleep.

My mind then went to how I was going handle Eli, not only is he the thorn in Quincee's side, but he is also thug number two who threaten Jimmy's life and knows where I live.

Then my phone rings and I cringe at what I hear.....

The End

About the Author

A native New Yorker; born in Manhattan, raised and residing in The Boogie Down Bronx. I spent my formative years in Spotsylvania Virginia, which is where I get my charm and my manners from, and why I consider myself a country girl at heart.

I am a proud single parent of adult fraternal twin daughters, who have blessed me with three precious grandchildren, and one still cooking.

A Navy Veteran…"The Sailor's Creed" is forever etched into my spirit.

Before being graced with my sister; I was an only child for twelve years, which left me with countless hours of alone time to spend with my thoughts.

Four decades, three degrees, and two careers later, my fantasy and dream of bringing my imagination to life, have come true.

Note from the Author

Thank You...You who are reading my words right now. I am honored by your support.

It's been an absolute delight to have introduced Quincee-Jane, Danny, Matt, Cheryl, and Toomey, in this first installment of The LoveGoode Trilogy Series.

I welcome your thoughts, opinion, and critique; whether, positive or negative.

Email me at **sisterwithapen@gmail.com**

Also feel free to leave a comment on **Amazon.com** or **createspace.com**

Coming Soon
Book Two
Three the Strong Way
(This Is Who I Am)

Labor Day Friday 2006
Tina's house
About half to midnight

All through the night, I had been watching Quincee work the room with her 'it' factor magic. My Lady can hold her own, anywhere. At the time, my back was to her and all of a sudden I got a weird feeling in my gut. When I turned around, I saw her standing in the doorway of the kitchen. Just then, that got-damn country bumpkin walked up to her. The way they were looking at each other; I knew right there that that country-fied bastard had touched on my woman.

My fists are balled as I am taking that first step towards Rainey. Matt holds me back by my left shoulder, while saying, "It needs to be handled; but, Not like that brah."

Before my brother's hand was off my shoulder, I already had a plan formulated, and was making my way over to Quincee's lying ass.

www.ingramcontent.com/pod-product-compliance
Lightning Source LLC
Chambersburg PA
CBHW021456240626
47154CB00002B/399